Halfling

Donna Marie Robb

This is a work of fiction. Any resemblance of any of the characters to persons living or dead is strictly coincidental.

First Edition

ISBN: 1539841545
ISBN-13: 978-1539841548

Cover image from Pixabay

Chapter 1

"My name is Remmi Clearwater and I was never mind-drained," I whispered to myself as I had every day for the seven years I'd lived in the Cavern Lands of Penumbra. This was a secret I had to keep. I'd be executed if anyone discovered I had a functioning brain and could perform illusion magic.

My name was all I owned, even if I was the only one who knew it. Just saying it softly helped me keep my sanity in this place, the gloomiest province in Dreamearth.

But today was different. A dream was finally scheduled to take place here, in several minutes, in the courtyard just outside the Main Cavern. Visitors from Realearth hardly ever entered Penumbra during their nightly jaunts. This was my one chance to finally escape.

My mind churned as I dipped the soaking rag back into the bucket and continued scrubbing the Main Dining Hall's endless marble floor. Without stopping, I glanced through the corner of my eye at my fellow drones. Their faces remained eternally impassive as they worked, their drained minds unable to think beyond their assigned tasks. Some, like me, scrubbed the floor, while others polished the countless glowstones that dangled on silver chains from the vaulted ceiling. My companions wouldn't be a problem.

Getting past Treb, our overseer, was another matter altogether.

He stood against the far wall tapping a thin, knotted whip against his boot. A shudder passed through me. My coarse tunic rubbed uncomfortably against the welts on my back from his last beating. He had simply been in a bad mood the other day and I'd been the closest target. Among all the drones, I was usually his favorite scapegoat. But I'd face much more than a mere lashing if he caught me at this.

A lock of tangled hair fell into my eyes but I didn't bother to brush it back. I had to act mind-drained and couldn't let such things distract me from my task.

"You lot keep working," he said, finally heading toward the door. "This room had better be sparkling when I get back." He slapped his whip against the floor for emphasis. The cracking sound echoed through the large chamber.

The other drones continued their tasks without hesitation. They had been given a command and were compelled to obey it. But not me. I scrambled to my feet the second he was gone and scuttled across the slick floor. I had to get to that dream! From what I'd heard from stray conversations, those Dreamearthlings who worked directly with Realearth Visitors carried portals that whisked them from one part of our world to the other in seconds. If I planned this right, I'd sneak through one of these portals and leave Penumbra forever.

I hurried to the tall door and cautiously peered through the crack. Crowds of pale Penumbran citizens, garbed in drab clothes, streamed down the cavern corridors, in the direction of the Main Square.

My heart throbbed in a rapid staccato. I had to be extra careful. I was taking an enormous risk by using my magic, but what choice did I have? I was sure I'd inherited this talent from Mother, who could also change her appearance through illusion.

I mentally pushed aside her advice to never reveal my gift as I stepped up to a large mirror and concentrated on transforming my coloring and clothes. It didn't matter if the other drones saw this; I practiced my magic in front of just them all the time. Their brains had been restructured to instantly tune out things that happened beyond what they had been ordered to do.

A tingling sensation that felt like droplets of warm honey dabbing my skin spread over me. I sighed with relief as I studied my now translucent, grime-free skin and storm-colored eyes. My dark, matted hair had turned smooth and white. The illusion had worked. Even my ratty work tunic had become clean and form-fitting, with a pleated skirt and cloth slippers. I now resembled a middle-class Penumbran girl.

I took a deep breath and, hoping I could hold the illusion long enough to reach the unfolding dream scene, stepped through the door into the main tunnel that led outside. The streaming crowds jostled me but luckily no one took notice. I thrust my shoulders back and held my head up, such a different posture from the one I daily used as a mere drone. I could feel the cold stone floor beneath my feet; they were still bare behind the illusion of shoes.

Rows of glowstones lined the rounded walls and ceiling, throwing down a golden glow that was richer than the misty daylight seeping through the cave's opening. I struggled to maintain a calm expression as well as my illusion. One slip of that . . . I didn't even want to think about what would happen if the wrong person noticed.

The damp cave smell was instantly replaced by the scents of mist and early spring sage as I stepped outside, into the Main Square that backed up to the Dusk Hills. If only I could do more than merely form illusions and actually make myself taller. I was small for my age, unable to see over the heads of the adult Penumbrans. A few had lifted little children onto their shoulders to give them a better view of the unfolding dream, which had already started.

Disappointment filled me when I finally found a gap. I could still barely see. Countless Penumbrans crowded the vast courtyard. Every Penumbran in the province had to be here.

Several dancers waltzed to eerie, echoing music. They swirled around small tables and enormous colored balls that were scattered everywhere. Some of the dancers were humans, while others had the heads of horses, pigs, and sheep. All were garbed in bright clothes, the males in elegant suits, the females in gowns that glittered against the milky sunlight that never could penetrate the constant fog. My breath caught. I'd lived so long in a land where the only hues were variations of black, white, and gray that I'd almost forgotten other colors existed.

I spotted the Visitor instantly, an old man who was chasing something I couldn't see from my angle, weaving with surprising agility around obstacles and dancers. I could see through him as if he were made entirely of insect wings.

I continued to inch forward, straining to hold my illusion, as I slipped through the tight crowd, but unable to take my eyes off the dream. I had been a small child when I'd last witnessed one. Where was the portal the dream actors used to transport themselves to Penumbra, then onto the next dream site? My plan was to get close enough and shift my illusion to that of one of the dancers. I was counting on the Penumbrans being so enthralled by the dream that no one would notice my slight maneuver. That part looked to be working. The second the dream ended, I would then slip with the actors through the portal. I didn't care where we ended up; even the Nightmare Realms had to be better than Penumbra. I'd finally be free.

My skin tingled as the illusion threatened to slip. I couldn't continue to hold it. *No. Not now. Please no.* I was still separated from the dream by hundreds of gaping Penumbrans.

Horror filled me as the Visitor vanished, waking in Realearth. Stunned gasps washed through the crowd, followed by thunderous cheers. Not only was my chance for escape ruined but my entire body tingled, shedding the illusion. I was now just a filthy, ragged drone again. At least everyone was still too distracted to notice.

I dropped to the ground and began to pluck out weeds from a crack, pretending to be intensely interested in the task and oblivious to what was happening around me. My hopelessly unruly hair fell over my face in tousled snarls. I winced as the crowds pushed past, some of them thrusting kicks at me.

"Out of the way, stupid drone," someone grumbled, kicking me extra hard. Pain shot through my side and rage trembled through me but all I could do was remain huddled on the ground, plucking out weeds one by one. I gulped deep breaths in an effort to remain calm. I was sick of putting up with this kind of abuse and unable to defend myself. I'd come close . . . so close, only to slip at the last moment. If only more dreams took place here, I might have had time to come up with a better plan.

Gradually the crowds thinned as the Penumbrans hurriedly returned to the caverns. That didn't surprise me since they despised the outdoors, preferring the comfort of their interlocking caves.

My despair deepened. Why had I even tried? Not only did I fail to get away, but it was now obvious I'd disobeyed Treb's direct order to stay in the Dining Hall and keep working. I'd be lucky if all I got was a mere beating! Hadn't my years as a drone in Penumbra taught me that such efforts were useless? I'd *never* escape from here.

When everything had quieted, I dared to raise my head and push back my hair. The courtyard was nearly empty. The dream actors, along with the tables and balls, were already gone. It was as if a dream had never taken place. Only two figures at the far end were left, placing items into a wheelbarrow. I could tell, even from this distance, they were not Penumbran. One was a stocky, bearded man, the other a lanky boy. Both had vibrant red hair and brightly colored clothes.

Did I still have a chance? I looked around. The place was otherwise deserted. I was safe.

I rose to my feet and paced closer, my bare toes scraping against the paving stones. My heart pounded.

I froze as they turned toward me. They were gathering objects that appeared to be made of soft, transparent clay. What should I say? I had longed to sneak away with these outlanders but now my mind was completely blank, as if I really had been mind-drained. My face burned with humiliation as I realized how filthy and rumpled I looked. I ran a hand through my knotted hair and peered down at my baggy, threadbare tunic, smattered with stains. My face was also smeared with grime. When had I even last had a chance to shower? I usually didn't give my appearance any thought. What good was that to a drone?

If only I was cleaner, more presentable, I thought in desperation, wishing my illusion hadn't faded so quickly. The familiar tingle of another one spread over me. The strangers gasped.

What had I done? My mind whirled in panic as I looked down. My knee-length tunic had transformed into a pale green gown that appeared to be made of fine silk. Even my hands, which, a moment ago, had been callused and caked with dirt, were now as smooth and clean as a Penumbran lady's.

The boy's vivid blue eyes, behind round glasses, widened. He had spiky hair and a narrow, freckled face.

Did my hair look smooth as well? I reached up to touch it. The prickling sensation returned as my fingers encountered thick, tangled locks. A mixture of disappointment and embarrassment slid through me. I was back in my tattered tunic, grubby hands and all.

My brief discomfort was instantly replaced by terror. I had just displayed my illusion magic before these strangers.

"How come you didn't return with the others?" the boy asked in an awed tone. His accent carried a lilt that was so different from the sharp, guttural tones the Penumbrans spoke. It was reminiscent of Mother's speech, the accent outland Dreamearthlings used. A stab of homesickness struck my chest. "Aren't you one of the Substitutes?"

Substitutes. I'd heard that word before and wondered what it meant but that wasn't my greatest concern. "Please don't tell anyone you saw me do this," I rasped. I'd spoken aloud so little these past years that my voice sounded strange to my ears. "I'll be in deep trouble if they find out."

The boy looked confused but understanding softened the man's face. It was round and ruddy, fringed by a neatly trimmed beard. His gentle eyes were green, swirled with brown. "We promise, my dear." I gaped up at him. I couldn't help it. It had been years since anyone had acknowledged me in a non-commanding manner, let alone spoke with such kindness. The wistful longing to return to outland Dreamearth grew even stronger and reminded me of how much I missed Mother. "I'm George Mimsy," he turned toward the boy, "and this here's my son Peter." Peter smiled and nodded. "What's your name?"

"Remmi." It felt good to say it to someone other myself. "Remmi Clearwater."

"Clearwater?" He rubbed his beard. "I've heard that before. How old are you Remmi?"

I closed my eyes, momentarily savoring the sound of someone else saying my name. It had been years since I'd experienced that. Whenever I was addressed, it was just "You," or sometimes "Pale Green Eyes." "Almost fourteen." My voice still sounded dry and whispery.

"Just like me," said Peter, stepping forward, his shoes tapping against the cracked flagstones. I looked up at him and felt a twinge of jealousy. Did he have any idea how fortunate he was to be free and have a father who obviously cared for him? "Dad's training me to become a Thought Collector like him."

6

"Thought Collector?" I frowned in puzzlement as my gaze strayed to the wheelbarrow. Distant memories from my early childhood stirred. Substitutes. Thought Collectors. Hadn't I heard of such occupations when I was a child? I had never understood exactly what they were and Mother would change the subject whenever I asked.

"That's right. You've probably lived much of your life in Penumbra which is hardly ever Visited." George plucked an object from the wheelbarrow. It was clear like glass but resembled a lump of wet clay. "This is a thought, a memory," he said, holding the object out for me. "Go ahead. Touch it."

I did so, cautiously. Images I didn't understand stirred in my mind. I was riding in some sort of vehicle that moved rapidly along a black road. Outdoor edifices, larger than those I'd seen in any village, lined that street.

I pulled my hand away. The images instantly vanished. "This was the Visitor's thought?"

George nodded. "When Realearth Visitors enter Dreamearth during sleep, they shed extraneous thoughts, like this. It's up to us Thought Collectors to gather them up for the Analysts to study. This particular thought fell off that Visitor who'd just had his dream here. We—"

He stopped suddenly at the sound of hurried, thudding footsteps coming toward us. I froze, my blood turning to ice. Someone had spotted me, a drone, freely chatting with these outlanders.

A strong hand grasped me by the hair and jerked my head back painfully.

Chapter 2

Treb. I knew it was him before he even spoke. "I figured the displaced drone was you, Pale Green Eyes," he hissed in my ear. His breath was hot and sour. Sharp chills sliced my skin like glass shards. "I didn't think any of you had the wits to find the way out here on your own." His pig-like eyes flashed, his wide face was purple with rage. "This is for wandering away from your station."

Before I could flinch, his thick fist slammed into my left cheek. Pain shot through me as I stumbled to the ground. The metallic taste of blood filled my mouth. I glared up at him for a second then turned my gaze to the ground, remembering I was supposed to be mindless. I'd felt the force of his hand often enough but, every time, had to resist the urge to fight back. To do so could cost me my life.

"You worthless pile of garbage," yelled Peter, his shoes scuffling the ground as he flew at Treb. "I'm going to pound you so hard—"

"Calm, son," said George. His deep voice held an undertone of rage. "Remember, we are guests here. Violence is not how we solve things. There are other ways to deal with cretins like him."

I felt his firm hand on my shoulder. "It's all right, my dear. I won't hurt you." He spoke slowly, as if I really were mind-drained. Relief flooded me. He wouldn't reveal my true nature in front of Treb, or even use my name. I blinked hard in an effort to clear my watery gaze yet still maintain a blank stare. "Are you all right? Can you stand?"

I swallowed and nodded as I focused on keeping my expression impassive.

Treb snorted. "You treat that thing as if it has feelings, as if it's an actual person."

"*She* is a person, you half-wit," Peter snapped. "She's not just a drone."

Fear tightened my chest. *No!* I wanted to scream. *Don't give me away . . .*

"This one's always been more trouble than the others," Treb snarled, giving me a shake. "It's also been beaten more but obviously not enough. It's due for a—"

"Don't you lay another hand on her!" shouted Peter, clenching his hands into fists. His face burned a shade that matched his hair. "She's coming back with us. We have a ghostsilk portal. We'll be out of here in two seconds." He started to pull what looked like a wadded piece of silvery cloth from his pocket. It shimmered blindingly against the weak sunlight.

Reluctant joy replaced my fear. My plan was actually working. I was going to escape Penumbra after all.

Treb crossed his arms over his barrel-shaped chest and glared at Peter and George. "Then we can have you arrested and imprisoned for theft. You must honor our laws while you are on our land. If not, the Dreamearth government will track you down. That drone is Lord Malcent's property."

"Property." Peter's voice rumbled with rage. "She should be working as a Substitute, not a drone. She can form illusions. We saw her transform, just for a sec—"

Horror sliced through me. Peter slapped his hand over his mouth and his eyes grew enormous behind his glasses.

"She can?" Treb glared down at me but his slate-gray eyes were shadowed with fear. Fear? How could that be? I could feel my legs shaking.

"We saw nothing of the sort," George said, forcing a laugh. "My son here just has an overactive imagination. I've probably been working him too hard. But we do need a drone to help us with our Thought Collecting. If this one's too much trouble, we'd be happy to take her off your hands."

"It's not for sale." Treb grabbed my ear and tugged. I bit my lip and forced my expression to remain vacant. "If you need a drone, look elsewhere. None of Penumbra's drones are for sale. Now get off Lord Malcent's property this instant or I'll alert his police. They do not take kindly to interloping outlanders."

I couldn't even look back at George and Peter as Treb dragged me across the courtyard and into the tunnel. I swallowed a yelp as I stumbled beside him, my ear burning with pain.

"I always knew there was something different about you," his sneered, revealing ugly, stained teeth as he pushed me against a wall. Some of the Penumbrans passing by stopped to stare, including a uniformed policeman. The sight of a drone getting disciplined was one of the few things they did for entertainment.

"Hold her," he said to the policeman as he reached into his pocket and pulled out a syringe. The big man grabbed my shoulder, pressing it into the cold, rough wall. My heart beat rapidly, straining against my chest like a bird urgently flapping a broken wing.

"You've served your purpose, Pale Green Eyes," Treb hissed, grabbing a needle from his other pocket and sticking it into the syringe. "As you can see, no one will care in the least if we are short one drone." He glanced back at the forming crowd then grinned down at me. "One little prick and your problems will all be over."

My blood froze. Treb had done this to other drones, those who had gotten sick or grown too old to withstand the hard labor. Their bodies afterwards were dumped without ceremony into the cesspool where all the bathroom waste went.

A sudden energy surged through me as Treb rolled up the sleeve of my tunic, prepared to prick my skin with that needle. I dug my heels into the stone floor and twisted, freeing myself from the policeman's grasp. I sprinted away, pushing through the shocked crowds who had never seen a drone move so fast.

"Don't just stand there, you idiots!" Treb yelled, his voice pounding in my ears with a throbbing echo. "That drone must die. She wasn't properly mind-drained. She showed her magic."

Several gasps whispered through the crowd but I didn't stop to listen. I had to find a place to hide, to plan my escape from Penumbra. I ignored the tiny voice in my mind that told me that was impossible, that I'd be killed before I even set foot outside these caves.

My legs burned as I raced down several corridors. I'd been a fast runner as a child but years of taking on a slow, plodding gait had stiffened my muscles. I bumped into several startled Penumbrans but kept going. All were too shocked to see a drone running that no one stopped me.

A large clock on one wall told me that it was nearing evening. Most of the drones would be in the kitchens, helping to prepare dinner for the Penumbran citizens. I could blend in there, take on the illusion of another drone, and figure out a place to hide. I headed in that direction.

"Attention Citizens," boomed the voice of an announcer over the loudspeaker that echoed throughout all the corridors. "Watch out for a scrawny female drone that looks to be about ten years old." I winced. Years of near starvation in Penumbra had likely stunted my growth. "Her one distinguishing feature is her freakish, pale green eyes. Drone Supervisor Treb discovered she has illusion magic. There is no knowing what else she can do. She is highly dangerous. Alert the police or Treb if you see her but do not approach her."

Dangerous? If I wasn't so scared, I would have choked out a laugh.

My empty stomach growled as I inhaled the blending scents of spiced cave fish, baking mushroom pies, and brewing coffee that wafted from the nearby kitchen down the corridor. I hadn't eaten anything all day and the aroma was torture. I forced the feeling away. I couldn't think of food.

I opened the door of a small supply closet and breathed with relief when I saw that no one was in there. It was dark but smelled of floor cleaners and detergents. I formed an image in my mind of the illusion I would take. I'd be a male this time, taller, with lighter but still unkempt hair, and brown eyes. The familiar tingle spread over me. I could feel the illusion of height and the appearance of my tunic, which hung loose on my slight frame, growing shorter. I even envisioned a pair of shabby shoes over my now seemingly larger feet. The shoes provided for us drones were all too big for me so I went barefoot.

I didn't have a mirror but hoped the illusion was successful. At least I no longer looked like me. A fear that I wouldn't be able to hold it long enough itched the back of my mind as I shuffled out of the closet, once again taking on the plodding drone gait. The sounds of banging pots and excited murmurs from the cooks and other kitchen staff filled the vast room as I entered. I hobbled toward a small group of drones that were peeling potatoes in a corner. They didn't even glance up at me as I grabbed a peeler and joined them.

I concentrated on holding my illusion as I scraped a potato, feigning an intense interest in the task. The cooks and their assistants chattered non-stop about this exciting day: first a dream, then a rogue drone. An incongruous feeling of pride filled me. I had created just as much chaos in this boring land as that rare dream.

All conversation stopped suddenly. I forced myself to keep peeling even though my hands shook. Through the corner of my eye, I saw Treb enter with a tall man. He was pale even by Penumbran standards and wearing an elegant gray suit.

Lord Malcent. Panic tightened my throat. The paid kitchen staff had stopped their work. The drones continued with their tasks, not bothered by the distraction. I forced myself to keep scraping that potato, even though I had removed all of its skin.

"Are you sure you checked all of them thoroughly?" Lord Malcent said as he paced toward us with his hands clasped behind his back. The sound of his voice scratched my skin. I struggled not to shiver as I dropped the potato into the bucket and reached for another. I could feel the tingle of my illusion threatening to slip as his eyes, as cold and colorless as ice, bored into me. I briefly closed my eyes and concentrated. The sensation faded. I began scraping again, pretending to ignore him.

"Yes, my Lord," said the head cook. "We looked over every drone as they were assigned their tasks. The female you are looking for is not here."

I allowed myself to breathe as Lord Malcent stepped away. "You idiot!" He strode up to Treb and grabbed him by the wrist, dragging him toward the nearest counter. "How could you let a mere *drone* outsmart you?"

"S-she's not an ordinary drone, my Lord," Treb whined. "The mind-draining obviously didn't work on her."

Scrape, scrape, scrape . . . I forced myself not to stare as Malcent placed Treb's hand on a cutting board, grabbed a knife, and, with one fluid motion, chopped off his index finger.

Every Penumbran in the room gasped. One woman screamed and sank to the floor. I kept peeling, along with my fellow drones who took no notice, straining to keep my expression blank.

"Next time it will be your whole hand," Malcent said to a whimpering Treb as he tossed the bloody knife into the sink. One of the cooks pressed a cloth napkin over Treb's injured hand. The white cloth instantly turned red. "This drone must be executed on sight." Malcent scanned the room. "If any of you spot her, kill her immediately. Don't even bother to call for the police. Halfling hybrids like her are a danger to our world and Realearth. She must be destroyed!" He smacked his hand into his palm. Treb flinched.

"She might have escaped, my Lord," said the head cook.

A grin stretched across Malcent's thin face. "That would deprive us of an execution fitting for an unruly drone but miles and miles of desert wasteland await her if she does. She'd never survive."

Despair settled like a stone in my chest as he glided from the room with Treb at his heels.

"Unless she figured out how to fly," I heard someone mumble.

Chapter 3

My skin prickled, warning me my illusion was about to fade. I didn't have the strength to hold onto it much longer. Malcent's command for everyone to kill me on sight clanged through my mind. I had to leave the kitchen with its array of knives *now*, before I was spotted.

I dropped the potato and peeler and stood, slowly making my way toward what passed as the drone bathrooms just off the kitchen. No one paid me any heed. Only bodily functions distracted the drones from their tasks.

My entire body tingled the moment I stepped through the door and shut it behind me. I glanced down, saw I was back in my tiny body, baggy tunic and all.

The drone bathroom was one big room with a row of toilet pits on one side and a wall lined with rusted shower nozzles on the other. A small alcove that contained shelves of folded drone tunics stood off to the side. All were worn, patched, and stained.

I'd probably be safe in here since the only ones who entered were my fellow drones. It was also likely one of the first places Treb and the police searched, or so I hoped. It had been days since my last shower. I studied my dirt-crusted hands against the dim light of the softly flickering glowstones along the creviced ceiling. My fingernails were clotted with ash. My tunic, which reeked of sweat, was coated with a layer of grime. I longed to wash and change into a fresh tunic but couldn't chance it. If anyone heard running water in here, I'd be dead in seconds.

I stepped over to the shower side and leaned against the cold, mossy wall. The stifling air smelled of sweat, soap, and the stench coming from the toilets.

I softly thumped my head against the wall as my thoughts churned. My entire body was shaking, both from the cold floor and the illusion I'd just held. That had been the longest that one had lasted. I would have been excited had I not been filled with icy hopelessness. What was I going to do?

If only I could escape back into the Collective Unconscious Forest. I struggled to stop shivering. That was where I had lived for the first seven years of my life, before Mother died and I was brought to Penumbra. If only I knew how far it was and in what direction it lay.

A suffocating despair filled my chest. Malcent was right. Some Penumbrans did leave, including one of his wives and her only child. I don't know how they did it. Perhaps they were able to obtain those portals the outlanders used.

"Unless she figured out how to fly." That statement flickered through my mind. What did that mean? I couldn't fly! I'd never even tried. The only ability I had that I knew of was illusion magic, like Mother.

It was hopeless. What was I going to do now? I slid down the wall, settling on the cold shower floor. I pulled my knees to my chest and rested my head against them.

A sudden fury at Peter surged through me. I'd been able to keep my guise of mind-drained drone for years. It was his fault I was in this predicament. How stupid I was to think I could escape with his help. I clenched my fists so tightly that my uneven nails dug into my palms.

The feeling softened as an image of Peter's bright blue eyes behind those round glasses flashed through my mind, filling me with unexpected warmth. I instantly felt guilty for my mental outburst. This was the first time in decades that outland Dreamearthlings had ventured into Penumbra. Penumbrans purposefully cut themselves off from the rest of Dreamearth and prided their independence. The Cavern Lands had their own farmers, merchants, weavers, bakers, and cooks to maintain a functioning civilization. Of course any outlanders would be ignorant of Penumbran customs. How could he possibly know that any drone caught exhibiting a functioning brain would be executed, not given a pass to escape?

And Peter and his father had been so *nice*. I'd grown so accustomed to scolds and strikes, as well as complete indifference, that I'd nearly forgotten people were capable of kindness.

15

I forced back these thoughts. They were distracting me from plans to escape. I'd spent my early years in the depths of the Collective Unconscious Forest where Mother had taught me basic hunting and gathering skills. I wouldn't be completely helpless out there. I could even cook what I caught . . . I did remember how to start a fire, didn't I? Perhaps I wouldn't die, as Malcent had said. Still, that had been the reason I had never tried to escape before.

I remained where I was as my fellow drones relieved themselves before settling in for the night. The sharp, acrid scent of their unwashed bodies filled the chamber. They wouldn't bathe unless commanded. By the smell, I was sure one of Treb's underlings would herd them all into the showers first thing tomorrow morning.

After the last drone left, I took a deep breath and slowly climbed to my feet. I would still need food and supplies, whatever I could find. They probably wouldn't last long but I required something to at least get me started. I had to be careful. The police were still on the lookout for me and night guards patrolled all public areas, enforcing the evening curfew and prepared to discourage any potential thieves.

I tiptoed back through the kitchen, where the drones lay huddled on the floor asleep, some softly snoring. I gingerly stepped around them, mindful not to awaken anyone. Even though they wouldn't notice or care what I was doing, I didn't want to take any chances. At least the other workers had gone to their separate bedchambers.

I stole some dried meat, bread, and cheese from the pantry, which I stuffed into a cloth satchel. I found an old, battered canteen in the storeroom and slowly, slowly filled it with water from a sink, straining to remain as quiet as possible. My heartbeat throbbed loudly in my ears.

I froze at the sound of heavy footsteps thudding toward the kitchen. "I think I heard something," said the gruff voice of a night guard. "It might be that missing drone. I'll take care of it." The sound of a stick slapping against his palm echoed as he drew closer. His shadow rippled along the wall. A few of the drones stirred.

Terror pulsed through me. My mind spun in desperation as I struggled to create an illusion of invisibility, frantically hoping I'd had enough rest since my last one. My entire body tingled as it grew diaphanous then faded completely. The satchel and canteen dangling from my shoulders also seemed to disappear as the guard surged into view.

I stood still, holding my breath, terrified that the guard could hear my loud heartbeat. He held his club aloft as he scanned the room with narrowed eyes.

Please, illusion, hold for just a few more minutes. Desperation burned through me. The last one had drained most of my energy . . . energy I still needed for my escape.

I sighed deeply and ducked behind the sink as the guard's attention turned to the suddenly restless drones. My skin tingled as the illusion faded.

"Get back to sleep, you lot," he grumbled as his boots scraped against the floor. I allowed myself to breath. He was leaving. Good. "No more peeps out of any of you, you hear?" he snapped.

I remained huddled behind the sink for several minutes, my entire body shaking. Droplets of sweat tickled my forehead and dampened the wisps of hair that had fallen over my eyes.

I had to get out of here. I glanced at the tunnel the guard had exited. That led to the main square where the dream had taken place that morning . . . where I'd met Peter and George . . .

I looked in the opposite direction. There was another entrance that opened out into a small courtyard which was where the kitchen staff gathered on their breaks. It backed up directly into the Dusk Hills, where they loomed at their highest point.

It would have to do although my exhausted mind and body protested climbing those hills in the middle of the night. Still, that was better than what I would face if I simply succumbed to sleep, which was what my body, drained from the illusion, was begging me to do. I drew in a deep breath and staggered to my feet, my stiff, sore muscles protesting.

Before I stepped through, I glanced back at the drones huddled in a ragged pile on the floor. Most of them had fallen right back to sleep after the guard's brief visit. A queer sensation plucked at my chest. They had been my only family here in

17

Penumbra; a silent family that said very little and was only interested in performing the most mindless tasks. I struggled to feel a twinge of sadness but the only emotion that came to me was relief. Relief that I was leaving, that my wits had remained intact.

"Goodbye," I whispered to the slumbering group, feeling they at least deserved some ceremony, even if they were completely unaware of it.

Dim glowstones painted distorted shadows against the tunnel walls. I headed toward the courtyard. My palms were slick with sweat. I moved closer to the opening. What if a guard was posted there? I forced myself to keep moving forward, one weighted step at a time.

The cool, early spring air, tinged with the scents of dew and sage, stroked my face as I emerged from the tunnel. My breath caught in my throat. A guard was posted there but he was slumped against the wall, his snores rumbling.

I almost laughed with relief as I started across the flagstone courtyard, toward the hills. They were mostly barren, fuzzed here and there with clumps of brush. A nearly full moon strained to break through the mist, shedding a soft glow and weaving confusing shadows. The moist, night chill seeped through my thin, threadbare tunic with an icy embrace.

"Who's there?" I heard the guard's muddled voice say.

I ignored him as I pushed myself to climb the steep incline, ignoring the bite of sharp rocks on the bottoms of my feet and the dry brush that scratched my bare legs. My tired muscles burned but the memory of Lord Malcent's command to have me killed kept me from collapsing into a heap of exhaustion.

I topped the hill and stared down at a valley that was a sea of jagged hills and deep chasms. It stretched endlessly in the vague moonlight.

The brief burst of joy I'd experienced moments before vanished. How was I ever going to navigate *that*? It was as if all of Dreamearth was made up of nothing but desert badlands.

Rapid footsteps, snapping twigs and crunching over rocks, filled my ears. I turned. Several men clad in the dull livery of Penumbran police were racing toward me.

"There it is," called the leader. "The escaped drone."

Chapter 4

Panic pierced my chest. I raced down the hill, away from the police. Better to face never ending badlands than a hoard of men who would inflict unspeakable pain.

I had just reached the bottom when one of them grabbed me from behind and forced me to the ground. "We knew you couldn't get too far, little half-wit," the man mocked, his breath hot on my cheek.

Searing rage blazed through me, overpowering my terror. I'd been bullied by these brutes ever since I was a small child and had to take it, for fear of my life. But that no longer mattered. If I was to die, I'd do so fighting. I squirmed and kicked as the men pinned me down and one pulled out a knife. My flailing foot made a satisfying smack against someone's face.

A sensation of triumph rippled through me as his curses filled my ears. I glanced back. The man had his hand pressed against his nose. Trickles of blood seeped through his thick fingers.

Good. I hope I broke it. I scrambled away.

"No, you don't," yelled another, grabbing my ankle. Pain shot through my entire body as I fell back onto the ground. Pebbles bit into my skin through my tunic. "You'll pay for that, wretch."

My mind whirled as my arms were jerked behind my back. Sharp, shooting pain jolted through my shoulders.

I had to form an illusion. It didn't make sense to hide my talent any longer. These men were going to kill me for that anyway. Fear gave me the strength to do this yet again.

My thoughts fumbled as I strained to recall pictures of monsters from the Nightmare Realms I'd seen as a small child. Something massive and hairy with knifelike fangs. Would that be enough to scare the police?

The warm honey-tingle of an illusion trembled over my skin. I could feel my body appearing to balloon to a massive size. Yes, it was only an illusion, not really me, but the strangled gasps of fear from the police revealed I was successful. To my relief, they stepped back, their boots shuffling against the dirt.

"Treb was right," one gasped. "This one somehow escaped the mind-drain. How was that possible?"

I rose to my feet. Pain twitched in my side but I ignored it. My illusion towered over the guards with a massive body made up of thick black fur. I suppressed a laugh as they gaped at me, their eyes wild with terror.

That won't last long, my thoughts urged. *Run!*

Already I could feel the illusion fading, once again revealing my short, scrawny body.

I raced up the next hill, which was a mound of large, jagged rocks. It scraped the bottoms of my feet with painful gashes but I pushed on.

"It's just an illusion, you nitwits," snapped the leader's voice, echoing across the desert. "You heard what Lord Malcent did to Treb. Let's go."

I tumbled down the other side of the hill, ignoring the rough surface that tore at my skin and snagged my tunic. The vibrating sound of thundering boots pulsed in my ears. My lungs burned, winded, but I didn't have time to rest.

I scrambled to my feet and stumbled over sharp rocks.

"We got you now. Your illusions don't scare us."

I didn't look back but I could hear them creeping closer, closer. Laughter echoed around me as I staggered to a halt at the edge of a chasm, knocking a few pebbles into it. They fell soundlessly, never reaching the bottom.

"Give up, little drone." I still didn't turn around. The voice and footsteps were still several paces behind. "We won't hurt you so bad if you come quietly."

I studied the chasm and ignored the murmurings behind me.

"Quiet. I think she's gonna jump."

"That would take care of our problem." The footsteps stopped. All I could hear from the police was heavy breathing.

The chasm was a few feet across but stretched for miles on either side. My only choice was to jump over it. That appealed to me more than surrender.

My heart was beating so hard that my chest ached. I backed up a few paces, raced toward the chasm, and leaped.

I kept my gaze locked on the far edge. I soared higher . . . I was going to make it . . .

Instead of landing, the ground dropped away beneath me. My feet were pushing against air, not dirt and rocks. I was flying? My mind fumbled, struggling to understand this. Had Dreamearthlings dreamed when they slept, I would have figured this was a dream. How was that possible? The cook who said I might discover this was right.

My heart felt as if it had lodged in my throat in terror as I drifted higher, my legs still pumping in a running motion. The Penumbran police continued to stare up at me with their mouths hanging open. I was scared but knew I couldn't stop. Better to keep flying than end up captured.

"This is terrible," I heard one mumble. "She can illusion *and* fly. What else can she do?"

"Lord Malcent only knows about her ability to illusion," another said in a trembling tone, before their voices faded in the distance.

My fear calmed when I found it was easy to remain aloft. All I had to do was gently kick my legs and stretch out my arms, as I'd often done as a child, floating down Forest rivers on warm summer days, sometimes joined by the other village children. The evening air was cool and whipped tangled wisps of hair across my face but the weightless sensation of flight filled me with a bubbling euphoria.

Did I always have the ability to do this? I peered down. I was now so high the land was buried beneath Penumbra's fog. The sky was thickly freckled with pulsing stars. I gasped. When had I last seen stars? A few puffy clouds scurried across them.

I faltered momentarily in panic as I realized that, in my desperation to escape the police, I had dropped the food and canteen.

I'd have to figure something else later. I gritted my teeth and continued stroking against the air as if I were swimming. I couldn't go back for it now. Exhaustion from forming that illusion seeped into my bones and muscles, making the effortless flight a struggle.

Was I far enough away from Penumbra and the police to land somewhere? I forced myself to look down.

The ground was still covered in a thick mist.

I'm too tired . . . I can't keep going . . . My eyes, whipped by the cold wind, ached to close. My muscles burned and my breath was ragged, as if I'd been swimming for miles.

The mists surrounded me. I blinked as unexpected warmth stroked my face, legs, and arms. I realized I was encircled by clouds. No, not ordinary clouds, as I'd often seen from the ground. These appeared to be animals with thick, cottony fleeces. Like clouds, they faintly resembled a variety of creatures: birds, dragons, horses, turtles, but distorted, surreal versions of these beasts. Against the moon's glow, they ranged in color from dark gray to brilliant white. Their eyes, which were mostly hidden by their downy wool, glittered with faint flashes of colorful incandescence that reminded me of a sunset.

You are tired, they seemed to say as one, their voices reminding me of wind stirring through tree branches, a sound that brought back nostalgic memories of my distant Forest childhood. *Lie against us and sleep. We'll carry you to safety.*

"You're . . . clouds?" I whispered, settling onto the back of one that appeared to be a long-necked horse. Its fleece was even softer than the fine silks worn by Penumbran noblewomen.

Yes, came the reply. *It's only the special few who know how to fly that can ride us. We come to the aid of fliers in need, including the ones you call "Visitors."*

Several questions stirred in my mind. I longed to release them but instead was overcome by the warmth and comfort of the cloud fleece that surrounded me, the soft whispering of the winds rushing by, and the steady, flying motion. I drifted to sleep.

I awoke to the feel of warm sunlight on my face and a gentle crashing sound. The air smelled of salt and a fresh wetness I couldn't identify. I opened my eyes and sat up. My breath caught in my throat.

A vast body of water greater than any pond or pool I'd ever come across in either Penumbra or the Forest, formed an endless expanse of dark, shimmering blue. It was tinted with rainbow hues that swirled in mesmerizing patterns. A thrill passed through me as I realized what I was looking at. I had heard such things described by some of the travelers who occasionally passed through the Forest, but had never seen one myself. It was an ocean, a sea. It sighed and swelled as if it were a living, breathing creature, forming froth-tinged waves that lapped the sandy shore several feet away. Sunlight shimmered against the water, coating it with scales of gold, shifting to blue, then back to gold. The glare made my overwhelmed eyes water. It had been years since I had seen the sun uncloaked by mists and fog. I rubbed a fist across them in an effort to clear my vision and blinked hard.

I was sitting on rippling white sand, on a small beach. Several clouds, which had vague animal shapes, scurried across the brilliant blue sky. Their fleeces gleamed with faint golden shimmers.

Had my flight and sleeping on top of a cloud all been a dream? If so, how was that possible? Only Realearth Visitors were known to dream.

Besides, that couldn't have been a dream. Panic swelled in me as I stared out to sea. My throat was dry with thirst and hunger tore at my stomach. The cloud animals dropped me off here. But just where was this place?

Chapter 5

I certainly wasn't in the Collective Unconscious Forest. The air was already hot and moist even though it appeared to be early morning. Sweat tickled my skin beneath the coarse tunic. The Forest, with its endless canopy of trees, had been pleasantly cool even in the middle of summer. And its winters . . . I shivered, not wanting to think about those. The thought instantly made me welcome the overbearing heat of this strange place.

A sense of disorientation overcame me as something inside told me it should at least be noon. Just how far was I from Penumbra? Was I safe from Malcent and his police?

Well, wherever this was, I had to find food and water. I rose to my feet. I heard my empty stomach softly growling beneath the constant churning of the waves. I cursed myself for having left behind the food and canteen.

I looked around. Rows of small, colorful edifices stood a short distance away, in the opposite direction as the ocean. Unusual trees scattered the terrain. Some were covered with large, colorful flowers while others were impossibly tall and spindly, topped with fanlike leaves.

Where was I? My mind spun in a daze as I trudged toward the town. The sand was already hot, searing the tough soles of my bare feet.

The village was bustling with shopkeepers setting up wares under brightly colored awnings and children chasing one another and shrieking. There were many others, most in groups or pairs, who meandered casually, simply taking in the sights. Some people rode bikes or drove small, motorized carts down the narrow streets. Delicious smells of wood smoke and cooking food clung to the air, mingling with the ocean's dominating scent. My stomach twisted, reminding me of my hunger.

I stared at the crowds in shock. Unlike the Penumbrans with their uniform pale skin and white hair, these people came in a variety of shades. Many of them had skin the color of dusk and woolly black hair, which made them seem almost otherworldly. Their clothes were of so many varying, brilliant hues that I, so accustomed to monochromatic Penumbra, had almost forgotten that colors other than gray and black existed.

This land was the complete opposite of Penumbra. Everything from the brilliant open sky to the dark-skinned people and their multi-colored attire was Penumbra turned inside out and upside down. I knew I should be relieved but a stubborn fear clotted my throat. Would these strangers know instantly from my drab tunic that I was a drone? People glanced at me and hurried past as if I carried some deadly disease.

I looked down and noticed a dusting of sand had been added to my grime. A feeling of unease washed over me as I realized what a mess I must be. My filthy, tangled hair kept falling over my face and my tunic was completely hopeless. Such things hadn't mattered in Penumbra where the citizens hardly noticed me.

I fought the urge to form an illusion since I didn't want to risk displaying that ability in front of strangers. What if they mind-drained or executed such people here as well? The dreaded word "Halfling" flitted across my mind. And now that I had discovered I could fly as well meant that I had to remain extra vigilant.

I moved slowly through the village, unsure of what stance I should take. Keep my head down and my shoulders slumped like a proper drone? Or should I move with a more natural gait? As far as I could see, there were no drones in this village. I passed a woman sweeping the front of a shop and took fleeting note of the intelligent expression on her otherwise sun-withered face. She was certainly no drone.

These thoughts evaporated as I came across a gurgling fountain in the middle of a square. A statue of a fish-like creature was posed on a slender pedestal at the center of the fountain. Water poured from its wide mouth into the pool below. A few small, dark-skinned children played around the fountain's edge, laughing and splashing one another.

I knelt beside it, cupped my hands into the sun-warmed water, and gulped in mouthfuls. It had a slight metallic taste that reminded me of Penumbra's showers but soothed my dry throat.

I could feel a renewed energy pulsing through me. I splashed water onto my face, soaking my hair and the front of my tunic. Perhaps I could wash away some of that grime, make myself at least slightly presentable. My next goal was to find food.

"That fountain's not for bathing," shouted a tall, shadow-dark man, hurrying toward me with a broom. His words vibrated with the staccato accent that I had heard mingled in the crowds. "Get outta here!"

I dashed away, ducking into an alley, and stood against the wall, gasping in deep breaths. This was all too overwhelming. There was too much color, too much noise. In the distance, over the babble of the crowds, music played. My chest grew so tight it hurt. If I wasn't so frightened, so worried about where I was going to find food, I would love this place. At least in Penumbra, even if meals were scarce for drones, I could always find something to eat, limited though it was. What was I to do here?

I glanced around the alley. It smelled of garbage but at least the surrounding edifices provided shade from that stubborn, ever-present sun.

Garbage . . . My insides surged with an incongruous mixture of hope and revulsion. I was used to stuffing stray scraps off of dirty Penumbran dishes into my mouth when no one was looking, before washing them. And I had foraged in the dumpsters more times than I cared to think about, searching for anything edible I could share with my fellow drones. Most of them were even hungrier than I most of the time since they lacked the initiative to scavenge for food and instead relied on the scant, stale scraps that Treb allotted them.

A mist of flies swirled around the garbage cans. I struggled to wave them away in annoyance with no success. At least Penumbra, with its cool, damp gloom, lacked such pests.

"Get away from there," shouted a woman in that odd accent, slamming the door of the shop behind her. "No beggars. Off with ya! Go or I'll call the authorities."

Ice shot through my veins. Would the authorities here return me to Lord Malcent? I fled from the alley, my feet padding against the concrete. In seconds, I was back in the sunlight and barely missed getting hit by a motorized cart. The driver honked and shouted rudely, using words I barely made out.

What was I going to do? I fought the urge to crumple to the ground in defeated frustration. My thoughts raced back to the Forest where Mother worked odd jobs to keep us fed and clothed. Could I do that here?

I studied the rows of multi-colored shops and restaurants as a spark of hope deep within my chest strained to ignite. If I could only locate a place to shower and a clean set of clothes, perhaps I could find work. I'd still be a drone, of course, since I didn't possess any other skills but at least here, from what I'd observed, no one was mind-drained. The owner wouldn't even have to pay me. Just food and a space on the floor to sleep was all I needed. Certainly anything I found here would be superior to the life I had led in Penumbra.

The sight of several glass balls of varying sizes displayed in a window caught my eye, distracting me from my thoughts. Curious, I moved closer. Images flickered in their depths. One revealed a heavily wooded scene that had to be somewhere in the Collective Unconscious Forest. Another focused on a frightened Visitor surrounded by monsters in a place that seemed to be made entirely of shadows. A flicker of warmth filled me as I observed another Visitor soaring amongst cloud beasts just like the ones that had carried me here.

They were displaying dreams as they took place throughout Dreamearth! Viewing Crystals. Such devices were illegal in Penumbra, although Lord Malcent owned one. I had seen it numerous times while cleaning his quarters. He claimed they only served to remind Penumbrans that they were merely just a small part of vast Dreamearth when he felt Penumbra should be their entire world.

My gaze snagged on one of the larger crystals. It showed Penumbra's Main Square, decorated with large, colored balls. Dancers with animal heads waltzed around the elderly Visitor.

My heart lurched. I stepped through the door into the shop, desperate to hear if there might be mention of me, and cringed as a bell jingled. I hurried over to the large crystal that played the Penumbran dream.

Disappointment flooded me as it was instantly replaced by a woman garbed in an elaborate purple gown with billowing sleeves that flowed to her feet. Her face was more pretty than beautiful, dusted with faint freckles, and lashes that looked much too long to be real fringed her golden-brown eyes. Her hair draped one shoulder in a braid that formed an alternating pattern of black and gold.

"It has been years since I'd participated in a dream in Penumbra," she was saying to an unseen interviewer. I stepped closer, my breath suddenly coming out in shallow huffs. "The last time was—oh, it had to be ages ago, a couple of decades at least." She released a tinkling laugh. "That was . . . let me see. Yes, I was an apprentice then. It was just me and my good friend and colleague Luna Clearwater."

"Mother . . . ?" I gasped. My mind whirled.

"We were both apprentice Substitutes, training under the same—"

"Out, out!" a gruff voice shouted as a large man grabbed my arm with a grasp that hurt. "I won't have any vagrants stealing from my shop."

In the next instant, he had hurled me through the door, the bell clanging loudly in my ears. I stumbled out onto the street where I was jostled by the streaming crowds and once again enveloped by that glaring sun.

That woman knew my mother. I staggered down the street in a daze, my mind now too occupied to focus on my empty stomach and how I was going to feed it. I knew so little about Mother's life before the Forest, let alone who my father had been. These were topics she had refused to talk about whenever I'd brought them up.

But that strange woman had said "Luna Clearwater." That was Mother's name. My mind fumbled to figure out the word "Substitute." My thoughts shot back to my meeting with George and Peter. Hadn't Peter mistaken me for one after he had witnessed my illusion?

I was so deep in thought that I, at first, barely registered I was leaving the village behind, heading back toward the beach. But this was a different beach than the one where the cloud beasts had dropped me. A short distance away, on top of a low

29

hill, stood a colorful, umbrella-shaped edifice with a thatched roof. Smaller, cone-shaped cottages surrounded it, dotting a lush landscape scattered with flower-covered trees with long, sinewy leaves. I could hear the cacophony of birds that filled those trees. My mouth watered suddenly as I spotted several bright red fruits peeping out from beneath those leaves.

Food. A rare joy pumped through me as I raced to the first tree and plucked one of the fruits from a lower branch. It was larger than my hand and had a firm, fragrant skin. I forced myself to resist biting into it as I tried to assess whether or not it was poison, something I had learned years ago in the Forest.

I looked around. Dried pits of these fruits, apparently pecked at by birds and eaten by other small creatures, scattered the sand. Those were the only clues I had that they were safe to eat. I eagerly took a bite. If I were to die, at least it would occur in such a beautiful setting, not back in dismal Penumbra.

My mouth instantly filled with a tangy, refreshing sweetness. The fruit was so juicy it dribbled down my chin and splattered my damp, stained tunic. It was by far more delicious than anything I had ever eaten in Penumbra. I took another bite, then another, until I had devoured it down to the pit, which I dropped onto the sand.

I instantly plucked another and gulped that one down as well. I ate a third fruit much more slowly as I gazed out toward the sea. The late afternoon sun was sinking toward the west, sprinkling blinding golden shards over the wrinkling waters. Several boats dotted the ocean, some hauling fish up into nets. A rare euphoria brought on by a full stomach flooded me. Perhaps I could survive on my own after all.

My thoughts quickly sobered as I realized I would have to live on more than fruit if this was to be my permanent home. Where else could I go? I needed a plan.

I returned my gaze to the fishing boats. Fish . . . My heart jolted as I remembered how my mother had taught me to catch fish in the Forest rivers. Even though I was now satiated, my stomach twisted with longing as I recalled the tender, slightly sweet meat she had cooked for me.

The colorful water was smooth here, gently lapping the shore in tiny waves. The tide had crept in since this morning. I paced toward it and waded in up to my ankles. The water swirled around my sore feet with faint, silky warmth, filling me with a soothing comfort. The shallows were so clear I could see the rippling golden-white sand, shells, and small darting fish in distinct detail. Further out, the sea deepened into such an intense blue it looked as if it had been dyed.

I locked my gaze on the fish. They were small and fast and glinted with dazzling iridescence against the sunlight. Even the fish in this place were made up of impossible colors, so different from the dull, gray fish that were harvested in Penumbra's deepest, subterranean depths.

I could make a net to catch some of these. I struggled to remember the techniques Mother had used to capture pond and river fish.

I formed an illusion of a finely meshed net over my arm then sighed. That would do no good. It was merely an illusion, completely useless. If only I could create solid objects instead of mere illusions! I allowed the image to fade.

I trudged back to the copse of fruit trees, my mind churning with a plan. I'd plait leaves into a makeshift net to catch some of those fish. I yanked down a fistful of leaves as I pondered building a fire. Did I still remember how? It had been years since I'd attempted that. If it didn't work, I'd eat them raw. My mouth was already watering at the thought. Then I'd bathe in the ocean, see if I could get clean enough to appear less like a beggar. That horrible word, which I'd been called all day, echoed through my mind. Was a beggar worse than a drone? Perhaps then I could find work, start a new life here.

I studied the leaves as I clenched my lower lip between my teeth. My hands suddenly felt so clumsy and unskilled. I stared down at my callused fingers that had done nothing but hard, menial labor these past several years. How could I possibly create something as intricate as a net that could capture tiny fish? *Just start braiding the leaves,* my thoughts urged, *like Mother used to do with your hair.* The thought prickled my chest with a sharp pain.

"So you're the strange beggar girl everyone's been talking about," said an indignant female voice, its words vibrating with that island accent I'd been hearing all day. "Did

31

you swim across the Archetypal Sea just to trespass on my property?"

Chapter 6

Terror jolted through me. I reluctantly raised my head. A tall woman was standing over me with her hands planted on her broad hips. She wore a loose shift patterned with bright hues and a matching scarf covered her hair. A pair of seashell earrings dangled from beneath her scarf. Her skin was that same unearthly dark shade that was common here.

I cringed, expecting the woman to aim a kick at me and demand I leave. Instead, she continued to stare down at me through flashing onyx eyes.

"Can you speak, girl?"

My mind churned with conflicting emotions. As a drone, I'd made sure to keep my head down and rarely spoke, even when a Penumbran citizen had given me an order. I remembered how easy it had been to talk to George and Peter. But they had treated me with a kindness I hadn't experienced since I was a small child. I didn't know what to expect from this woman whose property I had trespassed on, whose fruit I'd eaten, and whose fish I had planned to snare. I had been chased away by angry shopkeepers all day. Why would this stranger be any different?

My face burned as I stared down at my fruit-smeared tunic through a mesh of matted hair. My fingers were tinged red as well and I was sure my face fared no better. I'd be lucky if this woman merely shooed me away and didn't call the authorities to arrest me immediately.

"Y-y-yes, ma'am," I finally stammered in a strained whisper. An urge to scramble to my feet and dash away tugged at me but my body refused. Instead, I cringed, drawing my knees to my chest.

"There's no need to be frightened." The woman's tone softened as she squatted beside me. "I don't bite, at least not usually. Do you have a name? Mine is Periwinkle Piper."

My muscles relaxed slightly. Perhaps this woman wouldn't strike me or alert the authorities . . . yet. Still, a part of my mind urged me to remain wary. "I-I'm Remmi."

"You're a mess, Remmi, and you look as if you haven't had a decent meal in ages." I stiffened as Periwinkle's gaze lingered on the fruit stains. "Where did you come from? I know everyone who lives here on Sandman Island and I've never seen the likes of you. Of course, we get plenty of visitors here, both of the Dreamearth and Realearth varieties." Chills dashed across my skin. "You don't look like the typical tourist. I should know. I own this vacation resort and have plenty of guests come through." She jerked her thumb toward the umbrella-shaped edifice.

I shifted my gaze away from Periwinkle and looked out toward the sea. What should I tell her? How do I know she won't turn me in to Lord Malcent if I told her where I'd escaped from?

My eyes remained locked on the restless waves. Their whispers were as soothing as the murmurs of the cloud animals that had carried me here. I had to be hundreds of miles from Penumbra, separated by land and sea, but was still reluctant to put my trust in a stranger. That was something Mother had taught me. And I also didn't want to share my newfound ability to fly and ride on clouds with anyone. My illusion talent had almost gotten me killed. Would those gifts reveal to Periwinkle that I was a Halfling, whatever that was?

"I'd rather not say," I said after what felt like an eternity of Periwinkle patiently waiting for an answer. "But I need a place to stay." I looked down and fiddled with the hem of my tunic. Wisps of hair tumbled over my eyes. "I'd be willing to work for food and shelter, of course, if there's anything—"

"Well, I could use an extra hand with the serving and cleaning, especially during the prime tourist season, which is coming up." Periwinkle placed a hand on my shoulder. "But I expect hard work. If you prove to be a good worker, I'll let you stay on permanently."

I felt a grin touch my lips. "I'm used to working hard, ma'am."

"So I can see," Periwinkle said, rising to her feet and taking my hands to pull me up. "Come. Let's first get you cleaned up."

I struggled to find my balance on the uneven sand. It was still hot even though the sun was sinking and I practically had to hop from foot to foot as Periwinkle led me toward a sandy path lined with flowering plants. Afternoon was stretching into twilight. The sun, deepening to gold, lengthened our shadows and spilled unsteady glitter over the restless sea. The cooling air was tinged with scents of salt, brine, and firewood.

"I have a spare cottage on these premises that you can use during your stay. Most of my staff lives in the village but since you're not from around here, you'll need a place to sleep."

I followed her down the path. Several small, cone-shaped huts with thatched roofs scattered the grounds. A few people, dressed in colorful, casual clothes, strolled about or lounged on the grass. Children played with a ball a short distance away, shrieking and laughing.

This was all still so strange to me. In Penumbra, the children were expected to play quietly while the adults, dressed in evening finery, sat around, softly chatting and drinking. Even celebrations came off as solemn ceremonies.

Periwinkle led me to a hut that stood a short distance away from the others. It was made of a thick, reddish-brown plaster I didn't recognize, embedded with decorative seashells.

"This will be your home while you work here," Periwinkle said, opening the oval door. I blinked several times when we entered, struggling to adjust my sun-soaked vision. We entered a round room with a small bed in the center and a desk beneath one window. A fan dangled from the tapered, thatched ceiling. "The bathroom facility is right in here," Periwinkle said, pushing open a door to reveal a porcelain bathtub that had been carved to resemble a seashell.

The place was small and sparsely decorated but I loved it instantly. A dazed feeling overcame me.

"I get this all to myself?" This was far more than I'd expected. I would have been satisfied with just a spot on the kitchen floor in a location that far exceeded Penumbra but having my own private dwelling . . . It was as if I were a Visitor in the midst of an impossible dream. This place reminded me of the tiny cottage in the Collective Unconscious Forest Mother and I had lived in when I was small.

"Yes, as long as you do your job and don't get lazy on me. Now wash up and meet me back in the dining area. You will have dinner then spend the evening helping to serve the guests, under my supervision."

"Yes, ma'am." My stomach leaped. Did she just say I'd get dinner?

"I'll . . . do you have anything else to wear?" I felt my face flush a deep red as Periwinkle ran her gaze over my hopeless tunic. "No, you didn't bring any belongings, did you?" She shook her head and clicked her tongue.

"I-I lost them," I stammered, hoping this wouldn't lead to more questions.

"Well, no matter. I'll find you something." Periwinkle pulled at my tunic, tightening it against my body. "You sure are a tiny little thing. While you are freshening up, I'll check around for any spare garments. Sometimes guests leave things behind and never come back to claim them. There might be something that will fit you. It will have to do for now until you've earned enough money to buy your own clothes."

"Money?" I blinked up at Periwinkle. When Mother had worked the occasional odd job in the Forest, she usually received goods, not cash, in exchange. The Penumbran Citizens were also paid for their jobs but it was unheard of to do that for drones. The belief that we were supplied with food, shelter, and clothes was considered quite enough for our labors.

"Of course." Periwinkle sounded almost indignant. "Did you think I don't pay my staff? Now hop to it. It promises to be a busy night."

I slipped into the bathroom as soon as Periwinkle left and filled up the tub. I gratefully peeled off my tunic and stepped into the water. It momentarily scalded my feet and I winced as I gradually lowered my body into it. The heat warmed my face and gently lapped my skin as the temperature adjusted around me. I sighed as I lay back and closed my eyes.

It had been so long since I'd bathed in privacy. In Penumbra, I'd showered with all the other drones.

I luxuriated for some time, lathering myself with scented soap, enjoying the water's warmth against my sore joints and muscles. There was even shampoo, its fragrance that of lilacs that pinched my chest with wistful memories as I rubbed it through my knotted hair. Mother's hair had always smelled like that . . .

Memories of falling asleep in her arms when I was a small child, being kissed and sung to, flooded my mind. I closed my eyes and pictured her beautiful face with its high cheekbones and large, dark eyes. I remembered her lilting voice and sweeping brown hair that tickled my skin.

My thoughts shot back to that woman in the Viewing Crystal, the one who claimed to have known Mother. Who was she? How did she know her? My mind itched with helpless curiosity but I forced it back. Sandman Island was now my home. Mother was dead, and that woman was merely a stranger.

When I finished my bath, I dried off with a fluffy towel, savoring its soft feel on my skin. I glanced down at my filthy drone work tunic, crumpled in a corner. Periwinkle was going to find me something else to wear. Hopefully she would let me burn that rag.

I wrapped myself in the towel and stepped out of the steamy bathroom. Deep gold beams from the lowering sun spilled into the main room, speckling the cot and wooden floor. There was something draped over the bed.

My heart gave a leap. It looked like a simple white shirt. I slid it over my head, barely able to contain my excitement. It was soft and didn't scratch my skin like the coarse drone tunics I was used to. But, like those tunics, it hung loose over my skinny body and reached below my knees. At least it was stain-free and smelled faintly of detergent.

A pair of sandals lay on the floor next to the cot. I slipped them on but they were too big and felt strange on my feet. I pulled them off, preferring to remain barefoot. That shouldn't matter around here. Most of the guests I'd seen had been barefoot.

I found a comb and brush on the desk and, standing before an oval wall mirror, started to work on my thick, matted hair. I gritted my teeth as I tugged and pulled. A flicker of melancholy spilled through me. Mother used to brush my long hair every day when I was little, sometimes braiding it into a neat plait when it was just too unruly to properly smooth.

If only she were here now. My frustration flared as the comb continued to get painfully stuck in my hopeless snarls. She'd be able to fix this. I couldn't even remember when I'd last brushed my hair.

Sighing with exasperation, I searched the desk drawers, coming across pens, pencils, paper, and a pair of scissors. I struggled to keep my hand steady as I lopped my hair off just above my shoulders.

Deep brown locks tumbled onto the desk and floor in tangled drifts. I gathered them into the wastebasket and brushed loose strands off my new garment. My hair wildly floated around my head in uneven layers, but at least that was an improvement.

I noticed a dark smudge on my left cheek in the mirror. Hadn't I washed off all the grime? No, it wasn't dirt but an ugly, purpling bruise. I pressed my fingertip against it and winced. It was still tender.

Treb. I should be used to his bruises by now but anger bubbled in my chest. That was where he had last hit me, in front of George and Peter. Well, he no longer mattered. He was endless miles away, still stuck in Penumbra's sunless Cavern Lands, and short one finger, while I was now on a paradise island, ready to begin a new life.

Chapter 7

I headed toward the dining cottage keeping my head down, hoping no one would notice me. I feared the white shirt would act as a beacon, drawing peoples' attention. A part of my mind knew that was silly. Why would anyone here care if I didn't act like a proper drone? I hadn't noticed any drones since I'd arrived. But my body still tensed, urging me to remain alert.

I slowed my pace and glanced around. Families and couples strolled by the beach and small groups of adults stood around, chatting and sipping drinks. No one paid any attention to me. I allowed myself to breathe, drawing in scents of salt water mixed with wood smoke.

My gaze snagged on the western horizon. The sun was slipping into the ocean, transforming wisps of silken clouds into fleeces of molten gold and crimson. The sea had become an unsteady mirror, etching these glowing patterns onto its surface.

I sighed and strained to imprint that beauty into my memory. I had so rarely viewed such a sight during my time in Penumbra and it filled me with euphoria. Were those the clouds that carried me here? But these didn't resemble animals, just feathery wisps of glowing down. I couldn't understand how the other people could continue hurrying past, not even glancing at them, as if they saw this every evening. They most likely did. I continued on.

The dining cottage's walls were made entirely of glass, providing views of the sea and foliage from every angle. The high ceiling was shaped like the inside of an umbrella and sprinkled with colorful hanging paper lanterns. Paintings of exotic birds, animals, and flowers decorated it. Polished wooden tables scattered the room. A few people were eating at some of these. Rich aromas that I couldn't identify but made my stomach nag even harder soaked the air.

Periwinkle's eyes widened with delighted surprise when she saw me.

"My goodness, Remmi. I barely recognize you. That shirt's a little big, but it was the best I could find under the circumstances. I suspected it would fit more like a dress on you. But what's this?" She grabbed my chin and tilted my face back. "I'd thought it was grime but it's a nasty bruise." Her tone grew sharp with anger. "What happened, Remmi? Who did this to you?"

I swallowed and looked away. "It's really nothing, ma'am." My voice came out soft and whispery.

"I'd say it *is* something." Periwinkle was practically shouting. "Whoever hit you deserves a good thrashing. It wasn't anyone on Sandman Island, was it?"

"No, ma'am. He's far, far away."

"That's good. If he comes around these parts, I'll deal with him myself. And call me Periwinkle. The rest of my staff does."

She hurried me through an opening draped by a floral print curtain into a kitchen. This room was much smaller than Penumbra's cavernous one but it made me feel oddly comfortable. A slender young man was frying slices of meat on a grill as he sang in a strong, melodious voice. The scents made my mouth water so much that I feared I might drool.

"Andrew, this is Remmi," Periwinkle said to the man. "She'll be working with us, starting with this evening's dinner shift."

"Fine," he said sharply. His skin was as dark as Periwinkle's. He had black, shoulder-length hair that was fixed into several slender braids. "We're going to need all the extra hands we can find tonight. Morphia Nightshade's the Substitute in tonight's scheduled dream. She's eating here first. Everything's got to be perfect."

"Ease up, Son. We still have plenty of time before Morphia arrives," said Periwinkle. "But Remmi and I still need to have our dinner." She grabbed a wooden bowl, filled it with rice, vegetables, and chunks of fish, and dripped a thick sauce over everything. She handed me a bowl, along with a glass of cold water.

After she served herself, Periwinkle sat down at a small table just outside the kitchen. I crept to a corner and settled onto the floor with my food.

"What, by the First Visitors, are you doing, Remmi?" Periwinkle gasped. I nearly knocked over the water glass, fearing I'd accidently formed an illusion. "Why are you sitting down there?"

I shook my head. I couldn't think of anything to say. I was used to huddling in corners with the other drones, stuffing whatever scraps I could get my hands on into my mouth.

"Don't sit there gaping like a trapped fish, Remmi." Her tone was edged with impatience. "I already told you I won't bite. Sit, eat." She patted the chair next to hers. "You heard my son Andrew. Morphia will be here soon and we have to be ready."

"Who's Morphia?" I slowly stood with the dishes—the bowl painfully hot in one hand, the cup chilling the other—careful not to spill, and slumped into the seat. My mind spun. In Penumbra, it was unheard of for drones to share meals with their superiors. But I was no longer a drone, was I? A server placed a basket of steaming rolls in the center of the table.

"Morphia Nightshade?" Periwinkle cocked an eyebrow. "Where in Dreamearth are you from that you've never heard of her? She's a world famous Substitute."

"Substitute?" There was that word again. I feared all these questions might force Periwinkle to pry into my past, but I just had to know. "Dreams didn't happen too often where I was from."

"They're dream actors who illusion themselves into people the Visitor knows in waking life. Now eat up. She'll be here shortly."

Illusion magic. Like what I had. Was Morphia a Halfling too? If so, why didn't she fear for her life? Maybe only Penumbrans hated Halflings. But if that was so, then why had I been sent there when Mother died? And why had she always warned me never to use my magic?

The overpowering smell of the food pushed aside these questions.

I ate at first with hesitance, then ravenous greed. The fish was soft and held a spicy tang, the vegetables cooked to perfection, neither too hard nor mushy, and delicately seasoned. I had never tasted a more delicious meal and swallowed it down with the water. I took a bite of one of the rolls that Periwinkle handed me. It was rich and buttery.

To my disappointment, I filled up quickly and had to push back unfinished portions. Now I regretted having devoured those fruits earlier.

"Is that all you're going to eat, Remmi?" Periwinkle asked in a concerned tone. "You could use some meat on those skinny bones of yours."

"I-I . . ." I gulped and forced myself to look into Periwinkle's eyes. To my surprise, they weren't pure black but held a hint of dark blue that reminded me of the sky just after sunset. "This is more than I've eaten in a long time." I slipped the partially eaten roll into my shirt pocket, hoping she wouldn't notice, in case I got hungry later.

"That's all right." She gently touched my hand. I blinked. Her full lips curved into a slight smile and the edges of her dark eyes crinkled with fine wrinkles. "We'll fatten you up in no time. The fishermen bring in tons of fish every day and Andrew knows countless ways to prepare them. I guarantee that, even if you stay here for months, you won't repeat a meal.

"I'll also have to send you to school." I looked down. A strange, swooping feeling filled my stomach. It was illegal to educate drones beyond basic tasks in Penumbra. "You speak fairly well, Remmi, so I assume you've been to school before."

I felt my cheeks burn with a glow as intense as that sunset I'd seen earlier. My schooling stopped when I was seven, after Mother died and I was sent to Penumbra. Memories of snuggling in her lap when I was very small while she read me stories from books with colorful pictures, flitted through my mind. I secretly kept up the skill by reading snippets of books I'd found in some of the Penumbran bedchambers while I was cleaning. I had to be extremely careful, since I'd face a mind-drain at best if I was caught. "I did but it's been years."

"I'll teach you then, at first, to get you caught up." Her voice was gentle. "Starting tomorrow. I did that with my son Andrew before he started school. I can do the same with you. When you're ready, you'll attend the village school."

"Sorry to interrupt, Periwinkle," said a breathless server, hurrying up to our table. "But Morphia Nightshade just arrived."

My gaze darted around the dining cottage, which had filled up since I'd entered. Several of the diners had stopped eating and were peering toward the front door. They reminded me of the rarely excited Penumbrans when a dream had finally come to the Cavern Lands.

"Is the dream already starting?" Excitement filled me.

"No, Remmi. That won't happen till later. Dreams occur frequently here but when the actors and Substitutes show up ahead of time, they get special treatment." She stood and turned to the server. "Thank you, Percy. You and I will wait on Morphia and her people. Remmi, you stay beside me, since it's your first shift. Just follow my lead and observe. The rest of the staff will see to the other guests."

Shock jolted through me as a tall, stunning woman entered. She was the same woman I had seen in the Viewing Crystal, the one who claimed to have known Mother. She wore a similar wide-sleeved gown, except this one was dark blue instead of purple. As she glided into the dining hall, I caught a glimpse of her matching, jewel-coated shoes. They had slender, spiked heels. How did she not trip and fall in those? Instead, she moved with an elegant grace, her head held high. I couldn't help but stare. She put the Penumbran noble women to shame. I wasn't alone in my awe. Every eye in the room was fixed on her. Her hair, black with gold streaks, now hung loose and fell in ripples past her waist. She was trailed by three others, two men and a woman, almost as elegantly dressed.

That first woman had to be Morphia Nightshade. I ached to approach her, to ask about Mother and illusion magic, but knew how laughable that would be. I had no idea how to approach a person with such elite status. Why would she even *want* to talk to *me*? My insides withered at the absurdity of that situation. I was only a drone and had spent this entire day as a beggar.

"Welcome to Sandman Island, Mrs. Nightshade," said Periwinkle, with a bow of her head. "I hope you are enjoying your stay. Please, allow me to show you to our finest table."

Morphia merely acknowledged Periwinkle with a slight nod. She and her companions were seated next to a window that looked directly out onto the dusk-darkened sea. A vase of colorful flowers and a flickering candle stood at the center of their table. Percy appeared with a bottle of wine and filled their glasses.

My thoughts churned as the other diners returned to their own meals and Periwinkle tended to Morphia. I still couldn't figure out why some people with magic were called "Halflings" and turned into drones or executed, while others were treated like Penumbran nobles. What was the difference? It was best I not reveal that I could fly and create illusions until I had the answer.

A nudge from Periwinkle startled me. "I'll start you off with something simple, Remmi," she said, handing me a silver tray filled with steaming, buttery bread. "Take this to Morphia and her helpers, see if they need bread. If one person doesn't, just move onto the next. If they do, pick the piece up with the tongs, like this," she demonstrated, "and set it gently on the bread plate. Don't be nervous. I'll be right behind you."

My heart raced as I approached Morphia. *She knew Mother, she knew Mother . . .* repeated loudly in my head, blocking out all the other noise. I kept my eyes averted as I approached, as I'd done countless times in Penumbra when serving its citizens. The scent of her perfume overpowered the bread.

"Would you like some bread, Mrs. Nightshade?" Periwinkle asked from behind me.

"No, thank you." Morphia's voice was curt but polite. I felt her gaze flicker briefly over me before she returned to her conversation. I moved to the next person.

"Good job, Remmi," Periwinkle said, after I'd made my round, as she took the tray from me. Warmth filled me. I'd never been complimented on my tasks in Penumbra and didn't know how to respond.

I next helped Percy serve their salads, followed by the main course: baked fish on a bed of rice, encircled by vegetables that had been cut into delicate flower patterns. I kept my eyes downcast, not daring to look straight at Morphia or the others.

My thoughts battled, one part of my brain urging me to ask about Mother, the other to keep quiet. Even if I wasn't a drone, I was still doing drone work. What if asking her a question earned me a beating or got me executed? That seemed unlikely here, from what I'd seen, but I still couldn't let my guard down. My escape from Penumbra would have been in vain.

"You are doing well, Remmi," Periwinkle whispered. "But don't be afraid to smile."

Smile? I had to remind myself again that things here were different. Even so, the thought of displaying a facial expression that wasn't blank stupidity before people I was serving filled me with dread.

This isn't Penumbra, I silently repeated as Morphia and her group left to prepare for their dream and Periwinkle had me pass out bread and refill water glasses at other tables.

I attempted a hesitant smile with one small girl and, to my surprise and delight, she smiled back. That was something that had *never* happened in Penumbra and, despite my aching feet at the end of the shift and the noise that continued to vibrate in my ears even after the crowds thinned and silence dominated, a warm sensation of satisfaction spread through my chest.

"Let's get to the bonfire party where the dream's going to take place," Andrew said, tossing aside his apron after the last guest had left and we'd cleaned up. "It'll be starting in less than twenty minutes."

"And Morphia Nightshade will be there?" My insides tightened.

"Of course," said Periwinkle, starting in the direction of the beach. "She's the star of the dream, although you won't recognize her." A crowd was gathered there, around a large, dwindling bonfire. A few brightly dressed people played instruments: two strummed small guitars while three others blew into wooden pipes, creating a lively tune that others danced to in bouncy, springy steps. The rest of the group clapped along. A wistful sensation prickled my chest as I remembered long ago summer nights spent around campfires while music was played and stories were told.

"Because of illusion magic?" I practically had to run to keep up with her and Andrew since their legs were much longer than mine.

"That's why Substitutes are so highly paid. All Dreamearth companies tithe to them." *Like the Penumbran citizens to Lord Malcent,* I couldn't help thinking. "I even give my share, but we don't begrudge them that. They are some of the most important people in Dreamearth. All those who work directly with Visitors are."

"Are Substitutes Halflings then?" It was difficult to pry out that question but I had been aching to ask it all evening.

"By the First Visitors, no!" Andrew turned on me so suddenly that I cringed, fearing he'd strike me. The bonfire's smoke burned my throat.

"Easy Andrew—" Periwinkle started but he continued as if he hadn't heard her.

"Halflings are a different matter altogether. Don't *ever* let anyone hear you make such a comparison. People with just illusion magic are full-blooded Dreamearthlings. Halflings are anomalies that can illusion all right, but not just on themselves. They can manipulate the surroundings and even hurl people great distances with just a thought. They've even been known to cross over into Realearth and convince people they were blasted gods. They—"

"Daddy finally made it!" Andrew's anger faded as a tiny girl dashed up to him with her arms raised. Her hair, like her father's, was fixed into multiple braids. They were decorated with colorful beads that glinted against the firelight. A pretty young woman with another small child followed her.

"Faya!" Andrew swept the girl up and spun her around.

Memories of Mother holding me until I fell asleep, singing and telling stories, brushed my mind. But I never knew my father. Mother refused to talk about him whenever I asked. Was he the reason I was mistaken for a Halfling?

That had to be a mistake. I couldn't do those things Andrew had said, just create illusions . . . and fly. Could Morphia fly as well? That was another thing I wished to ask her.

"Dream incoming!" someone shouted above the laughter and music.

46

Everyone hushed as several figures in bright yellow jumpsuits scurried by, carrying sofas, chairs, and a toilet, which they scattered along the beach.

"What's all that for?" I whispered to Periwinkle.

It was Andrew, balancing Faya on his shoulders so she could see, who answered. "Props for the dream. This Visitor will be in desperate need of a bathroom but all she'll find is that toilet in full view of our group." He chuckled.

"How do you know this?"

"All the scheduled dreams on our island are printed in the *Dream Journal*, a weekly magazine. Well, at least what should take place if the Visitor sticks to the script. They have the power to change things. It's just that most of them don't know."

"Andrew may make his living at cooking," said Periwinkle, a grin crinkling the corners of her glittering eyes, "but his real passion is dream watching. Too bad there isn't any money in that."

"Hey, Mother, you know we need Visitors more than they need us," said Andrew.

A woman's voice called for our attention.

It was Morphia Nightshade. She had changed from the long-sleeved gown into a black, skin-tight outfit that emphasized her slender figure. Her feet were bare and her golden-black hair was pulled back into a single braid, the same way she'd worn it in the Viewing Crystal. I couldn't help noticing that, without those high heels, she looked much shorter, tiny even.

"The dream will take place in a few seconds," she said, her strong voice carrying over the crowd, overpowering the lapping waves and snapping flames. "This particular Visitor will appear to be a child, even though, in waking life, she is a newly married adult. According to the script, she is feeling nervous and unsure about her new role in life, which is why she has reverted to her childhood persona. I will portray the pet she had at that time, which has suddenly appeared on what she thinks is a family vacation. In her present waking life she is on a tropical vacation honeymoon with her husband, which explains why the scriptwriters have selected your island for the setting. You all must remember to remain silent observers. It is not your job to interfere with this Visitor, even if you feel an urge to help or torment her. That is reserved for hired actors and Substitutes like me. Are there any questions?"

I still ached to ask her about Mother but couldn't. Not in front of all these people. Had Mother also interacted with Visitors? Why had she kept that a secret?

Soft murmurs swept through the crowd but no one asked her anything.

"Good. Let the dream begin."

I gasped as Morphia appeared to melt. She sank to the sand in a crouching position, rapidly transforming into a small, fluffy poodle. She was using illusion magic in full view of a cheering audience. All of Dreamearth knew she and others did this and they were even paid for it. I still couldn't get over that.

A girl who looked to be no older than seven suddenly materialized. She was as pellucid as a ghost and her eyes darted wildly, as if she were struggling to take everything in.

"Mom? Dad?" she called in a high, piping voice. "Where are you?" She moved with a jittery gait toward a woman who was reading a newspaper on one of the sofas. "Excuse me. Have you seen my parents?"

"No." The woman didn't even glance up from her paper.

"What about my husband?" Her voice wavered with uncertainty. For a moment, her image blurred, briefly stretching into a tall woman who must have been in her twenties, before snapping back into a child.

"He's probably back at the hotel, where you left him," the woman said, flipping a page of her newspaper. It made a soft crinkling sound that was nearly drowned out by the constant stirring of the waves.

"Do you know where the nearest restroom is?" The girl tugged at her long blonde hair and hopped from foot to foot. Several people in the crowd laughed softly behind their hands.

I strained to choke back sudden anger. I had to remind myself that this was only a dream to her. She would soon awaken back in Realearth.

"There's one right over there."

An expression of relief crossed the girl's flushed face until she looked to where the woman was pointing. It was the toilet, standing out on the open beach, with all of us watching. She recoiled and backed away.

A twinge of sympathy twisted my chest. Her frustration pained me since I'd had no more privacy than an animal during my years as a drone.

Morphia, in poodle guise, began softly whining. "Rusty," the girl gasped, bending down to reach for her pet. "What are you doing here? I thought we left you at home. Do you know where everyone is?"

Morphia as Rusty wagged her tail, then turned and dashed across the beach, toward the starlight-frosted sea. The girl, transforming back into a woman, ran after her. I at first thought the illusioned dog and the Visitor were going to plunge into the ocean but, instead, they slipped through something silver, like a water shimmer, and disappeared. Memory stirred in my mind. Hadn't Peter pulled out a similar object when I'd first met him? The newspaper reading woman stood and followed, as did the yellow clad men, after they had quickly gathered up the toilet and furniture props. The crowd applauded.

Only one person from the dream crew was left, a man with a wheelbarrow, who began searching the sand for stray Thought Artifacts. Peter? George? I didn't recognize this man. My disappointment deepened as I realized Morphia wasn't coming back.

The crowd began to disperse. Andrew pulled his now drowsy daughter into his arms and handed her off to her mother.

"Where did they go?" I asked. "Did the girl . . . woman, wake up?"

"Not yet," said Periwinkle, pointing to the strange, shimmering object. The Thought Collector, having gathered what he could find, pushed his wheelbarrow through then followed, instantly vanishing. The shimmer disappeared a second later. "They entered the ghostsilk portal, which—"

"Why do they call them ghostsilk?" Peter had called his portal that as well.

"They are spun from the hair of ghosts that dwell in the Nightmare Realms. Only those who work directly with Visitors are permitted to own ghostsilk portals so they can travel to different parts of Dreamearth in seconds. That woman wasn't finished dreaming, she merely moved on to another location for a different segment, one where she is probably once again an adult."

I longed to ask if Morphia would be back but resisted. I'd found a home here. True, I was still doing drone work but I wasn't required to act like one. I had my own cottage and Periwinkle was paying me.

And I had to figure out why I'd been mistaken for a Halfling. I silently vowed to keep my magic to myself until then. I could still be in danger otherwise.

Chapter 8

I inched slowly beneath the covers of my bed and felt odd, as if I were some other person. It had been so long since I'd slept in a bed. Not since I was a child, living in a similar cottage in the middle of an endless forest. For the last several years, I had grown used to lying on a cold kitchen floor. This was strange, alien, and far too soft.

Sighing, I pushed the covers aside and settled on the hardwood floor. That was better but, despite the fragrant, balmy spring air that seeped in through the open window, I shivered. I missed the surrounding press of several warm bodies. I pulled off the bedcovers and rolled them up into separate mounds, which I placed around me, pretending they were my fellow drones. I squashed the pillow over my face to block out the invading moonlight.

I still couldn't sleep. The sounds were all wrong. Instead of the low snores and steady breaths of the other drones, the night was restless with the chirps, squawks, and hoots of outside creatures. Through all that, my ears picked up the sea's distant churning. I rose to my feet, closed the window, and returned to the floor between the makeshift drones. The island racket was only slightly muted.

As soon as I had drifted off, I was awakened by the crash of thunder and heavy pounding against the roof as if it were being bombarded by countless pebbles. The moonlight seemed to have transformed into brilliant lightning flashes that proceeded loud thunder blasts.

I shifted position as I turned my thoughts to the frequent but gentle Forest rains that would drift through the branches like wet weightless feathers. Were these heavy squalls a frequent occurrence on Sandman Island? If so, how did anyone ever sleep?

I managed to slip back to sleep and woke with the warmth of sunlight on my face. Panic jolted through me. I had overslept and would be—

It took a moment before my brain adjusted to these new surroundings. I was not in the dreary Penumbran kitchen but a sunlit room. The night noise had been replaced by overpowering birdsong, mixed with the distant crowing of a rooster.

I raced outside and hurried toward the dining cottage. I nibbled on the roll I'd saved from last night. It was now hard and dry but I didn't know when I'd get a chance to eat again.

The dirt path was only slightly damp and already the sun was hot. The humid air smelled of blending fragrances: flowers, the sea, and cooking food, which made my stomach twist in longing. Several resort guests were already out, enjoying the day, most of them lounging in the sun.

The dining cottage was crowded with guests, which other servers were attending. I grabbed a basket of bread and placed it on a table to show Periwinkle I didn't need to be told what to do, like a drone. The family sitting there stared at me with surprised expressions.

A wave of panic swept through me and I froze. What was I doing wrong?

"Not so fast, Remmi." Periwinkle pulled me away and steered me toward the hanging that led into the kitchen. "First, let's neaten you up a bit. You look as if you just tumbled out of bed."

I blushed as she pulled a tiny comb out of her pocket. That's exactly what I had done. I was so used to going straight to my tasks in Penumbra immediately after waking that it hadn't occurred to me things might be different here. No one had cared how drones looked.

Periwinkle ran the comb through my uneven hair. At least I'd cut off the nasty snarls. She then straightened my rumbled dress-shirt and stood back. "There, that's a little better. But I ought take you into town and get you some new clothes."

My mind fumbled with this information. Didn't Periwinkle say I'd eventually have enough money to do this? I'd never bought clothes before, even when I lived in the Forest.

Mother had always made mine. "B-but I only worked a little last night," I stammered. "I don't think I have enough yet."

"It'll be on me this time, Remmi."

"But—"

"Not another word. I'm in charge here. There's a little boutique not too far from here that sells clothes that aren't just for tourists. We'll go there right after breakfast."

"Breakfast?" I blinked at her in confusion. Drones had to be commanded to eat to keep their strength for work, but were only given left over scraps from Penumbra's kitchen staff at random times.

Andrew emerged from the kitchen with a steaming plate, which he placed on the table where Periwinkle and I had shared dinner last night, along with a glass of cold, orange liquid.

I recognized the contents on the plate, since they reminded me of special breakfasts Mother used to serve: pancakes and eggs. But these pancakes were speckled with dark brown dots that were slowly melting.

"What's—"

"Chocolate chip pancakes, to celebrate your first official day with us," said Andrew, displaying a dazzling white grin.

"Well, girl, don't just sit there gaping," said Periwinkle, joining me with her own breakfast as Andrew returned to the kitchen. "Eat up. We have a lot to do today."

I plunged into my breakfast. It had been a long time since I'd eaten anything so rich and overwhelmingly sweet. The orange juice was both tangy and sweet. In Penumbra, the drones were only given water.

"Come along, Remmi," Periwinkle said, once we cleaned up our dishes. "I'll put you on the afternoon shift so we have some extra time."

A dazed feeling overcame me as I followed her outside, to a motorized cart parked behind the dining cottage. "Get in," she said, sliding onto the driver's side. I did so, my mind still spinning.

A fragrant wind brushed my face as she drove the cart over a narrow dirt road, then shifted onto a paved one. A few people waved at her as we passed. The sea-scented air was already heating up and sweat tickled my skin.

Sharp discomfort prickled me as we passed the small shops and restaurants I'd wandered by yesterday. I averted my eyes when she parked near that fountain and got out. Would anyone recognize me as the filthy beggar girl from yesterday? My cheeks burned as I realized my hair was now too short to cover my face.

Periwinkle grabbed my hand and pulled me into the nearest shop.

"Hello, Periwinkle." A woman stepped out from behind a counter. I glanced up and saw she had the same night-dark skin as Periwinkle. Her multiple braids were decorated with beads. "What brings you here so early?" Her voice thrummed with that now familiar Sandman Island accent.

I shrank back, wishing I was invisible. A warning tingle rippled along my skin. No! I wasn't ready to reveal my illusion magic just yet. Not before I had a chance to find out more about Substitutes. I bumped into a rack of clothes, nearly knocking it over.

"This is Remmi." With a wide smile, Periwinkle pulled me forward. "Her parents went back home to Zephyr, leaving her here to work at my resort from now through the summer." She chuckled. "But, of course, being Zephyrites, they have no concept of warm weather and she came with all the wrong clothes. We need to purchase a few things."

I gaped up at Periwinkle. How could she lie so easily? Still, I couldn't help feeling grateful.

"Oh, Zephyr. The famous floating island." I bit my lip, hoping the shop woman wouldn't ask any awkward questions. I'd only heard of Zephyr in passing but knew so little about it. "There's plenty here that should appeal to a pretty girl like you."

Shock replaced my unease. She thought I was pretty? People had compared me to Mother when I was little but I was sure that Penumbra had drained away anything good about my appearance.

Moments later, Periwinkle had gathered up an armload of colorful garments and herded me into a small, curtained room.

"Try this one first," she said, as excitedly as if she were a small child. She held up a sleeveless dress with a fringed skirt. It was the color of new leaves.

I shook my head. It was much too bright. I'd draw attention to myself if I wore that. I turned my gaze to the other clothes. They were all a mishmash of brilliant shades. Didn't anything here come in black, gray, or brown?

"Oh, Remmi, come on," Periwinkle practically pleaded. "This will look beautiful on you. It matches your eyes perfectly."

Warmth touched my face. My eyes had been called "freakish" in Penumbra.

I sighed, turned my back to Periwinkle, and reluctantly removed the shirt-dress.

I froze when she let out a horrified gasp. "Remmi, your back. Who did that to you?"

My scars. I'd grown so numb to the beatings I'd been given during my years in Penumbra that I'd forgotten. I could feel my entire body burning in mortification. I snatched the dress from her and slipped it over my head. It felt soft and cool against my skin.

"It's nothing," I mumbled, unable to look at her.

"Remmi, stop saying that." She placed her fingers beneath my chin and lifted my face. Her dark eyes were wet. "That bruise, those scars . . . none of this is 'nothing.' It's *not* okay. If you don't want to tell me where you ran away from, that's all right. It's your business and I won't pry. Maybe such treatment was tolerated there but it's not at my resort. If anyone—and I don't care if it's a staff member or a guest—mistreats you in any way, you don't keep it to yourself, do you hear? You tell me or Andrew and we'll take care of it. Do you understand?" She raised her voice on that last part.

My eyes grew hot. It was a strange feeling since I couldn't remember when I'd last cried. I blinked and nodded. "Yes, ma'am," I whispered.

"Good. Now take a look at yourself in something that actually fits." She turned me toward the narrow wall mirror.

The dress did match my eyes. Its bodice emphasized my too-skinny waist and flowed down to the flaring, fringed skirt that reached just above my knees. I felt an urge to cover myself, as if I were naked, but struggled not to let this discomfort show. I wanted to please Periwinkle.

55

"It's beautiful. Thank you."

We left the shop with a large bag filled with sundresses, shorts, and several bright shirts. I wasn't sure if I'd ever get used to all those different colors. I wore the spring-green dress and a pair of sandals, decorated with colored beads. At least no one could now mistake me as the mysterious beggar girl I'd been yesterday. People noticed me but in a different way. I quickly averted my eyes before I could study their expressions but the looks seemed to be . . . approving. Was that even possible?

When we returned to the resort, Periwinkle began to teach me history and arithmetic over a lunch of grilled fish, cheese, and sliced fruit. After that, I got to work, washing dishes, taking orders, and clearing tables. The work was the same as that I had done in Penumbra, with even the nasty task of gutting fish added in, but I was surprised to find that I enjoyed it much more. No one scolded or slapped me and all the guests were in good moods, apparently happy to be here. Those I personally served even left me cash, which Periwinkle insisted was mine to keep. "Most of them tip very well here," she said with a wink. Andrew and his helpers sang, hummed, and chanted as they worked. No one had ever sung in Penumbra's kitchens. Only upper class Penumbran children were given music lessons. I longed to join in but knew, from past experience around campfires in the Forest, that my own voice was hopelessly flat.

If only I'd inherited Mother's singing ability. A wistful twinge pricked me as I washed dishes and listened to the others' tuneful harmonies.

It was strange to wash and get dressed each morning without someone ordering me to do so. Deliberately picking out something different to wear each day, instead of simply grabbing a drab tunic from a messy pile, felt like a tiresome chore. I repeatedly told myself I'd get used to it, that this was what normal people did. And I was now a normal person, not a "nonperson," as drones were often called. No one here saw me as anything odd, as something that needed to be mind-drained or destroyed. I just had to repeat that to myself every time I felt the tingle-threat of an illusion or an aching desire to fly again.

The days passed quickly in a whirl of activity, serving in the dining cottage, helping Andrew wash dishes, gut fish, and slice fruits and vegetables, tutoring sessions with Periwinkle, cleaning cottages, and helping the gardeners weed the grounds.

Nights were spent dancing and telling stories around a bonfire. Visitor dreams, as Periwinkle had promised, were frequent but Morphia Nightshade had yet to return.

I hung back in the crowd during these times, a silent observer as the rules dictated. I'd repeat my mantra that I was a "normal person" during each dream, to fight the urge to take on an illusion. My life depended on this for now. At least until I got a chance to ask Morphia, since she made her living performing illusions. Visiting Substitutes like her were continually treated as well as Lord Malcent and his family had been.

I was given one free day each week, which I often spent exploring the surrounding village. The rest of the island was made up of plush farmlands. Sandman Islanders, much like the Penumbrans, prided themselves on the fact that their land was self-sufficient, although they occasionally traded with people of Zephyr, which drifted by once a year. I found it amusing that that was where Periwinkle had told the shop lady I was from.

I also shared some of my free days with Andrew. He lived in the village, but would often invite me to join him and his family on the beach, where they taught me to swim in the ocean. I always made sure to wear a shirt over my swim suit to cover up my scars. After my humiliation with Periwinkle, I didn't want anyone to ask me uncomfortable questions, especially those that might make me reveal I'd come from Penumbra.

Ocean swimming was quite a different experience from the calm Forest ponds and flowing rivers of my early childhood. I quickly learned to enjoy diving under the waves and riding them, a sensation that reminded me of my cloud ride to Sandman Island. Sometimes the waves were so fierce that they'd knock me down and pull me under. I'd fight my way to the surface, coughing and sputtering, the salt water stinging my nose and throat. I was surprised to find I even loved that.

My skin deepened to a dusky tan and the sun painted my dark hair, which I continued to keep short, with reddish-gold highlights. Periwinkle's insistence that I eat at least three meals a day was starting to show. I was no longer so frail looking but had developed slight curves and my breasts began to bud. I was also sure I had grown a bit taller. Despite all this, I still stuffed rolls and other food items into my pockets when I thought no one was watching to take back to my cottage in case I got hungry during the night. I never wanted to experience that empty belly ache again. If Periwinkle or Andrew noticed, they didn't say anything.

Was I fourteen now? I remembered my birthday was in the spring. It was something I had almost forgotten during my years in Penumbra.

I gradually adjusted to sleeping in my bed at night instead of the floor, in between rolled up blankets. I silently repeated my mantra each day: "I'm a normal person now, no longer a drone."

I thought my troubles were over. I had never been so wrong.

Chapter 9

Loud knocking tore me awake early one morning.

"Open up!" yelled a gruff male voice. "We have a warrant to search each cabin for a dangerous Halfling that escaped Penumbra several weeks ago."

I jolted to a sitting position and glanced around the room. Luckily the curtains were drawn so no one could see me. A grayish, pre-dawn light seeped through them. I had to get away but the only way out was through the front door.

"I told you, there are no guests here," said Periwinkle's voice, sounding more angry than frightened. "I don't want to waste your time. I'm sure you're very busy and have—"

"Not too busy to execute a runaway Halfling, ma'am." The sound of pounding followed by the door lock breaking filled my ears. "We've already told you that this warrant's issued by Lord Malcent of Penumbra and signed by Dreamearth's other province leaders."

I scrambled out of bed. My mind churned with desperation. These men wouldn't listen to me if I tried to explain that Malcent was mistaken and I was more like Morphia, not a Halfling. They were set to kill me on sight.

I pressed my back to the wall as the door swung open. I squeezed my eyes shut and willed myself to turn invisible. I hadn't practiced illusion magic since I'd arrived here and my body felt reluctant. I dug my nails into my palms to hone my concentration.

"I find it hard to believe one tiny Halfling, a mere child, is the cause for so much ruckus," said Periwinkle.

A flicker of relief flashed through me as I felt the familiar tingle of an illusion taking hold.

"You must have heard, it's been all over the news," said a different man's voice. I dared to crack an eye open. Periwinkle was accompanied by two tall men in police uniforms. They wore dark blue instead of Penumbran gray but the style was identical. "A small part of the Collective Unconscious Forest has begun to disappear. Do you think that's a coincidence? Lord Malcent's Halfling drone escaped at around the same time that notorious Halfling, Njim, started appearing in Realearth, trying to pass himself off as a god there. Rumor has it he's struggling to convince them, not like in the old days—"

"And you think this child you're looking for is Njim?" Periwinkle forced a laugh.

"Not exactly, but we can never be too careful. There are a few Halflings out there who managed to escape the required mind-drains as infants. It's our job to find them and destroy them as quickly possible."

Sweat streamed down my face and my body shook as I struggled to hold the illusion. How long were they going to take?

"So," said the other man, plucking at the covers on my unmade bed, "no one is staying here?"

"This is a spare cottage," said Periwinkle. She glanced around, as if searching for me, while not making it obvious. "I haven't had a chance to send my maid in yet."

"Tell this maid of yours to clean the drawers as well," said the first man, as he shuffled through my nightstand drawer. I was so embarrassed I nearly lost the illusion. That's where I continued to stash pieces of food I managed to snatch from the kitchen. It was silly, I knew. Periwinkle would never let me go hungry but a small part of my mind still feared this was all an illusion and I'd end up empty-bellied back in Penumbra. "You're going to have a serious bug problem if she doesn't."

"I'll see to that." Periwinkle's eyes flashed with anger. Whether it was because my secret food stash had been discovered or the policemen were taking too long, searching every corner of my cottage, I wasn't sure.

Pain flooded my veins as I strained to continue holding the illusion and not move . . . not move. I was sure the men could hear my heartbeat, which was loud in my ears. Sweat completely soaked my nightgown, as if I'd been dunked in water.

"See. There's no Halfling here," Periwinkle said at last, opening the front door for them. "You've checked every inch of my resort, harassing my guests for nothing."

"Just doing our jobs, ma'am." The man's voice sounded weary, defeated. "It's our duty to rid Dreamearth of these Halfling vermin."

I collapsed to my knees the second the door slammed shut behind them. The room was spinning. I crawled into the bathroom, hoping I'd make it in time. My mouth was filled with thick saliva and my stomach heaved. I threw up into the toilet.

I wiped my mouth with the back of my hand and flushed. I hugged my knees to my chest and rested my head against them. I couldn't stop shaking. My stomach felt slightly better but my throat stung with bitterness and terror still gripped me.

What if those men came back? I had to leave, to fly away from the one place I thought was safe. But I was drained from holding that illusion for so long. I could barely even move, much less fly. My entire body ached.

What was it that gave me away as a Halfling, if it wasn't illusion magic? No one on Sandman Island had recognized me as one. Would they change their minds now? If Periwinkle didn't turn me in, would Andrew? I recalled how insulted he'd been when I asked if Morphia Nightshade was a Halfling.

"Remmi, honey, where are you?" I didn't answer as I heard Periwinkle enter the cottage, her flip-flops slapping against the hardwood floor. "You sure are a good hider. You can come out now. Those bully blowhards are gone. I made sure they were all the way through the ghostsilk before I came back here."

I still didn't say anything, just squeezed my knees tighter in a futile effort to stop trembling.

"Oh, there you are." I sensed her standing over me but I refused to open my eyes. Maybe I'd become invisible again, this time permanently, if I kept them closed. Ridiculous, I knew, but I couldn't help hoping. "Are you sick?"

I winced as I felt her cool fingers brush back my hair and press against my forehead. "No. You don't have a fever. Still, you have been working very hard and have had quite a scare. Take today off and get back into bed. I'll bring you some soup."

I didn't move until I heard the front door tap shut behind her. I staggered to the sink, splashed cold water on my face and brushed my teeth, cleansing the bitterness from my mouth. My stomach still felt queasy but I was sure that was more to do with fear than illness.

Periwinkle returned not long after I had climbed into bed.

"Here, this ought to settle your stomach." She handed me a bowl of chicken noodle soup and crackers.

She sat on the edge of the bed, stroking my hair as I cautiously sipped the soup. This was what Mother used to do when I was sick. I wished I could enjoy the taste through the sourness that still lingered in my mouth.

"Those men are really gone?" My voice came out as a choked whisper. I set the soup bowl on the nightstand.

"I made sure of it." Periwinkle's voice was annoyed. "They spent a couple of days searching the entire island. My resort was their last stop. There were no Halflings here, as they discovered." She winked at me. I was the one they were looking for, yet she spared me. I was filled with intense gratitude.

"What exactly is a Halfling?" I closed my eyes, unable to even look down at the comforter.

"They are people who have a Realearth parent and a Dreamearth parent and therefore belong to both worlds. Here in Dreamearth, it's something that happens when the man is dreaming. It's the other way around in Realearth."

I swallowed. "But why are they so hated?" I still couldn't open my eyes. I clutched the comforter in my hands.

"They aren't so much hated as feared. Since Visitors have the ability to manipulate our world—even if most don't realize they have that power—this magic is passed over to any Halfling offspring. Halfling magic works in both worlds."

I thought back to what Andrew had said. "So they can do more than just create illusions?"

"That's right. Halflings have multiple magical abilities, not just one. And those only grow stronger as they mature."

The coiling in my stomach grew more intense, threatening to release the soup and crackers I'd managed to choke down. Did that mean I was a Halfling if I could also fly? I remembered the fear the Penumbran police had showed when I flew away from them. But that still didn't mean I was a Halfling, did it? Had my father been a Visitor? No! I refused to believe that.

I managed to pry my eyes open but still couldn't meet Periwinkle's gaze. "Is that why . . . why their minds are wiped?" My throat was tight, painful, my words released in whispered gasps.

I saw Periwinkle nod from the edge of my vision. "It's a repulsive practice, in my opinion, but it's the law in every province that any woman pregnant with a Halfling must give her child up at birth. If she doesn't, she is severely punished." Bitterness stung Periwinkle's voice. "The babies are mind-drained and sterilized to prevent future breeding then placed in stasis until they are old enough to work as drones."

I'd been spared the mind-drain. Did that also mean I hadn't been sterilized? I struggled to keep my face composed. I was now fourteen but still had never experienced the monthly blood I had, on occasion, overheard women discussing. I shuddered as I remembered that none of the drones, including those who were older, ever had children. I had never given it much thought before, figuring it was due to lack of privacy and the fact that they couldn't make decisions on their own. But could this have been the primary reason?

Periwinkle had grown silent with her gaze fixed on the window. I managed to look at her. The invading sunlight plucked out the blue glints in her otherwise black eyes. "People have suggested to me I use drones as workers. It would save me money since they wouldn't have to be paid. They are merely mindless machines, I'd been told, programmed to carry out orders without question and to perform the most menial, unpleasant tasks, which would free me up considerably. I refuse to do that. That's nothing more than slavery and ought to be outlawed. But Dreamearth's major lawmakers firmly believe that mutilating Halflings protects both worlds."

"What about Njim? Didn't those men say he's causing trouble in Realearth?"

"Yes, him." Periwinkle sighed. "He's a prime example of why that ugly practice of mind-draining them at birth was started in the first place. Halflings who didn't abuse their great magical abilities managed to blend into society. But some became drunk with power. When they found they could cross over into Realearth and also work magic there, they pretended to be gods and demanded worship."

"Gods," I whispered. "Isn't that what Andrew said?"

Periwinkle nodded. "The First Visitors dreamed our world into existence countless eons ago. Many Realearthlings have a similar belief, that some god created their world. For all we know, there is some underlying force or even being that started all this. I've heard it called 'God' or 'Higher Power' by both Visitors and Dreamearthlings and it's steeped in deepest mystery. But the ancient Halflings who invaded Realearth pretended they were the personifications of such a being, and often multiple beings. Just about every civilization on Realearth worshipped these Halflings. Most were cruel and petty, using their powerful magic to harm, threaten, and create strife. Great numbers of Realearthlings have died in wars, fighting over which god or gods were the best. Sadly, such wars are still going on today in Realearth, even though it's been centuries since any Halflings have presented themselves as deities."

"Until Njim." My brain felt numb, as if I'd just experienced a mind-drain.

"Yes, until him. If those men were after you, I'd rather not know," Periwinkle said, rising to her feet. "You seem harmless enough."

"What about Andrew?" I couldn't get the glare he'd given me when I'd asked about Morphia out of my mind.

"He might have been swayed by popular opinion on the Halfling matter, but he still listens to his mother. If you don't give him any reason to suspect, he'll remain a good friend. Now get some rest." She leaned forward and kissed my forehead. Sudden moisture touched my eyes. I hadn't been kissed like that since Mother was alive. "If you are feeling well enough by tomorrow morning, I'd suggest you start attending the village school. You are certainly ready. You have an agile, intelligent mind, Remmi, and I don't want to see it go to waste."

I was relieved when Periwinkle turned her back to pick up the bowl and couldn't see the tears that spilled down my cheeks. The first tears I'd released in years.

Chapter 10

The Sandman Island School, nestled at the base of the foothills, was small with little more than a hundred students. These ranged from children that were barely beyond the toddler years to older teens.

"So you're Remmi Clearwater," the teacher, Mrs. Swan said, taking my hand as if I were a small child and leading me into a classroom filled with kids that looked to be around my age. "Stay here," she said, dropping my hand and leaving me standing in front of several rows of desks.

"Everyone, take your seats quickly." Her tone was brisk. A sensation of panic filled me as the students scrambled to their desks. It had been so long since I'd been in a classroom. I turned my gaze downward and stared at the scuffed floor tiles. "We have a new student, Remmi Clearwater," she said once the room had quieted. She placed her hands on my hunched shoulders. "She lives and works at Periwinkle's Resort."

The soft sounds of whispers and giggles filled my ears. "Check out her funny haircut," someone snickered.

If only my hair was still long and could curtain my burning face. My palms were slick with sweat but I resisted wiping them off on my dress.

"You can be seated, Remmi," Mrs. Swan finally said, pointing to the only empty desk, near the front. I tried not to let my relief show as I slumped into it.

"Hi," whispered a plump girl in the desk next to mine. "I'm Jenna Graystone."

A sick feeling wormed through me as I briefly studied Jenna's slate-gray eyes and long white hair that hung in a single braid down her back. She was Penumbran. The realization throbbed through my mind in a vibrating echo. Even though Jenna's otherwise translucent skin held a rose flush from exposure to the sun, she stood out in this class of tanned and night-skinned students. And, unlike the rest of us who wore shorts, cottony shirts, sleeveless sundresses, and sandals, she was garbed in a long-sleeved blouse, floor length skirt, and thick boots. A wide-brimmed hat was slung over the back of her chair.

What was a Penumbran doing here? I turned my face away from Jenna and focused on the teacher. All the Penumbrans I had ever known loathed the sun and preferred to remain in deep caverns. Even though I didn't remember ever seeing Jenna before, I feared the girl might have been sent here as a spy. Periwinkle had assured me I was safe once those police had left.

"Okay, class," said Mrs. Swan, "let's get started. Why are Visitors so important to us? Remmi, do you know?"

I stared down at my desk as I felt several eyes back on me. Why was she putting me on the spot like this? I searched my mind, trying to remember what I'd learned several years ago, but came up blank. "No, ma'am," I whispered, saying it more to the desk than Mrs. Swan.

I felt my face reddening again as soft laughter flittered through the room. "It looks like you've been replaced as the queen of stupid, Brilla," a tall, tanned girl with bleached blonde hair, who sat on the other side of me, opposite Jenna, whispered to the girl in front of her.

Anger battled with my humiliation. Was I no better than a drone, even if I'd never been mind-drained? An urge to hit that girl filled me.

"Shut up, Kaya," snapped the other girl.

"Does anyone else know the answer?" Mrs. Swan scanned the room. Jenna's hand shot up. "Jenna, you really should give other students a chance to answer questions." She paused for a moment but no one else offered. My tense muscles loosened slightly. Perhaps I wasn't so behind after all. "Okay, Jenna. Why are Visitors so important?"

"It's their thoughts that keep Dreamearth intact. Every time they enter our world, they shed Artifacts which are filled with their personal thoughts. Dream Analysts drain these Artifacts to study the liquid thoughts. They take notes, which they pass onto the Dream Scriptwriters, then empty these thoughts into the Life River at Dreamearth's end, which is made up of the thoughts that came before. It separates into tributaries, spills into our oceans, forms our clouds, and evaporates into the atmosphere. If the River were to dry up, our world would end."

"Excellent answer, Jenna." Mrs. Swan beamed down at her.

"Little Miss Know-It-All," muttered Kaya, glaring at Jenna. I sympathized, even though Kaya had called me stupid seconds ago. I hated Jenna even more.

"That is why we must respect every Visitor," Mrs. Swan continued, "even if they are often tormented during their brief dream jaunts."

The other kids openly mocked Jenna in between classes, tripping her in the hallways and thrusting kicks at her. I turned my head when she glanced at me, her moist eyes pleading, as if hoping she'd finally found someone to be friends with.

My conscience nagged me to at least smile back but I refused. Even though Sandman Island was now my home, Penumbra was too fresh in my memory. There was no chance in the Nightmare Realms I'd *ever* become friends with a Penumbran.

At lunchtime, I spotted Jenna sitting alone at a far table in the small lunch yard, her face hidden behind a book. She glanced up briefly as I stood there, my stomach more uneasy than hungry, as I struggled to figure out where to sit. *You're a normal person now,* played through my head, overpowering the fading drone instinct to huddle on the ground with my food.

Jenna waved at me to join her but I ignored her and continued to scan the rapidly filling tables. Kaya, Brilla, and a third girl, Pedra, had a table all to themselves. My face grew warm as they glanced my way then turned back to one another, whispering and giggling. Was I going to be the object of their derision after Jenna?

At least they were nothing compared to Treb and the adult bullies who'd tormented me for years.

I slid into an empty space at the end of a crowded table and stared out at the glittering sea beyond the school's grounds. Kids talked and laughed around me. I remained quiet as I nibbled the sandwich Andrew had made for me. It was as if I had performed an invisibility illusion, without putting in the effort. I was surprised by the relief I felt. I didn't have to answer any awkward questions and lie about from where I'd come.

And I wasn't signaled out like Jenna.

Each day was the same for her. The other students, but mainly Kaya and her minions, made fun of her weight, her freakish paleness, and frumpy clothes. She always ate lunch alone.

A part of my mind—the part that remembered how, not long ago, *I* was the freakish one—urged me to come to Jenna's defense. But I couldn't stop viewing her as an enemy and held back. Besides, I didn't have time for this. Even though Periwinkle had been an excellent teacher, my lack of schooling for years in Penumbra had set me far behind the other students. I stayed up late each night, after my work shifts, pouring over my studies, straining to understand obscure terms, and struggling to catch up.

One afternoon, class was interrupted by an announcement that a dream was about to occur on school premises. Murmurs of excitement fluttered through the classroom.

"The dream will take place in the hallway," Mrs. Swan said, herding all of us from the room.

I stumbled beside the others in a daze. This was the first time, in the weeks since I'd started, that an actual Visitor was scheduled to come here. Usually dreams happened in town, on the beaches, or at Periwinkle's Resort.

"I am Larry Nimbus, the director of the dream that is scheduled to occur in a few moments," said a balding, middle-aged man in an elegant indigo suit. "This dream has no Substitutes or other dream actors, just all of you, as extras." Excited gasps filled the hallway. "The Visitor will be a teen, like all of you. He will show up completely naked." A few of the girls tittered and nudged one another. "He will interpret this school as his own. In this instance, you are permitted to laugh and point, but don't overdo it." Larry scanned us with sharp, glinting eyes. "The poor kid is going to be humiliated enough. Lucky for him, this is scheduled to be a brief dream and he will awaken immediately after, instead of going on to another segment."

A moment later, the boy materialized. He appeared to be slightly older than me and his diaphanous dream body was as bare as a fish. He slunk down the hallway in a hunched position as my classmates laughed and pointed, just as we were instructed, although I was sure many were enjoying the experience.

I found it difficult to look at him, although I couldn't figure out why. In Penumbra, we drones, male and female, had frequently showered together and changed clothes in front of one another. None of us had ever thought much of this: it was just what we did. My chest twisted as I realized why this was so. Not only were the other drones incapable of thoughts beyond the mundane tasks we were forced to perform, but they likely had all been sterilized. Even if, by some remote chance, any of them were intimate, the possibility of conception was nil.

I forced the thought away and focused on my fellow classmates. I could see smears of blush reddening the cheeks of some of the girls, who couldn't stop giggling, while many of the boys were openly mocking.

Relief swept through me when the Visitor vanished. He'd likely be relieved that that embarrassing experience was "just a dream." That is, if he even remembered this event at all. According to Realearth Studies, which was my favorite class, many Visitors completely forgot their Dreamearth jaunts after awakening.

We all had a difficult time focusing that afternoon, thanks to the dream interruption, so Mrs. Swan released us several minutes early.

I shoved my books into my backpack and started toward the resort. I'd first go for a dip in the ocean. Then, after dinner, I'd spend a long night pouring over my books. At least it was a free day from work, giving me much needed time.

Through the corner of my eye, I saw that Kaya, Brilla, and Pedra had gathered around Jenna.

"Why do you wear that stupid hat?" taunted Pedra, snatching it off Jenna's head. "Are you afraid your ghastly marshmallow skin will melt?"

"Give that back!" Jenna cried as Kaya shoved her face down into the dirt and pinned her head down with her foot.

Several other kids gathered around, shouting in excitement. They always loved to watch Kaya and her minions torment Jenna. Some of them even joined in.

Just walk away, I told myself, forcing my thoughts to the pile of homework I had to complete. Jenna was not my concern. I took a few hurried steps, struggling not to look back.

"Eat dirt, white mole!" Brilla's grating voice was followed by the sound of her foot kicking flesh.

I turned around. Through gaps in the crowd, I saw Jenna curled in the dirt, moaning and clutching her side.

I stood still, fiddling with my backpack's strap. My chest ached. They were treating Jenna like . . . well, like a drone. Should I try to help her? She was still Penumbran and probably Lord Malcent's spy.

Another thought echoed through my mind. What would Periwinkle think if I walked away from this? I'd neglected telling her about Jenna whenever she'd asked me about school.

"Let's strip off her clothes so she'll have to go home as naked as that Visitor," said Kaya, tugging on Jenna's blouse. Jenna pulled back and, wincing in pain, struggled to stand. Brilla and Pedra pushed her back down.

"There's so many layers, it'll take forever," someone else said.

"A fat, naked Jenna's not something *I* want to see!" said another.

Jenna flailed and kicked as Kaya, Brilla, and Pedra tore at her clothes.

I rushed toward them. "Leave her alone." My voice came out as a strangled whisper. Everyone ignored me.

I pushed through the crowd to confront the trio. "I said." I struggled to make my voice louder but it still came out hopelessly soft. "Leave her alone." My knees shook. Speaking up in Penumbra would have gotten me killed. The fear, as ridiculous as it was now, still lingered.

Kaya tossed her long hair and laughed. "What? *You're* going to stop us?"

Laughter rang around me. The trio turned from Jenna to face me.

"Aren't you a serving girl and maid at that resort?" taunted Brilla.

"Just try to stop us, Mop Head." Kaya shoved me, hard. I stumbled.

Fury burned through me. I glanced at Jenna, now sitting up and staring at me, then focused on Kaya. She squinted down at me with small blue eyes that reminded me of Treb's.

She's a bully, no different than Treb and the Penumbran police. I narrowed my eyes at her.

She suddenly fell back, tripping over Jenna and landing on her bottom. Pedra and Brilla pulled her up. "Who pushed me?" She angrily scanned the crowd. The other kids mumbled and blamed one another.

I didn't see anyone push her—she was probably just clumsy—but a fleeting feeling of triumph passed through me. Memories of how I'd created a monster illusion to scare off Malcent's men filled my mind. If only I could do that again. Only not a monster this time. Something that would *really* scare them but not give me away.

The familiar tingle of an illusion crept over my face and body. I no longer cared about my secret vow not to use my talent. Morphia Nightshade performed illusions, after all, and everyone *loved* her. My body appeared to stretch, creating the illusion of a tall, dark-skinned woman in a tailored dress.

"I've had enough of this!" I yelled, changing my voice as best I could. "Leave Miss Graystone alone."

"P-Principal Foxglove," gasped Kaya, bumping against her friends. "We were only playing, having a little fun, ma'am."

"Fun," I screeched. I found I enjoyed the sight of all those terrified faces gaping at me. "This doesn't look like fun. School's out. If you all don't get off the premises, I'm telling your parents."

I bit back a laugh as they all dashed away in different directions, leaving Jenna still sitting in the dirt. My illusion suddenly faded. Jenna stared at me in shock then staggered to her feet.

A mixture of rage and panic filled me. What had I done by displaying my secret magic in front of a Penumbran, of all people? What if she contacted Lord Malcent and those police came back?

I started to hurry off but slipped on something. I looked down. My throat tightened. It was Jenna's crumpled hat, which someone had dropped. She slowly moved toward me.

Just run, my thoughts urged. Instead, I picked it up, brushed it off, and handed it to her.

"I—thanks for that. That was impressive." A grin stretched across her flushed, dirt-smudged face. Her clothes were rumpled and dirty. Parts of her braid had unraveled into pale wisps.

"Just don't tell anyone about this," I whispered, clenching my hands.

"But why? You really scared everyone with that illusion. You ought to train to become a Substitute. You'd be a great one."

"I—no. I have a job at Periwinkle's Resort. I . . . I can't use my illusion magic."

"Why?" Jenna sounded genuinely puzzled. "Does Periwinkle not allow it? You'd think that would please her. Substitutes are always welcome."

That was true. Was it possible I could become one? I felt a faint flicker of hope.

"With a talent like that, you really should consider it. I wish I could illusion. I've always wanted to work directly with Visitors, ever since Mother and I left Penumbra. I'll have to settle for being a Dream Scriptwriter or a Dream Analyst, though. If I'm lucky."

"You're from the Cavern Lands of Penumbra?" I decided to play dumb just in case there was a chance she recognized me as one of the drones. "The place ruled by Lord Malcent?"

Jenna nodded and began to unravel her braid. "Lord Malcent is my father."

Chapter 11

My chest tightened, making it impossible to breath. I should have known. Jenna was a spy, sent here to find me and take me back to Penumbra. Why hadn't I listened to my first instinct and just gone home?

"Mother and I left Penumbra a few years ago," Jenna said, sitting down on a bench beneath a wide, flower-covered tree. If she noticed my horrified expression, she didn't let on. She set her hat down and ran her fingers through her hair.

I remained standing, aching to run away but my feet stayed stubbornly rooted to the ground. Years as a Penumbran drone had trained me to submit to the needs of the Cavern Lands' citizens, especially those who, like Jenna, had been born into the ruling bloodline.

"I-I didn't think too many Penumbrans ever left the Cavern Lands," I managed to stammer out.

Jenna divided her hair into three sections and quickly braided it. "It's rare, I know, but Mother wanted a better life for us. Father had three wives, including Mother."

"B-but your last name." I still couldn't control my stutter. "I-I thought it was Graystone, not Malcent."

Jenna looked up at me and blinked. "Mother changed it after we escaped. I'd been friends with some peasant kids when I was little and their last name was Graystone. Of course, my father never approved." Her voice was tinged with bitterness. "I was supposed to be a proper daughter, which meant spending my days in quiet tasks like embroidery, which I was terrible at, and learning silly things like how to properly sip tea and sit without wrinkling my dress." She straightened her rumpled clothes, brushed off most of the dirt, and placed her hat back on her head. I stared but still couldn't quite meet her eyes. Aside from the smudges on her round cheeks, all evidence that she'd been roughed up earlier was gone.

I had always secretly envied the Penumbran children, especially the wealthy ones, who were given opportunities I knew I'd never have. Could it be some of them were unhappy? How was that possible? "Didn't you attend school in Penumbra?"

Jenna shook her head. "I had a tutor who taught me to read and perform simple mathematical sums but that was pretty much it. I learned how to sing from another instructor. My father had several children from two of his wives but I was the only one Mother was able to produce so she was the least favorite. I wasn't ever going to take Lord Malcent's place as ruler of our Cavern since I wasn't the eldest and merely a girl. No, at best I'd learn a craft but my main fate was to be married off to some minor lord from another Cavern and have as many children as I could to continue the bloodline. I'd be married now if we hadn't escaped."

I sank down on the bench but kept a respectful distance from Jenna as I struggled to process this.

"Have you always lived on Sandman Island?" Jenna asked after a long pause.

I looked down. My face burned and I feared my sun-tanned cheeks had turned a vivid crimson. I fiddled with the hem of my sundress. Chills swept across my skin despite the heat. "I grew up in the Collective Unconscious Forest," I murmured, keeping my eyes averted. At least it was a partial truth.

"Really?" Jenna scooted closer. "That was our first home, after Penumbra. We settled in one of the larger villages, where Mother made jewelry and painted pottery, crafts she had learned while growing up in Penumbra. We lived on the earnings from her sales. We've moved a few times, before coming here, where she opened her own shop. I doubt this will be our final home. I hope it's not. I hate it here." Jenna took off her hat and fanned her round, sweaty face. "Not only are the kids at school mean, but it's too hot and humid. It doesn't get much cooler even in the winter. The sun's too bright. And those frequent squalls and thunderstorms always wake me up in the middle of the night. I know I sound selfish, since I have so much more freedom now, but I miss Penumbra's cool caverns."

I shuddered. I could never fathom ever returning to Penumbra, even if, like Jenna, I had grown up as part of the ruling bloodline instead of a drone. I loved almost everything about Sandman Island. True, the kids at school were little better than Malcent's minions, but Periwinkle, her staff, and most of the resort guests treated me well. The constant smell of the ocean, and even the thunderstorms, which now lulled me to sleep, were comforting.

"Would you like to come home with me?" Jenna looked over at me with sparkling eyes. "Mother's still at her shop but she should be home soon. You'd be able to meet her."

I tensed. How long ago did Jenna and her mother escape Penumbra? Would the woman recognize me as one of the drones? I would have found that notion almost laughable if it didn't scare me so much. How many Penumbran nobles ever acknowledged drones? We were even ignored by the ordinary Penumbran citizens.

"We can work on our homework together," Jenna pressed, likely noticing my hesitation.

I felt torn. A tiny stream of sweat tickled my spine and my dress clung to my damp skin. I'd been looking forward to taking a quick dip in the ocean after school before starting on my homework. I studied Jenna, translucent-pale beneath layers of clothes, and strongly doubted she would be up for a swim. It was highly likely that the only bodies of water Jenna ever submerged herself in were baths.

Still, Jenna was the student that always received the highest marks, came up with the cleverest answers, and spent her lunch breaks reading. She could help me with my studies, and, by the First Visitors, I could use it!

"Okay," I heard myself say before I could change my mind.

A joyous smile spread across Jenna's sweat-beaded face. A twinge of guilt stabbed my chest for my initial hesitation. She walked with a bounce in her step as she led me to a small motorized cart. "Mother lets me use this since school is further away from our home than her shop," Jenna explained. "I had to get a special license to drive this."

I couldn't help but gape at Jenna as I slid onto the padded vinyl seat opposite the steering wheel. The only people who drove these carts were the elderly and a few other grownups, like Periwinkle. Everyone else walked or rode bikes, which wasn't that much of an inconvenience since Sandman Island was only around twenty miles across with just one main village.

A soft breeze blew in my face and stirred my hair as Jenna carefully maneuvered the vehicle down a narrow, winding cobblestone street that led deeper into the hills, away from the sea. The houses grew scarce and the foliage thickened. Just where did Jenna live?

She pulled up to a hill at the end of a long, dirt path. Where were we? There were no houses nearby, just a few short, wind-bent trees and a crevice in the side of the hill.

"Well, this is it," Jenna said, a faint flush brightening her pale skin.

"Where's your house?" I slid from the cart and looked around. It was quiet here, except for the sea-tinted wind stirring the trees, and a few stray seagulls gliding about. This had to be the most remote section of Sandman Island, far from the village and farmlands.

"Right here," Jenna said, stepping through the crevice, which turned out to be an opening.

I followed her. It took a moment for my eyes to adjust but, once they did, I saw I was in a small cave.

Sudden dizziness overcame me and my heart pounded. I leaned against the nearest wall.

"Remmi." Jenna placed a hand on my shoulder. "What's wrong?"

I took a deep breath and looked around. This dwelling was nothing like the Cavern Lands. The room was small with rounded walls. Paintings of colorful birds and butterflies decorated them, and a thick batch of multi-colored flowers stood in a vase in the center of a little round table. Four brightly painted chairs, which resembled oversized stools, encircled the table.

I allowed myself to breathe. "Nothing." I forced a smile. "Just too much sun. I'll be fine."

"That's why I always wear a hat." Jenna took hers off and hung it on a wall hook. "Mother made everything in here," she continued proudly as she tossed her backpack onto an overstuffed chair. "She should be home soon. Her shop is on the outskirts of the village. Would you like a snack, Remmi, while we do our homework?"

"Sure," I said, my eyes still scanning the room. I figured Penumbrans couldn't bear to live in anything other than caves and caverns.

Jenna rummaged through a small refrigerator. I stared at it, feeling a peculiar sense of awe at something so mundane. Even though I had lived on Sandman Island for months now, I still found these modern appliances fascinating. In Penumbra, meat was smoked for preservation and food was kept cold in the deep, lower caverns.

Jenna placed a plate of neatly sliced cheese and crackers onto the table, along with two cups of juice. A queer twinge stirred in my chest. It felt strange having a Penumbran serve me. The words, "Thank you," swelled in my throat but I found I couldn't release them.

A frustrating awkwardness overcame me as I sat next to Jenna, nibbling on the snacks and staring at a page of my Realearth Studies book. *You are her equal now,* I silently intoned as I re-read the same sentence over several times, but was unable to focus. I kept glancing at Jenna, who was mulling over a math problem, then around the strange little cave. I sighed and returned to my book.

If I was a Halfling, I'd have the ability to cross over into Realearth. Wasn't that a part of their magic? The thought filled me with a bubbling thrill, but I'd still prefer not to be one.

I forced these distracting musings away. I had a long list of homework assignments to go through, which I was sure would keep me up through the late hours. My drills with Periwinkle had paid off but, whenever I was stressed or tired, the words seemed to jiggle across the page like restless ants.

"I'm home, honey," a pleasant voice called from the doorway. I looked up to see a white-haired Penumbran woman step into the room, carrying several shopping bags. "I stopped at the market and thought I might—hello?" Her gaze locked onto me as Jenna rushed forward to help her with the bags.

I gulped and had to force myself to look into the woman's gray eyes. I'd been trained in Penumbra to keep my gaze averted whenever I was in the presence of important citizens and found this habit difficult to break. Like Jenna, the woman was soft and plump. She wore the same long, homespun skirts and broad hat, the latter which she removed and placed on a hook next to Jenna's, but moved with a regal grace.

I tugged at my memory, attempting to pull this woman's face from a past I was trying to forget.

"I see Jenna has made a new friend," she said, smiling at me. Her voice was pleasant and, although it was chipped with the harsh staccato of the Penumbran accent I had grown to loathe, it held an oddly lulling undertone.

"Mother." Jenna placed the bags on the counter then turned toward me. "This is Remmi. She's in my class at school and fought off some bullies." Warmth crept across my face. "Remmi, this is my mother, Felysa Graystone."

Chills danced across my skin as I shook her soft hand. I struggled to keep my eyes locked on Lady Graystone's and forced a smile.

"I'm pleased to meet you, Remmi," she said in an earnest tone.

"I-I it's good to meet you too, Lady Graystone," I murmured awkwardly and lowered my eyes. I studied the polished stone floor. My face burned as soon as those words were out of my mouth.

"Lady?" The woman laughed. "That's a title I haven't heard since I lived in Penumbra. You can just call me Felysa, Remmi. Everyone else does. You girls get back to your studies. This 'Lady' has a chicken to bake. Can you stay for dinner, Remmi?"

"Yes . . . ma'am." I still couldn't bring myself to say Felysa's name.

"Good. It won't be ready for a while so enjoy those snacks." Felysa clattered into the kitchen.

Jenna sighed. "Poor Mother. She works hard all day and then has to come home and make me dinner. I offer to help but she refuses. She wants me to concentrate on my studies." Jenna leaned close to me. "What I wouldn't give to have drones. That's one thing I miss about Penumbra."

I pulled back, a sudden rage searing my chest. I felt it rise like bitter bile into my throat, threatening to spill out like vomit. "Drones aren't work machines, they're people." My voice came out tight and raspy.

"No they're not," Jenna said, looking down at her math book. "They're nonpersons, dangerous criminals and anomalies that had to be subdued. At least they get put to good use."

I couldn't listen to this. I slammed my book closed and stuffed it into my backpack.

Jenna looked up in surprise. "Remmi, what are you doing? I thought you were staying for dinner."

"I-I have to go." I was so furious I could barely force out the words. I swung my pack over my shoulder and strode toward the cave's entrance.

"What's wrong?" Jenna hurried to my side but I brushed past her.

Chapter 12

I raced down the trail, my feet pounding softly against the dirt path, stirring up dust. I heard Jenna plodding behind me, calling to me, but she was too slow. I sped up, remembering the many foot races I had won as a child during village festivals in the Forest.

I briefly felt my body grow buoyant, weightless, ready to float off the ground, and slowed my pace. No. I couldn't take flight still in eyeshot of Jenna. I didn't know yet if flying was normal for Substitutes.

I felt a breeze brush against my wet cheeks. It was only then I realized I was crying. My throat ached. I stopped and looked back. Jenna stood in the distance, bending over at the waist and breathing hard. She had given up the chase.

I continued striding toward the main part of the village. I brushed angrily at my tears. I thought I'd made a friend. This reverie filled me with a bitterness that stung like poison. I wiped at my streaming eyes and, to my annoyance, realized my nose was dripping as well. I dug around in my pack, searching for a tissue. I should have known I could never befriend a Penumbran. What was I thinking?

It was late afternoon. The sun hung low in the sky, spilling liquid gold all over the restless sea. Beyond the usual array of small boats and buoys bobbing in the harbor, loomed an ominous pirate ship, its black Jolly Roger flag flapping in the wind. An enormous crowd, a mixture of tourists and Sandman Islanders, had gathered on the docks to watch.

My heart sank. I always found the unfolding dreams tantalizing but now I wasn't in the mood. I just wanted to return to my cottage, huddle on my bed, and attempt to forget what Jenna had said. But the only way back to Periwinkle's Resort was past the crowd-jammed docks.

The dream was already in progress. I decided to watch it, hoping it would take my mind off Jenna, but the crowd was so thick I could barely see what was happening. The Visitor, a small boy, was waving a wooden sword at a scruffy pirate with an eye patch and a peg leg, demanding that he release his baby sister.

"Does the boy know that pirate in waking life?" I whispered to a woman next to me. I longed to know if he was portrayed by a Substitute.

"Of course not," she answered with irritation, her gaze still locked on the dream scene. "Did you miss the announcement?" I nodded, feeling slightly disappointed. "It's the villain from one of his favorite movies."

I stood on tiptoe, struggling to see over peoples' heads, only to discover that, despite my recent growth spurt, I was still frustratingly short.

Just as I managed to find a gap in the crowd, the ghostly Visitor vanished, awakening in Realearth. Soft groans whispered through the crowd.

The pirate, who had colorful tattoos decorating his muscular arms and long scraggly hair, transformed into Morphia Nightshade. A plunging sensation filled my stomach. The groans instantly turned to deafening cheers as the woman smiled and bowed. A sea-tinged zephyr stirred her long hair into blending black and gold ripples.

Urgency tugged at me as I watched the beautiful Substitute glide toward a ghostsilk portal. The sensation quickly turned to crushing disappointment as the glimmering silk swallowed Morphia. What could I even say to her? My shoulders slumped beneath my heavy backpack. How could I ever prove I was Luna Clearwater's daughter?

The crowd dispersed as soon as the rest of Morphia's entourage followed her through the portal.

I was about to continue my homeward walk when I glimpsed a tall, lanky boy with spiky scarlet hair. He stood out even against the colorful crowd.

I felt a leap in my chest. Was it . . . ? Could it be . . . ?

He was gathering up gooey, transparent Thought Artifacts the Visitor must have shed during his dream, and tossing them into a wheelbarrow. A part of me felt I should be furious with him. He was the reason I had nearly been killed in

Penumbra. But, if it hadn't been for him revealing me, I'd probably still be stuck there.

"Peter!" I called, pushing my way through the crowd. I didn't care if my eyes were possibly red and puffy from my recent outburst. I knew I had looked much worse when I first met him.

He instantly straightened and looked around. His glasses slid down his long, sweaty nose. He pushed them back and stared down at me as I approached, his bright blue eyes growing enormous behind the lenses. "Do I know you?"

A sudden laugh escaped me. "I'm Remmi, the drone from Penumbra."

He stumbled back a pace and bumped into the wheelbarrow. His eyes grew even wider as they studied me. "I-it is you! Y-you look like the illusion you showed us, the green dress—" He stopped, his freckled face flushing a deeper red than his hair. "Only now it looks like you've seen more sun and your hair's shorter."

I felt my own face burn at that memory. I twisted the fringed hem of my sundress. It was the pale, bright green one Periwinkle had bought me when I'd first arrived, now slightly snugger and a bit shorter. At least I was presentable without having to illusion it.

"I-I'm so sorry." He looked down and shuffled his feet. "Dad and I . . . we thought you might be dead . . . all because of me. I was an idiot. I should have known. *Dad* let me know I'd blown it, believe me." He ran his hand through his hair but kept his gaze on the ground. "He tried to see if he could talk to Lord Malcent but the police forced him to leave. I felt awful, there was nothing we could do to for you and it was all my fault. We're only lowly Artifact Collectors. We couldn't tell a ruler of a province what he should do but believe me, Dad tried."

"That's all right." I touched his arm. He looked up but was unable to meet my eyes. "I got away. I now work at Periwinkle's Resort and am also attending school." I patted my backpack. I could feel my anger toward Jenna gradually receding.

Peter smiled. "That's a relief. I'm so glad you're . . . that you're not dead." His ears turned a brilliant pink.

"Where is your father anyway?"

"At a different dream site. He's now having me do my own gathering. Which reminds me, I've got to go. I'm scheduled at the next site in a few minutes."

"A few minutes?"

"Yeah. It's all the way in the Nightmare Realms but the portal will take me there in seconds."

"Will Morphia Nighshade be there?" Excitement pumped through me.

"According to the script, she is. Usually Dad is assigned to clean up after her dreams but it's my turn today." He puffed out his chest in pride.

I'd been waiting for this. A second chance to meet Morphia. Would I be able to talk to her without my throat closing up? I had to try, especially if she could tell me who my father was. If she could prove he was a Dreamearthling, I wouldn't have to live in fear that those police might someday return for me.

The frightened part of my mind rebelled, telling me I'd already wasted enough time at Jenna's and it would take hours to catch up on my homework, but I couldn't let such an opportunity slip away. It could be weeks, perhaps even months, before Morphia appeared in another Sandman Island dream.

"Could I come with you to watch this dream?" I winced at the nervous squeak in my voice. "I've never seen one that took place in the Nightmare Realms."

Peter looked down and ran a hand over his hair. "I'd like to have you come, Remmi, I really would, but I shouldn't. Not to the Nightmare Realms."

"Come one, Peter." Desperation burned within me. "I'm not afraid. I survived Penumbra. The Nightmare Realms are nothing compared to that."

He continued looking down. "Remmi, I-I just don't know. If anything happens—"

"Look, Peter." I leaned closer and stared directly into his vivid eyes. "You owe me one. You almost got me killed in Penumbra, remember?"

He made a low choking sound. Guilt washed through me but I didn't know what else to do. Not when Morphia, the key to my past, was just moments away, on the other side of that portal.

"Okay." His voice was resigned. "Just this once. I'll bring you back as soon as it's over."

"I'll never forget this. I promise." I followed him as he trundled his wheelbarrow toward the floating ghostsilk. It rippled like a gauze curtain in the ocean breeze. He pushed the wheelbarrow through then turned toward me.

"Have you ever entered one of these before?"

I shook my head.

"It's easy. Just step forward." Warmth filled me as he awkwardly took my hand. I felt a strange relief to find it was just as callused as mine. "It's really no different than walking through an open doorway."

I gulped, closed my eyes, and took a tentative step forward. Wisps that felt like fine hairs tickled my skin. "Keep going," instructed Peter's voice. "Just another couple of steps." The sensation disappeared, replaced by icy rain batting my skin. "That's good." He released my hands.

My eyes sprung open. We were in a rain-drenched forest of leafless trees. Through the sheets of rain, which soaked my clothes and hair, I could make out a man beneath a wide plastic awning, shining a dim spotlight on a silvery track. A second man, whose muscular arms were decorated with glowing tattoos, stood behind him. Another, whom I recognized as Larry Nimbus, the director of that naked Visitor dream, was also beneath the awning, seated in a tall chair.

"The dream is about to start." Peter's voice was nearly drowned out by the hissing downpour. "Look. There's the Visitor."

A young girl appeared beneath the awning, shielded from the rain. She sat against the tree, her back straight and stiff, too stiff. The tattooed man slipped behind the tree. He seemed to be waiting for something.

A vehicle I recognized as a car from my Realearth Studies class moved soundlessly down the track, toward the girl, its bright headlights blurred through the curtains of rain. A large truck followed, much too close.

The Visitor's eyes were wide as she watched the approaching vehicles, her face contorted in a terrified expression, as if she wanted to scream but couldn't. Her pajamas were sprinkled with a fine, glittery dust.

The car suddenly skidded and the truck slammed into it with a horrible crash. The sound vibrated painfully in my ears. Enormous flumes of fire and smoke billowed out from the wreckage then were instantly doused by the rain.

It was only a dream, a nightmare. I still clenched my hands into fists so tight my knuckles hurt.

The wrecked vehicles, now smashed together, continued soundlessly down the track, vanishing into the trees. When they departed, I noticed a body had appeared on the ground beside the terrified child. It was a woman. Her head was thrown back, partly severed from her body by a large glass shard sticking out of her neck. Blood spurted from the wound and seeped onto the damp, mossy ground.

I forced myself to study the dead woman. Was she Morphia using an illusion? Her face would have been breathtakingly beautiful if it weren't swollen and mottled with bruises. One dark eye was open and held a vague, unblinking stare, while the other was a bloody slit. Her shiny black hair spread over the ground.

"Mama," the girl choked, her voice a rasping gasp, "t-t-this is m-my fault. I-I can't move." She remained frozen. Her face was partially obscured by wisps of hair, as glossy and dark as the woman's.

Did her mother really die like that? Horror filled me.

The man behind the tree made a signal with his hands. Several shadowy creatures with glowing red eyes slinked from the trees and surrounded the girl. They growled, revealing sharp, silvery teeth that reminded me of thin blades.

I ignored the rain, which continued to soak my clothes and hair, as I moved toward them. I couldn't let them hurt that girl.

I was barely aware of the warm, prickling sensation that spread over my body, forming the monster illusion I'd used before. If it could scare off the Penumbran police, would it work on nightmare creatures?

"Go away," I shouted.

They turned from the girl in unison and dashed off into the trees.

"That's not in the script," yelled the tattooed man as he took off after them.

The girl stared up at me, her mouth open in a soundless scream.

What had I done? I instantly shifted my illusion, taking on the form of the mangled woman, alive and whole.

I knelt beside the ghostly Visitor and pulled her into my arms, the way Mother used to hold me when I was little. The sparkling dust coating the girl's pajamas slid off as if it was a sheath of gauze cloth.

"It's okay," I whispered. "The monsters are gone."

"Mama." The girl, who could now move, wrapped her arms around me. I was surprised at how solid the diaphanous Visitor felt. "Y-you're alive. You survived." The rain pattered upon the awning above us.

The child vanished. I fell onto the cold ground as the illusion faded. The rain suddenly stopped, as if on cue.

"What is the meaning of this?" yelled Larry, hurrying toward me. "This script didn't call for another Substitute." The spotlight man shined his light into my eyes, blinding me.

Chapter 13

"Larry, calm down," said a voice I recognized as belonging to Morphia Nightshade. The dead woman came to life, transforming into the famous Substitute. "Charlie, turn off that light. The dream's over." She gracefully stood and brushed off her dress.

"Why wasn't I told about a second Substitute?" Larry raged as Charlie obeyed Morphia. The flickering residue of the glare still danced before my vision. "This isn't what we rehearsed. What am I going to tell my boss?"

"I hadn't heard about a second Substitute either but she's a good one. And so young." Morphia grasped my cold hands and gently pulled me to my feet. "Did Lorelei Morningstar send you?"

"Who?" I averted my gaze.

"Who is this kid?" said Larry as men in yellow suits began to disassemble the wreckage. Peter crept by with his wheelbarrow. He didn't even look at me. Was he angry? Would he get in trouble because I forced him to bring me? Guilt gripped my chest. I'd only wanted to find out more about Mother, not cause trouble for everyone. "She doesn't even know who the head Dream Director of Visitor Visions is."

"Visitor Visions?" I asked.

"One of the major dream studios." Larry shook his head.

"Yet this child is extremely talented in illusion magic," Morphia said. I forced myself to look directly into her eyes. My eyelashes felt heavy, beaded with water droplets that blurred my vision. I blinked hard to clear it. To my surprise, she was not much taller than me. Her deep golden-brown eyes sparkled with an amused smile. I swallowed, struggled to speak, only to find my mind was suddenly blank.

"What's your name, love?"

"Remmi Clearwater." It still felt strange to give my full name even though I ought to be used to it by now. "I think you used to work with my mother, Luna."

"Luna Clearwater," Larry gasped. "I didn't know she had a kid."

Morphia's eyes widened. "I've always wondered what happened to her." She gently placed her beautifully manicured fingers beneath my chin and studied my face. "You're the spitting image of her, that's for sure, except for the color of your eyes. You probably inherited that from your father."

My heart leaped. "My father! Who was he? Do you know?"

Morphia laughed and ran her fingers through her shining black and gold hair. "Oh, Remmi, love, that's the wrong question to ask about your mother. She had many lovers, a different one practically every week, it seemed. Never one to settle down, poor Luna. Too picky when it came to men." Disappointment battled with my relief. At least it didn't sound like he'd been a Visitor. "She had everything going for her too, a great career, many admirers . . . but she just up and left one day, without even saying goodbye to anyone." She stopped preening and turned her focus back to me. "Whatever happened to your mother, love?"

I gulped. My gaze drifted back to Peter, who was now leaning against his wheelbarrow and gaping at us. "She died, several years ago."

"Oh, Remmi." Morphia's voice trembled. "I'm so sorry. She was like a sister to me."

"I'd like to learn how to become a Substitute," I caught myself saying. Something squeezed my heart. I wouldn't have to leave Sandman Island, would I? "Could . . . would it be too much trouble to teach me?"

Morphia blinked. "Oh, love, I'm an extremely busy woman. Do you know how many dreams I must perform in during any given—"

"You ought to consider it, Morphia," said Larry, in a whisper loud enough for me to hear. "You're not getting any younger, neither you nor your husband. Your popularity has been gradually waning."

"It has not!" Morphia blurted.

"Think about it," said Larry, raising an eyebrow. "When was the last dream you'd starred in that was broadcast over Dreamearth's Viewing Crystals?"

"There was that one in Penumbra," she said. I felt my heart lurch.

"Which was months ago. But with an apprentice, you'd get extra pay and publicity. Some of the other older Substitutes are—" He instantly stopped as Morphia fiercely glared at him. "I'm suggesting you consider it, is all."

"Luna's daughter as my apprentice," Morphia mumbled, more to herself than Larry or me. "That *would* stir up some well-deserved attention."

I looked from her to Peter. He had finished gathering up the girl's thoughts and was wiping his muddy hands on a rag. At least he hadn't gotten into trouble because of me.

"Larry, go on without me. I'm taking the rest of the day off. I have an apprentice to train."

"Now? What am I going to tell—"

"Let Lorelei know my plans. You're right. This is too good of an opportunity to pass up. She'll understand. Besides, the rest of today's dreams are just vague fragments that the Visitors aren't going to remember anyway. And they're not even going to be filmed."

Larry sighed. "Very well. I'll tell her." He disappeared into the ghostsilk.

Before I could think any of this through, Morphia wrapped her arm around my shoulders. "You're trembling, love," she said sweetly. "Now that I think of it, I really could use an apprentice. Why don't we discuss this at my home, over a cup of cocoa, after you've dried off and warmed up?"

My mind churned. Did I really *want* to become a Substitute? I had to admit the thought thrilled me, even though a part of me knew she would only train me for her own benefit. But perhaps she knew more about Mother's past than she let on so far.

That was what swayed my decision. Hot cocoa also sounded heavenly and I was freezing.

"Wait," I choked out as she gently steered me toward the ghostsilk portal, behind Charlie, who slipped into it carrying his equipment. "I must talk to Peter."

"Who?" Morphia raised an eyebrow. I looked in his direction. Even though the rain had stopped, it had flattened his hair to his head and speckled his glasses.

"Peter, the Artifact Collector." I hurried over to him. "Peter, I—"

"I heard." He grinned and took off his glasses to wipe them off on another rag. "Mrs. Nightshade might take you on as an apprentice. I don't think she's ever had one before." He slipped his now clear glasses back on.

"Thank you for—"

"Come along, Remmi, love," called Morphia, standing before the ghostsilk. "What would people think if I let you catch pneumonia?"

"You'd better go. I can't wait to tell Dad!"

I squeezed his hand then slipped through the portal with Morphia.

In the next instant, we stepped into an elegant room. I gaped. It was even larger than the vast Penumbran cavern rooms, its high ceiling carved with intricate patterns and dripping with crystal light fixtures. An enormous Viewing Crystal, flickering with distorted, silent images, stood in the center of the room. Windows, which took up most of the walls, looked out onto countless spired buildings. We were in a city. I had never been in a city before.

"My husband and I live in the heart of Nod, an immense city-province," Morphia said with a hint of pride in her voice. She took down the ghostsilk portal and folded it into a tiny square, as if it were nothing more than a handkerchief, which she slipped into a hidden pocket of her velvet dress.

"Fiona, come here," she called.

Seconds later, a slender girl who looked a few years older than me scurried into the room.

"Ah, Fiona, you are a punctual one," Morphia said with a wide smile. She spoke slowly to the girl, enunciating each word as if she were addressing a small child. "This is Remmi, who may become my new apprentice. She was caught in the rain during my last dream. Take her to the main guest bathroom to wash off. Give her one of my old dresses. Did you get all that, Fiona?"

"Yes, ma'am," Fiona replied in a monotone voice.

I felt as if an icy hand had gripped my heart and was tightening its grasp. Fiona's eyes were dull, impassive. I knew that look all too well. The despised word *drone* pressed against my mind, as if creating a deep, permanent imprint.

I pulled away from Fiona and silently cursed. Morphia had removed the ghostsilk portal. I had to get out of here but didn't know how. I was apparently in one of the upper apartments of an extremely high building. Could I still fly if I opened a window? It had been months since my escape from Penumbra.

"Remmi, go with Fiona." Morphia's voice was edged with concern. "You're dripping wet and will catch your death if you don't warm up and dry off."

I had a feeling Morphia was more worried that I had smeared mud over her immaculate carpet than she was about my well-being. I forced my gaze to settle on hers. I was still shaking but wasn't sure if that was due to the cold of my wet clothes or learning that she owned a drone.

"I can't stay, I've changed my mind," I mumbled, barely able to hear my words over the loud mashing of my heart. A clammy sickness clenched my throat as I looked at the girl. Fiona stood perfectly still, waiting to carry out her mistress's orders.

"Whatever is wrong, love?" Morphia stared at me with a puzzled expression.

"Fiona is a . . ." I couldn't say the word.

"A drone? Oh, I see." Morphia smiled. Her teeth looked blindingly white against her dark red lipstick. "You are one of those people who have a soft spot for those who have been mind-drained." I stiffened. "As do I, love, as well as my husband. It's true we have a couple of drones to help us care for our apartment but don't worry. We treat them well and make sure they are properly fed. Isn't that right, Fiona?" Morphia placed a gentle hand on her shoulder. The girl, who was slightly taller, looked down at her with vacant eyes.

"Yes, ma'am," Fiona said again in that same impassive tone.

I studied her. She was clean and dressed in simple but neat livery. Her face was softly rounded and had the glow of one who was well cared for. That was so different from the pale, pinched faces of my fellow workers in Penumbra. A flicker of guilt jabbed my chest as I realized that, since my escape, I had barely given them much thought. Certainly they had suffered just as much as I, despite their drained minds and blank expressions, and were likely suffering still.

Disturbing memories trickled through my mind like icy water as I followed Fiona down a long corridor. I recalled nights when I had lain awake in the drone huddle on the hard floor, my back throbbing from a recent beating, my hollow stomach pleading in protesting growls. The hunger usually hurt even worse than the lash. I shivered.

Fiona opened the door to a bathroom that was larger than my entire cottage on Sandman Island. "Thank you," I said. Those were words I'd *never* heard during my years as a Penumbran drone. The girl bowed her head in acknowledgment and shut the door behind her.

I peeled off my soaked clothes, which had been clinging to my skin, and stepped into a large shower with glass walls. I sighed as the water poured down on me like a refreshing, cleansing rain, coating me with intoxicating warmth, washing away the chill along with the mud. Not even the little shower over the seashell tub in my cottage felt that smooth. And Penumbra's drone showers, which never seemed to get warm enough, had pounded me like wet sand and held a metallic taste.

My thoughts churned. Morphia didn't know what had happened to Mother. Why did she quit her career as a Substitute to move to the Collective Unconscious Forest?

A distant memory tweaked my mind, one I had suppressed for so long since it filled me with disturbing emotions. The last time I'd seen Mother.

It had been over six years ago, during the winter when a fever epidemic swept through our village. My skin burned and sweated despite the pervasive cold, and my thoughts blurred in a sweeping array of nonsensical images, which was the closest any

Dreamearthling ever came to actually dreaming. My lids felt too heavy and my eyes hurt.

"We have to go to the hospital, little one," Mother whispered in a raspy voice. We shared a fur pallet on the floor of our tiny cottage. A crackling fire burned in the hearth. Mother's beautiful face was flushed and shimmered with a coating of sweat against the firelight. "So many have already died. If we . . . . we don't go, we'll . . . die too." Her words were forced as if it hurt to speak and her breathing was heavy. Ice even colder than the winter gripped my heart. "I'm so sorry, little one." She brushed back my hair and kissed my hot cheek. "I . . . tried so hard to hide you . . . to keep you safe. I just hope they won't find—"

I slid into a feverish darkness as Mother held me close.

She was gone when I finally gained consciousness. I was lying on an uncomfortable cot. The room, I noticed when I opened my eyes, was all white and overly bright with artificial lights that hurt. My eyes fell closed again.

Mother . . . I silently called as terror filled me. *Where are you?* I didn't even want to think the word "dead." She couldn't be. Mother was strong. She could survive anything.

I drifted to sleep again but when I awoke, I was not alone. A tall man in a white lab coat stood beside me. I was still too weak to sit up but I blinked hard, straining to make out his face. It was hopelessly blurred.

"Mother?" I croaked. "Where is she?"

He traced my cheek with his gloved hand. "Luna Clearwater, your mother, is gone," he said in a sad voice. Despair crashed through me but I was too exhausted to even shed one tear. I pulled the thin sheet up to my chin and stared at the wall. It wasn't blurry, like the stranger. I looked back at him and was still unable to make out his face. "She did an excellent job of hiding you all these years but now her secret has been discovered."

What do you mean? I longed to ask but talking was too much effort.

"They tried to mind-drain you, but I made sure that didn't work. You are to be sent to Penumbra to work as a drone." I knew about drones. A few worked in the Forest, usually helping shopkeepers with simple tasks. I was sure I could do that. "Only answer 'yes' or 'no' to any questions and *never* ask any. Keep your head down and avoid eye contact. Do what they tell you, or die."

This memory, mixed with my questions, slammed through my brain but never quite settled.

As I dried off with a soft, scented towel, I saw that Fiona had left me a short red dress, decorated with beads, and matching pumps. The garment was made of a soft, shiny fabric that felt rather slippery.

As I dressed, my gaze settled on my light green sundress, crumpled in a wet, muddy ball in the sink. Periwinkle had bought that for me. I rinsed it and rung it out as best I could. Perhaps it was still salvageable.

I draped it over one arm as I found my way back to the room I'd first entered. Morphia reclined on a pink settee in a nook that faced the windows. Late morning sunlight spilled through it, confusing me. Hadn't it been afternoon on Sandman Island, then the middle of the night in the Nightmare Realms? Just where in Dreamearth was Nod? How far was it from Sandman Island? Fiona knelt before her, painting her fingernails.

"Remmi, love, you look amazing in that dress." I blushed as Morphia settled her gaze on me. "Of course, if I decide to take you on, you'll have to visit my stylist. She'll fix your face and do wonders with that wild mop of hair." I tugged self-consciously at my short, damp locks with my free hand. "Why are you carrying around that ratty old rag?" She focused on the wet sundress. "I'll have my other drone discard that."

"No." I clutched it to my chest. It felt cold through the thin silk of the one I now wore. "I want to keep it."

"Really?" Morphia raised an eyebrow. "Any apprentice of mine would only be seen in the finest clothes."

I continued to stand there, not moving. I couldn't just toss it away as I'd done with that horrible drone tunic. "Yes. It was a gift."

"Oh, I see." Morphia sighed, resigned. "Mia," she yelled. Moments later, a second girl with a vapid expression hurried into the room. "Mia, this is Remmi Clearwater. Take that damp dress from her and launder it. And bring her a cup of hot chocolate."

Mia nodded and took the dress. Guilt filled me. I didn't want drones waiting on me. Was this something I'd have to tolerate as Morphia's apprentice?

"Don't just stand there, Remmi, love. Have a seat." Morphia nodded to a padded chair near her settee. I slid into it. A dizzy feeling overcame me as I peered through the window. The surrounding buildings were hundreds, maybe thousands of feet high. I thought of the impossibly high trees in the Forest. "I think I've seen you before." Morphia gently blew on her wet nails.

"I work at Periwinkle's Resort on Sandman Island." My face grew warm. "You ate dinner there before one of your dreams."

Morphia shook her head. "I'm often so many places in one day, love, that it's hard to keep track." She sighed as Fiona started on her other hand. "It's a good thing Hayden and I never had children, since our schedules are so crazy. He's a Substitute too. We've always been too busy to take on apprentices, although several of our other Substitute friends have. Some have even held auditions in order to find the best potential illusionists out there." She giggled. "I suppose I should count myself lucky that you came to me."

I stared at Fiona and picked at my own plain nails. My conscience tugged at me. Did I want to learn from a woman who owned drones, even if she treated them well?

Mia returned and handed me a warm mug filled with steaming hot chocolate. "Thank you," I said, locking my gaze with hers. She merely averted her eyes and slipped away.

I sipped the drink. It was rich and creamy and spread warmth through me.

I turned at the sound of soft footsteps padding behind me. A tall man strode toward us, coming from the direction of the staircase. His shaggy, shoulder-length hair framed a handsome, narrow face. I could see the slight bulge of toned muscle through his button-down shirt.

"Hayden!" Morphia scrambled to her feet, not waiting for Fiona to finish her nails. "You startled me."

"I entered from my ghostsilk through our bedroom," he said.

Morphia glided toward him and gave him a kiss. "Hayden, this is Remmi Clearwater. I discovered her during one of my dreams. She's a gifted illusionist, one of the best I've ever seen." Sudden pride filled me. It looked as if the talent that had nearly gotten me killed had transformed from a curse into a precious gift. "That's to be expected, since she's Luna Clearwater's daughter. Larry suggested I take her on as my apprentice."

"Luna had a daughter?" He smiled down at me with gentle gray-blue eyes. His voice was deep and kind. "Well, I certainly see the resemblance." He turned back to Morphia. "I think having an apprentice would do you good, dearest. Young Penny can be her client while she is training. This would be perfect since they are close in age."

"Penny?" I asked.

"Penny Brooks," said Morphia. "She was the Visitor you rescued earlier. She's been one of my primary clients ever since she was four, just after she lost her mother. She spends most of her visits in the Nightmare Realms, poor Penny. I can't count how many times she's been dusted with paralyzing powder. Her last dream was no exception."

"Paralyzing powder?" Was that the glittering dust that had coated her pajamas?

"It's often used on Visitors in the Nightmare Realms, making it impossible for them to move." She looked up at her husband with sparkling eyes. "I've been thinking . . . what will the public say when they hear the great Luna Clearwater had a daughter? And not only that. *I'll* be the one who'll have the privilege of training her."

Hayden swept her into his arms and spun her around. "I think it's wonderful. Luna Clearwater's orphaned daughter apprenticed to the famous Morphia Nightshade. That news will be broadcast over every Viewing Crystal in Dreamearth." My blood froze. Would that alert Malcent? Did he have any idea who my mother was?

"Larry said he'd talk to Lorelei but I still must contact Visitor Visions," said Morphia, once Hayden set her down. "They will *have* to film the dreams my new apprentice will be a part of. And there will be live interviews and—"

"Think of the extra company tithes," Hayden practically shouted. "And the response from the public at your wonderful deed. People will adore you even more."

"Wait!" I blurted. "Do we have to tell anyone? Can't I just work with Penny in private?"

Morphia tossed her hair and laughed. "I'm afraid she's going to be a shy one, Hayden. Fearful of the limelight."

"Just like her mother," said Hayden.

"Remmi, love, if you are to become a Substitute, you must get used to fame and all the little heartaches that go with it. But it's all worth it, trust me."

"But . . . but . . ." My mind fumbled. "Isn't it dangerous? Aren't there people who might kill us for our abilities?"

Morphia stroked her hair. "It sounds like you've been reading too many Nightmare Realm scripts, love. Yes, I'm not naïve. I know there are jealous people out there who wish they had our magic and could possibly plot to harm or kill us for that. But that's the same with talented, successful people everywhere, including Realearth. We shouldn't be stupid or careless, I agree, but you can't live your whole life in fear. Besides, there are many more who will look out for us.

"Now, I'll give you a night to think this over. Go back to Sandman Island and get a good night's sleep. It should be evening there now." She reached into her pocket and pulled out her folded ghostsilk. She tore off a fragile corner, and gave it to me. The fabric was so fine, thinner than a cobweb, that I could barely feel it in my hand. "Pieces of these portals can be used as communication devices. Just say my name into your ghostsilk patch and I'll come for you."

I glanced down at the dress, searching for a pocket. I didn't find one. "And this dress—"

"Keep it. It's yours," she said, hanging up her ghostsilk. "I'll be sure to save that other one for you. It's probably still in the wash."

"Goodbye for now, Remmi," Hayden said with a grin as I stepped toward the portal. I waved then hesitated.

"Just visualize where you want to go and walk into it," said Morphia.

I closed my eyes and, remembering how it was entering one with Peter, formed an image of the interior of my cottage in my mind. I felt the now familiar tickle-whisper of faint ghost hairs against my skin. The soft carpet beneath my feet hardened into smooth wood.

I opened my eyes. I was home, standing in the middle of my cottage, which suddenly seemed so tiny compared to Morphia's vast apartment.

It was small, true, but held a cozy warmth that Morphia's home seemed to lack. The back of my throat suddenly ached at the prospect of leaving this place. The setting sun filled most of the room with a rich, rosy glow.

I looked around, wondering if I could still see Morphia and Hayden watching me through the portal. I caught a faint gleam, like the reflection of a water shimmer, for a fleeting second before the ghostsilk vanished.

I paced the room, thinking. I'd have to leave Periwinkle's Resort if I accepted Morphia's offer. I found I loved Periwinkle as a mother, almost as much as I had my own.

But to train to become a Substitute . . . what Mother had been. Would I be safe from Malcent if I showed the world my talent?

A loud knocking at the door jolted me from my thoughts.

Chapter 14

"Remmi? Are you home yet? It's me, Peter."

I opened the door. His hair was still damp but he had changed into dry clothes. He pushed at his glasses, which were inching down his nose, with one hand as he hoisted my school backpack with the other. His eyes widened as they briefly studied me then quickly looked down. "Wow, Remmi! That's a different dress. You look . . . you look . . ." His face turned a bright red that made his freckles stand out.

"Is that my backpack?" My words came out in a rush, to cover up my own awkwardness.

"Yes. You . . . uh . . . you dropped this at that dream site." He shuffled his feet. I took the pack from him.

"Thanks." I tossed it onto my cot. "How did you find me?"

"You told me you worked here but I had to ask one of the workers where your cottage was." He looked around. "It must be pretty nice to have your own place. Ours is so crowded, between my parents and my siblings."

"Lucky you." A wistful longing tweaked my chest.

"So, what happened after you left with Mrs. Nightshade? Are you going to be her apprentice?" His cheeks deepened even more.

"I'm not sure yet. Maybe." I couldn't help smiling when I looked at him. I was sure he felt even more nervous around me than I did with him. "Would you like to take a walk, perhaps go into the village for something to eat?" I still felt hungry despite the crackers and hot chocolate. "Do you have time?"

Peter grinned and patted his pocket. "Dad lent me his ghostsilk portal when I told him about you and that I ought to return your backpack. My shift's over. I have school in the morning but I don't see why I can't stay for a bit."

The heat and humidity still clung to the air as we made our way to the village. The pirate ship was gone. Now a cruise ship was docked in the harbor so, even though no dreams were scheduled at that time, the narrow streets bustled with tourists.

I led Peter to a small sandwich shop near the beach. To my surprise, once we reached the front of the long line, he insisted on buying our food. Was this a date? I struggled to grasp that concept. I knew of such things but had never assumed something like this could happen to me. My life had never been even close to normal and I doubted that would happen any time soon.

Peter and I settled on the beach with sandwiches and sodas. I slipped off the red pumps, which were too fancy for the beach. Why hadn't I left them at the cottage?

We ate in silence for a while. My heart was racing and I could barely taste my food. I focused on the surrounding scenery and the constant lapping of the waves only a few feet away.

A crescent moon danced in and out from behind woolly clouds and a warm breeze, tinged with the blending fragrances of flowers and cooking food, brushed my face and fingered my hair. It was a beautiful night but I could already smell the approach of an oncoming squall.

I dug my bare feet into the sun-warmed sand and studied the clouds, which were mottled with moonlight and shadow. Some held the blurred shapes of different animals. I squinted in an effort to make them out: sheep, dolphins, and something that looked like a bird with an elephant trunk instead of a beak. An urge to fly amongst them, as I had done during my escape— which now seemed to have taken place a lifetime ago—tugged at me.

"I wonder if those clouds are watching us," I murmured, then instantly felt silly.

Peter laughed. I flushed, certain that what I had said sounded incredibly stupid. "I see them up close all the time in Zephyr."

"The famous floating province?" I'd learned more about it in school. It was described in one of my schoolbooks as a series of floating islands, called skylands, which were part of an archipelago named the Tears of the Moon. Some people lived on the skylands but most of the structures were attached to giant

100

silk balloons. These had to be constantly maintained. Bridge-like streets and glass staircases connected everything.

He nodded. "I live there."

"It sounds amazing."

Peter swallowed the last of his sandwich. "Not really. Not if you live there. But it is where the world-renowned Cloud Wranglers live and work."

"Are they the ones that herd cloud beasts?"

"Yes. They're like Substitutes, only instead of having illusion magic, they can fly. Cloud Wranglers come from all over Dreamearth to work in Zephyr. They basically control the weather."

"The weather?"

"Pretty much. Cloud beasts gradually absorb moisture from the air into their bodies. When they become too heavy, this water is released as rain. It is up to the Cloud Wranglers to round them up and take them to parts of Dreamearth that are experiencing drought." He sighed. "I wanted to be a Wrangler when I was little but I couldn't fly. You have to be born with that talent, just like illusion magic."

My skin chilled despite the heat. I resisted telling him that I'd flown from Penumbra and had been carried here on the backs of cloud beasts. What if my ability to do both would make people mistake me for a Halfling? A part of me felt I could trust Peter but I'd learned caution too well in Penumbra.

"Do you like Artifact Collecting?" Better to change the subject.

"For the most part. I get to travel all over Dreamearth but it can be nasty too."

"What do you mean?"

"Sometimes Dad has to clean up after Halfling mind-drains."

"Halfling mind-drains?" The sandwich I had eaten sat like a stone in my stomach. Sour bile rose into my throat.

Peter nodded and looked toward the sea. "Since Halflings are part Visitor, their thoughts come out as Artifacts that are drained into the Life River. I-I watched a mind-drain once." His face paled. He didn't look at me. "It was so horrible. This hose-like device was inserted into a baby's head. The thoughts that came out were tiny, like regular baby Visitor thoughts. They looked like marbles. Dad poured them into a bucket."

"And the baby became a drone." My stomach churned and bile slid into my mouth. *Please . . .* I begged my body. *Not in front of Peter!* I swallowed it down.

"Yeah." Peter's voice was toneless. "But first it had to be placed in stasis until it was old enough to work as one. That experience was so terrible that Dad said I wouldn't have to do that anymore, collect drained Halfling thoughts, until I'm older. But he hopes it never comes to that."

"What do you mean?" The breeze tossed wisps of my hair into my eyes. I brushed them back.

"Dad hates what they do to Halflings, turning them into drones. He's trying to figure out a way to fight this injustice." He turned and looked at me. His thin, freckled face, streaked with moonlight, looked almost handsome. "How did you end up a drone, Remmi? Especially since you hadn't been mind-drained?"

"I was mistaken for a Halfling because of my illusion magic but I was somehow spared the mind-drain."

"That's awful. Not that you weren't mind-drained." The color rushed back into his face. "But that you were mistaken for a Halfling."

I shrugged. "It no longer matters. That's in the past and I'm *never* returning to Penumbra."

Peter grinned. "I hope you become Morphia's apprentice. That will show them."

"I'm seriously considering it."

"Good." He leaned forward on his knees and gently touched my face. Ripples of warmth pulsed through my body. I feared he could hear the fierce pounding of my heart, which echoed in my ears, drowning out the waves, as his lips brushed against mine.

Peter pulled back. His blush was brilliant even against the faint light and I was sure my face was just as red.

"I-i-it's getting late and I have school," Peter mumbled as he began gathering up the remains of our dinner. "I'll walk you back."

I stood, brushed sand from my dress, and picked up the pumps but didn't put them back on. The wind, though warm, was growing stronger and the clouds were thickening, swallowing the moon. Hopefully we'd make it back before the rains started.

Rains likely formed by the cloud beasts I had ridden. I still couldn't mention that to Peter.

"I-I hope I'll see you again soon," he said at my door as he hung the ghostsilk portal in the air. The wind blew it into ripples as if it were the surface of a restless pond.

He kissed my cheek and vanished into the silk before I could answer.

Chapter 15

Warm rain batted against me as I raced toward the Dining Cottage to talk to Periwinkle. I was tired but didn't think I could sleep until I explained everything to her. I brushed my sopping hair from my eyes as I entered—it was time to cut it again—and searched the crowd for Periwinkle. Wasn't this the second time today I'd been caught in the rain? The wet dress clung to my skin.

She stood near the kitchen, talking to a sunburned man in shorts and a boldly patterned shirt.

"What're you doing here?" asked Percy as he glided by with a tray of drinks. "I thought you were off today."

"I am." I was aware of several people staring at me as I made my way through the restaurant. "I have something important to tell Periwinkle."

Her eyes widened as soon as she saw me. "Remmi! Shouldn't you be in your cottage, doing your homework?" She cocked an eyebrow. "And you're soaking wet. What, in all the provinces, made you come out in this—?"

"Ma'am, what are you going to do about my cottage's leaky roof?" the sunburned man asked in an irritated tone.

"I'm sorry, sir," said Periwinkle. "I'll send one of my men right away." She turned back to me. "Remmi, whatever it is will have to wait until tomorrow morning. You look exhausted. Get back to your cottage before you catch something. There are extra umbrellas in the kitchen." She turned and beckoned to the man. "Come, sir, and we'll see about that leak."

I stood still for several minutes, after they'd left. Murmurs mixed with the sound of the rain pattering against the roof. I took a deep breath and struggled to control the anger that threatened to emerge. Periwinkle was a busy woman and I'd caught her at a bad time. She ran this resort by herself, with just the help of Andrew and a few staff members.

Guilt tugged at me as I made my way back to the cottage. The rain was even heavier and thunder roared in the distance. Except for this warm, humid weather, the storm reminded me of Penny's dream in the Nightmare Realms.

The nightmare that was about to change my life . . .

After I'd dried off and changed into my nightclothes, I plucked the patch of ghostsilk off my nightstand and settled on the bed.

I saw my reflection against its silvery surface, as if it were a mirror spun from the finest silk. "Morphia," I whispered, barely able to hear myself over the pounding rain and rumbling thunder. "Morphia," I repeated, louder this time. "All you said I had to do was speak into—"

"I hear you, love." Morphia's face instantly replaced mine. "Have you come to a decision?"

"Yes." Nerves twitched through me but I spoke as confidently as I could. "I accept your offer. I'd like to be your Substitute apprentice."

"Excellent." She stepped back so I could see her entire body. It was as if I were peering at her reflection in a mirror, only in miniature. She wore a velvety, deep green gown. "I'll come for you right away. No need to pack anything, love. You'll get a whole new set of clothes—"

"Wait." I nearly crumpled the silk in my hand. Morphia's image briefly shattered until I straightened it out. "Sorry. Can it wait till tomorrow? I didn't get a chance to talk to Periwinkle and—"

"Who?"

"The owner of the resort on Sandman Island where I work." Irritation gnawed at me. Hadn't I told her that before? She'd even *met* Periwinkle that one time she'd eaten in the Dining Cottage. How could she have forgotten? "And I also must go to school—"

"School?" Morphia laughed. "Oh, love, you needn't bother. I have a private tutor all set up for you, right in my building."

"It's not that. I . . . I should at least tell my teacher that I'm leaving. And there's someone else I must talk to as well." My heart twisted as I thought of Jenna. It would be so much

105

easier if I just allowed Morphia to come for me this instant. I wouldn't have to explain any of this to anyone, not even Periwinkle.

But my conscience wouldn't let me. I owed Periwinkle so much and needed to set things right with Jenna. I already knew my mind would itch like a drone tunic if I left now.

"Oh, I see." Morphia grinned. "You need closure. Perfectly understandable, love. I'll come for you tomorrow evening, then, Sandman Island time, and meet you at the resort's dining establishment. I remember it now."

I struggled to calm my restless mind as I turned out the light and lay back on the bed. My life was changing so fast. If only the noisy night could overpower my restless thoughts.

*

As I hurried toward the Dining Cottage the next morning, I rehearsed in my mind what I was going to say to Periwinkle. The rain had vanished, leaving a clear, humid morning.

The familiar blending scents of Andrew's cooking struck my senses before I even entered the Cottage. They smelled delicious but I doubted I'd be able to choke anything down.

Periwinkle and another staff member were placing freshly cut flowers in small vases on each table, which they did each morning before the restaurant opened.

My throat clenched as I approached her. "Are you busy? I need to talk to you," I whispered.

"Remmi, honey, I'm so sorry about last night," she said, brushing her hands on her apron. Her seashell earrings jiggled. "You just caught me at a bad time. What was it you wanted to tell me?"

I forced myself to look into her eyes. Where should I start? "The Substitute Morphia Nightshade asked me to become her apprentice." The words, released so abruptly, sounded ludicrous to my ears.

Periwinkle's eyes widened. "Child, what are you talking about? A Substitute apprentice?"

I nodded. "I didn't share this with you but I can illusion."

"There is a lot I don't know about you, Remmi, but illusion magic? I'd like to see that."

I closed my eyes and pictured Andrew in my mind, his brilliant smile against dusk-dark skin, and the thin dreadlocks that brushed his shoulders. My skin itched with the familiar sticky tingle of an illusion.

Periwinkle drew in a sharp breath. My eyes sprung open. I looked down at Andrew's slender, muscled arms and sandaled feet. I seemed taller and even my clothes had changed.

Periwinkle sank down onto the nearest chair and waved a hand in front of her face, as if afraid she might faint. "By the First Visitors, girl!" she gasped, her scarf slipping to the side, revealing tufts of woolly gray and black hair. "Why didn't you tell me you could do this? Here I've had you wait tables and clean cottages when you have such a gift. Although I shouldn't be surprised. You are a mysterious one, Remmi, appearing out of nowhere and hiding from those foreign police."

I allowed the illusion to slip and settled into a chair next to Periwinkle. I took her hand in both of mine. "I'm grateful for all you've done for me, I really am. There is a part of me . . . a big part, actually, that doesn't want to leave. But I feel this is an opportunity I shouldn't pass up."

"Of course not, honey." Periwinkle tightened her grip. Her eyes were glossy with tears. "I wouldn't hear of it. It is a great honor to be a Dreamearth Substitute. Of course you should accept Morphia Nightshade's offer. Just promise me you'll be careful."

I wasn't sure what she meant but I assured her I would be.

I was so jittery that I could barely eat my breakfast. A part of me was tempted to pull out Morphia's ghostsilk piece from my pocket and ask her get me now. But Periwinkle insisted on throwing a party for me this afternoon. And I still had to confront Jenna.

I was surrounded by students the instant I stepped into the school hallway. At first I thought another dream was taking place until I realized they were all staring at me. My face burned. Several voices spoke at once.

"You're going to train under Morphia Nightshade?"

"Show us an illusion."

"You must be so excited."

All of this attention was so overwhelming that I just wanted to sink into the floor and hide beneath the polished tiles.

"How did you all know?" My voice was barely audible above the noise.

"It's all over the Viewing Crystal news," one boy said, his eyes shining.

"It is?" I could feel my bright flush receding, leaving my face ashen-pale. Just what was I getting into by agreeing to this? Was the whole world going to watch me? Would I still be safe from Lord Malcent?

Relief washed through me when Mrs. Swan herded us all into class.

I struggled to not look at Jenna as I settled at my desk. She sat with a lowered head, her face hidden behind an open book.

At lunch, Kaya, Brilla, and Pedra beckoned me, encouraging me to join them. I glanced from them to Jenna. The Penumbran girl sat by herself, as usual. Jenna had spent all her lunchtimes with her face buried in a book.

I didn't see a book this time. Jenna's face, beneath her hat, had a slightly swollen look, as if she had recently been crying. She gazed directly at me through storm-colored eyes that shimmered with unshed tears.

"Remmi, you are going to be an apprentice to the great Morphia Nightshade," Kaya said, her voice loud enough for Jenna to hear. "You can't possibly want to sit with that loser." She jerked her chin in Jenna's direction.

A sudden rage burned through me but I wasn't sure who it was directed at. I was still angry with Jenna for her attitude concerning drones but also had a sudden desire to punch Kaya.

"This is my last day here," I said coldly. "I'll eat with whomever I choose."

I strode from Kaya without looking back. Jenna's eyes widened as I approached her table. A fat tear slipped from her eye and trickled down her plump red cheek. She quickly brushed it away.

"I-I'm happy for you, Remmi," she said in a soft, shaking voice as I sat across from her. "But I don't understand why you ran off like that yesterday. Did I say something to offend you?"

Yes, very much, I longed to say but held back. I looked down and poked at my food, a thin slab of fish on a bed of rice, and a salad. Andrew prepared my lunches every morning, and they were always delicious, but I feared my tense stomach would reject it if I forced myself to eat.

I sensed Jenna's gaze burrowing into me. What could I say? Admit I'd been a Penumbran drone?

"I'm sorry," I finally whispered, more to my food than to Jenna. "I don't know why I acted that way." My stomach ached, as if my intestines had entwined into a tight knot. *That's a lie,* my thoughts whispered but I ignored them. I forced myself to look up.

"It's okay," Jenna said, her eyes still tear-filled. "I'm sorry too, for whatever I said." She took a nibble of her salad.

"You're lucky to be able to get away from here," she continued. "Although, I have to admit, there is a part of me that wishes you weren't going, especially since you're the first real friend I've made outside of Penumbra."

The thought of Jenna spending lonely days at school, where she would once again be the target of ridicule, angered me. It wasn't fair. My mind churned as I absently chewed my food, hardly tasting what I was eating. Now that I'd finally made a friend, I wanted to keep her. Even if she was Penumbran.

I reached into my pocket and pulled out the scrap of ghostsilk fabric Morphia had given me. I carefully ripped it in half. The delicate cloth tore easily, as if I were pulling apart a gauzy tissue. I handed one of the pieces to Jenna.

She stared at the portal-piece with wide eyes. Sunlight glinted against its shimmering surface, weaving silvery spangles across her face. "Is this part of a ghost—?"

"Yes." I smiled and nodded. "Morphia gave it to me. It should help us keep in touch while I'm away."

"I'd like that," Jenna said, rubbing the fragment against her cheek.

*

Periwinkle's entire staff, along with most of the village, showed up for my farewell celebration. I'd initially hoped to keep my illusion talent a secret. I looked around at the colorful banners and decorations that were streamed across the Dining Cottage. Now the entire island knew what I could do.

A stubborn melancholy clung to my insides like a damp rag as I feasted and danced by the hot bonfire with Andrew and his little girl Faya. This will be the last time I do this. I forced a smile.

Periwinkle held me close for several long moments after most people had left and Morphia stepped through the ghostsilk that suddenly appeared. Thoughts of how Mother used to hold me fleeted through my mind as I listened to the throbbing of Periwinkle's heart against my ear. Her body felt softer, more rounded while Mother's had been fragile, almost bony. Periwinkle smelled of the sun-soaked sea instead of lilacs. She stroked my hair.

"You know how often dreams take place here." Periwinkle pulled away. "We'll probably see each other even more than before." I wished I could believe her.

I then gathered up my belongings and followed Morphia through the ghostsilk. I turned back one last time to wave at Periwinkle, Andrew, and his family before I stepped completely through. The delicate hairs tickled my skin and brushed against my cheeks like the whisper-fine touch of butterfly wings.

Chapter 16

I stumbled from the portal into Morphia's elegant apartment. I suddenly felt so shabby and tiny in this place, garbed in a simple faded sundress and clutching a single backpack that contained all of my belongings. This wasn't much more than what I had carried out of Penumbra.

Morphia led me up a winding staircase to my room. My eyes widened as I stepped into it. My Sandman Island cottage could easily have fit in here and still had space to spare. The high, domed ceiling was deep blue, like dusk, and decorated with stars that flashed when Morphia flipped the light switch. A large light fixture, shaped like a crescent moon, dangled like a chandelier from the center of the ceiling.

An enormous, ornate bathroom was adjacent to this room and the closet was another room in its own right.

"I have a schedule planned out for you," Morphia said as I tossed my backpack onto the wide, round bed. The bedspread was patterned to resemble the sun. She ran her gaze over me, her golden eyes softening. "You look tired. While you had a full day already on Sandman Island, it is early morning here. Get some sleep and I'll have Fiona wake you in a couple of hours. You'll adjust to the time change quicker if you don't sleep all day. We have much to do before you officially begin your apprenticeship."

Morphia turned and gently shut the door behind her.

I kicked off my now worn sandals and dug my bare feet into the thick carpet. It was almost as soft as cloud animal fleece and came up to my ankles. I sank back onto the bed and closed my eyes.

I was exhausted but my body refused to settle. So much had happened in these past couple of days that my mind seemed incapable of processing it all. It felt like the mental equivalent of attempting to sculpt something recognizable out of watery mud.

The bed also felt strange, too large and soft, much different than my small Sandman Island one. I had trouble getting used to that at first. Perhaps I could adjust to this as well.

A longing to return to the island ached inside me. I stared up at the blinking stars through eyes that refused to remain closed. I missed the distant stirring of the surrounding Archetypal Sea, the frequent noisy thunderstorms, and the cacophony of restless birds in the tropical trees.

It was too quiet here. The only sound that filled my ears was my own breathing.

I managed to doze off for what felt like mere seconds when someone gently shook me awake.

"Miss Clearwater," said a timid voice. "It's time to get up. Mrs. Nightshade is waiting."

Groggy confusion momentarily blurred my mind as I sluggishly sat up. Fiona stood over me, patiently awaiting further instructions.

"Thank you, Fiona," I said, slipping my sandals back on and running a hand through my mussed hair. "That will be all."

Fiona simply bobbed her head and stepped through the door.

I sighed and stretched. Just what kind of day did Morphia have planned?

I stumbled downstairs, still feeling lost and disoriented in this apartment.

Morphia was waiting in the room I had entered on my first visit. I followed her into the hallway where we stepped into what appeared to be a closet. A moment later, I realized it was an elevator.

"My apartment takes up the entire top floor of this building," Morphia said.

After several minutes, the opposite door opened into an elegant lobby. My wide eyes scanned the vast room, taking in the plush furniture, the shiny, tiled floor, and an enormous chandelier that dangled from the high, domed ceiling. A few people in expensive looking clothes milled about. Not even Penumbra's fanciest chambers could compare to this.

"Don't gawk so, Remmi," Morphia whispered as she guided me toward a wide glass door. A doorman in fancy livery dipped his head at Morphia and smiled at me as he opened the door for us. A queer feeling surged through me.

This sensation deepened into an overwhelmed daze as we stepped out onto the crowded street. "Over here," Morphia said, taking my hand and leading me toward a sleek black town car parked in front of the building. It was large and roomy with soft leather seats. The leather's scent filled the air.

"Henry," Morphia said to the driver, a middle-aged man with weathered skin. "This is my new apprentice, Remmi Clearwater." He smiled and nodded at me. "Remmi, this is Henry, my personal driver and yours as well."

At least he wasn't a drone.

"I hope you had enough time to rest, Remmi," Morphia said as the car started cruising down the street. The surrounding buildings were so high they blocked the sun, washing the streets in shadow. "Because we have a packed day. First, we'll make you more presentable. As a Substitute, you will frequently be thrust into the public eye, often as yourself, not hidden behind the personas you will take on for your client. We must purchase you some decent clothes." Her gaze flicked over the faded blue sundress I wore. I felt blood rush into my face. "After that you have an appointment with my personal stylist Diana."

I swallowed and twisted my hands in my lap.

"Don't get me wrong, love," Morphia continued, likely interpreting my silence as sore feelings. "What you have on is perfect for Sandman Island but you are in Nod now. If you wander the streets dressed like that, people will see you as a tacky tourist, not a Substitute in training."

I turned my gaze to the window and watched the crowds flicker by. Perhaps it was a mistake to come here. After years of not belonging, I'd finally found a decent home on Sandman Island. Why did I have to leave it? Periwinkle felt like a mother, a replacement for the one I'd lost. Would Morphia ever be that, or would she simply be just a mentor?

"We'll have to go another way," Henry muttered under his breath as the car inched along in heavy traffic. "This street is closed for an upcoming dream. The main prop is a burning airplane, all for a Visitor who is uncertain about a business trip he is nervous about taking."

"Oh, yes." Morphia sighed. "I was originally offered that assignment but I turned it down for another commitment." She smiled at me and squeezed my hand. "You have such rough hands, love. Diana has creams that should do wonders for those calluses. And she can fix your nails, too."

"Why didn't we just use the ghostsilk portal?" I whispered. I had to change the subject but was curious about that as well.

Morphia tossed her head back and laughed, causing her hair to ripple. I fleetingly wondered if her original hair color was black or gold.

"Ghostsilk portals are only used for traveling long distances, usually from one dream site to another. For daily errands in cities such as Nod, we citizens are encouraged to use our own transportation. I admit that traveling like this does make us seem as mundane as Realearthlings are in their own world but it is silly to use our portals for just short jaunts. That doesn't stop *some* Substitutes from abusing the privilege, however." Morphia rolled her eyes. "Ah, here we are."

The car slowed to a stop in front of a large building that was painted with an array of brilliant colors. Mannequins in elegant clothes were displayed behind the wide windows.

I spent the next hour or so trying on countless outfits. There were slinky, strapless silk dresses, jewel-spangled gowns, filmy blouses with draping sleeves, lacy skirts, form fitting slacks, colorful scarves, and fur-lined coats. "You must be prepared for winter here in Nod," Morphia advised. "It gets bitterly cold, unlike your tropical island." I tensed. Cold winters were the worst. At least winter was still months away.

Even the nightclothes and underwear Morphia purchased for me were fancy, made of silk and lace.

Penumbran noblewomen didn't own this many clothes. She ordered a saleslady to package everything.

Morphia had me try on endless shoes after that. Many of these were high-heeled boots and pumps that felt uncomfortable and gave me an awkward, stumbling gait. "You must get used to walking in these, love," Morphia crooned. "In many of Penny's dreams, you will be portraying her mother, Bianca Del Mar, who had been a famous movie actress before her death. She often wore these kinds of shoes."

"Can't I just illusion them as I do other clothes?" I pulled off a pair of boots that came up to my thighs.

Morphia shook her head. "You can but your walk would be all wrong. If the persona you are taking on is wearing heels, you must be too. Looking natural is a lesson that I'm including in your Substitute training."

I sighed inwardly. My body was drained and I felt as if it were the middle of the night, even though sunlight spilled in through the skylights that lined the high ceiling.

"We mustn't forget jewelry," Morphia said, approaching a counter that displayed a countless array of sparkling necklaces and earrings.

I gaped. I had never worn jewelry before, not even the seashell baubles that were sold mostly to tourists on Sandman Island.

"We don't want anything too gaudy," Morphia said, picking up a thin pearl necklace and holding it to my throat. "You are fine-featured and still quite young. Anything too fancy will overpower you. Besides, you can always illusion jewelry. But we definitely should get your ears pierced." I winced at this notion. What did that entail?

The next stop was the beauty salon, a few blocks down. I wore a beaded pink blouse with billowy sleeves and a matching skirt. Even my pumps had been dyed to match. I was grateful they were flat. I wanted to avoid walking in high heels as long as possible. My earlobes, now decorated with tiny stud earrings, still slightly stung from the piercing.

I scanned the salon. The place was lined with mirrors and hair dryers and smelled of hairspray. A tall woman glided forward to greet us. "Ah, Morphia." Her blonde hair was swept up into an elaborate hairdo and her eyebrows were fine, pale lines. A gold nametag indicated this woman was Diana. "It's good to see you. And this must be your new apprentice. Remmi is it?" She grinned down at me, displaying teeth so blindingly white they looked artificial. "Oh, dear. You need much work, I can see." Diana's voice was tinged with an unfamiliar accent.

"That's why we're here," Morphia said, placing a hand on my shoulder.

My face grew hot as Diana led me to a vinyl chair in front of a lighted mirror. I felt as if I were once again a hopeless drone, despite my new clothes.

"You are actually quite beautiful," Diana said, studying my face. "You should see some of my other customers. But you need to show it off. Oh, those eyes! By the First Visitors, they really stand out against your skin, although too much sun is bad, very bad. We can't have you looking shriveled and old before your time, can we? And who cut your hair?" I remained silent, knowing it was futile to answer. Diana seemed to enjoy hearing the sound of her own voice. "It's such thick, lovely hair but so jagged, so sloppy. I'll trim it for now, just to get it even, but you really should let it grow long. And eyebrows shouldn't meet like yours do. They're full and dark—how I envy that—but desperately need some plucking. Your looks are like a garden, Remmi. Remember that. But they need constant pruning."

I bit my lip as Diana trimmed and plucked and applied a layer of cosmetics to my face.

Another woman massaged my rough hands with lotion and complained about the calluses. She filed my stubby nails, attached long plastic ones over them, and painted them with a sparkly pink polish.

"Don't touch anything until they're dry," she chided.

I had never worn makeup before and didn't particularly like it. My face felt like a mask, my mascara-coated lashes took up a part of my vision, and I had an urge to wipe off the glossy, fruit-scented lipstick as soon as it was applied. Lastly, Diana touched up my hair, framing my face in tiny, delicate ringlets.

"Remmi, love, you look gorgeous," Morphia breathed. "Diana does work wonders. Of course, you were pretty before but just look at yourself now. You're an entirely different person without even having to illusion."

I studied myself in the mirror. The image gazing back wasn't Remmi Clearwater, but a painted porcelain doll. This wasn't the Remmi who was used to hard labor, who loved to swim in the ocean, and who had once flown amongst the clouds. That mirror image was . . . just who was she? She was someone who looked too fragile to have done any of that, who might break into countless shards if she so much as moved the wrong way.

Chapter 17

"There's this lovely little café where we can have lunch," Morphia said when we were back in the car. "It will give us time to go over tonight's script."

"Tonight?" I gulped.

"Of course, love. You've already had an impromptu interaction with Penny. This dream, as well as those that follow, will be scripted. And beforehand is your interview."

"M-my interview?" My mouth had suddenly gone dry.

"Naturally. I must introduce you to all of Dreamearth as my new apprentice. The whole world will be watching this dream."

I twisted my hands in my lap and winced when I inadvertently pulled back one of the fake nails. It was glued on so tightly it felt as if it were one of my own.

"Take the car back, Henry," Morphia said as the car pulled up in front of a small, pastel edifice. A fancy sign that read "Convergence Café" hung over the door. "And have the drones put away Remmi's new clothes. I'll contact you as soon as we are ready to come home."

As I stepped out of the car, I noticed that Morphia had changed her appearance. She resembled a plump older woman with a scarf tied over her gray hair.

"Why did you illusion—?"

She broke off with a chuckle. "I'm too recognizable, love," she whispered as she guided me through the crowds, toward the café. "I don't need people bothering me at this time, asking for photos and auto—Oh, Remmi." Her tone suddenly changed. "Look up, love. Your feet know what they are doing. You don't have to stare down at them. And straighten your shoulders." She pressed her hand against my upper back. "That's it. Don't shuffle your feet so. Take smaller steps."

My exhaustion returned, quenching the excitement I had fleetingly experienced. Feeling once again like a drone that had been given a direct order, I obeyed Morphia. I lifted my head, thrust my shoulders back, and took a few hesitant steps.

"You're too stiff, Remmi, love," Morphia crooned from behind. "Keep that posture but walk naturally. Moving with grace is important for the role you will be playing for Penny. Bianca was well known for her graceful glide."

"Sorry." I felt my face redden and wondered if that blush was visible beneath the artificial one Diana had applied to my cheeks.

I struggled to concentrate on my movements while my senses were overwhelmed by the surroundings. The sidewalk bustled with crowds of people, many of them dressed in odd, colorful clothes, and traffic clotted the street. Several people I passed spoke languages I didn't recognize. Occasionally, ethereal Visitors, experiencing their dreams, flitted by. I was surprised that most of the people, except those I assumed were assigned to the dream, didn't even stop to watch, as if such things were a commonplace occurrence. Even though dreams were quite frequent on Sandman Island, they still attracted an audience there. And in Penumbra, they happened so rarely they were a cause for celebration.

I sighed with relief as we entered the café.

It was quiet inside after the noisy street with the roar of thousands of voices and cars honking and screeching. A fountain gently splashed in the middle of the room. A group of well-dressed people in their early twenties sat near the fountain. Other patrons were seated at tables scattered around the room.

Morphia, who had shifted back to her regular appearance, was greeted by a tall man in a suit.

"It's an honor to have you here again, Mrs. Nightshade," he said with a bow. People always bowed to Morphia. This uncomfortably reminded me of how the ordinary Penumbrans acted toward Lord Malcent and his family.

My thoughts started to stray to Jenna when Morphia placed a hand on my shoulder. "Thank you, Maurice. I'd like a table for my newest apprentice and myself."

Maurice smiled down at me. I returned the smile, briefly fearing the expression might cause my makeup to crack.

"Yes, yes, of course. Right this way, ladies."

He led us to a small table, next to the fountain, directly across from the chattering group. "The waiter will be with you momentarily," he said, handing us menus.

I scanned the menu. It was so different from the ones at Periwinkle's Resort, which were coated with plastic and decorated with shell and fish patterns. These menus were leather bound and opened up like a book. The dishes, which had odd names, none of which I recognized, were written in a fancy font I found difficult to read.

This felt strange. The waiter, almost as elegantly dressed as Maurice, filled our glasses with icy water. I had always been the one doing the serving.

"Would you ladies like a drink while you look over the menus?" he asked.

"Bring us each a glass of your finest white wine," Morphia said with a small smile.

I gaped. "Wine?" I whispered once the waiter had left. "I'm only fourteen." Periwinkle had refused to serve alcohol to anyone under twenty although I had seen kids not much older than me imbibing on the public beaches. It made them loud and rowdy. Some of the noble children in Penumbra often had wine with their dinner, I recalled, but their glasses held more water than wine.

Morphia grinned. "It's okay in Nod, as long as it's with a meal. Besides, this is a celebration of sorts, isn't it? This is your first official day as my apprentice." She lifted her glass once the wine arrived and took a graceful sip.

I did likewise, with slight hesitation. The liquid was a soft gold color and held a rich woody flavor. It increased the dazed feeling, brought on by the time change, which still clung like a stubborn mist in my mind. My lipstick left a pink smudge on the rim of the glass. I felt my face warm as I noticed that, even though Morphia was wearing just as much lipstick as me, her glass remained pristine.

"Your client, Penny Brooks," Morphia began, after we had placed our orders, "lives on the southern west coast in a large Realearth country that is called the United States, or America." I nodded. I had learned of this place in my Realearth Studies class. "She is twelve years old, an only child who lives with her widowed father, a respected neuroscientist."

"A neuro—" I shook my head. "What's that?"

"He studies the human brain and, interestingly enough, is fascinated by dreams." Morphia emitted a tinkling laugh. "At least according to his profile. Hayden's worked with him but he's never been my client. Your focus, however, will be on Penny and Bianca."

She paused momentarily when the waiter brought our salads. I picked at mine, feeling hopelessly awkward with my long, fake fingernails. How was I going to do any work with these?

"Bianca was born in Mexico, another Realearth country that is directly south of the United States, but left when she was a little girl," Morphia continued. "She met James Brooks at college, even though they were training in different fields. Bianca landed her first role in a movie just before they were married. She decided to keep her original last name since that was what she was known by. Bianca had to travel frequently for her career, often going overseas for weeks and even months at a time. She continued this even after Penny was born, which is quite sad since ghostsilk portals don't exist in Realearth. Realearthlings travel long distances by airplane, just like those Dreamearthlings who don't own portals, and can take several hours."

Morphia washed a bit of her salad down with a sip of wine. I put down my fork. My stomach tightened. I knew what was coming next.

"Bianca died in a car accident." I remembered the dream I had interrupted. "Penny, who was only four at that time, had been in the car with her mother, which is why she remembers the event so vividly. It's these nightmares that haunt her almost every night.

"Luckily tonight's dream is not a nightmare." I let out the breath I hadn't realized I'd been holding. "In fact, it should be fun for you." Morphia pulled the script from her purse and scanned it. "According to this, Bianca, who will be you, love, is strolling along a red carpet at a major awards ceremony. Penny will be in the audience, cheering for you, her mother. All you have to do is smile and wave at her."

Once the waiter brought our meals, I ate in silence, picking at my fish. It was good but couldn't compare to Andrew's cooking. Tender but bland in comparison, it was flavored with just a hint of lemon. Andrew had often added hot spices and rich sauces to his creations.

Loud laughter erupted from the table across from us. I looked up. A skinny, plainly dressed man with hunched shoulders was passing by that group, mopping the tiled floor.

"Look, it's one of those drones," one young man said to his companions, a nasty smile stretched across his face. "They're too stupid to notice anything. Watch this." He stuck his foot out.

The drone, focused on his task, tripped and stumbled face first into the fountain, splashing water all over the floor. The entire group hooted with laughter.

Rage surged through me and my face grew so hot I was sure it would melt off my mask of makeup. I leaped from my chair and strode toward the fountain.

"Remmi, what are you doing?" Morphia hissed.

I ignored her. The drone was struggling to stand but his worn shoes kept slipping on the tiles, sending him toppling back into the fountain. The group laughed harder and patrons at the other tables joined in.

I bent to help the drone up. Through his thin shirt, which was completely soaked, I could see several thick crisscross patterns. I choked back the bile that rose burning into my throat. I had similar scars on my back, but his were much worse, as if he had been whipped every day for years.

"It's okay, I've got you," I soothed as I grabbed the man's arms and, slipping on the slick floor myself, struggled to pull him up. He was heavy despite his bony frame but years of labor had made me strong. I eased him to his feet and held him steady. "Are you all right?" I asked gently, patting his shoulder. He simply stared down at me with vacant eyes.

"Hey, girl," called the young man who had started this. "What are you doing? You're ruining all the fun."

My fury returned. I wasn't sure if it was the wine or exhaustion but I suddenly felt drunk with an uncontrollable rage. "Fun?" I shouted, locking my gaze with that young man. His table shook, knocking down all the drink glasses with a deafening clatter but I barely processed that. "Tell me, what's so funny about tripping a man who's just trying to do his job?"

"Man?" laughed an attractive red-haired girl. "You act like he's a person. He's just a drone."

I clenched my hands into fists. My fake nails dug painfully into my palms but I didn't care. "Drones *are* people. In fact, they're more than ordinary humans. They're Halflings. In Realearth, Halflings have been gods. They could be gods here too if they didn't have their—"

"This drone is no Halfling," said Maurice, hurrying over. He turned to the drone. "Look at this mess you've made!" he yelled, his face turning a deep purple. "Clean all that up, including those broken glasses."

"Please, sir." My insides burned with desperation. I clutched Maurice's arm. I felt dozens of eyes burrowing into me. Morphia tugged at my sleeve, urging, "Remmi, let's go," but I brushed her off. "They caused this." I glared at the group. "He was just doing his work and they tripped him. And I don't know how those glasses broke. They just toppled over."

"Young lady, that drone is not a person but an it. It was a murderer before it was convicted and mind-drained, sentenced to life as a drone. It had brutally slaughtered three people, including one child. Why do you defend it?" His gaze locked onto mine.

I felt the blood draining from my face as Morphia grabbed my hand and pulled me away.

"Remmi, not all drones are Halflings," she said once we were back on the street and she had called for Henry through a tiny square of ghostsilk, like the one she'd given me. A steady rain was falling so we huddled under an awning. "I thought everyone knew that. Many are convicted criminals, the worse kinds such as murderers and rapists."

I swallowed. "I-I didn't know," I choked in a tiny voice.

Morphia, back in her elderly woman guise, stared at me through pale blue eyes. "It's actually quite an efficient system, when you think about it. What better way is there to rehabilitate such dangerous criminals than to drain them of their original personalities and force them to serve society by doing the nasty, menial jobs most of us would rather avoid? Citizen tithes pay for the prisons where many of them spend their nights but many businesses and companies thrive from the free labor. It's actually a win-win situation."

I remained silent during the ride back to Morphia's building. I stared through the window, my gaze snagging on the beads of rain oozing down the glass. So, not all drones were Halflings. How many of the drones I had worked with, slept, and showered beside for years in Penumbra had been monstrous criminals before their mind-drains?

Chapter 18

"From now on, you must watch what you say and do at all times, Remmi," Morphia said in a stern voice as one of Diana's assistants touched up my hair and makeup. Another worked on Morphia. We were back in her living room, getting ready for our interview and my dream debut with Penny. "Your little escapade with that drone ended up all over Viewing Crystal news." She pointed to the flickering images in the Viewing Crystal but I refused to look.

"It did?" My entire body went numb.

"Someone at the restaurant had a camera. Luckily rumor of that earthquake has distracted most people from you."

"Earthquake?" My throat was so tight the word came out as a rasp.

"Didn't you see that table shake and all the glasses fall down at once?" Morphia stared straight ahead as the stylist pulled her hair into an elaborate twist with intricate gold and black weaves. I didn't answer. I couldn't, even if I wanted to, since my makeup artist was now focused on my lips. Just how much touching up did I need anyway after Diana's handiwork this afternoon? "No, of course not, love." Morphia clicked her tongue. "You were so upset you probably didn't. Funny thing was, I didn't feel the ground shake. And no one else in Nod reported an earthquake. It was just centered on that table, which is strange. Wasn't that where those kids were sitting? The ones you yelled at?"

I nearly bit my lip through the thick coat of shiny gloss. I wanted to forget all about this afternoon. I shifted my gaze away from Morphia. Across the room, Lorelei Morningstar, the Dream Director, was speaking to the film crew. The reporter, Randal Wicks, a handsome, silver-haired man, stood to the side, murmuring to himself. I assumed he was rehearsing what he was going to say.

If only I could hear him. What was he going to ask me? Mother had been right. Perhaps I should have kept my illusion magic a secret. I now understood why she'd run away to the Forest and had never mentioned her career as a Substitute. Not if this was something she had to go through every day.

I took a deep breath in a futile attempt to calm my nerves.

"Remmi, love, have you heard a word I said?" Morphia shook my shoulder. "It's almost time. Put your shoes on and go stand over there." She indicated her ghostsilk portal that swayed in the still air as if caught in a breeze.

"Do I have to?" She held out the pair of high-heeled pumps I'd spent the afternoon walking in as part of the dream rehearsal, as Lorelei instructed me to "glide and straighten up." She'd been even worse than Morphia. My feet still ached. "No one will be able to see my feet anyway. Not in this dress." My gown, which reached the floor, sparkled with an array of rainbow colors every time I moved. The spike-heeled shoes perfectly matched it. Even my hair had been sprayed with a substance that made it glitter.

"What did I tell you about Bianca, Remmi?" Anger tinged Morphia's voice. "Now—"

"Nightshade. Clearwater. You're up," barked Lorelei, a large woman with short hair that was such a bright buttercup yellow I was sure it had been dyed. She was the first person I'd met who bossed Morphia around.

"Stop dawdling and put on those shoes," Morphia hissed. Her eyes flashed.

I stood several inches taller in the heels but they pinched my feet and made my ankles wobble. I took a step forward and tripped on the gown. I stumbled, nearly crashing into the Viewing Crystal, when Morphia grabbed my arm. My face burned. Would the humiliation never end?

"I take it you've never worn a long dress before?" Her tone had softened. I shook my head. I longed to snap, "What do you think?" but held back. Of course she wouldn't know. She didn't know anything about my past, besides Mother, and I wanted to keep it that way. "Lift up the front, like this, but gracefully," she said, demonstrating with her own lengthy dress.

The concentration I put into that, as well as keeping my head high, shoulders back, and to not break my neck, helped me ignore the hushed murmurs coming from the crew.

"We're losing time, ladies," said Lorelei, grabbing me by the shoulders. "Clearwater, you stand right here." She pulled me to the edge of the ghostsilk. "Nightshade, you're here, that's it." Morphia stood on the opposite side of the ghostsilk, poised and elegant, as if she had done this countless times. There was no doubt she had. "Good. That's good. Wicks, you're on."

Lorelei stepped aside as Randal approached. Charlie shone a bright light on us. It reflected off my gown, blinding me. I squinted, struggling to see.

"Smile, Remmi," Morphia whispered.

Randal faced the camera and started speaking. "Good evening, everyone," he said in an overly enthusiastic voice. "This is Randal Wicks, here live in the penthouse of famed Substitutes Morphia and Hayden Nightshade. Morphia has just taken on her first apprentice, the beautiful Remmi Clearwater."

I smiled as broadly as I could but my knees shook beneath the massive skirts. I prayed I wouldn't topple over. Through the corner of my eye, I could see our images wavering in the depths of the enormous Viewing Crystal. This was the first time I'd ever appeared on one. Well, second, counting this afternoon at the café. Could everyone see the terror on my face?

"You may be surprised to learn that Remmi here is the long lost daughter of world-renowned Substitute Luna Clearwater. This comes as a surprise to everyone since, until now, no one knew Luna even had a daughter. Tell me, Remmi, where have you been hiding all these years?"

I froze as he turned toward me and thrust the microphone in my face. Sweat tickled my skin beneath the gown. I resisted the urge to scratch and fidget.

"I-I lived in many places." I winced at the squeak in my voice. It was a slight truth but I didn't want to say too much. Was Malcent watching? Would he recognize me behind all the makeup and sparkles? At least he didn't know my name. It was my anonymity as a drone that could possibly spare me.

"Could you elaborate, Remmi? You are such an enigma, we all want to know more about you."

127

I cleared my throat. My heart pounded. "I was working on Sandman Island when I first saw Morphia, as part of a dream. I knew I had to find her because I'd always wanted to be a Substitute." Okay, that was a lie since I'd only recently found out what a Substitute was, but I'd sooner move to the Nightmare Realms than tell the world I'd been mistaken for a Halfling and worked as a drone for many years.

"Did your mother live with you on Sandman Island?" Randal pressed.

A drop of sweat trickled into my right eye, stinging it. I blinked rapidly. How deep was I going to go with this lie?

"Can't you see you're upsetting my apprentice?" Morphia said in a dramatic voice that sounded fake to me. She pulled me close and pressed her cheek against mine. Her skin was impossibly soft, like a baby's. The scent of her perfume was so strong I almost thought I'd pass out. "She's on the verge of tears, poor dear." She sniffled. "Luna was practically my sister. We'd known each other since we were kids and were even apprentices together, when we were the same age as Remmi is now. And then I found out that she's . . . she's . . ." She sobbed and clutched me tighter.

"I'm so sorry to upset you, ladies," Randal said. I was secretly grateful to Morphia for distracting him from prying into my past. I continued to blink my irritated eye. "Now that we know she's gone, the world grieves with you."

"Luna might be gone but she lives on in her daughter, whom I've taken upon myself to train." Morphia pulled back and cradled my face in both her hands. Her eyes were liquid, reminding me of melted honey. "It's like having dear Luna back, only now, I get to be the mentor."

"There you have it, folks." Randal grinned as he faced the camera. "Morphia Nightshade is taking time away from her incredibly busy schedule to train her first apprentice, her best friend's long-lost daughter. Isn't that—"

"Pardon my interruption," said a plump, partially bald man, sticking his head through the ghostsilk, "but the dream is starting in two minutes."

My heart leaped into my throat. Lorelei signaled to Morphia from the sidelines.

"Time to form your illusion, love, just as I told you," Morphia said, her brilliant smile broadening even more. She murmured something to the Viewing Crystal. Seconds later, our images vanished, replaced by a beautiful woman, the one I recognized from Penny's last dream, only whole and uninjured. Her shining black hair was swept up into an elaborate style and her exotic eyes shone as if they were made of highly polished mahogany. "It's a simple one for your first official dream," Morphia whispered. "You don't have to change the dress, just your face and hair."

I shrank back, wobbling in those pinching pumps. Even though I was beautifully dressed, I felt hopelessly unqualified. How could I possibly pull this off when in all my short life, I'd only been a drone and a serving girl? Such a skill required much more than mere illusion magic. I struggled to remain steady as I closed my eyes and concentrated, allowing Bianca's likeness to sweep over me. I felt the familiar, sticky tingling all over my skin.

"Perfect," breathed Morphia, stepping back so the camera could focus on me. The onlookers applauded. The man had disappeared back into the ghostsilk. I peered into its reflective surface and saw that my illusion was successful. Bianca's reflection, though slightly marred from the rippling, stared back at me.

Morphia gently grabbed my arm and pulled me toward the portal. It transformed into a silken window filled with lights and cheering crowds. "This dream is taking place nearby, in downtown Nod," she said. "You've had some practice walking in those heels. Don't forget what I taught you. Head up, shoulders back, small steps." I walked into the portal, my insides a swirling mass of nerves. "That's it. Good. Be proud. This is one of the highlighted dreams, one of few among millions that will be shown throughout Dreamearth."

As the familiar tickle-whisper of the ghost hairs brushed against my skin, I could feel that the thick carpet beneath my wobbling feet changed in texture, becoming thin with the hardness of concrete beneath. I stood on a long, red carpet. Brilliant lights shone everywhere. This was even worse than the one that had nearly blinded me during that awful interview.

Velvet ropes on either side formed an aisle, each holding back crowds of screaming, cheering people. The cameraman slipped through the ghostsilk behind me, still filming, followed by Lorelei.

"Bianca! Bianca, over here," several people shouted, flashing cameras in my face. I staggered, blinded.

Panic washed over me. My chest tightened, making it difficult to breathe. My heart was beating so fast I could almost hear it over the deafening noise that assailed me. Sweat prickled my forehead and dripped down my back.

My skin tingled with the sticky sensation of the illusion threatening to slip. No. This couldn't happen. Not on my first dream assignment, and one of the highlighted dreams to be displayed on every Viewing Crystal in Dreamearth. I squeezed my eyes closed—bright flashes flickered against the darkness of my lids—and struggled to bring Bianca's image back into focus. I was now Bianca Del Mar, glamorous actress, mother to Penny. The effort made me light-headed.

"Mama," a high, piping voice shouted. "Mama, over here. Look at me."

I pried my eyes open and, taking a deep breath, scanned the crowd. I had never been the center of this much attention and the tightening panic was returning. It dissipated only slightly when my gaze alighted on Penny, standing out against the mass of people, transparent in her Visitor guise. She was frantically waving and jumping up and down, an enormous smile on her face, her sleek black ponytail bouncing.

I smiled and took a hurried step toward her. I'd completely forgotten what Morphia had told me about slightly lifting the front of my dress when I walked. The ridiculous skirts tangled around my foot, sending me toppling to the carpeted ground. A wave of pain jolted through my right knee. The crowd drew in a single gasp. The sensation of warm honey dripping all over my body momentarily distracted me from the haze of discomfort.

"Mama." Penny surged forward. "Mama, are you okay? You—" She suddenly skidded to a stop, gazing down at me.

I averted my eyes, focused on my hands. One of the fake nails had broken off and my fingers were still knotted with calluses, despite the efforts of Diana's assistant. My illusion had completely slipped, right in the middle of the dream. The crowd gasped and whispered. Penny drew back and frantically searched the crowd, looking for her mother.

She vanished in a shower of Thought Artifacts that scattered the ground.

I was instantly surrounded by the onlookers who were babbling at once. "Are you all right, Miss?" "Perhaps we should call a doctor." "Is there one around?"

Lorelei's shrill voice cut through all the others. "Nightshade, get over here and see to your apprentice."

Only one person thought to help me up. "Can you stand?" asked a familiar voice, one that filled me with warmth.

Relief mixed with humiliation flooded me as Peter, with his wheelbarrow standing a short distance away, bent and held out a hand.

"Here, lean against me," he said, gingerly struggling to pull me up. I draped an arm over his shoulder. His body, beneath his shirt, felt firm. His glasses were sliding down his nose but he ignored them.

"She'll be fine, boy," Morphia said, stepping through the portal. To my relief, the cameraman and his crew were packing their equipment. Lorelei stood to the side, wearing a menacing expression. I hardly cared. Morphia grabbed my other arm and, with Peter's help, steadied me on my feet. My knee throbbed and my ankles threatened to buckle in those stupid heels. I kicked them off, sending them skittering across the pavement.

"Remmi," Morphia shrieked. "I paid good money for those. Boy, go pick those up. I've got her."

"I'm okay. I can walk," I snapped, pulling away to gather up the shoes. My knee throbbed but I didn't see what the big deal was. I'd experienced worse pain before.

"Remmi, are you okay?" Peter looked down at me, his eyes worried behind his glasses.

I forced a smile. "I'll be fine. I—"

"Artifact boy!" shouted Lorelei. "Leave the apprentice alone. Get those Artifacts gathered before they are stolen off the streets and placed on the black market."

131

Anger pumped through me. She was treating Peter like a drone. And Morphia wasn't much better. I should just head back to Sandman Island. All I had to do was picture my cottage as I stepped through the ghostsilk—

"Stop daydreaming, Clearwater, and get over here," snapped Lorelei. Her eyes shone a deep blue, like the sky just after sunset. That effect had to be another artificial enhancement.

I staggered toward her, still tripping on my gown and clutching those awful pumps in one hand. "Goodness, you move like you were raised in the wilderness," she said, grabbing my arm and hurling me through the ghostsilk back into Morphia's living room.

I bit my lip, afraid that if I spoke I'd say something I'd later regret.

The sudden silence was almost deafening, marred by the residue noise that still lingered in my ears. Only a few of the crew were left, gathering up the last of their equipment. Mia was cleaning up after them and Morphia lay back on a couch. Fiona held an icepack against the woman's forehead. I would have laughed if I wasn't so angry and exhausted.

"Have a seat, Clearwater," said Lorelei, shoving me down next to Morphia. I dropped the pumps onto the floor. "Nightshade, sit up and listen to me." Morphia eased to a sitting position and handed the icepack to Fiona.

"I understand this is your first dream, Clearwater." Lorelei's voice softened only slightly. "But this is a big business and we can't afford many screw-ups, not for dreams that are broadcast throughout our whole *world.*" She slammed her fist into her palm with a sound that made Morphia jump. "Visitor Visions is just one of many companies that work directly with Realearth clients during their brief jaunts. We need their discarded thoughts to feed the Life River. There's a rumor that it's starting to recede and that a part of the Collective Unconscious Forest has begun to vanish." A sudden chill crept down my spine. Isn't that what those police had said to Periwinkle months ago when they'd been searching for me? "At least, it's just untouched wilderness at this point. No one really knows what's causing this but we all need to be on our toes and keep each Visitor in our world long enough to accumulate as many thoughts as possible.

"You've done well in the past, Nightshade," Lorelei continued as she rose to her feet. "Enough to earn the respect of millions of Dreamearthlings. You and Luna Clearwater both, before she disappeared. If you want to hang onto all of this," she glanced around the large, fancy room, "I'd suggest you work harder with this new apprentice of yours. The fact that she's Luna's daughter has gained you much affection but you both have to shape up. Is that clear?" She glared down at us with her oddly artificial looking eyes.

"Can't I train in private first?" I asked, standing up, only to regret it since my knee still throbbed. I sat back down.

Lorelei smiled coldly. "There are countless dreams taking place at every minute, throughout all of Dreamearth. Only the most interesting are filmed for the entertainment of our Dreamearth viewers and they are *usually,* but not always, those that feature Substitutes. If you want to be highly paid and earn fame, you must be willing to be filmed. Most Dreamearthlings would kill to possess illusion magic and have the opportunity you've been given. Don't blow it."

She strode toward the ghostsilk and turned back to us before entering. "A film crew will be here tomorrow morning, at nine o'clock sharp, to film your tutoring session. Try not to be so clumsy this time." She disappeared into the portal, followed by the last of the crew.

"Tutoring session?" Hadn't Morphia mentioned something about a private tutor before?

I looked up and was horrified to see an image of me, as Bianca, toppling over in Penny's dream playing in depths of the Viewing Crystal. I turned away as Bianca's stunning face was replaced by mine. I could barely hear the sound but I caught laughter in the background and an announcer's voice saying, "There's apprentice Remmi Clearwater's first dream. Let's hope she can remain on her feet for the next one."

"Turn off," Morphia shouted at the Viewing Crystal and grabbed the icepack back from Fiona, who had continued to stand there. The images instantly vanished. Morphia let out a weary sigh. I had a feeling she was already regretting having taken me on. I felt likewise. "Did you think you'd be allowed to slack off on schoolwork? Education is very important for Substitutes."

I knew I should be grateful, especially since the main thing I'd resented in Penumbra was the lack of education and opportunities, but I was so tired and mortified that I couldn't even think of that.

"Here, let me take a look at your knee."

"It's fine," I said, even though, now that the evening's turmoil had calmed, it throbbed with pain.

"Just let me see." Morphia pushed me back and slightly lifted my rainbow skirts, exposing my leg. "We can't have you limping around like an injured puppy on top of everything else. Oh, this is awful!" she gasped.

I looked down and practically burst out laughing. "It's just a bruise. I've had lots of them. It'll heal in a few days."

Morphia sighed. "That's a relief. Only wear pants and long skirts until then." She placed the icepack on my knee. I winced as the chill seeped through my nylons.

"What's that for?"

Morphia gave me a puzzled look. "To ease the pain, of course."

"Oh. Okay, thanks." I felt my lips tug into a smile. That was actually nice of her. The coldness did help soothe the throbbing. Now that we were finally alone, except for Mia and Fiona, I could quiz her about Mother.

"You heard Lorelei," she said before I could open my mouth. "We have a lot to do to form you into real Substitute material. Your illusion magic is excellent, but you must practice holding those illusions longer. Some Visitors stay for up to a half hour at a time. Fortunately, we are not scheduled for one of Penny's dreams for a few more days, so that will give us plenty of time to rehearse for the next one." My eyelids felt as if they were weighted by rocks. Morphia's voice continued to wash over me as my eyes drooped closed.

In the next instant, someone shook me awake.

"You've worn out your new apprentice, dearest," said a man's voice. "Let her get some sleep."

My eyes flew open. I was still on the couch with my knee now numb from the icepack. The man I recognized as Morphia's husband Hayden grinned down at me. "How did your first dream go?"

"Hadn't you heard?" Morphia snapped. "It was shown over all the Viewing Crystals. They're probably still replaying it. It was a disaster. Remmi tripped on her gown and—"

"Well, if I remember correctly, *you* fell off a winged horse on your first official dream," he said with a laugh.

I nearly laughed myself when I noticed Morphia's face reddening beneath her heavy makeup. "Really?" I removed the icepack.

"It was a flying dream, of all things and, I, well, can't fly. Luckily a Cloud Wrangler caught me." Her eyes took on a dreamy look. "He was handsome too and—"

"You know, Remmi here will probably perform better if she gets some rest," said Hayden. "Off to bed with you now. No more dawdling."

I stood. A twinge of pain shot through my knee.

"Don't forget your shoes, love," Morphia said, handing me those loathsome pumps. I reluctantly took them and moved slowly up the stairs.

I dropped them onto the floor the moment I entered my room. I stripped off the gown and its silly petticoats next, until I was just in a slip. I left them in a pile next to the shoes. I was amazed by how much lighter I felt.

I thought about leaving them on the floor until I realized this would only create more work for Mia and Fiona. With reluctance, I carried the bejeweled pile to the closet.

Someone had already hung up all of the clothes that Morphia had purchased for me. The leaf-green Sandman Island sundress hung among them. It looked limp and forlorn next to those fancy new garments. My mind swirled. I should be ecstatic but felt more concerned. Did I really need *this* many different outfits? This was more than triple the number of garments I'd ever owned in all of my previous years put together. Perhaps it made up for the time when I was a drone who didn't own anything, when even the ratty, overlarge tunics I wore daily were public property.

Fiona and Mia must have put away these new clothes. Perhaps I could give them some. But then both girls were taller than me.

I was about to enter the bathroom to wash off the mask of makeup still plastered to my face when I heard a familiar female voice calling my name. Jenna? My weary mind struggled to make sense of this as I searched the room. How could she have—?

My gaze snagged on a shining scrap of silk lying crumpled on the dresser. It was a piece of ghostsilk, the other half of the one I had given to Jenna.

"Remmi," Jenna exclaimed as I smoothed out the silk and stared into it. Jenna's face came into focus, shimmery and unsteady, as if it were a reflection on a restless puddle. "Wow. Look at you. It's only been your first day as a Substitute and you're already so fancy."

I flushed. "I'm about to wash it all off. I hope I don't have to look like this every day. How's school?" I stifled a yawn but didn't want to turn Jenna away. I didn't know when I'd get the chance again, if the second I had spent with Peter this evening was any indication.

Jenna made a face. "The same, only worse without you." Guilt tugged at me. "I still enjoy my classes more than most people. But my life has to be boring compared to yours. I caught your interview and first official dream on our Viewing Crystal over breakfast."

"You did?" I shriveled inside. "Oh, by the First Visitors, I'm so embarrassed."

"Don't be," Jenna soothed. "You looked incredible. I wish I could illusion like that. I have to go now. Class is about to start."

Jenna faded away before I could say anything more.

Warmth mixed with sadness filled my chest as I neatly folded the ghostsilk scrap and placed it back on my dresser. I no longer cared that Jenna was Penumbran. I already missed her.

I vigorously scrubbed my face, leaving the washcloth thickly coated with makeup grime. It was worse than washing ash and dirt off my face after a day's drudgery in Penumbra. I tried to rinse it out to save Fiona and Mia the extra work. I finally gave up, wrung it out, and slung it over a towel rack.

I was too tired to choose from the array of nightclothes that now filled several of my drawers. I settled onto the bed in my slip. Despite my exhaustion, sleep was a long time in coming.

Chapter 19

After I had showered, I stood, wrapped in a towel, before my open closet for several minutes, feeling hopelessly overwhelmed. What was I going to wear? There were too many choices. For a fleeting, irrational moment, I found myself longing for the mornings in Penumbra when all I had to do was grab a tunic from the pile. That certainly had been much simpler.

I finally opted for jeans, a type of pants which, aside from initially trying them on at the shop, I'd never worn, and the plainest shirt I could find. I slid my feet into a pair of flats and hoped Morphia wouldn't make me practice gliding in high heels today but strongly felt I would be disappointed.

Lastly, I stared at the cosmetics Morphia had purchased for me from Diana and my heart sank. I didn't feel like completely painting my face as Diana and her assistants had done. Since I was going to be filmed again this morning, I applied just a slight dusting of blush to my cheeks and a touch of lip gloss. I had washed out the curls, leaving my hair to once again float around my head in an unruly mass. I brushed it in a futile attempt to get it to lie flat. At least it was now neatly trimmed.

I crept downstairs to find, to my surprise, Hayden in the kitchen. He wore a checkered bathrobe and his shoulder-length hair was pulled back. He smiled at me as I hesitantly approached. Mia was setting the kitchen table and Fiona was slicing up ham, cheese, and onions at the island counter.

"Ah, the new apprentice is up bright and early," Hayden said, grinning as he set a frying pan on the stove. "I heard you had quite an eventful evening."

I nodded. My face burned.

"Well, I hope you are well rested."

I nodded again, feeling awkward. I couldn't think of anything to say.

"I'm making omelets but, if you don't want one, I can fix you something else."

"No, an omelet will be fine." I shifted from foot to foot. "I'll help. What would you like me to do?"

"Nonsense, Remmi." Hayden chuckled. "You're our guest. Sit down. Breakfast will be ready shortly."

"Will Morphia be joining us?" I glanced around but didn't see her. "The film crew should be here soon."

"You'll have to forgive her. She likes to sleep late but she never fails to miss an engagement."

I settled at the table and tapped my fake fingernails against it, noting the one on my right index finger that had broken off last night when I fell. Could I remove the others just as easily? I pulled at one but it hurt, as if I were trying to tear off my real nail. I returned to tapping them, feeling restless and fidgety.

This was so unnatural. I listened to the sizzle of eggs in the frying pan. I was used to working, not sitting idly for minutes that seemed to stretch into hours.

The scents of frying onions and ham filled me with a sudden, piercing melancholy as my thoughts turned to Periwinkle and Andrew. They were probably eating dinner while I was about to have breakfast. The time difference made my mind spin.

"Here you are, Remmi," Hayden said, setting a plate with a steaming omelet and browned toast before me. He slid into the seat across from me with his own plate. Mia set down two tiny china bowls, one filled with butter, the other with salsa. Fiona served me a glass of orange juice and Hayden a cup of coffee. Both girls then stood back with their hands clasped in front. This made me uncomfortable.

"Aren't they going to join us?" I knew that was a stupid question, especially since I had served as a drone in Penumbra. I remembered many seemingly endless mealtimes when I and a few others would stand against the wall for hours as the diners casually ate and chatted, in case the Penumbrans needed something such as their glasses refilled. I had always despised this. I preferred cleaning filthy toilets and scrubbing floors to just standing there with my feet aching and my empty stomach grumbling. Drones *never* ate with their superiors. I instantly looked down and spooned salsa over my omelet, longing for Andrew's spicy cooking.

"They've already eaten," Hayden said. "But they are here if we need anything else."

"I'm sure I'll be fine," I said, smiling at the girls. They simply nodded in acknowledgement.

"You heard her, girls," Hayden said kindly. "We can manage. Thank you."

They dipped their heads in unison and moved away.

"You didn't think the shaking table yesterday was just an accident?"

"I'm sorry?" I nearly choked on my food. I took a sip of orange juice. My thoughts raced back over yesterday. So much had happened that my memories all blurred together.

"The table at the Convergence Café." He raised an eyebrow. "It couldn't have just moved on its own."

I frowned and looked down. "Did Morphia tell you?"

"It was all over the Viewing Crystal news, my dear. That, and you coming to the defense of a drone. That was extremely noble of you. Very few people are willing to speak up for drones."

My cheeks burned. I'd wanted to forget all about yesterday. I glanced toward the stairs, hoping Morphia come down this second. At least she would be a distraction.

"You were quite agitated, Remmi, were you not?" I could feel his gaze on me.

"I was angry, the way they were treating that drone . . . But I don't know what moved the table. They've been saying it was probably an earthquake."

"Have you never been in an earthquake, my dear? They shake *everything,* not just one object. Is this the first time something's moved when you felt angry?"

I put my fork down. My stomach was so tight I couldn't eat anything else. My thoughts swirled, suddenly alighting upon Kaya, when I'd attempted to stand up to her in Jenna's defense. Something invisible had pushed her. A sudden chill seeped through me.

"What are you saying? That I can move things with my mind, in addition to illusion magic and—" I clamped my mouth shut.

"And?" Hayden cocked his head.

"Just . . . in addition to illusion magic. I should really check on Morphia." I scrambled from the table.

"Be careful," Hayden said. His grin, which I had thought pleasant before, now unnerved me. "She's liable to bite your head off if you see her without her makeup."

"I'll—" The sound of a buzzer went off.

"That's the crew," Morphia called from the top of the stairs. So she was up, after all. "Hayden, darling, could you see to them? I'll be right down."

"No. I'll do that," I said, relieved for a chance to get away from Hayden and his awkward questions.

"I'll let you girls have your day," he said, pulling out a ghostsilk and removing his robe. He had on jeans and a shirt underneath. "I have to get to work."

Relief filled me as he vanished through the portal. The elevator door opened.

Several people stepped into the room. I recognized the reporter Randal Wicks among them.

"Good morning, Miss Clearwater," he said, his smile as big as it had been last night. "I hope you're ready for your next Viewing Crystal segment." He brushed past me before I could answer and motioned to two men in matching shirts that had the name Visitor Visions embroidered on their pockets. One man held a small camera, the other what appeared to be a folded light. "Greetings, Mrs. Nightshade," he said, bowing his head to Morphia as she glided toward him. She was clad in an form-fitting pantsuit. "You're as lovely as ever. I was told we'd be filming in the study."

"Of course. This way, fellows." She led them into a hallway.

A tiny, squat woman entered next. She had a book-filled tote slung over one shoulder. Two women I recognized as Diana's assistants from yesterday followed her. "So you're Remmi Clearwater," she said, extending a hand for me to shake. Her rich voice belied her size. "I recognize you from last night's interview. I'm your tutor, Professor Amanda Flit." I stared down at her, surprised that she only came up to my waist. Her deep auburn hair curled around her wizened face that reminded me of a rough, brown coconut.

"Right this way, ladies," said Morphia, beckoning us all into the hallway. I gasped. I hadn't seen her entire house and wondered how many rooms it contained. "The study is the door on the right."

A mahogany desk dominated the center of the large room. Bookshelves lined the walls and two leather chairs stood beside an ornate, unlit fireplace. A wistful feeling squeezed my chest as I remembered huddling before a fireplace years ago with Mother as she read to me. Our cottage had been much smaller and plainer but this room had a cozy feel that the others in Morphia's vast home seemed to lack.

"Remmi and Professor Flit will sit at the desk, so you can set up here," Morphia told Randal and his men. She turned and stared down at me; her high heels added several inches to her height. "Remmi, love, *that's* what you chose to wear?" She wrinkled her nose. "Well, there isn't time for you to run up and change. At least you'll appeal to a large portion of the audience, the young people and proletariats, mostly." She grabbed my hand with its broken nail and shook her head. "But we're still going to have to fix you up. You there," she snapped her fingers at the stylists, "see what you can do to make her appearance more presentable. And fix her broken nail."

The women led me to one of the leather chairs. A basket of fruit sat on the small, round coffee table that stood between them. I was tempted to snatch an apple and tuck it into my shirt but resisted. It had been a while since I'd hoarded food and the urge was gradually creeping back. Thanks to Hayden's cryptic questions, I hadn't been able to finish breakfast.

"I need to know a bit more about you before we start, Remmi," said Professor Flit, taking a seat in the opposite chair as the stylists began to work on me. Her feet didn't even touch the floor.

"I'm sorry, love," said Morphia, standing over us. "I didn't have enough information to give Professor Flit. Well-known Substitutes like me have very little privacy. Every detail of your life will eventually be revealed throughout Dreamearth."

Discomfort filled me. I couldn't tell *anyone* about Penumbra. That would alert the wrong people.

"I attended school in the Collective Unconscious Forest when Mother was alive," I said as one of the stylists curled my hair with a hot iron. "After she died I . . . I lived elsewhere and eventually found my way to Sandman Island." I had to push the words out. How could this not lead to more questions? "That's when I returned to school on the island." My palms were moist, as wet as my freshly manicured nails. I resisted wiping them off on my pants.

"That had to be quite an adventure," breathed Randal as the stylist fluffed my hair. "I'll get that story out of you yet but, for now, the focus is on your lesson."

The stylists, finished with their work, backed away as Professor Flit and I were led to the large desk. She spread her books over its surface. I was bathed once again in a spotlight and the camera was aimed at me. Randal broke into his familiar wide grin. I tensed. Here I was again, showing my freshly made up face throughout Dreamearth. At least I didn't have to prance around in spike heels this time.

"Randal Wicks here, back once again in Morphia Nightshade's home, where her new apprentice, Remmi Clearwater, is to begin her first private tutoring session with Professor Amanda Flit. Since Substitute apprentices must travel throughout Dreamearth on any given day, it is difficult for them to attend regular school. Professor Flit has been tutoring apprentices for over twenty years."

Amanda smiled shyly at the camera, then looked down and opened a book. "Let's get started, shall we? Remmi, can you tell us who the leaders of each of Dreamearth's eight provinces are?"

I took a deep breath. That was something I knew. "Yes. The Collective Unconscious Forest is ruled by King Hubert and Queen Lavonda. The Sandman Island looks to Queen Selene. Both Zephyr and Nod elect presidents: the current presidents are Lars Seacrest of Zephyr and James Cirrus of Nod. Lord and Lady Neval are the Nightmare Realm's leaders, and, for

Penumbra," my voice cracked. I cleared my throat and forced the hated name from my lips, "Penumbra's leader is Lord Malcent."

"Very good, Remmi. Many of my students couldn't name all the leaders before I started working with them." My palms were still wet but my tight chest loosened. I had been a mediocre student at best at the Sandman Island School, especially when compared to students like Jenna. "Now can you name the Emperor, the leader who is in charge of our world?"

I bit my lower lip as my thoughts darted back to what I had learned since my return to school. "This office is temporary, a five-year term. The Emperor is appointed by the province leaders and their advisors. Dreamearth's current leader is Emperor Stark."

"That's correct, to a point, Remmi," said Amanda. "But, in all the excitement of your becoming Morphia's apprentice, you likely missed it. Lord Malcent of Penumbra has just been selected as Dreamearth's latest ruler. It was just announced this morning, Nod's time. He will be officially sworn in two months from now and his eldest son Randal will take over as Penumbra's new Lord during his reign."

It was as if everything had suddenly frozen, except for my heart slamming in my chest. I almost forgot about the light shining on me, the rolling camera, and Professor Flit and all of Dreamearth waiting for my response.

"M-Malcent of Penumbra," was all my numb lips could mumble. It was neither a question nor a response.

"*Lord* Malcent, Remmi," corrected Professor Flit. "Soon to be Emperor Malcent. According to the Viewing Crystal news clips, the entire province of Penumbra has been decorated for the ongoing celebrations." She laughed. "Its citizens are wandering around in a daze, having never seen so much color in their lives."

That I could believe. But Malcent as Dreamearth's new Emperor? I forced myself to display an impassive expression, something I was an expert in thanks to my years as a drone. If I revealed the horror that was ripping through me, it would only lead to questions I didn't want to answer.

"Now, let's move on to Dreamearth history," said Professor Flit, opening up another book.

I struggled to focus as she drilled me on Dreamearth history, Realearth languages, and my favorite subject, Realearth Studies. The back of my mind echoed with *Malcent will be Emperor, Malcent will be Emperor* . . .

I was learning about Realearth phones when a ghostsilk portal suddenly appeared in the middle of the room. Randal made a slashing motion with his hand at the cameraman.

A tall, gray-haired man in a dark suit stepped from it, trailed by several men and women with burlap bags slung over their shoulders. One of the men was George Mimsy. His eyes were shadowed by dark circles but they brightened briefly as they flickered over me.

"Why now?" Morphia groaned. "This was all going so well. You'll have to come back later. We're in the middle of something important."

"I can assure you this is far more urgent, Mrs. Nightshade," said the tall man. "It concerns both you and your new apprentice. Pack up your equipment and leave," he said to the crew. "I'm here to speak to Mrs. Nightshade and Miss Clearwater in private. This is not meant for Viewing Crystal entertainment."

Chapter 20

"We'll continue your lessons tomorrow, same time," said Professor Flit as she gathered up her books and followed the others out of the study.

"What is the meaning of this?" Morphia fumed, once the man made sure the group had left the apartment. Her cheeks flamed a harsh red through her thick layer of makeup. "Can't you see we were in the middle of filming my new apprentice—?"

"I am Bruce Sparks, a representative of the Ministry of Thought Artifacts."

"What does that have to do with us?" asked Morphia, her arms folded.

"Everything you Substitutes do involves our company, Mrs. Nightshade," said Mr. Sparks. "The Ministry of Thought Artifacts is the most important institution in all of Dreamearth. We outsource Dream Actors like you, as well as Thought Collectors," he nodded at George and the others. "And we hire countless Dream Analysts who drain the Artifacts of their most important essences to learn about each Visitor. Those who empty the liquid essences, after they've been studied, into the River and haul the discarded Artifacts to the Thought Dump are employed by us as well. You Substitutes may think you're the most important people in all of Dreamearth but you're merely cogs in a giant machine that processes the thoughts of billions of Visitors."

Morphia stared at him through eyes that looked ready to shoot fire. "What is this about?" I said before she could say anything I was sure we'd both regret. My mind was still on Malcent. Was he the one responsible for whatever was wrong? My hands and feet were filled with ice.

Mr. Sparks nodded to the Thought Collectors. They tipped the contents of their bags onto the desk. A mini avalanche of numerous Artifacts tumbled out, jiggling as if they had been shaped from gelatin.

"Those are fresh Artifacts, collected from dreams that occurred within the last hour."

I glanced at George. His face was impassive but his eyes held a worried glint.

"Is there something wrong with the Artifacts?" A faint relief stirred within me. This didn't seem to have anything to do with Malcent.

"You tell me, Miss Clearwater," said Mr. Sparks. "Pick one up and have a good look."

I did so. It had a squishy texture, like soft rubber; my fingers formed indentations. I could see straight through it. The faces staring at me looked distorted. It was similar to the one George had shown me in Penumbra. Similar, but not the same.

"I can't see any images, sense any thoughts."

"Very astute, Miss Clearwater," said Mr. Sparks. "It's blank, devoid of any thoughts. All the other Artifacts here are the same. This has been happening with many Visitors, for weeks now, and the numbers continue to grow each day. There is less to pour into the River. So far, the damage has been gradual."

"Is that why a small part of the Collective Unconscious Forest has started to recede?" Discomfort squirmed within me. "I'd heard that had something to do with a Halfling named Njim." It disturbed me to bring that up but I felt it had to be said.

"That's one speculation that's floating around," said Mr. Sparks. "But I don't see how one Halfling who's crossed over can affect the private thoughts of hundreds of Visitors. That's never happened before, not in the history of both worlds."

"I still don't understand," said Morphia, her voice holding an irritated undertone. "Why did you come to me? *I* have no control over my clients' thoughts."

"Mrs. Nightshade, the Ministry has researched the matter. Your client, Penny Brooks, was the first Visitor to start producing blank thoughts."

"What does that mean?" I said. "She seemed pretty normal to me, except that she was traumatized by her mother's death." I could relate but didn't say so.

"That's what our scientists are trying to determine, Miss Clearwater." Mr. Sparks motioned again to George and the others, who instantly started gathering the Artifacts back into their bags. "The best hypothesis they can come up with so far is that Penny is the carrier of a disease that affects Visitor thoughts. That it's contagious and gradually spreading. If this keeps up . . ." He shook his head. "Let's just hope a cure or solution is found before it's too late."

"What are we to do in the meantime?" asked Morphia.

"Just the same as always," said Mr. Sparks. "Keep working with your Visitors. We need all the Artifacts we can get and hope some contain the proper thought-essences. Oh, and don't let any of this leak out to your news guys. We don't want to start a worldwide panic."

George was the last to enter the ghostsilk. He briefly took my hand in a firm grip and squeezed. "I'm glad to see you're doing so well, Remmi," he whispered, giving me a wink. "I'll be sure Peter gets to do his collecting after some of your dreams." My heart briefly soared. He turned and disappeared.

"You heard the man," Morphia said, once the portal vanished. "We are going to push on as if we hadn't heard any of that."

"Are you sure?" Discomfort wormed through me. "That sounds really serious."

"Consider this part of your training, love. As Substitutes, we must remain focused on our clients and their dreams. The world can fall apart around us but the Visitors will keep coming. Without us pretending to be those they are familiar with, they will just waste their time here, wandering aimlessly."

"But Mr. Sparks said—"

"I don't care what he said." Morphia's eyes glowed harshly. "We are not merely cogs." She took several deep breaths. "He just wasted part of our day with something we have no control over and we have a packed schedule. You have an interview this afternoon, then you will observe one of my dreams. The director on that set will probably have more questions for you." Exhaustion was already seeping through me. "Then you will spend the entire evening practicing your illusions. You must not let your illusions falter for at least a half hour. That, and practice walking in a long dress and high heels. We can't afford another mishap like last night."

I reached for that apple when she wasn't looking and took a bite. It was tasteless and waxy. I spit out the piece into my palm. This apple was made of wax. Why would anyone put out fake fruit?

"This," Morphia said, grabbing the artificial apple from me and throwing it back into the basket, "is what we must avoid. Good thing the film crew wasn't here to catch that or it would have been all over the Viewing Crystals. Now come along."

Chapter 21

I spent the following days preparing for Penny's next dream, in between tutoring sessions with Professor Flit, and seemingly endless interviews. Morphia had even requested one of the stylists to pick out my clothes each day.

Morphia went over the dream with me the night before rehearsals were to start.

"The first part of the dream is going to reenact Bianca's fatal accident," Morphia said, sitting beside me on the living room couch with the script in her hand. It was late but at least it was just the two of us, not the entourage of crew and stylists that seemed to accompany us everywhere. "It will be similar to the dream you walked in on, with one minor change."

I struggled to push back what Mr. Sparks had said, about Penny having been the first Visitor to drop blank thoughts. Even if Morphia didn't think that was anything to worry about, I was determined to watch Penny throughout the dream and see if anything unusual happened.

"You, as Bianca," Morphia continued, "will be sitting behind the steering wheel of a car, pretending to drive it. Don't worry, love. You won't actually be driving this vehicle," Morphia hurriedly said before I could even ask. "It will be pulled along a Nightmare Realm road on tracks. Penny, in her Visitor guise, will appear in the backseat." Morphia shuffled through the script's pages. "A heavy rain will be falling, just like before, since that ties into Penny's memories of that night. This is a reoccurring theme for her. An enormous dragon will suddenly appear in the middle of the road and—"

"A dragon? That's not what happened before."

"That's right, love. That's what the script says. Don't forget, Penny was very young when this accident happened so her memory isn't so . . . well, sometimes it twists the details." She cleared her throat. "This dragon will pluck you out of the car in its mouth and place you on the ground while Penny—"

"Wait!" I clenched my fists. "The dragon will *what?*"

"Don't worry, love." Morphia laughed as she patted my knee. "You are perfectly safe. Nightmare Realm monsters are harmless. They only *look* scary. Besides, Adam Winter, an esteemed Monster Trainer, will be right there, making sure the dragon handles you gently. You'll have rehearsed it numerous times before the actual dream. Once the dragon releases you, you still have to do your part and illusion Bianca's death. You remember what I looked like when you first walked in on Penny's nightmare?" My neck felt suddenly stiff but I forced myself to nod. "Well, illusion that, complete with the blood and glass slab sticking out of your severed throat. Let me see you try that."

I scrunched my eyes closed and forced that horrible image into my mind. Seconds later I felt the familiar sticky-tingly sensation of a successful illusion.

"Excellent!" breathed Morphia. "It looks good . . . but the left eye needs more bruising. Focus on that without losing the rest of the illusion."

Keeping my eyes squeezed tightly shut and shaking with the effort, I concentrated on that eye.

"Very good, Remmi," Morphia said. "Open the one good eye and let's see how long you can hold this illusion."

I cracked open my right eye. The Viewing Crystal was off and I could see Bianca's mangled image reflected against it, too distorted to make out. Sweat tickled my back as I began to count the minutes. The illusion part was easy: it was the strain of holding it that drained my energy. I felt it would be easier to hold my breath.

"Beautiful, Remmi," Morphia said after an eternity. "You can release it now." Her words swept through me like a cooling breeze.

I took a deep, grateful breath and allowed the gruesome illusion to fade.

"That was nearly twenty-five minutes, love," Morphia said, her gaze fixed on the large, wooden clock that stood against one wall. My limbs felt limp just from that effort alone. "Luckily, for this dream, you only need to hold this image for a few fleeting seconds." I sighed with relief. "The prop workers will enter after this 'accident' and throw a ghostsilk portal over both you and Penny, transporting the two of you to another location. This will take place in Zephyr." A thrill passed through me as my thoughts briefly touched on Peter. "It will be a surreal depiction of Penny's bedroom. You will need to re-image Bianca, but just as her regular self."

Morphia shuffled the script's pages. "According to this, Penny may ask you to sing since her mother had often sung to her when she was small."

My face burned. "I-I can't sing," I balled my hands into fists.

"Nonsense." Morphia laughed and tossed her hair. "Any idiot can sing a simple tune. Give it a try."

I tugged at my fingers and cleared my throat. A tune that Mother used to sing briefly touched my mind with comfort as I recalled the warmth of her body, the delicate fragrance of her hair. I struggled to imitate the melodious lilt of her voice and cringed at the sound of my own, which was childlike and dissonant.

"Oh, dear." Morphia wrinkled her small, freckled nose. "You were right. I'll see if I can hire a professional singing coach to help out. Voice illusions are possible but it takes years to gain perfection. Luckily Visitors aren't too picky if your voice doesn't sound like that of the person you're portraying. Your singing won't be all that great for this next dream—Lorelei will probably throw a fit—but it's something we'll have to seriously work on."

I gulped in a deep breath. Working as a Substitute was harder than laboring as a drone in some ways.

*

I was exhausted when Morphia finally released me to go to bed but I had to contact Jenna. If Lorelei was going to be directing this upcoming dream, I needed it to go as smoothly as possible.

I picked up the ghostsilk scrap and sat back on my bed. A twinge of guilt plucked at me. This was the first time in days that I'd had time to contact Jenna and I needed something from her.

"Jenna, are you there?" An uneasy feeling overcame me as I remembered that soon Malcent would be Dreamearth's Emperor. I wasn't sure how that was going to affect her.

"Remmi," she said in a sleepy voice. An image of her face appeared, slightly distorted through the wrinkled silk. She sounded as if she'd just woken up.

"Yes, it's me. I'm sorry. Did I wake you?"

"I was about to get up anyway. I've started summer break from school, so I get to sleep in a bit on days when I'm not helping Mother at her shop."

"I heard about your father." I swallowed. "Are you going to be okay?"

"A tropical island is probably the last place anyone would look to find a Penumbran. Besides, he'll be too busy running the world to worry about Mother and me." Something clenched inside me. I hoped she was right. "I've been keeping up with all your interviews on the Viewing Crystal and in magazines. I can't wait to watch your latest dream."

"About that." I swallowed. I had to be careful or my plan could expose Jenna. "I have to sing to my client in one scene but I can't. Sing that is. I sound terrible."

"Are you sure? Sometimes people think they're worse than they really are."

"No. I really am. But, believe me you don't want me to demonstrate. Didn't you say you had voice lessons in Penumbra?"

Jenna's tiny, sleep-tousled image nodded. "Yes, starting as soon as I could talk. A beautiful singing voice is a main selling point for Penumbran brides belonging to ruling bloodlines."

"Sing something for me."

Her cheeks deepened to a brilliant pink. She burst into a brief ballad. Her voice was strong and lilting, causing chills to ripple along my arms. I felt a stab of jealousy and forced it back.

"You're really good," I said with a wistful catch in my throat when she finished. "I was thinking . . . you could sing for me, pretend to be my voice for that dream while I just move my lips."

"How?"

153

"Through the ghostsilk. I'll wear a shirt with a front pocket and tuck my ghostsilk scrap into that pocket. Only your voice will be heard."

Jenna's eyes brightened. "So I get to be part of an actual dream!" Her voice shook with excitement.

"Yes. The dream will be playing live on the Viewing Crystals, at noon Zephyr time, which shifts. You may have to—"

"Don't worry. I'll check that day. I believe it's currently somewhere over the Archetypal Sea. I'll start singing as soon as you give me a signal. Do you have to sing any particular song?"

I told her the lyrics, which I remembered from the script. Luckily it was a quick, simple ditty with just a few lines. Jenna sang it back to me perfectly.

My mind was restless as I climbed into bed. I turned off the bright moon chandelier but kept the ceiling stars flashing. I let my thoughts drift as I stared at the tiny, pulsing lights. Bedtime was the only chance I had for solitude but I was usually so tired that I fell instantly to sleep.

I'd been a Substitute apprentice for several days now but had learned nothing more about Mother. Was all the nagging and constant primping and preparing for dreams worth it?

I had to escape, even if briefly. The last stop on Penny's dream would be in Zephyr, Peter's home.

I formed a plan as sleep gradually overtook me.

Chapter 22

I followed Morphia into the dusky Nightmare Realms for Penny's dream and watched as the prop workers rolled a sleek, silver car onto narrow tracks that lined the asphalt street. Lorelei was already there, directing the crew. She wore a deep purple suit and her hair had been dyed to match.

Beyond her towered Windstreaker, the dragon that was to pluck me out of the car at a crucial moment during the dream. Even though I had rehearsed this scene several times—her teeth were merely nubs that barely mussed my clothes—the sight of her still made my breath catch. She dwarfed the spiky trees that surrounded the area and her hide was blacker than the roiling clouds overhead. Her folded wings, which resembled a bat's but were as large as sails, had a diaphanous texture. She stared down at me through heavily ridged eyes that glowed golden-red like a pair of setting suns. Her trainer, Adam Winter, who was smoking a cigarette, leaned against her haunches.

"Hello, Windstreaker," I said, stroking the side of her wedge-shaped head. Her thick hide felt oddly smooth, almost velvety. A deep purring sound like distant thunder rumbled in her throat. "Are you ready for today's dream?"

"She says she is," said Adam, dropping the cigarette and crushing it beneath his boot. "Isn't that right, girl?" He planted a kiss next to her smoking nostril. "You've both had a lot of practice. This should go smoothly."

"She actually spoke to you?"

"Of course." Adam rubbed the rough ridge above her eye. "One of the first things I learned as a Monster Trainer was how to communicate with them. Most dragon breeds are easy since they speak telepathically." I thought of the cloud beasts and how they had spoken to me through my thoughts. "All I—"

"Miss Clearwater!" Lorelei's razor-sharp voice sliced at my ears. "Stop playing with that dragon and get over here. The

155

dream is about to start." Both Windstreaker and Adam gave me apologetic looks.

"Your client is deeply asleep and entering the REM stage," said Lorelei as I hurried over. "Assume your illusion and get into the car." A crewman held the car door open for me.

"Just like we rehearsed," said Morphia, standing beside me.

I closed my eyes and, once again, felt my face and body mold into the likeness of that gorgeous, graceful woman. Once I felt the honey-droplet tingle along my skin, I knew the illusion was successful.

"Good," said Lorelei, giving me a rare compliment, "now get in."

I slid behind the steering wheel as the door slammed shut. A heavy rain began to fall on cue in slanting, gray sheets. The unseen Cloud Wrangler hired for this dream had signaled the cloud beasts. The car raced smoothly along the tracks. Its speed gradually increased and the windshield wipers slapped uselessly at the rivulets of water running down the windshield. I could barely see Windstreaker's massive form straight ahead.

Ignoring the cameras aimed at me, I placed my hands on the steering wheel. Just as I'd rehearsed, I counted down the seconds it would take for Penny to appear. Three, two, one . . .

I nearly jumped as the Visitor girl popped into the back seat. A stand-in actress had portrayed Penny during the rehearsals but her sudden appearance still slightly unnerved me. I took a deep breath and stared back at her through the rearview mirror. Her hair was loose and she was clad in strawberry print pajamas.

"Don't worry, *mi Corazon*," I said, reciting the first line I'd had to memorize. Morphia had worked with me to get the cadence of Bianca's unusual accent just right. "We'll be home soon."

Penny's large eyes widened and her face paled. "I don't like this, Mama. Can't you just pull over?"

"No. This is the quickest way. In a few minutes we'll be nice and warm at home, with Daddy." I focused on Windstreaker straight ahead, her wings flared, her breath smoking through the rain, drawing closer, closer. Any second now, the car's top would open and she would pluck me out with her mouth. I just had to stay focused and be ready to illusion the gore once she set me on the ground. It would look like the dragon had mauled me. I hated doing this to Penny but had no other choice.

With a shudder, I closed my eyes and formed a picture of dead, bloody Bianca, complete with the partially decapitated head.

The tingling just started when I heard the unclicking of my seatbelt and slender arms grabbing me, pulling me out through the suddenly open door.

Icy wet needles batted my skin as I tumbled into the mud. Someone was on top of me. I pried my eyes open. It was Penny. She leaned over, her long hair soaked and dripping into my face. She wore a broad smile.

"I did it, Mama. You're safe."

I stiffened and strained to hold the illusion of unharmed Bianca. Morphia had warned me this could happen. It wasn't our job to change the scripts but strong-willed Visitors did this quite frequently.

Two prop men hurried forward with a ghostsilk portal, flinging it over us. My surroundings spun.

When they stilled, I blinked rainwater out of my eyes. My mind whirled with a sensation of disorientation. Penny and I were sitting on a large bed with food trays in front of us. She had somehow dried off but I was soaked beneath my illusion. Water seeped from me onto the bedspread. I quickly formed another illusion to make it look dry.

Our food was an odd mishmash of cookies, meat I didn't recognize, and mushy vegetables. A drinking glass, shaped like a boot, was filled with a pale red liquid I knew was food coloring mixed with water to resemble wine. Penny's cup was a rubber sneaker.

I briefly scanned the room as I gathered my thoughts and waited for Penny to speak, as the script for this scene dictated. This place wasn't so much a room as an enormous basket, approximately the size of my bedroom at Morphia's. It didn't have a ceiling but was attached to a great silk balloon that hovered above like a giant, multi-colored jellyfish. The thatched walls of this place were bright yellow and a single window looked out onto an endless blue sky.

We were in Zephyr. A flicker of excitement passed through me. Peter was scheduled to gather up Penny's thoughts after this dream.

Several other beds scattered the basket-room. Small groups of people were seated on each one, sharing trays of food. Their drinking glasses also resembled shoes. Servers carrying more trays wove between the beds. This basket-bedroom-restaurant droned with several voices speaking at once, intermingled with the clinking of dishes.

"I quit ballet," Penny said. She looked down and toyed with her food. None of it went into her mouth, which didn't surprise me. I had learned a while back that Visitors rarely ate during their dreams, even in restaurant settings.

"You quit?" I blinked at her as I strained to focus on what she was saying. At least she was following the script in this segment.

Penny nodded and looked up. Her wide brown eyes studied my illusion-concealed face for approval. "Yeah. It just wasn't for me. I didn't have the coordination and the teacher wasn't going to let me dance on points anyway. It's something to do with my back. Nothing serious but she felt I might hurt myself if I tried them. You're not disappointed, are you, Mama?"

"Of course not, *mi Corazon*," I said as I placed my hand over hers. She felt solid, despite her ghostly appearance. Her hand was soft, and, unlike mine, not marred by calluses. "Is there something else you prefer?" It felt odd playing the mother, especially when I had no such experience. It had even been years since I'd been a daughter. The sudden thought tightened my throat.

Penny's face relaxed into a smile as she nodded. "I joined the soccer team at school and am one of the best players." Her voice trembled with pride. "We're on summer vacation now but I practice almost every day. Isn't that right, Dad?" She turned suddenly and looked around.

I followed her gaze. This was another line that deviated from the script. All I saw were the dream extras. No other Substitute had been hired to portray her father.

"Dad?" My voice reflected my confusion.

"Yes, Mama. You'd be so proud. He invented a device that records dreams. I can now see you all the time."

My face tingled as Bianca's illusion threatened to slip. I struggled to hone my focus. From what I could tell, the only camera in the room was filming this dream live over the Viewing Crystals.

"Mama, say something. Don't tell me you've already forgotten Dad." Her voice sounded thick with tears. "I know it's been a while but you haven't, have you?" She clutched both my hands and squeezed so tight it hurt.

I tried not to wince. "No, I haven't," I whispered, drawing Penny close. Her smooth hair held a faint fragrance and her soft cheek was warm. "I could never forget your father, *mi Corazon.* Nor you." The words felt strange on my tongue.

"Mama, sing to me, like you did when I was little. Before . . ." Penny blinked, releasing a slender trail of tears onto her cheeks.

Here it was. Penny had returned to the script. I nodded and tapped my shirt pocket, which was hidden by the illusion. Jenna, please be there! "I will," I murmured. "Lay back and close your eyes." Penny did, the tear traces faint against her diaphanous, olive cheeks.

I stroked Penny's hair as Jenna's voice sang through the pocket. I moved my lips and hoped it look natural. My heart was beating so hard I feared it would overpower Jenna.

Jenna had only sung one verse when Penny's eyes sprung open. She sat up, gaping. Jenna continued singing but I bit my lip. My entire body tingled as Bianca's illusion completely vanished.

Penny blinked at me briefly in confusion then snatched the silk dangling from my pocket.

"Mama?" she whispered, staring into it. Jenna's startled face peered back.

Chapter 23

The silk fluttered to the bed as Penny vanished, spilling Thought Artifacts all over the floor.

"That's it. Wrap it up," Lorelei called to the crew as she stepped forward. The room exploded with chaos as beds were pushed aside by prop workers and the dream extras scurried on to their next dream assignments.

"What is this?" She snatched up the piece of ghostsilk. Jenna's frightened face instantly vanished. Lorelei glared at me with deep purple eyes flecked with gold. Hadn't they been blue before?

My face burned. "I-I had a friend do the singing for me."

"Well, there'll be no more of this." I bit back a scream as she ripped the gauzy cloth to shreds. "A Substitute never cheats. If you do such a thing again, you will be out, do you hear me? You can go back to waiting tables, or whatever it was you did at that resort, and forget about becoming a full-fledged Substitute."

I lifted my chin and stared straight into her unnatural eyes. "That would be fine—"

"Please, Ms. Morningstar, give her another chance," Morphia said, gently pulling me close. I struggled to pry myself from her iron grasp. "You have to admit, she's an outstanding illusionist for one so young. How many Substitutes can do what she does at her age? She's just a bit . . . unschooled, if you will. I'll work with her on that."

"You'd better, Nightshade. I'll give you one more chance to whip your apprentice into shape."

She whirled from us and stomped into the ghostsilk portal.

"I told you we'll work on your singing," Morphia hissed, her clutch on my arm turning painful. Her long nails dug into my skin. "Why do you insist on getting us in trouble? Do you have any idea how important this is to me?"

My anger evaporated as Peter trundled in with his wheelbarrow. I struggled not to show my enthusiasm in front of Morphia since, to her, Thought Collectors were regarded as little more than drones.

"I wonder if these thoughts came out blank," I said, pulling away from her and picking up an Artifact. To my dismay, I didn't detect any images. I reached into my pants pocket and pulled out a folded piece of paper. My clothes were damp from that tumble into the rain but the note was only slightly wet at the edges. Hopefully it hadn't smeared too badly. I placed the Artifact against it and pressed them both into Peter's hand. He pushed at his glasses and gave me a shy smile. Warmth filled me.

"Remmi! Leave those Artifacts alone," Morphia yelled, grabbing my arm and pulling me away. "You're not a common Collector. Substitutes must *never* soil their hands on Visitor thoughts. Now come along." She pulled out her own ghostsilk. "We have a dinner engagement in Nod, which we're already running late for, followed by a press conference. And," she plucked at my shirt, "you still have to change out of those wet clothes."

Prop workers had taken down the façade walls. A blast of cold air struck me. I shivered in my wet clothes but at least I now had a view of this section of Zephyr. I'd read up on this province to research my secret plan but still felt awed by my surroundings, as if I were a Visitor caught in a dream.

Zephyr was made up of countless sphere-shaped edifices of varying sizes, ranging from office buildings to single residences, all joined together by railed streets and held afloat by thousands of enormous balloons. I'd learned that hundreds were employed day and night to keep the balloons fueled and repaired. The Zephyrites that filled the streets wore thick, fleecy garments that were bright, even by regular Dreamearth standards. I felt as if I were drowning in color. Even the surrounding sky appeared to be a deeper shade of blue. Vehicles that resembled giant kites frequently flitted overhead.

"Hey, isn't that Remmi Clearwater and Morphia Nightshade?" a young man shouted, pointing at us.

Several people stopped and turned.

161

"Yeah. They just filmed a dream here."

"Remmi, come *on*," Morphia urged, tugging me through the ghostsilk as the herd of Zephyrites stampeded toward us.

I only had a second to glance back at Peter before I tumbled into Morphia's living room and she pulled down the ghostsilk.

A feeling of joy battled with my irritation at Morphia and anger at Lorelei for destroying the one thing that kept me connected to Jenna and Sandman Island.

Peter had been reading my note.

*

I forced myself to stay awake that night after Morphia had finally let me go to bed. I glanced over at the small clock on my nightstand. It was a little after midnight, which was around six in the evening current Zephyr time. I had to look up this information on the Viewing Crystal before I even made this plan.

I reached into my nightstand drawer and grabbed a couple of cookies I'd swiped from the dinner event Morphia and I had attended earlier. Ever since I'd taken a bite out of that wax apple in the study, I'd started hoarding food again. Morphia would have a fit if she ever found out. She wouldn't understand since she ate as little as possible to maintain her figure but, between interviews, press conferences, and dream rehearsals, my mealtimes were sporadic. I doubted Morphia would let me starve but this gave me a sense of control.

I devoured the cookies as I plunged into my enormous closet to search for winter clothes. Zephyr was cold and often windy because of its altitude. I pulled on a pair of thick pants, a sweater, a fur-lined coat, boots, and a knit scarf.

I thought about packing a few things in case I decided to make this escape permanent and return to Sandman Island. Something squeezed my chest as I thought of Penny. Even though I'd only worked with her in a couple of dreams, I knew I couldn't just abandon her. We shared a wound when it came to mothers.

I had to retrieve Morphia's ghostsilk. I'd studied a map of Zephyr ahead of time so could find my way around. I'd told Peter, in the note, to meet me at the glass staircase that led to the famous floating islands at seven thirty, but I wanted to get there early to scope everything out.

My heart jumped around in my chest as I crept down the hallway toward the bedroom Morphia and Hayden shared. Had she gone to bed when I had or was she still awake? Worse, what if Hayden was in there with her? I hadn't seen him since my first morning here, which had been fine with me, but what if I walked in on them while they were . . . ?

I shook my head in an effort to erase that embarrassing image. I was tempted to forget the ghostsilk and just fly to Zephyr but that would take far too long, even if I once again rode on the backs of cloud beasts. Besides, I'd only flown that one time. What if that had just been a fluke?

I continued toward their bedroom. If they were awake, I'd just pretend to be half awake and had lost my way to get a snack in the kitchen. Although I didn't know how I'd explain my clothes. Would she see through an illusion of pajamas? My heart increased its pulse as I slowly eased the door open. Snores vibrated through the vast room. I held my breath as I entered, relieved it was as thickly carpeted as mine. My footsteps were soundless.

I could barely see in the darkness but my chest leaped with joy when I noticed the faint, water-shimmer glow of the ghostsilk hovering right beside the bed.

I held my breath and tiptoed toward it, fearing any noise would wake them. No, not them. Just Morphia. Hayden's side of the bed was empty.

I forced back a laugh as I glanced down at Morphia soundly sleeping and snoring. Her hair was a rumpled mess of black and gold against her pillow and a thin trail of drool streaked her chin. Her face, covered in cream, shone a ghastly white against the ghostsilk's faint glow.

I was sure Morphia would murder me if she awoke this second, and not just for the jaunt I was about to take.

I gasped as a second ghostsilk appeared in the room.

"Hayden, is that you?" Morphia mumbled sleepily.

Chapter 24

That had to be Hayden returning from a dream site. I formed an image in my mind of the glass staircase and dashed through the portal. Relief filled me as I felt the gauzy tickle of ghost hairs, followed by a blast of cold air.

I stood before the seemingly endless staircase. It reflected the twilight sun's rich gold. The ghostsilk flapped rapidly in the brisk wind. I grabbed it before Morphia could figure out what I'd done. Before I folded it up, I tore off a small piece from one its edges, just as Morphia had initially done. But the ghostsilk had been whole. Had she repaired it afterwards? Well, I needed another piece. Lorelei wasn't going to take away my chances to communicate with Jenna. I slipped both ghostsilks into the pocket of my coat.

I studied the staircase, which connected Zephyr to the archipelago of floating islands—or skylands as the book called them—named the Tears of the Moon. Crystalline rails ran along either side of it. Intense awe filled me. The numerous skylands varied in size, some no bigger than boulders, others larger than Sandman Island, all hovering in empty space. The more massive ones were interconnected by other branching glass stairways. Faint mists clung to some of the skylands like the shredded remnants of ghostsilk portals. A couple of the largest skylands were speckled with houses and small buildings. People lived there. An endless array of the colorful balloons and spherical edifices of downtown Zephyr stretched to the west of the skylands.

What kept the skylands afloat? Not even the books could answer that. Balloons were needed to hold up the buildings in the downtown section, but the skylands seemed to hover on their own, like the moon.

I still had an hour to wait before Peter arrived. That gave me time to explore.

I'd read that the stairs, even though they looked fragile, were strong enough to support the weight of a large adult.

I leapt onto the first step. The sound of my boots tapping against it created a tinkling sound that reminded me of wind chimes.

A brief sensation of dizziness filled me as I looked straight down, through the glass. The Archetypal Sea undulated far, far below, its dark blue waters tinged with the swirling rainbows of Visitor thoughts. Clouds, taking on vague animal shapes, drifted beneath me.

An intense longing to fly suddenly filled me. I glanced around. There was no one here.

Chimes rang in my ears as I jumped to the next step, and the one after that, willing my body to become as light as ghostsilk.

I shrieked with elation as my jump turned into a graceful glide. I soared higher as I kicked my feet and stretched out my arms. Several cloud beasts, some gauzy wisps, others thick and fluffy, brushed against me with impossibly soft fleeces. I briefly wondered if any of them were the clouds that had carried me to Sandman Island but then felt silly for having such a thought. What were the odds of that? There had to be thousands, perhaps even millions, of cloud beasts. And they were all shaped from the essence of Visitor Thoughts.

Dreamearth needs us more than ever. The voice in my mind was not my own but it was as if the speaker had read my thoughts. Was a cloud beast speaking to me or its companions? *Fewer of us are being formed.*

"What do you mean?" Dread tightened my chest.

The nearest cloud beast, which resembled a fat, gray sheep, turned its dewdrop eyes toward me. *We don't know the cause. But Dreamearth needs our rain. Without it, our world will dry up and gradually fade. Have you come to guide us to a drought-plagued land?*

"I'm sorry." I shook my head and drifted higher. "I'm not a Cloud Wrangler and I can't stay long."

What did the cloud beasts mean that fewer of them were being formed? Did this have something to do with the blank thoughts Penny and some of the other Visitors had been leaving? There still appeared to be plenty of cloud beasts here in Zephyr.

This worry was pushed aside as I soared higher. Wind whipped at my face and rippled through my hair. My chest swelled with such an intense euphoria I almost feared it would burst. Why had I jumped so quickly at the opportunity to become an apprentice Substitute just because I'd learned that Mother had been one? I should have waited and become a Cloud Wrangler apprentice instead.

It was becoming difficult for me to breathe. I strained to pull the thin, icy air into my lungs. The sky was now dusk blue and stars glinted against it. A sharp, crescent moon loomed directly above me, larger than it appeared from the ground. A momentary giddiness filled me as I wondered if I could reach it if I kept flying. The only problem would be lack of air . . .

"You've flown too high," said a familiar voice that sounded far away. Unlike those of the cloud beasts, I heard it with my ears, not my mind.

Was I hallucinating? I looked down. The skylands and Zephyr's countless balloons looked like grains of colorful sand. I'd left the cloud beasts far below, except for one. It hovered beside me, shaped like a fuzzy, exotic bird.

"Did you . . . say something?" My words came out in breathless gasps. It hurt to speak.

The creature winked at me, then transformed into Hayden.

I screamed and plummeted.

Chapter 25

My stomach leaped into my throat as I plunged downward at a rapid speed. The wind numbed my face. I flailed, struggling to regain control when a strong hand gripped my arm.

"That's it," Hayden, flying beside me, soothed. "Smooth your flight. Good." He gently guided me. We drifted downward, heading toward a small, deep green skyland.

I slowed my speed as we drew closer, closer, closer. I stumbled onto a field of tall grass that was as fine as hair. Hayden landed gracefully beside me. His long hair was pulled back into a ponytail but wisps of it blew across his face.

"What . . . how . . . ?" My words were faint wheezes. I crumpled onto the ground into a ball, pressing my head against my knees and took deep breaths. I feared I might pass out. The thin grass tickled the side of my face.

"Take your time, Remmi," Hayden said, kneeling beside me and stroking my back. "You've had quite a shock. Don't worry. Morphia didn't see you. She takes a little something to help her sleep and was unconscious again the moment I saw you disappear."

"Y-y-you can fly too?" I finally managed, slowly lifting my head. My surroundings tilted. I closed my eyes.

"Yes. I have more magic than the average Dreamearthling and it looks like you do too."

A chill that was not from the wind blowing through the grass filled me.

"With practice, you too could do this." I opened my eyes. He waved an arm. At first, nothing, then the ground rumbled and shook. I pressed my knees to my chest.

The earthquake suddenly stopped. "You did that? Shook the skyland?"

Hayden grinned. "Just a little. It isn't much more than shaking a table, only I've taught myself to control it. And that's not all. My illusions can extend beyond myself."

I blinked up at him. "What do you mean?"

"I can manipulate the surroundings, like this."

He snapped his fingers. Snowflakes drifted from the sky, even though I didn't see any cloud beasts overhead. They fell first in delicate patterns but then turned to thick swirls. They brushed my face with icy kisses and thickly coated the grass, turning it a white that glimmered against the brightening moonlight.

The air had grown even colder. I gritted my teeth and pulled up the hood of my coat. I hated snowy winters. Mother had died in the middle of one.

"Please. Make it stop."

"It's merely an illusion, my dear." He waved his hand and the snow instantly vanished. "I just wanted to show you what you could be capable of."

I swallowed. "Are-are you a Halfling?" I cringed as I remembered Andrew's reaction when I'd suspected Morphia of being one.

"I don't go around calling myself one, since that would be deadly for my reputation but, yes, my father was a Realearthling."

Bile rose into my throat. I now wished I hadn't gulped down those cookies so fast. If that dive I'd taken earlier hadn't dislodged them, Hayden's words threatened to.

Did that mean I was one too? No. I'd continue training with Morphia and working with Penny and see if I could find out who my father was. If he was somewhere in Dreamearth, then I could prove Hayden wrong.

"I'll make a deal with you," he said, grabbing my hands and pulling me to my feet. "You keep my secret and I won't mention that you have extra talents outside of illusion magic."

"Deal," I said, looking him straight in the eye as I shook his hand.

"Good." He pulled out his ghostsilk. "I'll leave you to your little jaunt. Morphia should sleep for a little while longer but watch your time." He hung up the ghostsilk. It rippled in the wind. "Oh, and just be careful while interacting with your clients during their dreams. You don't want to accidently step out of them."

Before I could ask what he meant, he'd already disappeared into the ghostsilk.

What time was it? I looked around, disorientated. Hayden's sudden appearance had shaken me but I still didn't want to miss Peter.

Relief flooded me as I found the staircase leading from this skyland. It was just a few feet away. Standing on the opposite end, at the edge of downtown Zephyr, was a tiny figure with bright red hair.

"Peter!" I shouted, my voice hoarse from screaming. I jumped up and down and waved my arms.

It took a moment before he spotted me and waved back.

I pushed through the hair-like grass and leaped onto the stairway. I resisted the urge to fly as I climbed down toward him, taking two steps at a time. He also stepped onto the staircase and started toward me with the ease of one who'd climbed this numerous times.

"Geez, Remmi," he gasped as we met halfway, "what were you doing all the way out there?"

"I got here early so I could explore a bit." I touched my wind-burned cheeks with numb fingertips. They had to be as blazing red as a sunset.

"I-I'm glad you came. It's good to see you again, alone."

"I'm sorry for—" I started, my intention to apologize for the way Morphia and Lorelei treated him but my words were cut off as he pulled me toward him. A mixture of joy and awkwardness filled me as I melted into his embrace. He seemed even taller and his body was firm with slim but well defined muscles. He smelled of soap.

He pressed his lips against mine. My heart raced and my breath caught in my throat as his tongue brushed mine, his fingers stroked my wind-tousled hair.

He pulled back suddenly, his cheeks flaming and glasses fogging. I stared up at him, both relieved and disappointed.

"W-we should be getting back," he stammered, straightening his rumpled shirt.

"Getting back?"

"When I told my parents you were coming, they asked me to invite you over for dinner. Do you want to come?" His eyes were pleading.

I nodded, almost too breathless to speak, and squeezed his hand. "Of course." I ran my fingers through my hopeless hair and straightened my clothes. Peter still held my hand as we continued down the crystal stairway, leading back to downtown Zephyr.

Moonlight flooded the floating city, glinting against windows and making the balloons shine. The blending fragrances of cooking food mixed with incense filled the air. The winds were getting even stronger, causing the smaller balloons to dance.

"What are those?" I asked, pointing at a few of the kite-like vehicles that darted overhead.

"Kitebikes. They are the closest most of us, outside of Cloud Wranglers and Visitors, can ever get to flying," his tone was wistful, "but I won't be able to learn to ride one until I turn eighteen. I'm saving most of what I earn from my Thought Collecting apprenticeship to buy one as soon as I can.

"My home is just over here." He tugged me toward one of the smaller spheres. Three steps led from the skypath to its front door.

A small, thin woman greeted us. She had dark hair but her eyes were as blue as Peter's. She had to be his mother. George towered behind her, grinning.

"Phoebe, this is Remmi, the one I had told you about," George said, taking my coat and hanging it on a hook next to the door.

She smiled and took my hand. "It's so nice to finely meet you, dear," she said. "I'm so glad everything worked out for you. It must be exciting to be an apprentice Substitute. It's such an honor to have you dine with us tonight."

My face grew hot. "Thank you, ma'am." I wasn't sure what else I could say.

"You're Morphia Nightshade's apprentice!" piped an eager young voice. A small red-haired girl hurried over and gazed up at me with large, admiring eyes.

"We've watched all your dreams and interviews on our Viewing Crystal," said a skinny boy the same size as the girl. He had a thin, freckled face like Peter but his hair was dark.

"Don't crowd her like that," Peter scolded them in a half playful manner. He turned to me. "This is Timothy and Giselle, the annoying twins. You'll have to forgive them. This is the first time they've met an actual Substitute. They'll probably bombard you with questions all through dinner."

"That's all right." I smiled at them. "Ask anything you want. But I'm not really a Substitute just yet. I'm still just an apprentice."

"That doesn't matter," said Timothy, his gaze still locked on me. "You still get to be a part of actual dreams!"

"Let's all sit down to dinner, shall we?" said George, holding a chair out for me.

The meal was one that I'd never had before, consisting of something that I first thought was chicken. But the bones were more delicate than those of chicken and the meat had a sharper, tangier taste.

"This is tovu bird," George explained. "They mostly live on the surrounding skylands. It's not something we eat every day but, having you over is a special occasion, I'd say." He winked at me.

The meat was accompanied by potatoes and a strange salad that seemed to be a combination between the hair-fine grasses that covered the tiny skyland and multi-colored flower petals, mixed in a vinegar dressing. The other kids and I drank a reddish, berry tea while George and Phoebe sipped wine. So this was what it was like to have dinner with an actual family. A wistful sensation tugged at me.

"I'm afraid that, once Lord Malcent becomes Emperor, I'm going to be forced to perform more mind drains," George said, his voice solemn.

I nearly choked on a mouthful of food.

"But that won't be for at least a few more weeks," Phoebe said. "Perhaps by then someone can bring him to his senses, make him see that mind-drains are barbaric."

George shook his head. "Not that stubborn old goat. He's stuck in his ways. Why, he's even used non-Halflings who hadn't been mind-drained as drones." He looked at me. I stared down at my half eaten meal. What if Hayden's hint was correct and I was a Halfling? Not even Morphia and other Substitutes could fly and move things with their minds. "Didn't you catch his latest interview? He says he's going to clamp down even harder and search out Halflings that have somehow escaped the mandatory mind-drains as infants. And the other leaders are backing him up, thanks to that infamous Njim."

"Does that mean I'll have to perform mind-drains too?" Peter's face had turned a sickly shade of white.

George nodded slowly as if his head had grown several pounds heavier. "I'm afraid so, son. Thoughts are all part of our job."

"Is it too late for me to pull out of my apprenticeship then and become something else?"

Fear gripped my throat, making it impossible for me to eat or even talk as conversation drifted around me. I had only weeks to find out who my father was and prove I wasn't a Halfling. But what about Hayden?

Everyone grew silent as a ghostsilk suddenly appeared. Morphia, clad in a nightgown and matching robe, stepped through it. She hadn't even applied her makeup. Her face blazed such an intense red her freckles looked white against it.

Chapter 26

"Remmi, get back this instant." She stomped over to me and grabbed my arm in a painful grip. "Do you realize how much—?"

"Please, Mrs. Nightshade," said Peter, rising to his feet. "She was just having dinner with us. We invited her."

Morphia glared at him, then glanced around the tiny cottage and wrinkled her nose in distain. "You're lucky the news crews aren't here to report this," she said, completely ignoring Peter. "Now come along. You've wasted enough time already."

"Just let me get my coat," I said, pulling away from her. As I grabbed it, I smiled at Peter and his family. "I'm sorry about this. I hadn't exactly cleared it with Morphia." I could hear her tapping her slipper-shod foot against the floor. "Thank you for dinner. It was delicious."

"You're always welcome in our home, Remmi," said Phoebe.

"Wait," called Timothy. "Before you go, could you autograph this for me?" He thrust his napkin at me, along with a pen.

"Mine too," chimed in Giselle.

"I can't wait till I can tell everyone at school about this," Timothy said as I scribbled a brief note and my name on each of their napkins. Morphia's *tap-tap-tapping* drummed in my ears.

"How did you find me?" I asked once we were through the ghostilk, which I assumed had to be Hayden's, and back in her living room.

"Ghostsilk works when you envision a person, as well as a place. Had you known that, you probably wouldn't have taken your little excursion. What, by the First Visitors, were you thinking? And where's my ghostsilk?"

I tossed my coat and scarf onto the couch, then handed her the portal. I was roasting. I snuck the torn off piece into my pants pocket.

She bit her lip so hard that it appeared to disappear. "There's a piece missing."

"To replace the one Lorelei tore up." I hadn't slept and Morphia was grating my nerves like sandpaper.

"Do you have any idea how expensive it is to get these rewoven? The barbers who cut ghosts' hair in the Nightmare Realms charge a fortune for each lock. I only gave you that scrap so you could contact me. What in all of Dreamearth did you need it for?"

I sighed and plopped down onto the couch. Exhaustion saturated my entire body. "To keep in touch with a friend." It seemed futile to lie.

"Remmi, get one thing straight if you are to become a full-fledged Substitute. You must leave all your previous friends behind. We Substitutes run in elite circles and our old friends merely get in the way. It would be a major embarrassment if a news crew caught you having a meal with lowly Thought Collectors."

A sudden rage tore through me. I surged to my feet. "Then perhaps I'm not cut out to be a Substitute. I'll pack a few things and return to Sandman Island." I started toward the stairs. My words were serious. I ached to return to the island, although the urge to possibly learn more about who my father might be tugged at me. And then there was Penny . . .

"Remmi, love, no." Morphia scrambled to my side and clutched my hand. I felt my lips curve into a smile. I had leverage. She *needed* me as her apprentice for the extra publicity. "Please don't be so hasty. If you need time off here and there, just let me know. But within reason."

I turned to face her. Her liquid-honey eyes were damp.

"I can live with that. But—"

"Good." She steered me into the dining room where Fiona and Mia had set out breakfast. "We can go over the script for Penny's next dream while we eat."

I scanned the platters of rolls, bread, and fruit and balked. I was full from dinner with Peter's family. "Okay. But I have a favor to ask first." I leaned in close and locked my gaze with hers. "I want you to tell me everything you know about Luna

Clearwater, my mother. You must have *some* idea who my father is."

"Oh, love, hardly anyone in Dreamearth even knew she had a—"

"Just tell me, or I'll walk out and return to Sand—"

"All right, all right." She shook her graceful, manicured hands. "To tell the truth, Remmi, Luna and I weren't exactly friends. In fact, we were rivals. We both worked for Visitor Visions and interacted with many of the same Realearth clients. That's when I first met Hayden."

She laughed bitterly. "She and I were in love with same man but he initially chose Luna. I'll be honest with you, love." She patted my hand. "I was *elated* when your mother seemed to vanish off the face of Dreamearth. That left Hayden for me."

I felt as if something heavy had rolled over me. "H-how long ago did this happen . . . when she disappeared?"

Morphia bit into a strawberry and chewed it slowly. "Oh, who can keep track? Fourteen, maybe fifteen years. But the important thing is, I ended up with Hayden while Luna never seemed to settle down."

I stared down at the fruit platter as I struggled to make sense of this.

"Is that enough for you, love? Let's go over this next dream."

Could *Hayden* be my father? Did that make me a Halfling, then, if he was one? Perhaps that explained my extra magical abilities.

Chapter 27

"This particular dream will occur two nights from now . . . Remmi, love, are you listening?" She shook my shoulder.

I blinked and looked at her. How could she not see it? Shouldn't this upset her, just a little?

I struggled to push aside those distracting thoughts. If Morphia didn't notice the obvious, *I* wasn't going to point it out to her. I made a mental note to ask Hayden about it when I saw him . . . if I could figure out how . . .

"Yes. Sorry. Go on."

"Bianca won't feature in this one," she continued. I wasn't sure if I should be relieved or disappointed. "And it will be a fun dream, not a nightmare." I decided on relief. "You will be portraying Penny's best friend Tabitha Conner."

She grabbed my hand and tugged me toward the living room Viewing Crystal. Several images, displaying various dreams occurring throughout Dreamearth at this time, flickered in its depths, weaving a confusing kaleidoscope.

Morphia tapped the Crystal. "Show us an image of Penny Brook's best friend Tabitha Conner." The images faded, replaced by one of a girl who was Penny's age. Like Penny, she was tall for her age with a slim, athletic build. She had light brown skin, hazel eyes, and dark, tightly curled hair that reminded me of a native Sandman Islander's. To my chagrin, this twelve-year-old was also taller than me.

"Now, form an illusion of her," Morphia instructed.

I closed my eyes and concentrated. Transforming into Tabitha was almost effortless, much easier than impersonating elegant Bianca. I figured this was because I had more in common with a tomboyish kid than an elegant movie actress.

"Excellent. Now shift back and let's go over the script. Even though this should be an easier dream for you, it will be quite involved and, like the last one, will include two separate scenes. Lorelei will be directing again, so everything must run smoothly." Her voice was tense.

We settled back at the dining room table, which had now been cleared. The script was several pages long and was to start in a section of the Collective Unconscious Forest I had never visited, in a copse made not of trees but giant lamps.

"I know the Forest is a vast place," I said, "but is it safe?"

Morphia blinked at me with a confused expression.

"That rumor that a part of it has disappeared." My irritation was returning. Morphia didn't seem to notice much beyond her limited, personal world.

"Oh, Remmi, love, of course. Visitor Visions wouldn't place any of its Substitutes in danger." She returned her focus to the script. "Penny's paternal grandmother Alice had a penchant for collecting unusual lamps, which she had picked up at various yard sales and swap meets. I'll portray Grandma Alice in this scene. All you and Penny have to do is kick a soccer ball back and forth. I'll yell at you both to be careful and not break anything."

A rare joy filled me. This dream sounded like fun, where I could just be a kid and re-experience, even for a few moments, a carefree childhood that had been cut far too short. I already knew I'd prefer portraying Penny's friend over her mother.

"Your main responsibility here will be to lead Penny toward a ghostsilk portal, which will transport the two of you to the outskirts of Nod for the next dream segment. This will be a distorted version of a world famous Realearth amusement park that Penny has been to several times. Again, you will join her here as Tabitha. According to the script, she will want to ride some indoor roller coaster but as soon as you both get in line, she will remember that she has forgotten something important and needs to go home to get it."

Morphia looked up from the script. "As soon as Penny walks away, drop Tabitha's illusion. She will return shortly to look for her friend but won't be able to find her. You can either return back here or blend into the crowd as you wait out the rest of Penny's dream, which should end shortly after that. Your client will be lost, frustrated, and perhaps even close to tears with panic. Do not attempt to comfort her. She is at a point in her waking life where she is just beginning to long for independence, at least according to the Analysts. As such, it is important that she work this out on her own, even if it means waking up. Is that understood?"

"Yes," I said.

*

Over the next two days, I attended lessons with Professor Flit and spent the afternoons preparing for Penny's upcoming dream. Morphia took me up to the roof of our building to practice kicking a soccer ball around.

Several photographers from different dream journals followed us. The pictures of me in rehearsal were to be included in articles describing this upcoming dream, which would be broadcast throughout Dreamearth.

The humid summer heat beat down onto the tar and the city fumes were overwhelming. I ached for a fresh, tangy ocean breeze. If I was still on Sandman Island, I would be swimming in the sea, not kicking a ball around on a hot roof that burned through the soles of my shoes.

I also felt hopelessly awkward and was sure that Penny would notice, even in the dream, how uncoordinated her supposedly athletic friend had become. Why was it I'm only graceful in either the air or water?

I hadn't been able to get in touch with Jenna through the new ghostsilk shred. What was wrong? Had I not tore it off correctly? I pushed back my concern that her father might have captured her when her face was briefly revealed over the Viewing Crystals at the end of Penny's last dream. She was safe on Sandman Island. I had to keep telling myself that to protect my sanity.

And why was Hayden never home? Now that there was a slight possibility he could be my father, I really needed to talk to him. Morphia claimed he was always at different dream sites. Since so few of his dreams were ever filmed, he had to work harder.

"I expect this dream to run smoothly, Clearwater," said Lorelei as we stood in the lamp forest, waiting for Penny to appear. Today, her eyes blazed a fiery green and her hair was an

178

even brighter red than Peter's. "This is your final chance. If even the slightest thing goes wrong, I'm pulling you. Do you understand?"

"Yes, ma'am," I said, taking on Tabitha's likeness. I ignored Morphia's terrified expression.

The camera crew stood behind us, prepared to begin filming the moment Penny showed up. One man counted down the seconds, "Three, two, one . . ."

Penny appeared on cue. She wore shorts and a loose T-shirt. Her long hair was pulled back into a ponytail.

"Hey, Penny," I said as Tabitha, quoting the script and holding out the soccer ball. I dropped it onto the spongy ground. "Let's practice our moves."

"Okay, Tabby." Penny's voice was emotionless like that of a mind-drained drone. A disturbing feeling clamped my chest. Her eyes, which had lost their usual sparkle, were locked on the ball. Did this have anything to do with her empty thoughts?

"Be careful, girls," called Morphia's voice as she stepped out in the guise of an elderly woman, from behind a fat lamp tree. She wore a broad hat and a floral patterned housedress. Wisps of grayish-white hair floated around her plump face. "I don't want you breaking any of my lamps."

"Okay, Grandma," Penny said in that same toneless voice.

Just focus on the dream, I reminded myself as I gently kicked the ball. The surrounding lamps were as tall as trees but came in different shapes and widths. Some were round and bulbous, like pumpkins, others slender, resembling fancy street lights with lacy lampshades. These colorful shades concealed the sky, just like the thickly leaved branches in the Forest. Brilliant lamplight shone everywhere, weaving confusing shadows like multiple suns.

I missed the ball a few times as I focused on maintaining Tabitha's appearance, and had to chase after it. When Penny got the ball, she kicked it skillfully along as she wove gracefully in and out through porcelain lamps. She didn't even come close to breaking any.

"Are you all right, Tabby?" she asked, coming to a stop and tugging at her ponytail. Relief washed through me. She was back to her normal self; her dark eyes were bright, her diaphanous face flushed. Why had she acted so strange before? "You seem to be a little off in your game."

Before I could answer, Morphia reappeared as Grandma Alice. She stared down at us through light green eyes webbed with fine wrinkles. "I'm making lunch," she said with a smile. "What would you like?"

"Grilled cheese sandwiches and lemonade, please," said Penny, jumping up and down. "And hot-fudge sundaes for dessert."

A table, covered with these foods, which was pushed through a portal by one of the prop workers, appeared to materialize before us.

"Can you see us, Dad?" Penny called as she sat down at the table. She looked up and waved.

Ice flowed through my veins as I followed her unsteady gaze. I didn't see any other Substitute pretending to be her father, which wasn't even in the script.

"What are you talking about?" I asked, deviating from it myself but I had to know.

"Dad's filming this dream."

I glanced back at the camera aimed at us from behind the ghostsilk. I was even more confused. Visitors couldn't perceive ghostsilk, even in their dreams, and that included anything it covered. She shouldn't have been able to see that camera.

There was something else going on with her besides blank thoughts. Could it somehow tie into those? Hadn't she mentioned something about her father recording dreams before?

Morphia nudged me, reminding me it was time to move on to the next part of the dream, the amusement park section.

"C'mon, Penny, let's keep practicing," I said, grabbing the ball from her and clumsily kicking it through the ghostsilk.

"Yes, Tabby," she said in that same simpering tone she'd used at the start of this dream. She stood and dashed after the ball, into the portal.

I leaped in after her, expecting to step into a crowded amusement park.

Instead, I was in what appeared to be a girl's bedroom, softly lit by a nightlight. I was completely naked and could feel the carpet beneath my bare feet.

A non-diaphanous Penny with loose, sleep-tousled hair was sitting up in the bed, gaping at me through wide eyes.

Chapter 28

She was hooked up to an odd device that lay on her nightstand. Rectangular in shape, it was the length of a large book and emanated a soft beeping sound.

I stared back at her. This wasn't the amusement park but Penny's bedroom. And what, by the First Visitors, had happened to my clothes?

My illusion had slipped. With my mind whirling in panic, I formed an illusion of the shorts and shirt I had been wearing just seconds ago.

How did this happen? Was it possible that the dream's location had changed at the last moment and no one had bothered to notify me? If so, how did that explain my sudden nudity? And why did Penny look so solid?

A sudden realization struck me. Somehow I'd ended up in Realearth. How was that possible?

"You look familiar," Penny said. Her tone was so casual I was sure she thought she was still dreaming. That was a relief. It would give me time to slip away without her ever knowing I was really here. "Have we met? Do you go to my school?"

I glanced around, searching for the ghostsilk portal. I couldn't find it. Even though Penny still thought she was caught up in a dream, that wouldn't last long. Any minute now, she was sure to realize she was awake.

I closed my eyes and envisioned Bianca, this time with loose hair and a silken nightgown. My entire body tingled, starting from my scalp and trickling downward.

"Mama?" Penny gasped in a barely audible whisper.

"Yes, *Corazon*. Now, go back to sleep."

I drew back my shoulders and lifted my head as I stepped toward Penny's bed, struggling to imitate Bianca's graceful gait as Morphia had instructed. I crept carefully so as not to trip on any of the wires attached to that strange machine.

I settled on the edge of the bed and, pulling the blankets over her so she wouldn't feel my bare skin beneath the illusion, placed my arms around her. Penny's glossy, sleep-tousled hair smelled faintly of strawberry-scented shampoo. I stroked that hair.

Sing, my thoughts commanded. My throat tightened. If only Jenna could provide my voice once again.

I sang softly. My voice sounded reedy and dissonant to my ears.

My face burned as Penny drew back and stared up at me through wide brown eyes. "You don't have to sing, Mama," she whispered sleepily. "Just hold me."

Relieved, I tightened my grasp and rubbed Penny's back in circular motions. She sighed, shut her eyes, and leaned her head against my shoulder.

I studied the room as I waited for Penny to drift off. The faint, grayish glow of predawn was already seeping through the window. This room, except for Penny's bed, looked nothing like the basket-bedroom-restaurant in the dream that took place in Zephyr. It was painted with delicate pastel shades and cluttered with dolls and stuffed animals. Posters of sports teams covered the walls and a couple of gold trophies glinted on Penny's nightstand. I felt a twist of wistfulness in my chest as my gaze scanned her book-lined shelves.

My arms ached with Penny's weight. Her breathing had settled into a steady rhythm. Taking extreme care not to wake her again, or accidently detach any of the wires connected to her, I slowly, slowly eased her back onto her pillow. She didn't wake up.

Would she now return to Dreamearth? I allowed Bianca's illusion to slip. Would I be able to follow her? I waited for a few breathless seconds but no portal appeared.

I stood and tiptoed to Penny's closet. A colorful array of garments filled it. I wasn't comfortable stealing from my client but what other choice did I have? A clothing illusion would eventually fade.

I pulled on a pair of jeans, only to find, to my mortification, they were too long. Penny was only twelve and she was taller than me. I cuffed them around my ankles. I put on a pink shirt decorated with the decal of some Realearth cartoon princess. Even Penny's shoes were too big, but not by much. They would have to do. I slipped my feet into a pair of loose fitting loafers then tiptoed toward the door.

Penny stirred, threatening to awaken again. I had to get away *now.* It was doubtful I'd be able to convince Penny a second time that she was still dreaming.

My heart was beating so loudly I feared Penny and anyone else who dwelled in this house would be awakened by it. I knew Penny was an only child who lived with her widowed father, so there was at least one other person I might disturb.

What if James was already up? I slipped from Penny's room and carefully shut the door behind me. What would *his* reaction be if he caught me creeping through his house? He'd likely suspect I was a thief and call the authorities. At least Realearthlings didn't mind-drain their undesirables . . . or so I had learned in Realearth Studies. I desperately hoped that was true.

I held my breath and attempted to tread quietly. *Be graceful, just as Morphia taught you,* I silently pleaded as I stepped as lightly as I could. To my horror, most of the house had hardwood floors, and the soles of Penny's shoes made a light tapping against it. I heard soft snoring coming from behind one door. That had to be where James slept. I slipped off the shoes in an effort to walk silently.

My palms were so slick with sweat that I had to continually keep wiping them off on the jeans, switching the shoes from hand to hand to do so. I continued down the hallway, lined with photos. The light spilling in through the windows was dim but, among these pictures, I caught glimpses of Bianca and Grandma Alice. A queer feeling twisted my chest. We Substitutes were likely inferior shadows to the actual people we portrayed. Why was it that the Visitors accepted us without question as their loved ones in dreams?

I sighed loudly with relief when I saw the hallway ended in stairs that led directly to a foyer by the front door. I crept down slowly since the stairs were also wood and felt slick beneath my bare feet. I fought an urge to slide down the rail.

My hands were shaking and my palms were so wet that I fumbled with the knob for several seconds. It made an awful rattling sound I was sure filled the entire house. Why wouldn't it open? My mind whirled in panic when James's snoring, which I could hear all the way down here, stopped.

I studied the door. My breathing came in shallow, ragged gasps. The lock was just above the knob. I twisted it with a trembling hand as I heard the sound of rustling coming from upstairs. Fearing I might keel over with fright, I pulled the door open, dashed outside, and accidently slammed it shut behind me.

Stupid! Stupid! Stupid! I mentally scolded myself as I raced across the lawn. The thick, cold dew drenched my feet and the bottoms of the jeans. I ignored the discomfort and ran down a sidewalk lined with elegant houses and flowering trees. The concrete, scattered with leaves and flower petals, was hard beneath my feet but I refused to stop until I was sure no one was following me.

I finally slowed and looked around. Through the trees, I could see an ocean, starting to glitter against the emerging sun. It was a soft gray-blue, dull compared to the brilliant incandescence that tinged the Archetypal Sea.

Struggling to fight a choking panic, I put the shoes back on and continued walking, having no idea where I was going or what I should do. I remembered it was late summer here as well and, even though it was early, the damp morning air was starting to grow hot. It wasn't quite as humid as warm days on Sandman Island but would likely get close. In some ways that I couldn't explain, this was similar to parts of Dreamearth but also entirely different. Did the air seem heavier? I breathed deeply. The smells were different. The scents of summer foliage blended with sharper, pungent odors I couldn't identify. This was Dreamearth turned inside out, a place that relied on technology, not magic. Clouds were simply banks of mist, not living creatures that rescued tired fliers in danger of falling.

Cars occasionally whizzed by on the street. I froze every time one passed, afraid I'd be instantly noticed as an alien, a foreigner, but not one of them stopped.

A few joggers hurried by from time to time. They merely smiled at me and one woman even mouthed a polite greeting. No one was at all surprised by my presence.

Could I pass myself off as a Realearthling?

After I had walked several blocks, the houses gave way to strip malls lined with shops and restaurants. The traffic was heavier here and the crowds had thickened. My empty stomach leaped as I smelled, through the stench of car fumes, the familiar, comforting scents of breakfast cooking. A fresh desperation gripped me. What was I going to do? Was I stuck permanently in Realearth? I had grown used to eating regularly these past several months and feared I'd weaken with hunger if I didn't find food soon.

I settled on a brick wall to think this over, figure out what I should do.

My thoughts darted back to my arrival on Sandman Island all those months ago. Then I had been filthy and destitute. But I had changed and experienced so much since then.

I searched the street, grazing over shops and restaurants. This city wasn't all that different from Nod and, thanks to Realearth Studies, I was sure I knew enough about Visitor culture to get by. Perhaps my accent was slightly different but hopefully it wouldn't be all that noticeable. I should be able to find work for a while until I figured out a way to return to Dreamearth.

I scoured my thoughts for a reasonable plan. My abilities to illusion and fly were my greatest assets but they'd be useless here. What else? At least I'd had some schooling since I'd left Penumbra. That should help.

I felt a momentary leap in my chest, which instantly plummeted. There was something else I had learned from Realearth Studies: most places didn't hire anyone under sixteen, at least not in the United States, where I'd ended up.

I could lie about my age. I glanced down at the cartoonish shirt in despair. Between that and my size, I probably looked more like eleven than sixteen.

My empty stomach rumbled. I fixed my gaze on the nearest restaurant, which was open for breakfast, and took a deep breath. The owner could be as nice as Periwinkle. I leaped off the wall and started toward it, breathing in the blending scents of coffee, bacon, and pancakes.

Chapter 29

Groups of people filled the restaurant. Most sat at booths and tables, while others waited to be seated. Was I doing the right thing? I scanned the large room and stood behind a large family. Very few people were alone. I studied the bustling servers, dressed in neat livery, who scurried about with trays or coffee pots. At least none of them appeared to be drones.

Of course they wouldn't be. Realearthlings didn't perform mind-drains.

This slightly calmed my unease but I still felt so unsure. I was in a different *world*, although there were plenty of similarities. Would getting a job here and a place to stay be as simple as it was with Periwinkle? A nagging doubt itched at me but what other choice did I have? The only Realearthling I knew was Penny and that was only through her dreams.

My gaze strayed to a flat, rectangular Viewing Crystal that was placed high up on a wall, like a picture. No, not a Viewing Crystal, I recalled from Realearth Studies. Here they were called televisions and worked differently. Channels were changed by remote controls instead of voice activation. They also provided entertainment, not just news, and certainly not clips of various dreams.

"There you have it folks," said a beautiful, dark-haired reporter who spoke into a microphone. She was on a street surrounded by crowds of people. "Has God, who now goes by the name Njim, finally appeared, or is it all a great hoax? What do you think?"

My blood chilled. Njim? The Halfling who had been crossing over into Realearth?

She shoved the microphone at a man in a business suit. "We shouldn't jump to conclusions this soon. This could all be a stunt, some sort of movie promotion."

I allowed myself to breathe. Good. At least some Realearthlings had doubts. Perhaps this would discourage Njim and he'd return to Dreamearth, maybe even turn himself in.

"But he's been seen in other places," the newscaster continued. "Didn't he make an appearance in Boston last week?"

Before the man in the suit could respond, another man stepped in. This one was younger with long, unkempt hair. He was carrying a large sign with the word "Repent" in bold red letters.

"Don't you people get it?" he exclaimed, staring through the TV screen with wild eyes. "God has returned to judge us all. Now is the time to—"

"How many in your party, miss?" I started and pried my gaze from the screen. A young woman in a server's uniform stared down at me from behind a "Please Wait to be Seated" sign and held several menus. Her eyes, fringed with long, curling lashes that had to be fake, shone with impatience.

"I'm alone," I said, straightening my shoulders. The woman raised her eyebrows. "I'm here to ask for a job." My mind raced back, straining to recall what I had initially said to Periwinkle. At least I no longer looked like a beggar, even in clothes that weren't mine. "I'd be willing to—"

"A job?" The woman's gaze slid over me, lingering on the pink T-shirt. Her lips, painted with bright red lipstick, curved into a smirk. "Is this some kind of joke?"

"No, ma'am." I swallowed. This woman was certainly no Periwinkle. "I don't have any place to go and—"

"How old are you?" Her voice softened and her eyes lost their hard edge.

"Sixteen." The lie tasted bitter on my tongue. I doubted the woman believed me.

"Wait here. I'll get my manager."

I breathed deeply in an effort to calm my rapid heart as I turned my attention back to the TV. The news blurb about Njim had been replaced by an ad for dog food. Disappointment filled me. I had been hoping for more information, in extensive detail, concerning Njim. If he was living in Realearth, wouldn't many Realearthlings know him personally? Or was he just good at hiding?

A middle-aged man approached me. An annoyed expression played across his face as he studied me. "Are you the kid looking for a job?" he asked, glaring down at me. "This had better not be a prank."

I gulped. My throat was suddenly dry and my hands felt clammy. I resisted the urge to wipe them off on Penny's pants. "It's not a prank, sir. I need a job and a place to stay." I forced myself to look directly into his eyes, which seemed to soften. Realearthlings did things differently here. I could already sense he was not going to be as obliging as Periwinkle.

"You don't appear to be homeless," he said. "And I certainly don't believe you're sixteen." My face grew hot. Why had I even bothered to lie? I was terrible at it. But I had an uncomfortable feeling that that wouldn't be my last lie. No Realearthling would ever accept that I just fell out of a dream world. The vast majority didn't believe such a place existed. That was the one detail from Realearth Studies that snagged in my mind. "You also don't sound like you're from around here. Where are your parents?"

My discomfort increased, gnawing at my insides. I should turn and run. But where would I go? I'd only encounter this same problem at different places.

"My mother died when I was little and I don't know who my father is." That, at least, was truthful. I wasn't yet sure about Hayden but determined to find out.

"Don't you have any belongings?"

I averted my gaze. "I-I . . . they were stolen."

"You were robbed?" The man didn't sound as if he believed me.

"Y-yes, sir." My vision settled on the tiled floor. I was certain he'd chase me away, just as the shopkeepers had done when I'd first arrived on Sandman Island.

He sighed. "Come with me. I'll make some phone calls. There are places that take kids like you."

I allowed myself to breathe as I followed him into a back office. It was small and the desk was piled with papers. A framed photo of the man posing on the beach with a large dog stood at the center of that desk, next to small gold sign engraved with the name Joe Henderson. I took a seat against the wall.

Where was he going to send me? I folded my hands in my lap to keep from fidgeting. Hopefully anyplace in Realearth would be better than Penumbra. I was determined to find a way back to Dreamearth . . . as soon as I figured out how. Was it possible to re-enter without a ghostsilk portal?

Joe spoke briefly into a plastic object on his desk with a curling chord then turned his attention to a television-shaped contraption with a keyboard. He ran his fingers over the keyboard, making tapping sounds.

I struggled not to gape as I searched my mind for the information I had gleaned in Realearth Studies. More than anything, what I had learned in that class was going to be the most useful while I was here. The thing Joe had spoken into was a telephone, I recalled, a more primitive one than those cell phones I had also read about. And the television-like artifact was a computer monitor. Such a thing linked Realearthlings to their world, like Viewing Crystals did with Dreamearthlings.

A server entered carrying a plate and a glass containing an orange liquid. He smiled uncertainly at me as he handed these to me then left before I could thank him.

The plate held toast soaked in butter. The smell made my mouth water. I eagerly devoured it, washing it down with the juice, which had a sweet, tangy taste. Orange juice, I realized as I drained the glass. Dreamearth had that too, although there it had a richer flavor and had been thick with pulp. This was bland in comparison. Was that the way with everything in Realearth?

I turned my attention back to Joe. He was once again on the phone, speaking so softly I couldn't hear him. Who was he contacting? I wasn't sure what I should be feeling. Scared? Nervous? Excited? At least my hunger had been satiated.

I realized I actually felt numb, as if this wasn't really happening. Was that how Realearthlings felt when they were Visitors in Dreamearth?

"The police will send an officer over to talk to you in a bit," Joe told me, after he'd hung up the phone and taken the empty dishes from me.

"The police?" Terror gripped my heart. So he *had* called the authorities. But what exactly had I done wrong, aside from lying? My memories shot back to the brutal Penumbran police and how they'd chased me after my escape from the Cavern Lands. At least I could still illusion in Realearth. That thought filled me with a faint comfort.

"Don't worry." Joe's tone was gentle. He crouched down to be eye level with me. "They aren't going to arrest you. They'll just take you down to the station and ask a few questions. If you don't have parents, as you say, you'll have to be placed somewhere. There are some pretty nice foster homes out there."

"Foster homes?" I blinked, feeling incredibly stupid. I didn't remember Realearth Studies mentioning anything like that. Perhaps we hadn't gotten that far.

"Yeah. You're probably too old to get adopted but kids like you get taken care of, at least until you're eighteen." He stood and paced to his desk where he grabbed a magazine. "Here. It's an old issue but it should keep you entertained while you wait. I'll be back in a few minutes so don't even *think* of stealing anything."

He strode through the door. I glanced down at the magazine. The cover displayed a beautiful woman in a sparkling evening gown. She had to be one of those actresses, movie stars, as Bianca had been. I flipped through the pages without really looking at them.

My gaze strayed to Joe's desk. If I could still illusion in Realearth, could I also fly and move objects with my mind?

I focused on the gold sign with Joe's name and strained to move it. At first, nothing happened. I squinted my eyes and concentrated harder. *Move, move!* It suddenly shot off the desk and collided with the wall just above my head, then clattered to the floor at my feet.

At that moment, Joe entered, trailed by a tall man in a dark blue uniform with a gold badge on his chest. A Realearth policeman. My emotions were a swirl of elation and fear. If he intended harm, at least I was ready, armed with magic that no full blooded Realearthling possessed.

"I'm Officer Gabriel Diaz," the man said in a gentle voice. He smiled as he gazed down at me. He was young, perhaps not much more than a decade older than me, and had dark, curly hair and a coppery complexion. "What's your name?"

I swallowed. It was a fair question. "Remmi." My voice sounded high and trembling. "Remmi Clearwater, sir."

Officer Diaz jotted that down onto a pad he carried.

"I'd like you to come with me, Remmi," he said softly, as if he were coaxing a frightened animal. "You aren't in any kind of trouble. I'm not arresting you. We just need to find out a little more about you."

My mind nagged me to run away. No one would believe me if I told the truth.

I must find a way back to Dreamearth. I retrieved Joe's name sign from the floor. But, in the meantime, I ought to trust these Realearthlings. They hadn't given me any reason not to. Joe was even nice enough to feed me. I was prepared if anyone threatened me.

"This fell on the floor," I said as I handed him the gold sign. Another lie. He merely looked at me quizzically. "And thank you for breakfast."

I followed Officer Diaz out of the office.

Chapter 30

He led me to a black and white car parked in the restaurant's lot.

Feelings of loss surfaced as endless rows of shops, restaurants, and houses flickered by. Where was he taking me? Would I ever see my Dreamearth friends again? Why hadn't they tried to get me back once I crossed over into Penny's room? And why had my clothes disappeared?

I was jolted from my thoughts as the car pulled into a lot in front of a plain brown building.

The inside bustled with people, most of them wearing the same dark uniform as Officer Diaz. He took me into a private office and sat down behind a desk.

"Have a seat, Remmi," he said. "I'd like to ask you a few questions." Unlike Joe's office, his was neat and free of clutter but had a similar telephone and computer. He pulled out his notepad and looked over it. "According to Mr. Henderson, you claim that you don't have any parents. Is that correct?"

"Yes, sir. I was hoping I could locate my father." Did I say that out loud?

A look of relief flitted across Officer Diaz's handsome face. "You have a father. That's promising. What is his name?" His fingers were poised over the computer's keyboard.

My heart plummeted. *Idiot,* I inwardly scolded. Of course he'd need a name. "I-I don't know, sir. He disappeared before I was born." Well, it was a truth of sorts. If I was correct about Hayden, he didn't even live in this world.

Officer Diaz momentarily closed his eyes and ran his thumb over them. He sighed before continuing. "Remmi, I can't help you if you don't even know that basic information. Do you have any living relatives?"

Images of my Dreamearth friends filled my mind: Peter, George, Jenna, Periwinkle . . . They were my only family but were in a place I hadn't yet figured out how to return to. Depression sat like a lump in my chest. "No, sir."

"You have a slight accent I can't quite place. Are you even from the United States?"

I bit back a sudden urge to laugh. *Not even close,* a part of me itched to say. "No, sir. I don't remember where I was born but I lived with my mother when I was little, until she died. After that, I lived in . . . various places, until I found myself here, with just the clothes I'm wearing." I glanced down at the garments I'd taken from Penny's closet. It wasn't the entire truth but not exactly a lie either.

"Then we have no choice but to place you in foster care. But first we have to do a few things."

Officer Diaz drove me to a medical facility where I was examined, pricked with a needle that drew my blood, and a nurse studied the old scars on my back and asked several uncomfortable questions.

I then had to sit in the waiting room for what seemed like an eternity while one of the doctors met with Officer Diaz.

"The doctor gave you a clean bill of health," he said when we returned to the police station. "You aren't carrying any diseases, although there is indication that you've been abused in the past."

I clenched my fists and stared at the floor. I was relieved when he continued speaking after several moments, without forcing me to comment. "For now, Remmi, we'll place you in a temporary foster home. There is a woman who runs a group home not far from here. She's had a recent vacancy. One of the kids she was fostering just got adopted by a family. You can stay with her until we can get a social worker to take on your case and find a more permanent home for you."

A permanent Realearth home. I wasn't sure if that should fill me with joy or dread.

The sun was already sinking low in the sky as Officer Diaz drove me to the foster home. "This woman—she likes the kids to call her Aunt Olga—she'll treat you right." His voice was soft, almost a whisper. I cringed as I wondered what the doctor might have told him about my scars.

The neighborhood we passed through looked worn, as if it were much older than Penny's, where all the houses had been beautiful with neatly manicured lawns. Although some of these

195

homes were fairly large, the paint was peeling and weeds mottled the grass. Several even had bars on the windows. I fought back the growing uneasiness slowly swelling within. Just how many homes were I destined to live in before I found something permanent?

Officer Diaz pulled the car into a cul-de-sac where several kids played in the street. We slid into the driveway of a large house at the very end. This one was neatly painted a bright white with blue trim. The lawn was dry but flowers decorated a windowsill.

Some of the children gathered around us as Officer Diaz led me up a narrow stone path to the front door and rang the bell.

Moments later, a large, middle-aged woman in a loose, floral-patterned dress answered the door. She had a wide, wrinkled face fringed by feathery wisps of brown hair.

"This is Remmi Clearwater," said Officer Diaz after he had greeted the woman. "I must warn you that she only comes with the clothes on her back."

"Remmi, is it?" The woman's smile was strained, her eyes tired and bloodshot behind thick glasses. "Come on in. You can call me Aunt Olga. All the kids do. I have some spare clothes left over from some of the other kids you can use. You are small enough. Thank you, Officer."

"Good luck, Remmi," Officer Diaz said, tipping his hat before he turned back to his car.

A dazed feeling overcame me as Aunt Olga pressed her fingers to her lips and emitted a shrill whistle. A few of the kids who had been playing in the street raced toward her, their flushed faces beaded with sweat. They seemed to range in age from around nine to twelve.

Was I the oldest? Aunt Olga herded us all inside. "This is Remmi Clearwater, who will be joining us for a while," she told them. My stomach nudged me as I caught the scent of something cooking on the stove.

The house was cluttered with toys and knick-knacks. "Remmi, you will be sharing a room with Linda over there." Aunt Olga pointed to a girl who looked to be about sixteen. She was slumped in front of the television in the messy living room and wearing a sour expression. "Linda." Olga raised her voice. "Get over here and meet your new roommate."

The girl mumbled something under her breath as she reluctantly heaved to her feet and shuffled toward us. She was thin, something her baggy clothes couldn't conceal, and had straight black hair that appeared to be dyed. She glared down at me with icy blue eyes.

"Damn. I thought I'd finally get a room to myself."

"Linda," Aunt Olga scolded. "Watch your language while you're under my roof, do you hear. You're not so old that I can't wash your mouth out with soap."

Fear flickered across Linda's pale face. "Yes, Aunt Olga," she said, looking down. I caught the hint of a sneer in her tone.

"Good. Now you girls get acquainted while I go check on dinner," said Aunt Olga, turning away. The other kids sprinted into the living room to play. One young boy had already changed the channel Linda had been watching.

Linda grabbed the front of my shirt and pulled me forward. "If you touch any of my stuff, I'll beat you black and blue."

Rage broiled through me. Here was another bully, just like Treb and those girls who had tormented Jenna. "You just try," I growled, pulling back. Linda still clung to my shirt. "I'm much stronger than I look."

I mentally shoved against Linda, just as I'd done with Joe's name sign earlier. Linda shot backwards, landing on her bottom several feet away.

"Wow! You really are strong," exclaimed the boy who had taken Linda's seat in front of the TV. "How'd you do that?"

Before I could think of an answer, Linda scrambled to her feet and dashed into the kitchen. "Aunt Olga!" she wailed in a voice that made her sound much younger. "Remmi pushed me."

Despite the glow of triumph the filled my chest, I was determined not to stay here for long. I just *had* to get back to Dreamearth.

My new bed was small but reasonably comfortable, reminding me of the one I had slept in on Sandman Island. A freshly laundered scent clung to the sheets. Linda's bed was on the opposite side of the room but the girl had slipped away, to meet up with some boy. Just as well. I at least got this room to myself tonight.

Even though my mind was bloated with a myriad of thoughts, I fell asleep quickly.

I found myself in a meadow, sprinkled with flowers of every color. Their blending fragrances were so strong they made me dizzy, like Morphia's perfume. One side of the meadow stretched into a cliff that looked out onto endless blue sky. The other side was attached to a glass staircase that disappeared into a fog.

This had to be one of Zephyr's many skylands. Relief flooded me. I had returned to Dreamearth.

A ghostsilk shimmer appeared a short distance away. Hayden stepped through it.

I raced toward him. "I found my way back!" was what burst from my mouth ahead of the big question I wanted to ask him.

He grasped my hands. They were large and strong and knotted with calluses. He peered down at me with a smile. "You are dreaming, my dear."

"What?" I looked down. My body appeared solid, not diaphanous like a Visitor's.

"Visitors' bodies only look like ghosts to Dreamearthlings," he said, letting go of my hands. "You've discovered *the* main perk of being a Halfling." His eyes sparkled but his expression remained sad. "Congratulations. You've found out how to cross over into Realearth."

"So I really am a Halfling, or part Halfling?"

"There's no such thing as part Halfling, my dear." His tone grew hard, bitter. "All Halflings are sterile."

"But only if they'd been sterilized," I said, my flickering hope refusing to wane. "Isn't that what they do to Halflings that are turned into drones, aside from the mind-drains?"

"Mind-drained criminals are sterilized. Halflings don't need to be." I sank to the ground. I was back to the beginning, of not knowing who my father was.

"Remmi, you don't have much time since you'll awaken soon and there are things I need to tell you." He knelt beside me. "Since this is your first dream, there is no script to follow so I will speak freely."

"But what about . . . ?" I glanced around. We were alone.

"No cameras, Viewing Crystals, or an audience either. Unlike Morphia, I prefer anonymity."

"Where is Morphia?" She was going to be *furious* that this happened. She and Lorelei both. I felt oddly relieved. Perhaps I could forget about becoming a Substitute and return to Sandman Island. I'd also have more time for Peter and Jenna.

"The charges against her were dropped, thank goodness. Visitor Visions has been acquitted of any responsibility since no one had known."

"Known what?" My initial relief was quickly turning to panic.

"That you, my dear, are a Halfling. You may have been in denial up till now but your stepping out of that little girl's dream has proved it to all of Dreamearth."

I was glad I was already sitting since my legs would have given out. "But you're one as well. A Halfling, I mean. How have you been able to keep your secret?"

"The same way you did, until now, my dear. By only revealing the one magical ability I was known for and not showing off the rest. We Halfling Substitutes must practice extreme caution when working directly with a client since we can step out of Dreamearth if our client awakens prematurely. That's what happened to you. You followed her right out of her dream."

"What if it had been Morphia?"

He grinned. "Nothing. She merely would have entered the ghostsilk and ended up back where she started."

"There's another thing I don't understand." Even in my Visitor form, I felt my cheeks growing hot. "My clothes disappeared when I stepped through."

"Of course they did. Not even Halflings can carry objects belonging to one world into another. Only ghostsilks, which are invisible to full-blooded Realearthlings." My eyes strayed to the portal hovering like a water shimmer behind him. "This includes anything you might be wearing. Visitors often purchase and obtain souvenirs when they are here but those items disappear the moment they awaken. Those Halflings who've crossed back and forth have always made sure to have clothes waiting for them on either side." He chuckled.

"You mustn't return to Dreamearth in your solid body, under any circumstances. Too many people were watching Penny's dream on their Viewing Crystals and saw you disappear. It's all over the news that you're a Halfling." Despair settled like a boulder within me. "You will be a regular Realearth Visitor here in Dreamearth when you sleep. As such, you are safe and considered harmless. Realearth is your home from now on. Dreamearth's rulers have been alerted and the police in every province have been ordered to keep an eye out for you." A sharp chill jolted through me.

I felt my body flicker. "You are waking up, Remmi. You are now one of my clients. I took it upon myself to request you, as one Halfling to another, although that's just my little secret." He winked. "This is the last time you will see me as myself in your dreams."

He and the colorful meadow were fading. "Morphia said you had worked with Luna Clearwater. Do you have any idea who my father is?"

My eyes flew open before I could hear his answer. I was lying on the bed in my new room, trapped forever in Realearth.

Chapter 31

I struggled to push aside the depression that threatened to overwhelm me. The thought that my father existed somewhere in this world gave me a sliver of hope.

The problem was I didn't know where to start. What if he lived on the other side of the world? Realearth travel was much more complicated since they didn't have ghostsilk portals. Or what if he was dead?

The sensation of emptiness grew stronger. I didn't have *anyone* in this world if I found my father was deceased, or would have nothing to do with me. A world I knew so little about despite Realearth Studies. Would I ever belong to a family?

Aunt Olga enrolled me at the local high school, as a freshman. I was overwhelmed by the size of the campus and the noisy crowds. An intense longing for the tiny school I had gone to on Sandman Island, which could practically fit into one of this school's classrooms, flooded me on the first day. I also missed the private sessions with Professor Flit and, although I was sure I'd made quite a bit of progress during my weeks as Morphia's apprentice, the school work was daunting.

I forced myself to study hard, often working late into the night at the kitchen table after the others had gone to bed, until I started to make decent grades. I wistfully acknowledged that I would never be a stellar student, due to my years of educational neglect, but I was gradually catching up.

I practiced my illusion magic in private, when I was in the bathroom or shower, concerned I might lose it if I lapsed. Even though forming illusions was useless in Realearth, a desire to return to Dreamearth if things didn't work out with my father, lay curled up deep inside me.

During breaks from my homework, when no one was looking, I moved pencils and plastic cups with my mind. Although Linda still acted coldly toward me, she no longer threatened, not since I had mentally thrown her across the room.

Still, I knew I should be prepared just in case. I needed to keep my secret abilities honed.

Aunt Olga assigned each of us kids a rotating list of chores: washing the dishes, laundry, vacuuming, and cleaning the bathrooms.

"Man, this is so lame," Linda whined one Sunday afternoon as she and I folded laundry. "Why does she load us down with so much work? I have better things I can be doing, you know."

"What, like watching TV and texting your friends?" I rolled my eyes. An unexpected laugh burst out of me. I couldn't help it.

"What's so funny?" Linda glared at me.

"You think you have it so bad here. This is nothing! At one of the places where I lived, I spent hours washing floors, scrubbing stinking toilets, weeding gardens, and cleaning fireplaces, for thousands of residents. This was every day. I never had time to play or goof off and I slept on a hard kitchen floor with several others. I sometimes even went for days without food."

"Where is this place?" asked Theo, a ten-year-old boy who poked his head out of the bathroom. His eyes were wide with terror. "Will Aunt Olga send us there if we're bad?"

I chuckled. "Don't worry about it. It's very far from here."

"Like in a whole other country?"

"You could say that."

I had to admit that I found this foster home a near paradise when compared to Penumbra. The food wasn't as good as that on Sandman Island, but at least it was plentiful and I was fed regularly.

The one thing that frustrated me was my frequent inability to recall my dreams. I knew that dreaming was a new thing for me but this bothered me nonetheless. Dreamearth was my first *home*, after all, so why couldn't I linger, even if I was only now allowed to do so as a ghostly, harmless Visitor?

The main reason, I had to admit, was that my dreams would be the only way I could learn about my father. I didn't have his name to go by here in Realearth, which made searching on the Internet useless. Was he even alive? Did he have a family? I desperately wished for one. I missed my Dreamearth friends but figured being permanently stuck in Realearth wouldn't be so bad if only I could work this out.

Of the dreams I did remember, they were usually mundane, taking place at school—or what looked like an alternate version of my school—and were certainly scripted: I was either taking a test that was written in illegible gibberish, running hopelessly late for class, or caught naked in the hallways. This was bitterly disappointing since I ached to take a fleeting "vacation" to Sandman Island and visit Periwinkle, frolic once again with Peter on the Tears of the Moon, or soar with the cloud beasts. Why weren't the scripts allowing me to do those things? Was this part of my punishment, aside from physical banishment? I pounded the pillow afterward, drawing sleepy confusion from Linda. "Just an irritating dream," I explained with a shrug.

As Hayden had explained in my first dream, he never revealed himself.

I finally had a vivid dream, after weeks of trying, but it wasn't anything I'd expected.

I was in a small, sterile cell made entirely of dull gray stone. That was uncomfortably familiar. Penumbra! My Visitor body shook with terror. What was I doing here? This was the last place I expected to dream about. Visitors hardly ever entered Penumbra. I knew that well.

"Remmi?" said a weak voice from the ground.

I blinked and looked down. Jenna was huddled against a wall, her head on her knees that were pressed against her chest. Her usually neat braid was a mass of loose, grimy wisps.

"Jenna?" Straining to remain in the dream, I knelt beside her. "Is that really you?" I hoped that she would turn into Hayden or Morphia or any other Substitute.

Jenna blinked. Her eyes were red and rimmed with dark circles, as if she had been crying. "Father's men captured Mother and me," she whispered. "It turns out we weren't even safe on Sandman Island. Somehow they were able to find us."

Guilt pierced my chest as I remembered the dream where I had utilized Jenna's singing voice. Could that have alerted

Lord Malcent to her whereabouts? Or was he now Emperor Malcent? First Penny and now this. Why did I keep hurting people?

"Treb is mind-draining Mother in his office," she choked. "I-I'm next. We're going to spend the rest of our lives as Penumbran drones."

"No!" I clenched my fists. I felt the tug of wakefulness threatening to pull me out of the dream. I noticed a ghostsilk hovering right beside me. I grabbed it before anyone could snatch it away and could barely feel the cobweb-fine fabric against my fingers. "I promise I won't let that happen. I'll come for you. I'll—"

"You can't." Jenna leaned toward me. Her normally round, rosy face was thinner and pale. I wondered when Jenna had last been fed. "You realize you're a wanted Halfling? If you enter Dreamearth in your solid body, you'll—"

"I don't care," I said, just before I jolted awake.

I sat up in bed and looked around. The moon, dancing in and out of clouds, lit my room with a wavering glow like white firelight.

Linda was sleeping soundly. The crumpled ghostsilk shimmered in my hand.

I scrambled out of bed and unfolded the portal. Jenna was in danger and Felysa was likely already a drone. Forget the rules. I had to return to Dreamearth and help them.

Chapter 32

I paused. Was I simply going to step into the ghostsilk and go straight to Jenna without a plan? And I'd arrive there naked since I'd be crossing back into Dreamearth. The whole thing was suicide. I stood still for several seconds, staring at my rumpled reflection, distorted against the wrinkled silk, as I struggled to figure this out. There wasn't time. I had to go now. It was probably too late for Felysa but I could at least save Jenna.

I stepped through the ghostsilk, forming an image of the alcove where the drone tunics were kept. Luckily, Treb's office was adjacent to the kitchen, close to that alcove.

I felt the familiar cold floor beneath my feet, smelled the sickening-sweet stench of sweat, human waste, and mildew mixed with soap coming from the nearby drone bathrooms. No one was around. I wrinkled my nose as I plucked a stained, tattered tunic out of the all too familiar pile. I had hoped never to don one of these again. The coarse fabric scratched my skin, threatening to bring back a flood of disturbing memories. I pushed them back. This was not the time to be fussy. Jenna needed me. What if I was already too late?

Clinging to the ghostsilk, I crept toward Treb's door. I drew in a deep breath as I cautiously eased the door open. I didn't have time to react as a beefy hand with a stump for an index finger reached out and jabbed a needle into my arm.

"We were expecting you," Treb said, holding a syringe tipped by a silver needle as he stared down at me through squinty gray eyes.

A numb sensation spread through my body, turning my limbs to rubber. I held up the ghostsilk. It was only then that I noticed one of its corners had been torn off. Malcent slithered out from behind a corner and grabbed it. He was accompanied by a well-dressed woman with black and gold hair.

"Mor . . . phia . . . ?" I could barely choke out her name as I wobbled on my unsteady legs.

"You betrayed me, love," she said, her painted lips curving into a cold smile. "I'm merely returning the favor."

"You shall be paid handsomely for your excellent acting," said Malcent. His water-pale eyes gleamed as he studied the ghostsilk. "This is a remarkable device. Able to whisk a person thousands of miles away with a mere thought. I've always wanted one." He turned his icy gaze to Morphia.

"It is yours, then, Your Eminence," she said, dipping into a graceful curtsey. "I can always get another."

My consciousness wavered as my legs buckled beneath me. I crumpled onto the cold, hard floor at their feet.

Idiot, I cursed myself. I had fled from Penumbra all those months ago to escape the lethal injection Treb was going to give me and now I had willingly walked right into it. I'd just wanted to save my friends. I should have known that Jenna has been merely Morphia hidden behind an illusion and recognized the torn edge immediately. At least Jenna and Felysa were still safe on Sandman Island . . . but for how long, once Malcent became Emperor?

"Try flying away now, little bird," Malcent mocked. I winced as he bent down to stroke my cheek with his fingertip. "You aren't dying," he continued as I began to sink into darkness. "In a few days, I will be Dreamearth's Emperor. How auspicious, to have a public Halfling execution after my Crowning Celebration." His words blurred in my ears. "I don't yet know how you shall die but I assure you it will be slow and painful. I'll have to do some research. I do know one thing for certain: I shall get my inspiration from the Realearthlings. They've come up with some creative executions in the past, especially for those who have revealed themselves to be Halflings in *their* world."

Darkness swallowed me.

I awoke slowly, groggily. I was lying on cold, damp stone. My hands were shackled behind my back with iron cuffs. Chains rattled when I struggled to move. My mouth tasted like stale dust. Where was I? The place was dark, chill, and smelled of mildew. I had no idea how much time had passed. The not knowing made my brain itch, like a rash I couldn't scratch.

I tried to swallow but my throat was as dry as sand. Would they even bother to feed me while I was in here? Would dying of hunger and thirst be preferable to whatever execution Malcent might come up with? I remembered learning in Realearth Studies the terrible ways ancient Realearthlings executed their undesirables: live burnings, crucifixions, hangings—

Terror worse than anything I could imagine facing in the Nightmare Realms suddenly gripped me. I found myself longing for a mind-drain over facing a painful, humiliating death. Would returning to a drone's life be the more preferable option? It was now doubtful that Malcent would grant me such a choice.

The ache in my arms and shoulders pulled and burned, becoming unbearable. I had to shift my arms.

I strained to sit up and pressed my back against the wall. My entire body vibrated in agonizing protest as I wiggled, rocking back and forth, to work my hands under my bottom. My fingers scraped painfully against the stone floor but I didn't care. My muscles were on fire as I lifted my body, using the wall for support until my shackled wrists were under the backs of my knees. Sweat, which quickly chilled, soaked the drone tunic, tickled my face, and stung my eyes.

I rested for several moments, breathing deeply then slowly, slowly worked my hands out from under my legs. The shackles were attached to long, rusted chains that tangled around my legs.

I could move objects with my mind. A faint spark of hope flickered through me. I focused on the metal cuffs, which were faintly visible now that my vision had adjusted to the darkness.

I imagined them unlocking and falling to the ground. My face burned and my forehead throbbed with the intense effort. A droplet of sweat settled at the edge of my nose with an agonizing itch but I forced myself to ignore it.

After what seemed like an eternity, the shackles broke apart. I felt a leap in my chest. The chains slid onto the cement floor with an echoing clatter. I looked around as I untangled them from my legs and rubbed the circulation back into my wrists. I was in a cell that was only a few paces across and didn't have a door.

No door or even bars? A choking panic gripped me. I studied the walls. They stretched up to a ridiculously high ceiling where a trap door was embedded.

If I could fly in here, I'd be able to reach it. I rose slowly to my feet. My entire body ached, my stiff joints creaked in protest. I had never before flown without a running start. Could I become airborne just by jumping?

I stretched in an effort to loosen my tight muscles. Then I bent my knees, focusing on that buoyant sensation that filled me whenever I flew, and jumped. I floated off the ground but landed with a heavy thud seconds later, my feet slapping painfully against the cold floor.

"Again," I hissed through gritted teeth before despair could overtake me. My voice echoed through the narrow chamber.

I tried twice more before I was able to hover several feet above the ground. Elation swooped through me. By moving my arms, I could glide up and down the lengthy walls as if I were underwater.

I could fly in here, so now what? I alighted back onto the ground. I needed a plan to escape Penumbra . . . again. I still had to be careful. I sighed. My escape this time would be even trickier than before since I not only had to get out of this dungeon but find a way to return to Realearth. The only way to do that was through a ghostsilk portal. At least Malcent now had one thanks to Morphia.

My relief was short lived. I'd have to enter his quarters to retrieve it, if that was where he decided to keep it. It was a chance I had to take. Images of different illusion disguises flitted through my mind. Malcent, one of his current wives, a drone . . .

None of these prospects appealed to me, especially since I had completely lost track of time. What if it was night and Malcent was in his bedchamber, along with one of his wives? And any drone caught wandering the corridors after the evening curfew could expect a beating or worse. I shuddered as the prospect brought up a flood of disturbing memories I had to force back.

No. It wasn't safe to illusion anyone's likeness. The only option would have to be invisibility.

I gulped back the terror that threatened to overwhelm me as I leaped back into the air. I grazed the wall as I flew upwards toward the trap door, drawing closer, closer.

I pushed against the wooden door to find it jammed shut. My stomach felt as if it had become dislodged as I plummeted downward. I clawed at the wall as I struggled to remain airborne. *Focus, Remmi,* I inwardly shouted, pedaling my legs in an effort to hover as I figured out what to do. Was the door locked or merely just heavy? Could I blast it open?

I drifted slowly up toward it. The effort to remain in the air and push aside the door with my mind at the same time was almost overwhelming. Sweat tickled my skin and my head felt as if it were about to explode as I fixed my gaze on the thick wooden planks that made up that hatch.

I sank lower as I mentally strained against the door, which proved to be much harder to manipulate than the small objects I usually practiced on. And it was trickier than shoving a person. It remained wedged shut. I couldn't see the lock, which had to be on the outside. Burning frustration filled me. How was I going to get out? This was impossible.

I could already feel my energy fading from the struggle of remaining airborne and my useless attempts to blast open the trap door. Even the rank air seemed thinner, more difficult to breathe. If I didn't succeed this time, I would have to settle back down onto the uncomfortable ground and rest before trying again. Malcent's threat rumbled through my mind. How much time was left before my execution?

Anxiety pumped through me, filling me with determination. I picked up the discarded shackles and swung them at the hatch as I shot toward it.

A loud shattering filled my ears as I thrust the manacles through the wood. Success. I had splintered a narrow gap in the door.

"The drone," shouted a man's voice as I pulled my head and shoulders through. "Lord Malcent was right. She could escape. Call for back up."

My brief elation dimmed. Two Penumbran policemen stood over me. Fear wavered in their eyes. One held a raised club while the other pulled a device from his pocket and spoke into it. "Attention, police." His voice blasted through the corridor. I was sure all of Penumbra could hear it. "This is Gregor. The captured Halfling drone is trying to escape. We need back up immediately."

I dodged as the other man swung the club at my head. I forced myself through the narrow hole, suddenly grateful for my small size, and flung the shackles at the two men, striking one of them in the face. They staggered back, cursing. I slipped around a corner. The thunder of countless boots stomping through the corridor filled my ears. The entire Punumbran police force was after me.

"Where is the Halfling drone?" asked a gruff voice.

"Over there," said Gregor.

I was shaking so hard I could barely focus. *Invisible, invisible,* I silently chanted, both in an effort to illusion and to calm my racing heart. My body grew as diaphanous as a Visitor's and then disappeared altogether.

I froze and held my breath as the tap-tapping of boots approached me. The slate gray eyes of several policemen seemed to stare straight through me as they searched the corridor.

"Where did she go?"

"She's a Halfling. They know many tricks. Lord Malcent isn't going to like this. Keep looking."

I backed away and started in the opposite direction. I was relieved my feet were bare even though the floor was cold. That made me soundless as well as invisible.

I dashed toward the kitchen. I knew I could get my bearings and figure out which direction Malcent's quarters were from that since, to me, the kitchen had always been Penumbra's main hub. I had been in them several times, to clean, so knew where they were.

It was late. The only Penumbrans who prowled the corridors in this section were the night guards. A brief urge to check on my erstwhile drone companions tugged at me. Were they all right? Was Treb mistreating them? Anger shivered through me at the thought of him.

I pushed these feelings back. The police could be here any moment, looking for me. I had to find the ghostsilk and return to Realearth before my illusion faded.

The chambers I passed through grew larger and more ornate as I neared Malcent's private quarters. Slender stalactites dripped from the ceilings like shimmering icicles and the tapestries that decorated the walls displayed the only colors found in Penumbra.

I took a deep breath as I stepped up to the silken hanging that draped the entrance leading into Malcent's bedchamber. A warm, flickering glow shown through the opaque fabric and I heard the crackle of flames. A fire was lit. Did he sleep with a fire burning at night? I had only been in his chambers during the day.

I glanced down to make sure I was still invisible then slipped through the curtain.

Malcent's chamber was the largest in Penumbra, almost as big as Morphia's living room. A glowstone chandelier dangled from the high ceiling, flooding the room with a rich golden glow that reminded me of twilight. The fire, dancing in the fireplace at the far end of the room, added to that luminescence. There was a sunken, carpeted area to the left of the fireplace with a large, four-poster bed.

My heart lodged in my throat. A single lump in that bed was softly snoring. Malcent? Drifts of long white hair spread over the pillow. No. That had to be the wife he had chosen to share his bed with tonight. Lady . . . what? I couldn't remember. The only wife of his I knew was Felysa.

Malcent sat at a mahogany desk that stood against the wall, close to the bed. It was lit by a single glowstone lamp. His back was to me. Sticking out of the pocket of his dressing gown was a swath of gauzy silk that absorbed the chamber's golden light. The ghostsilk.

I held my breath as I slowly crept toward him, reaching out a hand I couldn't see. Closer . . . closer . . . almost there.

My hand became visible just as my fingers brushed against the airy silk. Malcent turned and stared directly at me.

Chapter 33

"I had a feeling you'd try to escape and come looking for this." He pushed the ghostsilk deeper into his pocket as he rose to his feet. I darted back with my eyes fixed on that pocket. Malcent paced toward me. His slippers padded softly against the carpet. "But I didn't think you'd outsmart my police." His narrow face broke into a grin that didn't reach his icy eyes. "I must admit, you're much more clever than I gave you credit for. You are far too smart for a drone."

I'm not a drone. I've never been mind-drained. I longed to say that but the words died in my throat.

"I had planned to have your execution broadcast all over Dreamearth via Viewing Crystals the day after my Crowning Celebration," Malcent continued, still walking toward me, forcing me to back up. I could feel the heat of the fire growing gradually warmer. "You were to serve as an example for all Halflings who dare escape the system but perhaps, given your abilities, such overthinking was foolish on my part."

I winced as my feet touched the stone hearth. It was hot. The fire roared and crackled in my ears. I now realized how large the fireplace was, as tall as a doorway, with flames that reached higher than me.

Malcent's grin widened. "No. This will be much more fun and for my eyes only."

Terror filled me as the fire's heat seared my skin. The smoke coated my lungs with bitterness and stung my eyes.

I forced back the urge to cough as I reached toward his bulging pocket. The ghostsilk was my only chance to escape. He wouldn't be able to follow me into Realearth. He grabbed my shoulders with a painful grip.

I strained to push him aside with my mind but he remained where he was, his grasp tightening. Furious that my magical energy had been spent blasting open the dungeon hatch and an invisibility illusion, I stomped hard on his foot. Rage flashed in his eyes as he let go of me.

The woman in the bed stirred. I blinked to clear my burning eyes.

"You're going right into the fire," roared Malcent, his voice filling the room with a disturbing echo. He clutched my arm, his nails digging into my skin. "I'm not taking any more chances with you."

I pulled back, falling onto the carpet. A fireplace poker leaned against the grate. I scrambled to my knees and grabbed it. Malcent bent close, reaching for me. I slashed him across the face.

His anguished yell filled the chamber as he staggered back, his hands pressed against the bloody gash that streaked his left cheek. I pushed my hand into his silken pocket and, ignoring Malcent's curses and the woman's screams, pulled out the ghostsilk.

Jenna's image sprang into my whirling mind as I flung the portal over my head. Even though she had been illusion-concealed Morphia in my dream, would she still be in danger once her father became Emperor?

I was instantly soothed by the familiar hair-tickle against my skin. As soon as the carpet beneath my feet was replaced by rough ground, I crumpled the ghostsilk into my fist so Malcent couldn't follow me. I stood still for several seconds, gulping in deep breaths and struggling to figure out where I'd ended up.

I was in a forest surrounded by trees with spiky, moss-veiled branches. It was nighttime but the area was softly lit by several round glowstones that dangled from some of the branches. The air was cool and smelled of moss and wood smoke. A girl with short, blue-streaked hair was bent over a pen, feeding several creatures that appeared to be dog-sized centipedes with metallic hides.

I was in the Nightmare Realms, where it was always night. I thought back, struggling to figure out how I'd ended up here. I should have returned to Realearth but, in my desperation to get away from Malcent, my mind had pictured . . .

I focused on the short-haired girl. Jenna? She was thinner but toned, not starved as Morphia's illusion had appeared in my dream. She was clad in black leather pants, a matching tunic, and her hair was so short it looked boyish. I stepped closer, snapping a twig.

She looked up. "Remmi?" A brief smile flickered across her face. She strode toward me, her boots crunching over gravel. "You aren't safe here. But I'm glad you're here, even if you shouldn't stay." She gave me a tight hug then pulled back. "You look awful, like you've really been through something. What happened? They say you're a Halfling. Is that really true? There's a million things I've been dying to ask you."

I stared at her, my mind reeling. I didn't know where to start.

"I look different, huh?" Her cheeks flushed a pale, bright pink. "The Nightmare Realms agree with me. It's always night here so I don't have to deal with the hot sun anymore."

"You . . . you live here now?"

She nodded. "Our class got to visit here on a field trip, where Master Monster Trainer Adam Winter introduced us to his menagerie of beasts. The other kids were terrified but not me." Jenna raised her chin. "I was fascinated and volunteered for all of Adam's demonstrations. There's nothing scary about those monsters. They're just like big, ugly puppies. Adam took me on as an apprentice Monster Trainer. Mom's even set up a shop here. But instead of earrings and sundresses, she now sells giant rubber eyeballs and skeleton hand backscratchers. Novelty items, but it's still a living."

"Jenna, that's wonderful," I said.

"Shhh!" She glanced around. I tensed as the sound of footsteps crunching over pebbles filled my ears. "Father's not Emperor yet but he's already acting like he is. He's got spies in every province. I know someplace safe, where even they won't go."

She grabbed my hand and led me past large enclosures containing odd and frightening creatures I'd never seen nor heard of. There were serpents with curly-cue bodies, enormous coal-black monsters that looked to have been made of jagged boulders, and humanoid beasts with glowing green skin and tentacles in place of legs. They all made low, growling noises as we hurried past.

"Don't be afraid," Jenna whispered. "They are all quite gentle, much nicer than they appear. Their main job is to scare Visitors but not harm them."

"I'm not afraid." A foul stench filled my throat and nostrils. I resisted the urge to gag.

"Here we are, the mammoth slug enclosure." We ended up at the edge of a deep, moss coated pit. At the bottom, in a wide chasm, I could see at least two creatures that appeared to be the size of adult elephants but were shapeless blobs with slimy, mushroom-colored skin. They grazed on the moss with fish-like mouths. The smell that emanated from that pit reminded me of a filthy latrine that hadn't been cleaned for months.

Jenna giggled and wrinkled her nose. "No one will come near us here. We're safe, at least for now." She locked her gaze with mine. "Is it true, then? About you being a Halfling? I saw you disappear out of that girl's dream on our Crystal but I didn't want to believe it."

Dread tightened my chest. Why hadn't I returned to Realearth where I now belonged? "I'm afraid so." I squeezed the wadded up ghostsilk tighter. I could barely feel it. I had to remind myself it was still there. I had to be ready in case Jenna turned on me.

"Wow!" She widened her eyes. "I've never met an actual Halfling before. Well, not one that wasn't a mind-drained drone." She frowned as she studied my tunic. "But why are you dressed like one? A drone?" Worry crossed her face. "They didn't try to mind-drain you, did they?"

"Your father did capture me but he threatened more than a mind-drain."

"What? How?" Jenna's hand flew to her mouth.

"Morphia tricked me. I—"

"Your own mentor?"

"Yes." My chest ached. That wound was still fresh but I felt I shouldn't be surprised. All Morphia had ever really cared about was her own reputation. "I dreamed you and your mother had been imprisoned by your father and I rushed to rescue you after I awoke. It was all a trick." I swallowed the bitterness that threatened to clog my throat. "But I fought him and managed to get away. He even has a wound to prove it."

"You stood up to Father? And escaped?" Jenna's eyes were wide with admiration.

I nodded.

"It would take a Halfling to do that. He's terrified of them."

"And you don't mind that I am one?"

Jenna looked down and kicked a pebble. "My feelings are mixed, Remmi. Not so much with you. You've stood up for me. You're my friend, after all, and I knew you had special magic even before I found this out. But there's been a lot of upheaval throughout Dreamearth since you crossed over."

"Because of me?"

"Yes. Father has police everywhere, even though he's not Emperor yet. It's his mission to wipe out every Halfling that escaped the mandatory mind-drains."

"And all the other province leaders are going along with this? Even the current Emperor?"

Jenna nodded. "Everyone's on high alert because of that Halfling Njim. And more and more Visitors are leaving behind blank thoughts. It's all over the Viewing Crystal news. The River is drying up and more of the Collective Unconscious Forest has disappeared."

"And they think it's all Njim's fault?" I thought about what Mr. Sparks had said. "They can't blame this on one person, can they? Even if he is a Halfling?"

"There isn't any conclusive evidence but who else can they hold responsible? You picked a fine time to step out of a Visitor's dream, Remmi."

My head spun. I sank down onto a mossy boulder, fearful I'd collapse into the slug pit if I continued standing. "There has to be something we can do to stop all this madness," I said, more to the giant slugs than Jenna.

"Do you mean fix the Visitors' dreams, stop my father from becoming Emperor, or stop the vendetta against Halflings?" Jenna said, settling onto the ground at the edge of the pit. I assumed she must have done that before since she didn't seem at all bothered by the stench or the ground's slimy texture.

217

"All of it," I mumbled. "But we should just pick one, for starters."

"Well, Father and his Halfling search are rolled into one. I'd talk to him if I thought he'd ever listen to anything I had to say."

"No, Jenna." I fastened my gaze on hers. "I don't want to endanger you. But maybe the other leaders would listen."

"Doubtful." Jenna plucked gobs of moss from the ground and tossed them down to the slugs. The creatures happily slurped up the morsels. "They may have their own ideas when it comes to their individual provinces, but they are merely puppets under the Emperor."

"But Malcent isn't Emperor yet. Isn't his Crowning Ceremony still days away?"

Jenna shook her head. "It's close enough. He's as good as Emperor now. The current Emperor is so old he can barely stand without help. From what I heard, he can't wait to retire and just go lay on a beach somewhere."

"There's got to be something." I leaned back on the boulder and stared up at the dark, misty sky through masses of barren branches.

I suddenly remembered what Peter had told me, just before I'd accepted Morphia's offer to become her apprentice.

"Peter," I shouted, sitting up. My voice echoed through the woods.

"Quiet, Remmi," Jenna hissed. "We're hiding, remember? Not that anyone's out there but while you're here, we've got to be careful."

"Sorry," I whispered. "I just thought of someone who might help." I looked down at the ghostsilk still wadded in my hand and damp with sweat. "I have this friend, an apprentice Artifact Collector. He and his family . . . well, they're against the mutilation of Halflings. It isn't much but it could be a start."

I smoothed out the ghostsilk and hung it in the air.

"What are you doing?" Jenna scrambled to her feet. "Are you returning to Realearth? I'd rather you not go but you really should. You'll be safer."

"No." I stood and straightened my shoulders. "I know the danger I'm in but I don't care. I already beat Malcent once. Besides, this is my fight too. I'm going to find Peter."

Chapter 34

Jenna grabbed my arm and pulled me away from the ghostsilk. "You'll do no such thing. If you even take one step toward that portal, I'm tossing you right into the slug pit." I already teetered on its edge. I took a giant step back. "You're a wanted criminal, remember?"

"Okay, I won't. But just let me touch it so I can visualize Peter. You'll just get tangled up in the silk without a visual of a place or person. I could describe him to you but I don't think the ghostsilk works that way. Once I mentally create a visual, you should be able to go up to him, wherever in Dreamearth he is at this moment, and convince him to follow you." I gave her a brief description of Peter.

"I'll find him." Jenna peered at her rippling reflection against the portal's surface.

"Tell him—"

"Don't worry. I'll improvise." She winked at me. "I'm good at that."

I placed my hand on the gauzy silk. It felt like a non-sticky spider web. I formed a picture of Peter in my mind, tall and lanky, his eyes an impossible shade of blue behind round spectacles.

I crept back the moment I felt my hand enter the portal, tickled by countless hairs in the ghostsilk weave, and motioned for Jenna to enter.

I remained out of sight for several long minutes. My restless heart refused to calm. What was I doing by involving my friends? I should have just returned to Realearth. What if I got them in trouble?

As the minutes passed, I felt tempted to peer into the ghostsilk. What was taking Jenna so long? Worries tickled my mind. Peter could be anywhere in Dreamearth. What if it was a crowded place?

"I don't understand why you have to pull me out of class for this," I heard him say as he stumbled from the portal. "Some other Collector could—"

His eyes grew enormous behind his glasses as they settled on me. "Remmi?" His face became a shifting kaleidoscope of conflicting emotions: joy, fear, and confusion. "What are . . . how . . . ?" He held out his arms but then suddenly pulled back, as if he'd changed his mind. My heart shriveled. "It's true then, what they've been saying all over the Viewing Crystals?" Worry shadowed his eyes.

I forced my head to nod.

"That explains it then. Why you were a drone in Penumbra." He scanned my tunic. "Wasn't that what you were wearing when—?"

"What?" Jenna's shriek stung my ears. "You were a *drone*? How's that possible? You'd obviously never been mind-drained."

I grimaced. "I was very good at faking it."

"I'm not sure if I would have remembered you. Mother and I left when I was pretty young, around eight or so."

I thought back. I'd arrived in Penumbra when I was seven and we were around the same age, so our paths might have crossed. A laugh formed in my throat but I pushed it back. "Not to be rude, but when did Penumbrans ever acknowledge drones, unless they wanted something from them?"

Jenna's face burned a hot pink. "That's true. Oh, Remmi, I'm so sorry. I never would have guessed."

"It's all right." I squeezed her hand. "I tried to avoid Penumbrans as much as possible back then, anyway. You were long gone before the dream that caused so much excitement, the day I was almost killed—" I bit back the rest of that sentence. Peter was staring at the ground and shuffling his feet, his ears burning the shade of his hair. "Anyway, that's all behind me. Take down that portal, please, before someone finds us." Jenna snatched it out of the air and folded it into a tight, neat square, which she handed back to me. "We have much bigger problems at this time."

"Is that why you brought me here?" Peter said, glancing down at the slug pit then quickly averting his eyes. He looked as if he were about to throw up. I'd almost forgotten about the stench.

"This is the safest place that I can think of," said Jenna. "We won't keep you too long."

"Peter." I stepped closer to him. He didn't back away. "You'd told me that your father was trying to come up with a way to fight what they do to Halflings. Has he come up with any ideas?"

Peter flushed and shook his head. "He's been even more secretive about his opinions, now that Malcent will be taking over as Emperor. We're sure there are other Halflings out there, besides you, who don't want to make themselves known because they are afraid of being mind-drained or worse." I thought of Hayden. "Most, I'm pretty sure, would just like to live ordinary lives like you. But things are a bit complicated right now."

"A bit?" Jenna snorted.

"So many of the Artifacts I've collected lately have turned up blank. Everyone, from us Collectors, to the executives who run the Ministry of Thought Artifacts, have tons of theories but no solutions."

I hadn't realized I'd been chewing my lower lip until I tasted blood. "Have you seen mine? My thoughts?" I felt suddenly naked, vulnerable. If they weren't blank, what did they reveal? But if they were . . . I didn't want to consider that but had to hear the truth. "Are they . . . ?" My voice faded.

Peter forced a smile and squeezed my hand. Sudden warmth flooded my chest. "Your thoughts are normal, Remmi. Dad made sure to check after your first dream."

"At least there's some good with me being banished to Realearth," I rasped. "But how long will it last? What if it's some sort of Realearth epidemic?"

"That's one of the theories," said Peter. "But we still don't know for sure and many people think the Halflings are to blame."

A chill passed through me.

"Mostly that darn Njim," said Jenna. "But now, thanks to Father, *all* Halflings are suspect."

"Your father?" Peter stared at her wide-eyed.

Jenna nodded. "He's Lord Malcent, the soon-to-be Emperor, but it's nothing to brag about, believe me. And no, it's not an advantage, so don't even bother asking. I haven't seen him since I was eight. He probably doesn't even remember me."

Conflicting feelings filled me. I ached to stay here in Dreamearth with my friends, my *true* family, but I couldn't endanger them. Besides, I doubted Njim and the blank thoughts were things that could be solved in Dreamearth.

"I'm going back to Realearth." I forced the words from my throat before I could change my mind. "I'll do the research there, see if I can find any clues as to what is causing some Visitors to leave blank Artifacts, as well as who this Njim might be." And also search for my father. I didn't add that last part out loud.

"That's an excellent idea, Remmi," said Peter with a slight catch in his voice.

I struggled to remain strong as he and Jenna embraced me before I hung up the ghostsilk. I lingered a little longer in Peter's arms. He seemed to have warmed up to the fact I was a Halfling. At least I had two Dreamearth allies. Possibly four. My thoughts turned to Periwinkle but I forced them back. I couldn't risk getting her in trouble. And Hayden I only saw in my dreams, hidden behind the illusions of familiar Realearth faces.

I allowed Peter to enter the portal first.

Then, without looking back, I formed an image of the bathroom I used at Aunt Olga's and stepped through. It was a relief to finally shed that itchy drone tunic. I allowed myself to breathe when I saw that the bathroom was empty and dark, except for the bright moonlight that smeared the opaque window.

A surge of triumph filled me as I folded up the slightly marred ghostsilk. It had been Morphia's and briefly Malcent's. Now it was mine. I could bodily return to Dreamearth at any time, although it would be foolish to do so. But still, just the knowledge of the possibility was a comfort.

I wrapped a towel around myself and, clutching the ghostsilk, tiptoed down the carpeted hallway toward my bedroom. At least it was late enough that everyone was sleeping but I had no idea how long I'd been gone.

Careful not to wake softly snoring Linda, I put on my pajamas, tucked the ghostsilk into my pillowcase, and sank into a sleep where my dreams were quickly forgotten.

Chapter 35

"When did you get back?" Linda asked as she roughly shook me awake. I reluctantly opened my eyes and stared up at her. "Aunt Olga's gonna kill you." Her pale eyes gleamed with amusement.

I scrambled out of bed to quickly shower and dress. Linda was right. I was in for it.

The second I stepped out of the bathroom, Aunt Olga grabbed me by the arm and dragged me into the living room. "Where have you been?" Her eyes blazed and her face was flushed an unpleasant red. "I called the cops, you know, and filed a missing person's report." She practically hurled me onto the worn couch.

"I . . . I . . ." I stared down at the cluttered coffee table to avoid her fiery stare. "I'm sorry. I left to look for my father." Those words burned my throat. That was something I had to do so it didn't feel like a complete lie.

"I don't believe you," she snapped, leaning her wide face close to mine. Her breath smelled of coffee and cigarettes. "I bet you ran off with some boy and came crawling back the second he dumped you."

My cheeks burned. I clenched my hands into fists. I could hear whispers and giggling coming from the kitchen where the other kids were having breakfast.

"They still haven't found a social worker to take on your case," she continued, flopping onto the couch beside me. She took several deep breaths before continuing, as if yelling at me had worn her out. "What with budget cuts, they just don't have the staff to send so it—"

She stopped and waved a chubby fist at the others who had gathered in the doorway to watch. "Get your butts to school, all of you," she rasped. "You're late as it is. I'm not in the mood to be called into the principal's office today."

I kept my gaze fixed on that coffee table. It was chipped on one edge. If Aunt Olga made me any angrier, I could knock it over with just a thought.

"If this happens again, Remmi, I'm washing my hands of you. You can live on the streets, as far as I care. Now, you better get to school. You've missed enough school as it is and I'm not signing any note. You'll have to think of something to tell your teachers."

I didn't say anything as I slipped past her, just gave the table a slight mental nudge, spilling toys and magazines all over the stained carpet.

Aunt Olga was still shrieking, claiming the house was haunted, as I grabbed my backpack and hurried out the door.

The determination to find my Realearth father raged within me, even stronger than before.

I was still sure the best way to do this would be through my dreams. True, dreams were carefully scripted but, if there was one thing I'd learned as a Substitute apprentice, it was that those were merely guidelines, not etched in stone. They could be changed.

After school, I checked out several books on dreams from the local library.

I sat by the window in the living room and forced myself to tune out the other kids' hooting laughter as they watched some noisy TV show. The title of the first book I opened was *Lucid Dreaming: Take Control of Your Dreams.* Chills crawled across my skin as I started reading the first page. How did Realearthlings know so much about dreams when their jaunts into Dreamearth were so brief and often forgotten? I remembered how Penny had taken over the dream where I, as Bianca, was supposed to be mauled by Windstreaker.

Was that the cause of Visitors' blank thoughts? I mused, turning my gaze toward the window, at the small backyard. The dry lawn was mottled with dirt patches. That was a mystery I still couldn't figure out.

Blank thoughts or not, Visitors could manipulate Dreamearth. That's when they reveal their true potential.

Each night, I fingered the ghostsilk tucked into my pillowcase and resisted the urge to slip through it when Linda was asleep. No. I couldn't re-renter Dreamearth in my regular body no matter how much I was tempted. I had to discover my father's identity as a Visitor.

What about the Life River? I thought as I lay in bed one night. It was receding but that was only because less new thought-essences were being added to it. But it still contained countless trillions of Visitor thoughts and memories. My father, whoever he was, had to have left behind thought-essences.

I fought the despair that threatened to overwhelm me as I gradually drifted to sleep. How could I possibly find the memories of one human out of multiple trillions that had all mixed together and been dispersed throughout Dreamearth? It was impossible.

What about the ghostsilk? I forced myself to stay awake a little longer as I reached into my pillowcase but didn't pull it out. I could barely feel it in my hand. If it could take me to anywhere in Dreamearth, and return me to Realearth, could it take me back in time?

I knew ghostsilk didn't work that way, but as a Visitor in complete control of a dream, I would make it so.

Mother . . . sleep was pressing against me, drawing me in. She was the key. I formed an image of her as I drifted off.

My Visitor body stepped through the ghostsilk . . .

. . . into the cottage I had lived in as a child. Mother sat beside a small, arched window that peered out into the Forest. Sunlight, splintered into golden rods by the thick branches of surrounding trees, spilled onto Mother. Her back was to me. Her thick, brown hair glistened with reddish-gold highlights.

Intense longing filled me. I stepped closer, catching the scent of lilacs. "Mother," I whispered.

She didn't hear me. Why should she? I'd traveled to the past and was no more than a ghost. I didn't exist yet.

Or did I?

Mother gently rocked and hummed to a bundle of white cloth she held in her arms. Brief joy spilled through me as her lovely voice filled my ears. It had been so long since I'd heard it.

"She's beautiful, like you," said a male voice at my side. "And she has my eyes."

Startled, I nearly awoke. A tall, diaphanous man with a boyish face stood beside Mother and gazed down at the bundle. He was a Visitor. How could that be? Could two Visitors share the same dream?

Then I remembered. I'd entered the past and was looking back on a memory, his perhaps.

Was he my father? I looked from him to the infant. It, like Mother, had olive skin and a full head of russet-brown hair. But its huge eyes were a brilliant spring green. I stared up at the Visitor's face. He didn't notice me. Through his glasses, I could see his eyes were the exact same color as the baby's. As mine.

Still, who was he? I didn't have a name and couldn't ask. My rapid heart lodged in my throat.

He knelt beside Mother and kissed her cheek. "I know I'm dreaming, that this isn't real," he said, grasping the baby's doll-like hand. Her tiny fingers wrapped one of his, barely able to reach all the way around. A smile stretched across his ruddy face. "But when we finally have our own child, I bet she'll be just as beautiful."

I gasped as I looked at Mother, to see her reaction. But she wasn't Mother. She was Bianca.

Chapter 36

He disappeared an instant later. The baby that had been me blinked in confusion.

I nearly jolted awake but struggled to remain in the dream. The infant vanished as Mother-Bianca transformed into Hayden.

He stood and paced toward me.

"What's this?" I managed to gasp. "What did I just see?"

"You tell me." He grinned down at me and tugged at the end of his ponytail. "This was your discovery."

"I thought . . ." My body was urging me to awaken but I refused. "I thought you weren't going to appear as yourself in any of my dreams."

"I decided to make an exception this time. Don't worry. This isn't being filmed so we can speak freely. I'm not the attention hound my wife is." I gritted my teeth at the mention of my former mentor. "Did you not want to find out who your father was?"

I nodded. "I still don't know. I'm sure that baby was me but I don't understand why you were both Mother and Bianca."

"Think about it, my dear," he said as he paced the room. Was this really my childhood home or merely a façade? "Who's Bianca's daughter?"

"Penny." My throat tightened. "Penny Brooks, the client I'd worked with. But that baby wasn't Penny. At least it didn't look like her. It looked like, well, me."

"You're close . . . so close, my dear." Hayden spoke slowly, as if I had been mind-drained. "You and Penny have more in common than you think."

I felt my Visitor body waver, threatening to vanish into wakefulness. *No, just a few more minutes,* I silently pleaded. "She's more than just my client?" My thoughts spun. "That tall man with the green eyes. Is he Penny's father?"

Hayden nodded his head eagerly. "So close, my dear. So close."

"And . . . mine too?" I sank down onto the chair facing the window and clutched its armrest. I figured if I held onto something, I could remain in Dreamearth longer.

"That's right. Your father was . . . is Dr. James Brooks, also Penny's father. He had been a client to both Luna and me, of course in different roles." He laughed. "In fact, I still work with him on—"

I couldn't hold onto the dream any longer. I was awakening. I scrambled out of the chair and grabbed the ghostsilk just as my eyes flew open.

I lay in bed, draped by the ghostsilk. It glowed faintly against the darkness.

I started to fold it up as I glanced over at Linda across the room, snoring into her pillow, and nearly laughed. Why was I so concerned with hiding it? I kept forgetting that Realearthlings couldn't perceive ghostsilk.

Excitement pulsed through me. I'd never get back to sleep now. I knew who my father was.

It wasn't a trick, was it? I recalled, with embarrassment, the dream I'd had of Jenna, who'd turned out to be Morphia.

But then, Morphia could only create illusions on herself. So, unless I really did slip back in time to peer at a dream Penny's father—and mine—had had years ago, Visitor James and infant me had to be Hayden's extended illusions.

But why did he wait so long to tell me?

Well, it no longer mattered. Now I knew.

I crept down the hallway, into the bathroom, and hung the portal in the air. Would it work in Realearth as my own magic did? The ghostsilk reflected the room like a silken mirror. *Please, please work.* I figured I wouldn't lose my clothes since I'd be traveling within Realearth. I took a deep breath, formed a visual of James Brooks, and slipped into the portal.

Instead of the filaments merely brushing against me before giving way, they tangled around me, netting me like a fish.

Sighing with frustration, I carefully peeled it off, fearful of ripping the delicate fabric, and folded it into a tiny neat square.

No, I'd just have to find him the Realearthling way. I returned to my room and slipped the ghostsilk back into my pillowcase.

*

I looked James Brooks up on the Internet first thing the next morning, before anyone was up. His name was everywhere, listed as the inventor of the Dream Catcher, a device that could not only look into dreams but record them.

"So many people forget their dreams just after waking," he was quoted. "But just imagine if you could record all the adventures you experience in your sleep and then replay them the next day, watch them as you would a movie on DVD."

A sharp chill shivered through me. The Dream Catcher. Did Penny have one? Was that the strange device that had been hooked up to her that night when I'd stumbled out of her dream? I recalled how she'd talked about her father filming us, even though she shouldn't have been able to perceive the Dreamearth cameras. The Dream Catchers were selling all over the United States—even the President owned one—and were soon going to be available overseas.

This filled me with a sensation of dread, although I wasn't sure why. Enough books have been written about dreams. Some had even been written by James . . . or Father. Was it really so wrong for Realearthlings to record dreams? Something just didn't feel right about this.

Did it have something to do with the depleted thoughts of so many Visitors and the gradual drying up of the Life River? Or was that all just a coincidence? Frustration flooded me as I leaned back and rubbed my still sleep-heavy eyes.

My heart sank when I managed to find his address. He lived on the other side of town. In my rapid escape from his house weeks ago and my placement at Aunt Olga's, I hadn't realized just how far it was.

I didn't bother to leave a note for Aunt Olga. She didn't believe me before, when I'd said I left to look for my father. Why would she believe me now, when it was the truth?

This plan *had* to work.

Besides, I already knew Penny . . . kind of.

By using an invisibility illusion, I slipped out early from my last class. A longing to fly directly to James's house tore at me as I boarded the bus but I couldn't do that in Realearth, especially not in the middle of the day.

I stared at the passing scenery during the long ride. The seedy neighborhoods gradually slipped away, replaced by palm trees, lovely homes, and ocean views. Longing to have James as a father and Penny as a little sister squeezed my chest. Nerves pulsed through my body as the familiar neighborhood slid into view.

I kept wiping my sweaty palms onto my jeans, which did little good, as I tried to work out what I could possibly say. Perhaps this was a stupid idea. My legs felt like wet paper as I stepped off the bus and headed in the direction of Penny's street.

Everything that swept through my head sounded lame. I was comforted by the fact that, as the famous inventor of the Dream Catcher, he would be open to the possibility that a dream world existed. At least I was living proof of that. My heart grew even more rapid as I neared Penny's house. It might actually be a good thing if Penny discovered I was in her bedroom that night.

Penny's house was easy to spot. It was the bright color of melted butter and stood out like a beacon from the others, which were soft, pastel shades. Penny was already home from school, kicking a soccer ball around on the wide front lawn.

"Yes!" she shrieked, jumping up and down as she effortlessly shot the ball between two shrubs some distance away.

"That was a good move," I said. Now was my chance.

"Thanks." Penny strode closer, tugging at the end of her ponytail. Her face was flushed and tiny beads of sweat glistened on her forehead. My mind fumbled for the proper words. *I'm your half-sister from Dreamearth. No. That sounded insane.*

"You have an interesting accent," Penny continued, cocking her head to one side. "I can't place it. The closest I can guess is British, but it's not quite that either. It's really pretty. Are you from around here?"

"Penny, there is something I need to tell you," I said. "It will sound pretty incredible but—"

"How do you know my name?" Penny widened her eyes. "Do you go to my school? You're not in any of my classes but you look familiar. You've been in some of my dreams, so I must have seen you somewhere."

Heat rushed to my face. "Your father . . . He invented the Dream Catcher, didn't he? That device that can record dreams? I-I read about it on the Internet." My stomach clenched with sudden nerves. "Is he home? Please, I'd like to meet him."

The sparkle in Penny's eyes suddenly dulled to a blank expression, one I'd seen too often on my fellow drones. "Yes, miss," she said in a toneless voice. "He's working in his office. I'll take you to him right away." She turned and strode up the path leading to the front door.

A disturbing feeling stirred within me as I followed her. Something was not right with Penny. One moment she seemed to be a normal kid, the next she acted as if she had been mind-drained. Was that why her thoughts continued to come out blank? Was the Dream Catcher the cause?

I felt suddenly dazed as I entered the familiar foyer and trailed Penny into a room that was set up like an office. Unlike the rest of the house, which was neat and beautifully decorated, this room was filled with clutter. James sat at a desk scattered with paper piles and framed photographs of Penny at various ages. I recognized him from my dream, a slim, middle-aged man with glasses and thinning sandy hair. He frowned at the screen of his laptop as if struggling to figure something out.

"Dad." Penny's voice had regained its former vibrant tone. James looked up and removed his glasses. My heart lodged in my throat. "This is . . ." Penny bit her lip and peered down at me. "I'm sorry. I don't know your name."

"Remmi," I gasped, my mouth suddenly dry. "Remmi Clearwater."

A grin stretched across his youthful face. "Nice to meet you, Remmi," he said, standing to shake my hand. I dared to look up into his eyes. Just like in my dream, they matched mine. "Do you know Penny from school?"

Thoughts whirled through my head so rapidly I could barely focus on what he was saying. They raced ahead as I imagined James adopting me, with Penny as my sister. I'd finally have a permanent home, something that had been taken from me years ago.

But first, I had to convince them of something impossible.

"I doubt it, unless you're in high school, Penny. I recently—I'm a freshman, although my school is a long ways from here."

"You're in high school?" Penny widened her eyes in surprise.

I flushed. Despite several months of regular meals, I still remained thin and small for my age. I remembered how even Penny's clothes had been big on me. Had my growth been permanently stunted from years of near starvation in Penumbra?

"I just thought you might go to my school since you keep appearing in my dreams," Penny continued. "Dad's invented the Dream Catcher but you already knew that. Who doesn't? Isn't that why you wanted to meet him?"

I swallowed hard and willed my rapid heart to calm to a slow, steady beat. It refused to comply.

"She's right, Dr. Brooks," I said, locking my gaze onto a stain on the carpet. "It sounds fascinating." My words came out so rapidly I feared he wouldn't understand anything I was saying. "I've also come across some of your books. Do you really believe that an alternate dream world exists?" My heart leaped into my throat. I was sure if I coughed, it would spring from my mouth and flop all over the floor.

Penny let out an exasperated sigh. I looked up at her. She tugged at her ponytail. "He does all right. He's made a ton of money off that Dream Catcher, but a lot of people still think he's nuts."

"Penny!" James exclaimed.

"I'm sorry, Dad. I know you're a genius and all, but come on. Dream worlds aren't real. Not even the Catchers can prove that."

A strange feeling wormed through me. I knew this was a common belief in Realearth but it still was strange to hear such a thing, especially coming from someone I'd worked with as a client. My throat tightened.

"I originally invented the Catcher for Penny," James said, slipping his glasses back on and sitting once again at his computer. "I wanted to record her dreams so we could look them over together the following day and analyze what was troubling her. You see, she had been suffering from terrible nightmares after her mother passed away." His fingers tapped the keyboard. "Would it be okay if I showed Remmi one of your dreams, Pumpkin?"

"Of course, Dad." Penny's voice was toneless. She had slipped into that odd, mind-drained mode. It seemed to occur every time someone asked her a question or gave an order, even an indirect one. My hands hurt. It was only then that I realized how tightly I'd been clenching them. Was the Dream Catcher somehow responsible for this? But how? Her thoughts, and those of many other Visitors, had come out blank but that didn't make any sense. What did blank Thought Artifacts have to do with Catchers, which merely recorded dreams?

James didn't seem to notice Penny's sudden change. He frowned at the screen as his fingers dashed across the keyboard. "This was one of the dreams I'd downloaded from the Catcher." He turned the screen toward me. "Don't worry, Pumpkin," he winked at Penny, "it's not an embarrassing one."

For Penny, I couldn't help thinking as I fixed my gaze on the screen. A mixture of horror and elation filled me. The scene of me as Bianca appeared, as clear as if it had been recorded in high definition. I winced as my image staggered awkwardly down the red carpet in that sparkling, rainbow gown. I felt the blood drain from my face as I watched the illusion-Bianca turn toward Penny before toppling to the ground.

The woman's image instantly dissolved, to be replaced by me. Visitor Penny, a ghostly, diaphanous form, skidded to a stop then scanned the crowd for her suddenly missing mother until she disappeared. I looked down. My face burned.

"That *was* you, Remmi," Penny shrilled. "That means I've had to have seen you somewhere. I just don't remember. If you don't go to my school or aren't on an opposing soccer team, then where? I couldn't have just made you up and here you are. That would be too weird. Even weird by Dad's standards."

"I do know you Penny, but not how you think."

Her face paled. "What are you talking about?"

Both she and James stared at me. Now was my chance. I took a deep breath. "I-I come from . . ." I struggled to pry the next words from my throat. "You are right, Dr. Brooks. What your Catchers have been recording is a real place. There another world, which people, Realearthlings like you, visit in their dreams. It's called Dreamearth. I'm from that world." I returned my gaze to that same stain on the floor. This had to sound crazy, even to James. "It was my job to interact with Visitors, which is what we call dreamers, by making myself resemble people they know in waking life."

Silence.

A chill passed through me. They wouldn't believe me unless I showed them. "I'm able to change my appearance through illusions . . . like this." I closed my eyes and concentrated, forming an image of Bianca in my mind. I could feel the familiar tingle start at my scalp and spread through the rest of my body.

"You . . . you pretended to be Mama?" Penny gasped.

Guilt struck me as I pried my eyes open. Perhaps I should have taken on someone else's likeness, like Tabitha's. All the color had drained from Penny's face and she looked as if she were about to faint.

I allowed Bianca's illusion to fade. "This was just an illusion. I've portrayed your mother in some of your dreams."

"This has to be some kind of trick," James breathed. He pointed at the laptop. "I've dreamt about Bianca for years, even before . . ." His voice faded.

A burning sensation like acid filled my entire body and my heart mashed around in my chest. Mother . . . The word caught in my throat.

Penny sobbed and sank to the floor with her face buried in her hands. James scrambled over and knelt beside her.

"It's okay, Pumpkin." James stroked her back in a circular motion. Penny's shoulders shook. "Your mother was quite famous, so a lot of people know what she looked like.

Remmi could have used . . . I don't know, but there has to be a logical explanation. There always is."

"I-I had thought that was really Mama, at least the good dreams, coming to visit me from the dead." She lifted her head and glared up at me through drenched eyes. Tears streaked her cheeks. "How could you do such a thing? Do you know how evil that was?"

"Penny, I'm . . ." My voice broke. I should never have come. I'd ruined everything. I couldn't tell James I was his daughter now. Intense remorse and depression filled my body like poison. "I'm so sorry. We're called Substitutes, those of us who are able to illusion the likenesses of people you know, or knew. Our job is to comfort, not harm. I know that isn't an excuse but—"

"Go back to your dream world," Penny said bitterly as she rose to her feet. "I hope I never see you again, even in my dreams." She dashed from the room, slamming the door behind her. I could hear the clatter of her sneakers on the stairs, followed by the slamming of her bedroom door.

James stood and glared down at me through eyes that glowed against his anger-red face. He was so tall. I may have inherited his eyes but not his height.

"I don't know what to think of this." His voice quavered, as if he were struggling to control his temper. I flinched out of instinct as memories of Treb and the Penumbran police barged into my mind. Would he strike me? "If this is a practical joke, it was a cruel one to play on us." My shame deepened. Why hadn't I thought this through before I took on Bianca's likeness? "You claim to be from a dream world—Dreamearth you call it—yet here you are. And you appeared in the footage of Penny's dreams more than once. All my Catchers can do is record the images produced by the amygdala, but this doesn't conclusively prove that an actual other *world* exists. If this is true, can you show me this world?"

A sinking sensation filled me. I slipped my hand into my pocket and could barely feel the ghostsilk's wispy hairs against my sweaty fingertips. "No sir. You wouldn't be able to cross over, only in your dreams. I can because I'm a . . ." A sudden hope leaped into my chest. Now was my chance. "A Half—"

"Of course not." James's tone was sharp. "You're nothing but an expert illusionist who used public information about my dead wife to play this prank. You'd better go." He strode to the door and opened it. "I have to see to Penny."

He grabbed me by the arm and half pulled, half dragged me into the foyer. "If you come anywhere near my daughter," he hissed as he opened the front door and shoved me through, "I'll call the police." A shiver passed through me. "Is that clear?"

"Yes, sir." I couldn't meet his eyes.

He slammed the door behind me.

I moved down the path as if I were a Penumbran drone once again, with my shoulders slumped, my feet dragging, and my hair hanging over my face. Despair washed through me with a drowning sensation. I'd had a chance to finally have a real family and I'd blown it. Seriously blown it. How could things have gone so wrong? Not only didn't James and Penny believe me, but they now hated me. I couldn't get the sight of James's eyes, eyes just like mine, blazing with loathing, out of my mind.

A hardness clotted my chest. It was a familiar feeling, one I'd grown accustomed to in Penumbra, to keep the hurt and loneliness away. For a long time, I'd even forgotten how to cry. The tears refused to come now, as if all the fluids within me had been sucked dry, even though my throat ached.

All hope of being reunited with my Realearth father had died. I was permanently stuck here with no real home, no family. Aunt Olga was going to kick me out once I returned. I'd either live on the streets or, if I was lucky, remain in foster care until I turned eighteen. I fingered the ghostsilk in my pocket but didn't pull it out.

Chapter 37

Twilight seeped through the trees and sparked against the distant sea as I slowly made my way toward the nearest bus stop. It would be dark by the time I got home, and I'd have to face up to Aunt Olga. I didn't really care. If all she did was kick me out, that would be nothing. I was used to worse.

I was jostled as people streamed off the bus and those of us waiting stepped on. I huddled into a seat near the back and closed my eyes. The roar of many voices speaking at once hummed in my ears as the bus started moving. I struggled to tune out the extraneous noise and my own horrible thoughts and just let my mind go blank. I didn't even want to fall asleep and briefly return to Dreamearth. The thought of that depressed me. I belonged to neither world. My brain refused to settle and instead kept replaying my horrific encounter with my Realearth family, focusing entirely on all the terrible things I'd said and done.

Things that caused my own father to throw me out of his house.

James would never know he had a Halfling daughter from Dreamearth. Perhaps that was for the best.

I was slammed forward as the bus screeched to a sudden stop. People around me swore and gasped. My eyes flew open. We had traveled some distance from Penny's and were in the heart of downtown Los Angeles.

"There's no gettin' through this street," the bus driver announced over the roar of voices. "Something's goin' on up ahead."

"It's that god that's been appearing in the news," someone else said.

My blood froze. Njim?

"Let us off!" another person yelled.

I scrambled to my feet as the bus's doors jerked open. Frustration pulsed through me. I struggled to squeeze past the people jamming the aisle. Others were huddled in their seats or trying to crawl beneath them in terror.

By the time I stepped off the bus, the city street was clogged with people and traffic had come to a dead stop. People stepped out of their cars and stared straight ahead.

"I will end all wars," a voice boomed from above. I bit my lip hard as I looked in its direction. The direction everyone else was. A glowing giant I recognized as Njim from news blurbs and websites hovered in the air, appearing almost as large as the tallest building. The crowd cheered, a sound that nearly deafened me.

"I will make your world into the paradise it was meant to be." He waved his muscular arm. The surrounding buildings transformed into giant trees with wide trunks and shining silver leaves that softly swayed. My thoughts briefly flickered back to my Forest days. The sky overhead was suddenly a kaleidoscope of rainbows that overpowered the dull street lights. Thousands of butterflies with jewel-like wings filled the air.

The crowd gasped as one, completely entranced.

I pushed through the tight mass of people. Njim, despite his size, was too far away for me to reach. How long would his illusion last?

"This is a lovely scene, don't you agree?" he continued, his overpowering voice somehow gentle. The crowd murmured approval. "But how would you like to see it snow, here in Los Angeles in late September? Do you think it's impossible?"

He snapped his fingers and the butterflies transformed into snowflakes that settled on peoples' heads and clothes.

"It's rainbow snow!" someone shouted, followed by more exclamations.

"Of course it is," Njim boomed. "Nothing is impossible with me."

I was never going to reach him. People were packed much too tight, making it near impossible to squeeze through. There was no use hiding what I could do. The crowds were focused on Njim anyway.

I leaped into the air. My flailing legs accidently kicked a few heads. I mumbled an apology but needn't have bothered since everyone was too entranced by the illusion of colored snow falling all around to notice what I'd done. Swirls of these fake flakes danced around me as I rose higher and higher above the crowd, brushing my face with a slight chill. They didn't dampen my hair and clothes the way real snow would have. The thrill of flight nearly overpowered my urgency to confront Njim. I sped toward him, squinting to see through the flurries. My hair whipped across my eyes, making this even more difficult. I now wished I hadn't taken Diana's advice to let it grow long.

I slowed my speed as I drew closer to him. His incandescent face was the size of my Sandman Island cottage but so handsome it was almost painful to look at. His eyes, glowing like twin suns, hurt my own eyes but I forced myself to stare directly into them. I felt as if I were an insect as I hovered before him, a tiny, insignificant creature that he could so easily swat away.

It's only illusion magic, I reminded myself. I swooped closer to get his attention and ignored the shocked murmurs from the crowd.

"I don't know who you are but you've got to stop this," I shouted, although my voice was faint and breathless from the flight. I felt thousands of eyes on me as I floated besides this being they all viewed as Realearth's newest god. I caught a glimpse of TV cameras trained on us from below. Now my Halfling status would be revealed to all of Realearthlings as well . . . even if they didn't know what that was.

"Remmi. I thought you'd finally join me," Njim said softly in a familiar voice. His image flickered briefly, revealing a man with a narrow face and long, loose hair.

"Hayden," I murmured as I sank to the ground. My legs buckled as I landed. I dropped onto the cement. "I-I can't believe—"

"You all saw her fly, did you not?" Hayden blasted in Njim's voice as he regained the image. The illusions of trees and colored snow instantly vanished. "This simple child here is proof of the magic I can bring to your world." I glared up at him as a boiling rage filled me. Hayden had been Njim all along. Why had he pretended to be my friend, a Substitute in my dreams? "Just imagine what your world would be like if you could all fly like this. No more waiting in long lines at airports and sitting on planes for endless hours when you can just think about where you want to go and fly there in an instant!"

Gasps rose from the crowds. Countless people had fallen to their knees. I studied their faces. Some looked terrified, others elated. They actually believed him?

"I must go for now, but I'll be back." Njim raised his arms. A glittering mist suddenly surrounded him in swirling drifts. Another of his illusions. Through it, I saw him pull out the ghostsilk and slip into it, vanishing instantly, leaving a pile of clothes on the street.

The mists and ghostsilk faded. I was stuck in the crowd, also kneeling on the ground where I'd dropped. I rose to my feet. I had to return to Dreamearth and confront him.

But before I could do that, I was engulfed by people. "Who are you, girl?" "How did you fly like that?" "I don't see any wires." "Do you know Njim personally?" "Is he really a god?"

Anger tightened my chest. I looked directly into a TV camera that was aimed at me. If all of Realearth was watching, I must warn them. "Pay no attention to Njim," I said with as much confidence as I could muster. Beads of sweat tickled my forehead and trickled down my face. "I know him well. He is no god. Just a fraud who knows a few tricks. Don't be fooled by his illusions. He taught me some. Stand back and I'll show you."

If Hayden could be a god, then I could be a goddess. An image formed in my mind of a giant, ethereally beautiful woman. A sharp tingle covered my entire body as I felt the illusion stretch to a great height. I rose off the ground so I could actually look down on the crowds. Awed gasps from thousands thrummed in my ears, telling me the illusion had been successful.

Chapter 38

The masses were huddled on their knees and more than one camera was trained on me. I glanced down at the image I had created. My skin was now translucent, glowing with iridescent undertones. Brilliant platinum hair, spilling past my illusion's slender waist, sparkled with tiny crystals against the street lights. I was garbed in a gauzy gown that looked as if it had been woven from butterfly wings.

I shifted my gaze to the crowds, every person staring up at me with utter adoration. An intense sensation of glory, of triumph flooded me. No wonder Hayden and other Halflings couldn't resist the lure of godhood, the joy of feeling such intense love from thousands of Realearthlings. Isn't this what I had desired during those lonely years in Penumbra, when I'd toiled in miserable obscurity?

Fight it, Remmi, a small voice at the back of my mind pleaded. *Don't become like Hayden and those others who inspired the mind-drains.*

With bitter reluctance, I allowed the illusion to fade and floated to the ground. A faint depression seeped through me as I found myself back in my diminutive mortal body. I felt deflated, even as more gasps shivered through the crowd. "See?" I said, facing the nearest camera. "It's just smoke and mirrors. I'm just as human as any of you."

I then pulled out my ghostsilk and hung it in the air. My best option was Morphia's penthouse. The thought filled me with dread and it was a gamble, but it was most likely where Hayden would have gone. It's where he had his clothes. I formed an image of my Substitute apprentice bedroom and stepped through.

The sudden silence that filled my ears was nearly deafening. The familiar threads brushed against my skin—my bare skin—as my feet sank into the too-thick carpet. I stood still for several moments, drawing in deep breaths. The room was dark, except for a nightlight plugged into one wall that emitted a soft glow.

Even though I knew that no Realearthling could see the ghostsilk portal, let alone glimpse Dreamearth through it, I grabbed the silk and folded it into a tiny square.

I turned on the crescent moon light and scanned the room. It still looked the same. Had Morphia kept any of my clothes?

I padded toward the wardrobe. Everything was gone, except for one item, the pale, bright green sundress I'd refused to get rid of. Morphia had probably figured it wasn't worth her attention but I happily slipped it on. It smelled of laundry detergent but still reminded me of the sea, of Periwinkle. I even found my Sandman Island sandals, pushed into a far corner of the vast closet.

Once I was dressed, I tucked the ghostsilk into a pocket. It was nighttime here. How late was it? Was Morphia asleep?

I found I was angrier at her over her ignorance of Hayden than her betrayal of me to Malcent. How could she *not* know her own husband, whom I assumed she'd been married to for years, was not only a Halfling but had been sneaking over into Realearth to become the latest deity? True, she never had noticed anything beyond her limited vision, but this was ridiculous.

I should wake her and tell her, just to be spiteful. I bit back a bitter laugh as I stepped from my former bedroom. What would her beloved publicity hounds say to *that*? I could almost hear the Viewing Crystal news blurbs: "Famed Substitute Morphia Nightshade is married to the Halfling trickster Njim."

"I knew you'd follow me here," said Hayden's voice from below. Rage boiled through me. He stood at the foot of the stairs, wearing a suit similar to Malcent's except that it was dark blue instead of black.

"So, you're the mysterious Njim." I folded my arms and glared down at him.

"In the flesh, as I really am," he said, dipping into a low bow. "Luckily you had the foresight to end up in your old room or that could have been extremely awkward, I must say." The calmness of his tone irritated me. Was that what he wanted?

"After you left, I convinced the Realearthlings that you were a fraud, nothing more than a skilled illusionist." My words echoed against the high walls and ceiling.

He cocked an eyebrow. "Really? You're so sure you *convinced* them? Realearthlings can be taught to believe anything but it takes skill."

"I can perform illusions too." I cringed at the childish squeak in my voice.

Hayden chuckled and shook his head. "Oh, Remmi. You are much too young and inexperienced for this. But it's so cute you even tried. I've made sure the Realearthlings would remain convinced that my claims and illusions are real."

He turned and strode into the living room, straight up to the window overlooking the city. The buildings glimmered with light.

I scurried after him. "What do you mean?" Dread had shoved aside my fury.

"Aren't you tired of it, Remmi?" Hayden's demeanor had suddenly changed. He sighed and leaned against the wall, his gaze still fixed on the window. "Always having to hide who you really are, to conceal your multiple talents?"

I stiffened and clenched my fists. My jagged nails bit into my sweating palms. The word "yes" formed on my lips but I couldn't release it. I merely tipped my head into a nod.

"Just like you, my mother had hid me away from the authorities to protect me from the mind-drain," he said in nearly a whisper. "But, also like you, we were eventually discovered, and I was again spared the mind-drain by a kindly stranger. I was older than you had been before you were sent to Penumbra, closer to twelve. I still had to work as a drone, pretending to be a brainless automaton, putting up with all the indignities I'm sure you know all too well." He looked over at me. His eyes were wet. "It was sheer torture."

My thoughts staggered around in my head, struggling to comprehend this. I was finally able to latch onto one question. "How did you know how old I was?"

"Remmi, my dear, *I* was the one who prevented your mind-drain."

My legs could no longer support me. I sank onto one of the settees facing the window. I stared at the buildings as I strained to process this. I didn't know how I should feel, grateful or angry. "Why did you do this?"

"I loved Luna before I married Morphia but she was enamored with one of her Visitor clients."

"James Brooks." Grief stabbed at my chest and painfully twisted.

"She disappeared into the Collective Unconscious Forest after she found out she was pregnant with you. I had my ways of spying on her but left her location a secret until you both were discovered." I shivered as memories of that horrible winter barged into my mind. "I was able to spare you from the mind-drain but not Luna." His eyes glimmered with more than tears.

"What do you mean?" I croaked. "Mother's dead."

Hayden pulled a ghostsilk from his breast pocket. "No. Luna isn't dead."

Chapter 39

"Mother's alive?" I peered up at Hayden, expecting this to be a trick. I longed to give in to joy but could I trust him?

"In some ways, yes." He hung up the ghostsilk and ran his fingers over it, causing it to waver. Once it stilled, I could see several clumps of misshapen hills through it. "Follow me."

I did so, with a restless mind and throbbing heart. The hills, stretching endlessly like ripples, looked as if they were made from old, opaque glass. There were hundreds, perhaps thousands, or even millions of them, surrounding us like frozen waves. The sky above was a pale, drab gray. This scenery reminded me of Penumbra's surrounding badlands; an eerie, surreal version. A river snaked through it in the distance. Its waters were made up of rainbow hues so brilliant I had to avert my eyes.

"This is the dumping ground for discarded Thought Artifacts," Hayden said. "Once their essences are drained, the husks are discarded here." He made a sweeping gesture with his arm.

"Where's my mother?" Icy desperation clutched my heart. I scanned the surroundings.

Hayden pointed his finger in the opposite direction of the fulgent river. Several people, clad in ragged, filthy tunics, shoveled scattered glass objects into piles, forming a new hill. A gruff overseer with muscular arms stood nearby, watching them as he tapped the handle of a whip against his boots.

My blood chilled. *Drones.* Even thinking that word made me shiver. The drones were forming a new hill out of Thought Artifacts. Did Peter and George know about this?

"The nasty job of sweeping them up into hills is done by drone labor." His tone was solemn. "It saves the Ministry of Thought Artifacts tons of money since drones don't have to be paid. This was the place where I worked when I was younger. I assure you, it's even worse than Penumbra. But not all drones are Halflings." I nodded numbly, recalling my embarrassing mistake at the Convergence Café. "That's the case with most of these. The worst criminals often get sent to work at the Thought Dump after their mind-drains. One of the main crimes against the government is infidelity with a Realearth Visitor and becoming pregnant."

I felt as if all the surrounding Thought Artifacts had toppled over me, crushing the air and life from me. Mother was alive but . . . Wouldn't death be preferable to life as a mind-drained drone? "Which one is she?" I hurried closer, my feet crunching over glassy sand and pebbles. Hayden followed.

These drones were even more filthy and disheveled than my erstwhile Penumbran companions. Their grime-clotted tunics were so threadbare that they were nearly transparent and some even gaped with wide holes. They might as well have been naked. I felt the urge to avert my eyes. I smelled the stench of unwashed bodies even from several feet away, a scent that grew stronger as I neared the grubby group. There were obviously no showers or decent bathing facilities in this dump.

Hayden guided me toward a slumped, barefoot woman who was kneeling on the ground, slowly piling now empty thought vessels into a miniature hill. Her face was concealed by greasy, matted hair.

Burning tears rushed into my eyes. "Mother . . . ?" I choked, kneeling beside the stooped woman. I ignored the sharp pebbles that bit into my knees. "Mother, it's me. Remmi." Holding my breath so as not to inhale the strong, unwashed scent emanating from her, I brushed back her knotted hair. "I'm older now. Do you recognize me?"

Her face was gaunt, her delicate cheekbones jutting through grimy, nearly diaphanous skin. Watery, vacuous eyes stared back at me. "I don't know." Her voice was completely toneless. "It doesn't matter. I must make hills." She turned back to her task.

Warm tears tickled my cheeks. I clutched Mother's hand and pulled it to my chest. Her callused fingers felt like fish bones. I feared they'd break if I held them too tight. "You're coming back with me, Mother." She instantly straightened, ready to obey. My heart briefly soared. I had almost forgotten about Hayden. "You'll—"

"Hey, no interferin' with my drones," yelled an overseer, hurrying over with his whip raised. "You, drone, get back to work." Mother knelt back onto the ground and returned to piling up Artifacts. The man continued to approach, an evil gleam in his eyes. Even though drones were always willing slaves, some people thought it fun to beat them for no reason. I knew that too well. He wasn't going to hurt Mother.

I stared straight at him and mentally pushed, sending him flying into a hill some of the drones had been working on. Thought Artifacts toppled over him. The other overseers rushed to help him.

Mother continued her task. "Mother—"

"It's no use, Remmi." Hayden whispered. I felt his strong hand on my shoulder, pulling me behind a hill. "She would obey you without question, but only because orders are all she knows. And you'd merely draw more attention to yourself, which we can't afford at this time."

Despair overwhelmed me. I slumped to the ground and buried my face in my hands. My parents were alive but I might as well have remained the orphan I always thought I was. My Realearth father didn't want anything to do with me and Mother was a drone who had no idea who I was.

"I'm not trying to become Realearth's latest god for my own ego," Hayden said. "My goal is to help all Halflings and drones like your mother. I promise I can heal her. You just have to hear me out."

I raised my head. "How? No one has ever reversed a mind-drain before."

"Come with me, Remmi." Hayden held out his hand to me. I took it. He pulled me to my feet. "I want to show you something."

He guided me toward the River. "Do you know what this is?" The waters, nearly as brilliant as sunlight, undulated with impossible colors, swirled with intricate patterns. I could only glance at it before my eyes became dazzled by the light.

"Isn't it the Life River, made up of Visitor thoughts?"

"That's right, my dear. It is what keeps our world in existence. What do you think would happen if it completely dried up?"

I chewed my lower lip as I pondered the blank Thought Artifacts the Visitors, starting with Penny, had been shedding during their dreams. Did that have something to do with Hayden, acting as Njim?

I drew my gaze to the River's banks. The pale sand surrounding them was damp. Further up, the sand was dry and crumbly, as if it had been touched by water that had dried some time ago.

"I . . . I believe the world would end. Doesn't it need Visitor thoughts?"

"Dreamearth and its full-blooded denizens do, but we Halflings don't."

The fury I'd felt earlier returned, filling me with a boiling bile. I turned on him. "It's you that's been drying up the River," I yelled. My voice echoed eerily against the countless Thought Hills. "I won't let you do this. I'll stop you." I had no idea how I'd do this, but determination burned through me.

"Remmi, my dear." Hayden placed a hand on my shoulder. I pulled back and glared up at him. "It's not what you think. Dreamearth won't be destroyed forever. We could remake it. We and other Dreamearth Halflings. You aren't the only one I managed to spare, just the only one I'd been able to locate, so far. We can truly become gods by doing more than just tricking people with illusions. We can make Dreamearth into the world we want it to be, where Halflings are revered as they deserve to be, not turned into mindless slaves.

"Your mother, too, can be remade, with her mind once again whole. Isn't that what you want more than anything, Remmi?"

I froze. To have Mother back again, after years of believing she was dead? And now . . .

My gaze drifted to the ragged drones in the distance, dutifully piling hollow Artifacts into more hills. My heart clenched. I couldn't tell Mother apart from the others.

Temptation tugged at me. My thoughts raced. Mother and I reunited, with her mind restored. Could there also be a way for me to get James and Penny to like me? If we could somehow share the same world, I'd have a complete family.

Depression drowned out the joy that strained to emerge. What I wanted was impossible, no matter what Hayden was promising. In order to remake Dreamearth, it would first have to be destroyed.

My thoughts darted to Peter, Periwinkle, and Jenna . . . they'd have to be remade as well. As would every other person.

"No, Hayden." I backed away, my feet crunching over Artifact shards. "I want no part of this."

"That's fine, Remmi." Hayden's voice was resigned. "I can do this all on my own, with James Brook's help."

"James . . . my father?" My heart twisted.

"My dear, I *inspired* him to create the Dream Catchers. I had to be subtle, so as not to be caught. But he's a genius and figured it out quickly."

"The objects that record dreams?" Penny's blank expression, whenever she was given a command or suggestion, barged into my mind. My blood chilled. Did her Thought Artifacts become blank *after* she started using the Catcher?

And what about the blank thoughts from the other Visitors? Didn't James say that he'd sold many of these Catchers?

"The Dream Catchers . . ." My throat was so tight I could barely release the words. "They are mind-draining machines, aren't they? They are turning Visitors into drones."

"You have that partially right, my dear." Hayden grinned. His eyes shone with the River's colorful reflection. "The Catchers have given me an advantage over ancient Halflings, who only had their magical abilities to convince Realearthlings they were gods. But modern Realearthlings . . . well, they are not so easily swayed. Not with all the technology and movie magic available in that world. They need a little more, shall we say, persuasion. But who wants to be a god to a bunch of mindless drones? No. I've inspired James to unwittingly tweak the Catchers. As they record dreams, they take away the Visitors' free wills but leave their personalities intact. As long as they continue using the Catchers, they will do whatever is commanded of them. Just think, Remmi." The light in his eyes increased in intensity. "If you join me in this, we can not only be reunited with other Halflings out there, but Dreamearth and its people will be remade to respect us and, with the mass-produced Catchers, Realearthlings will do likewise."

I stared at Hayden, my breath coming in sharp gasps, my cheeks flaming with rage. I couldn't believe what he was saying. I pulled out my crumpled ghostsilk.

"Are you going to run back to Morphia?" He folded his arms and cocked an eyebrow.

"Morphia?" I barked out a bitter laugh. "By the First Visitors, never. She betrayed me for a huge ransom from Malcent. It must have been all over the news. But, even so, you're *married* to the woman. Why do you know so little about each other?"

Hayden shrugged. "We've been a little more than passing roommates for years now. She shares so little with me and I could care less about the mindless garbage that is spewed all over the Viewing Crystals. Oh, and it's now *Emperor* Malcent, by the way."

I felt as if something heavy had rolled over me, choking out my breath, even though I already knew.

"Of course, we don't have to remake *every* Dreamearthling," he said, leaning close to me. "We'll be the ones in charge in the new Dreamearth."

That was tempting. A world without Malcent, especially Emperor Malcent, would be far superior. But it still wasn't right. I had to stop Hayden.

But how? What could I do to stop him, if thousands of Realearthlings were already using Dream Catchers? I needed to go somewhere to think, to figure this out. I hung up the ghostsilk.

"I take it I'm on my own then," said Hayden. "Very well, Remmi. Go back to Realearth. Become the ordinary teen you obviously want to be. Forget about your mother."

Chapter 40

His words hit me sharply in the chest as I stepped into the silk. Faint hairs brushed my skin.

I didn't visualize Realearth but the eternal evening of the Nightmare Realms. I pulled the portal down once I was through and tucked it back into my pocket.

A thick mist clotted the cool air. Through it, I could hear faint voices.

"Buzzlesnouts are extremely shy," I heard Adam say. "So you must be as silent as possible in your approach. Just leave a piece of chocolate, their favorite food, here, and they will sniff it out. Go ahead, try."

I remained where I was, afraid to move. From the sound of it, Adam was in the middle of a lesson.

"Okay, here I go," Jenna whispered. "I just place the chocolate here like—" A twig snapped. "Oops! Sorry."

"It's all right. Just try it again."

I wasn't sure how Adam would react toward me, so I slid behind a twisted tree and waited. I'd approach Jenna once her lesson was over.

I didn't expect a thick mass of fur, which reached higher than my waist, to come bounding at me out of the fog. I bit back a yelp as it pounced on me with its front paws. It was a three-headed dog that stood nearly as tall as me. I pressed against the tree as it bathed my face with three hot tongues. It then dropped down to all fours and pranced in a circle, its single tail wagging. One of the heads barked.

"Shhh!" I hissed, stroking its coarse fur.

"What is it, Fred?" called Adam's voice through the fog. "Can't you see we're busy?"

Six glowing eyes stared up at me and three noses twitched. The tail kept wagging. The middle head whined as Fred leaped on me again to resume licking my face.

Boots crunched over pebbles, coming toward us. "What are you doing, boy? Get over here."

Fred dropped off me and loped toward Adam with lowered heads and a drooping tail.

I rubbed dog spit from my face as I peered around the tree. Too late to form an invisibility illusion. Only fog wisps separated Adam from me.

"You look familiar," he said as he crouched down to stroke one of Fred's heads. "Aren't you that Halfling who—"

"Remmi!" Jenna gasped, racing toward me. "You're back. You shouldn't be but I'm glad—"

"You've been keeping in touch with her?" said Adam.

"Not much." Jenna shrugged. "It's a bit hard when she's all the way in Realearth. But it isn't right that she's stuck there. Dreamearth is her real home and she should be able to stay permanently."

"I'm all for that," Adam said, turning his gaze to Fred, who relieved himself against the tree. "But don't forget who the new Emperor is, Jenna."

"Father. I know. If I had my way, I'd sic Windstreaker on him, chop him up into little pieces, and toss them into the slug pit."

"Jenna!" Adam glanced around, as if afraid someone might be listening. He pulled a cigarette from his shirt pocket. "You shouldn't talk that way about the Emperor, even if he is your father. I'm off duty now. Go on home before your mother accuses me of working you to death. And Remmi, get back to Realearth before—"

"I can take care of any police," I said, feeling oddly confident. I focused my gaze on a nearby boulder and sent it flying several feet, knocking down a skinny tree.

Both Jenna and Adam, unlit cigarette dangling from his lips, gasped.

"Okay, Remmi, I believe you." Adam lit his cigarette and whistled to Fred. "You girls are on your own. If I run into any police, I haven't seen you. Jenna, we'll continue with our buzzelsnout lesson in ten hours."

He strode away, cigarette smoke mixing with the fog, and Fred bounding at his heels.

"Remmi, it's not that I'm not glad you're back because really I am, but why are you here? Did you find out anything more?"

"Where do I even start?" My voice came out as a sigh.

Jenna placed a hand on my shoulder. "Why don't you join Mother and me for dinner? Perhaps things will look better after a good meal. That's what Mother always says."

I doubted it but the mention of food made my stomach leap. I couldn't remember when I'd last eaten. Maybe things would look remotely better after dinner and a few hours of sleep.

I followed her to an enormous tree. It looked like a Realearth baobab I'd seen in a book once but was as wide as three Sandman Island cottages standing side by side. A cave-like opening yawned in the center of its massive trunk.

"This is our new home," she said as she pushed aside the thick leather hanging that covered the entrance, allowing me to enter.

I gaped as I stepped into a round room with gnarled, wood walls. The place was even cozier than Jenna's cave on Sandman Island. The furniture was plush and colorful paintings decorated the walls. A small fire flickered in a tiny grate and several glowstones dangled on vines from the high ceiling, washing the place with a comforting light.

I caught the pleasant scents of cooking meat and warm bread. I'd almost forgotten that this was in the heart of the Nightmare Realms.

"It smells like dinner is almost ready." She led me into the kitchen, which was even more brightly lit than the living room. "Mother, you remember Remmi? I told you she's not anywhere near as dangerous as some people on the Viewing Crystals claim."

"My goodness, but you made quite a commotion a few weeks ago," said Felysa, drawing me into her arms. Unlike Jenna, she was still round and soft.

"I told her she could stay for dinner," said Jenna.

"That's fine," said Felysa, returning to the stove. "I always make extra. But no running out this time, you hear?" She winked. My cheeks burned as I remembered the last time I'd been invited to stay. "But we'll have to make this an early night.

I have to go to my shop in a few hours and I'm sure Adam has something interesting planned for Jenna."

Dinner consisted of a tangy, unfamiliar meat that was actually quite delicious, cooked mushrooms, a salad, buttery bread, and iced berry tea.

After the meal I sat, swaddled in a thick, fuzzy blanket, on the soft couch in the living room, beside the fire. Their small Viewing Crystal flashed silent images on the coffee table. None of them depicted me. That was a relief. Perhaps I was already old news. Jenna huddled beside me. Felysa had gone to bed.

"Things are bad." My voice was so soft I could barely hear it over the crackling flames. Jenna leaned closer.

I told her all about Hayden, that he was really Njim, and that he inspired the man, who happened to be my Realearth father, to invent the Dream Catcher.

"And it's these Dream Catchers that are not only spying on Visitors' dreams but draining their thoughts." Jenna repeated what I'd just told her as if she couldn't believe it. "Does Peter know?"

I shook my head. "We need to tell him and his father and the other Thought Collectors, although I don't know what they could do. Right now, the Dream Catchers are only sold in the country where I ended up, but soon they will be all over Realearth." I thought of the Life River with its receding waters. If Hayden got his way . . .

We had to stop him somehow.

My thoughts turned to Mother but I forced them back. As much as I longed to free her, I couldn't afford to lose my focus. I had to come up with a plan but had no idea where to start.

We watched the Viewing Crystal for a while to see if there was any developing news. No mention was made of the River, Njim, or even me. All that played was a series of crazy dreams, not one of which featured Morphia as the leading Substitute.

I felt a faint surge of satisfaction. Maybe, since losing me, she had lost her popularity with the public. Or perhaps she was able to retire on Malcent's payment.

I was about to silence the Crystal and go to sleep after my third yawn—Jenna was already snoozing beside me—when Periwinkle's face flashed within its depths.

Several blue-suited police officers were dragging her from the Dining Cottage toward a ghostsilk portal. Her hands were cuffed behind her.

"She's innocent," Andrew yelled as he raced toward them, trailed by the rest of the staff. "How was she to know that stray child was a Halfling?"

Reporters swarmed Periwinkle and the police, blocking their entrance to the portal.

"Ms. Piper," one said. "Is it true you had a Halfling child that was taken from you years ago? Is that why you protected this Halfling?"

Periwinkle's eyes stared directly at me through the Crystal. "I've always felt what is done to Halflings is wrong." Her voice was clear and strong. "I know my saying so amounts to treason, according to our new Emperor, but I don't care. I'll stand by my beliefs."

"You do realize the punishment for having knowingly employed and protected a Halfling is a mind-drain?" said another reporter.

Ice clotted my throat as Periwinkle straightened her shoulders and said, "So be it," in a resigned tone.

Chapter 41

I pulled the ghostsilk out of my pocket.

"Remmi, what are you doing?" Jenna stared at me, her eyes wide.

"Didn't you just see that newscast?" My hands were shaking so hard I dropped the silk. "Periwinkle has just been arrested, all because of me."

Jenna stood. "You're not going anywhere." She snatched up the ghostsilk and balled it into her fist.

"Give that back!" I stood to grab the portal but she raised her arm over her head.

"No, Remmi. Do you realize the danger you'll be in if you reveal yourself? I'm going to feed it to my monsters so you can't do this."

I sighed. "Jenna." It was an effort to keep my voice from trembling. "I must go. Periwinkle was more than just my employer. She was like a mother to me and even protected me, at great risk to her own safety. If I don't, she'll be mind-drained . . . turned into a drone." I fought back the image of Mother that suddenly barged into my mind. "Besides, I'm a Halfling. I escaped Penumbra twice. There's a reason why we are so feared." My tone was firm, holding more confidence than I felt.

"Very well." Jenna took a deep breath and handed me the ghostsilk. "I'm positive they've taken her to Father's main palace, which is at the heart of Nod's capital city. That's where those who've been arrested for crimes against the government—and that would include giving refuge to known Halflings—are sent ever since Father took office."

"I don't need to know that. I just need to focus on Periwinkle as I step through."

"And do what? You can't just waltz in and rescue her. You'd only make her a fugitive like . . . well, like . . ."

"Like me."

"I was trying not to say that."

"Look. She doesn't have much time." We had to come up with a plan but the seconds were slipping away. "Okay. I'm going to focus on Malcent. He's the one that must be confronted if this craziness is to stop." I hung up the ghostsilk.

"Wait." Jenna clutched my arm before I could step through. "I'm going with you. After all, he is my father." She spat out the last word as if it were a curse. "But we're not going without back up. Just give me a second."

She squeezed her eyes shut. Her mouth moved soundlessly. After several seconds, she opened her eyes and looked down at me. "I just spoke to Windstreaker and told her to meet us there."

"Meet us?" I frowned. "You said they brought Periwinkle to Nod. Isn't that awfully far without a ghostsilk?"

"She can fly around the world in slightly less than an hour. She won't get there as quickly but that's the best she can do. She'd never fit through a ghostsilk portal."

I felt as if my heart were about to leap from my body as Jenna and I entered the portal. We stepped into what appeared to be a large conference room. Malcent sat at the end of a long, shiny table. Men, all in dark suits, sat at the table, on both sides. I assumed we'd interrupted a meeting with his advisors. Large, muscular men in police livery lined one wall.

A grin flashed across Malcent's face as he looked in our direction. "Well, well, well," he said, rising. He was dressed in his usual black suit but a dark purple cape draped his shoulders. "Our little Halfling bird has returned." He turned to the man sitting closest to him. "You know what we prepared. Bring the camera crew in here."

"Set Periwinkle free," I demanded, pocketing the ghostsilk as a few of his advisors hurried from the room to fulfill his orders. My voice echoed.

He paced toward me, flanked by his police. An ugly, jagged scar stretched across his left cheek. "Grab her before she tries any tricks," he commanded his men.

"No, Father." Jenna stepped in front of me. "No one is going to lay a finger on her without going through me."

Malcent's mouth crooked into a smirk. "Just look at you, my own daughter. You look like some non-Penumbran hooligan.

259

And since when did you start befriending drones?" He flicked his colorless gaze over me.

Jenna lifted her chin and glared directly at him. "I've been training monsters and going to school, studying more than needlepoint." A sneer tinged her voice. "What do you think of that, Father?"

"Get both of them, you idiots," Malcent hissed at his police.

One man grabbed Jenna's arm but, in one fluid motion, before I had a chance to react, she punched his face. He staggered back with his hands over his bloodied nose.

We were instantly surrounded by more men. One yanked my arms behind my back. Pain shot through me, fueling my rage. I mentally pushed, sending several of them flying across the room and crashing into the wall.

My triumph was fleeting. Something soft spilled over me like a fall of the finest sand. I was covered with a glittery dust.

Paralyzing powder.

A numb sensation seeped through me. My legs gave out. I toppled onto the polished wood floor. I strained to move my head, limbs, anything, but couldn't. Through the corner of my eye, I saw Jenna lying next to me, coated with that same dust.

"A little of that goes a long way," Malcent said, gazing down at me. His thin, scarred face cracked into a grin. "It's time for your public execution." He stepped away from me.

Murmurs and footsteps, clattering over the floor, filled my ears. "Set the camera over here," Malcent said. "There, yes, that's good. Pick her up and put her on that gurney."

A policeman roughly picked me up. I longed to kick and bite but remained limp, as if I were made of rags. He dumped me onto a narrow table. Wisps of hair hung over my face, tickling my skin and marring my vision. I could only blink my eyes.

Malcent paced closer. One of the policemen handed him a sharp knife.

"My estranged little daughter cannot move to help you now." His voice echoed and throbbed in my ears. "But she, along with the rest of Dreamearth, will watch as you slowly bleed to death from a thousand cuts." I strained to mentally push against him but nothing happened.

He moved his knife closer. My heart was the only part of my body that moved, throbbing in my chest like frantic humming bird wings. "You may be paralyzed, little bird, but you will be able to feel everything. Now, where to start first." He rubbed his pointed chin as if deep in thought. "I could begin with your pretty little face, cutting it up just as you did to mine." He traced his fingertip along the scar. "But I'll save that for last, ending by gouging out your eyes. I want you to see what I'm doing."

He lifted my limp left hand. His fingers were cold. He folded down all my fingers except the index one. "Let's start with the removal of your fingers, one by one."

I couldn't even bite my lip as he began to slice through my skin. The pain burned and a thin trickle of blood spilled onto the table. The agony honed my focus. I turned my thoughts to the dust. *Lift off me.* Tears tickled my cheeks.

A ghostsilk portal appeared right behind Malcent but I didn't let that distract me. Dust specks drifted upward in swirling patterns, sparkling softly. I could now move my arms. I struck out at Malcent, knocking the knife from his hand. It clattered onto the floor.

Peter hurried through the ghostsilk and grabbed Malcent from behind. "This is for hurting Remmi," he blurted, slamming his fist into Malcent's face. The man stumbled back and fell.

I sat up and brushed the rest of the dust off me. "Peter," I gasped. "How—"

"I came the moment I saw what was happening on our Viewing Crystal," he said, dashing to my side and pulling me into his arms. Warmth filled me. He lifted me off the table and set me down. "By the First Visitors, you're bleeding all over the place."

I'd almost forgotten about my cut finger. My blood speckled the floor and table and stained our clothes. He ripped a shred of fabric from his shirt and wrapped it tightly around my finger. "This should staunch the blood."

"Thanks." I hurried over to Jenna, still on the ground and coated with the powder. I brushed it off. It fell away in clumps. She sat up slowly, as if she had just awakened. I helped her to her feet.

"Don't just stand there," Malcent called to his men as he staggered to his feet. "You can't—"

A loud rumbling sound filled the room. A wall and part of the ceiling collapsed, spewing dust and rubble.

Windstreaker towered over us, her eyes glowing and the sun reflecting off her black hide.

"It's about time," Jenna gasped, hurrying toward her.

Chapter 42

I raced after Jenna, toward Windstreaker. She placed her enormous wings protectively over us and bent her long neck downward to glare at Malcent and his men. Peter grabbed his ghostsilk and darted out of the way. The cameraman continued filming.

Windstreaker's eyes glared a harsh red, as if coals burned behind her irises. She shot a thin stream of fire from her mouth, singeing the edge of Malcent's cape. He leaped back and stared up at the dragon. Both fear and rage flickered across his face.

"I can speak to Windstreaker through my thoughts, Father," Jenna said, patting one of the dragon's haunches.

"Stop sniveling, you cowards," Malcent yelled at his scattered men. "Nightmare Realm monsters are harmless." They still looked as if they didn't believe him.

"That's only because they've been trained," said Jenna, her lips curling into a smirk. "But I can command Windstreaker to roast you to a cinder with just a thought, and her natural instinct will kick in."

"Now, are you going to release Periwinkle?" I said. "It doesn't look like you have much choice, between my Halfling magic and a dragon."

Malcent glared at me. "You haven't won yet, little bird, so don't get cocky. I'm still Dreamearth's Emperor and my word is law."

"You won't be Emperor for long if Dreamearth fades away because the Visitors aren't producing enough thoughts." My voice sounded calmer than I felt.

"So that rumor is true then?" asked one of the advisors.

"It is not," Malcent snapped. "Pay no attention to this Halfling and her filthy lies."

"Those aren't lies," said Peter, striding toward us, his initial fear of Windstreaker evaporated. "I know firsthand. I'm an apprentice Thought Collector. If you want to see, I can show you. More and more thoughts have been coming up blank."

"Why, then, is this the first we're hearing of this?" asked another advisor.

"The Ministry of Thought Artifacts wanted to keep this a secret, to avoid creating a panic," I said, all too aware of the cameras trained on me. Was I making the situation even worse? "But it won't remain a secret for long, if this continues. I . . ." I swallowed. The next words were almost painful to release. "I know what the problem is. If I'm to stop it, I'll have to cross over into Realearth."

"Liar," Malcent roared. He started toward me but several of his men, advisors and police, stopped him. His usually icy eyes flashed with fury. "Don't tell me you all believe her. She's a cursed Halfling, an anomaly that doesn't belong to either world. Haven't any of you studied history? Halflings are notorious liars, tricksters, and the cause of so much trouble in both worlds."

"Remmi is the only one who can save us," said Peter. He crept beneath Windstreaker's draping wing and took my hand. It was sweaty and callused. A comforting warmth spread through my chest. "I trust she can do this."

I pulled out my ghostsilk. The thought of confronting my Realearth father again after our disastrous first meeting squirmed within me. I forced myself to ignore it. Shutting down the Dream Catchers was the only way. Just how this was to happen, I wasn't sure.

"But before I go, I demand you release Periwinkle."

"She's in a holding cell in the palace," said the first advisor. "She hasn't been mind-drained—"

"Yet," said Malcent with a sneer. "She will only be released if you succeed in your endeavor, little bird. But, if you fail, she will be mind-drained and you and I will continue where we left off." He tilted his chin toward the blood-speckled gurney. "And, if you fail and decide to stay in Realearth, I'll still call for your friend's mind-drain."

"I'll return, whether I succeed or fail."

"Remmi, what have you just promised?" Jenna said, her eyes dark with worry. "What you're doing is . . . well it's . . ."

"Impossible?" I hung up the ghostsilk. "Maybe it is but I at least have to try. Only a Halfling can do this and Hay—Njim is no help." I pulled both her and Peter close. "While I'm gone, I want you to do me a favor."

"Anything, Remmi," said Peter. His eyes were wet, making his glasses slightly fog.

"Make sure Periwinkle is safe."

"Of course we will." Jenna patted Windstreaker's smoking snout. "No one will *think* of mind-draining your friend with a dragon guarding her." Windstreaker snorted.

"Wish me luck," I whispered as I faced the ghostsilk. My reflection against its rippling surface looked like a tiny, frightened child.

"Good luck," said Peter and Jenna at once.

I plunged into the silk before I could talk myself out of this task.

My sundress and the shred of cloth around my cut finger dropped away as I stepped into Penny's room.

Chapter 43

Penny sat at her desk, in front of her laptop. She screamed the second I was through the ghostsilk.

"Wha-how—" Her eyes were wide as they scanned me.

I dashed behind her bed for cover. "Penny, I need clothes now," I said in a commanding tone. "Bring me some!"

Her expression instantly turned impassive. "Of course, miss." She walked stiffly to her closet and pulled out a pair of jeans and a T-shirt.

"Thank you," I said as she handed them to me.

Just as before, the pants were too long. I was about to cuff them when I heard James shouting, "Penny, are you okay?" followed by his heavy footsteps pounding up the stairs.

"That strange girl is back," she said as I pulled the shirt over my head. Her eyes shifted from vacuous to outraged.

James slammed open her door. "What are you doing here? I thought I—"

"She appeared out of the air, Dad, and she was naked."

His eyes widened. "I thought those clothes looked like Penny's." He pulled a cell phone out of his pocket. His ruddy face flushed an even deeper red. "I don't know what sort of thrill you are getting from these pranks but I've had enough. I warned you once al—"

"Please, sir." I grabbed his arm. "You've got to believe me. I was telling the truth when I said I was from a dream world." I pointed to the ghostsilk then remembered they wouldn't be able to see it. I took it down and stuffed it into the pants' pocket. "I can't show you directly but your Dream Catchers are gradually destroying it."

He let out an exasperated sigh and focused on his phone. "Yes, get me the police," he said into it. "It's an em—"

I honed my focus. The phone shot out of his hand and flew onto Penny's bed.

"Did you do that, Dad?" Penny gasped.

"No, I did. I told you, I'm from a dream world and I can work magic." I took a deep breath and settled my gaze on the flat, rectangular device on Penny's nightstand. That had to be the Dream Catcher. "Dr. Brooks, your Dream Catchers are not only harming my world but Penny as well."

"I don't understand." The intense color faded from his face. "If this is more—"

"Penny, bring me the Dream Catcher," I said.

Her face instantly went blank once again. "Yes, miss," she said in that same dull tone. She paced toward the nightstand and picked up the device.

"See what I mean?" I looked up at James.

"Penny? Don't tell me you're in on this joke."

"What are you talking about, Dad?" She focused on the Dream Catcher she was holding and frowned. "I don't get it." Her gaze turned to me. "When you asked for this, I felt an overwhelming urge to obey." She placed it back on the nightstand. "I can't explain it but it was like I just *had* to, or else." She looked me up and down. "The same when you asked for my clothes. And how you turned into Mama. Are you a witch or something? Dad, I thought you said magic didn't exist."

"It doesn't. Penny, I've always told you there's a natural explanation for everything."

"Then how do you explain my urge to obey?"

"Now that I think of it, you have been less rebellious lately. When I ask you to do something, you just do it. You used to put up quite a fight."

"Yeah, and it's a pain in the butt, especially at school. My teachers like it but it's awful with the kids. That pig Margery Priggs has had me throw away her stinking trash after lunch every single day and I do it without question. It's like I can't say no and tell her where to put it, like I used to. And a lot of other kids are doing whatever they're told. Some of the teachers, too, which is fun."

"Do you know if they own Dream Catchers? Those people that are obeying every command?" I asked.

Penny shrugged. "I don't know. Maybe. My best friend Tabitha," I felt a brief twinge in my chest, "has one and she's also been doing whatever anyone tells her."

James shook his head. "This is impossible. I didn't design my Dream Catchers to change personalities. They merely record dreams."

I remembered what Hayden had told me, how he'd inspired James to create them, including the partial mind-draining aspect. At least the symptoms would disappear after the person stopped using the Catcher.

"Have you used your Dream Catcher?" I asked James.

"At first, to test it out. But I designed it mainly for Penny, because of her nightmares."

"Did you have an urge to do what people asked?"

He stared at the ground and ran a hand through his thinning hair. "Now that I think of it, I did find myself saying and doing some things I wish I hadn't just because people were requesting things and demanding answers. But that eventually faded. I was sure it was because fame was all so new to me and I wanted to make a good impression."

"This may sound far-fetched," I said, slowly, remembering how badly my last encounter with my Realearth father had gone, "but you are familiar with the so-called god Njim?"

James snorted. "A god indeed. More like a fraud who knows how to use a lot of special effects and mind tricks."

"I believe he's real," Penny said, her eyes bright.

"Now, Penny, haven't I gone over this with you before?" said James, placing a hand on her shoulder. "Didn't I tell you that claims of gods and magic must stand up to scientific scrutiny?"

"Njim does. I told you he appeared at my school and performed all these amazing things. They weren't just mere tricks. His magic was real."

"Like this." I closed my eyes and concentrated. I had never before performed an illusion that wasn't directly on me before and hoped this worked. As much as I despised winter, I envisioned snowflakes falling around me.

A sharp chill raced along my skin.

"No way!" gasped Penny.

I opened my eyes. Flurries of snow drifted from the ceiling and swirled around us. They landed on the carpet in icy drifts.

"This is impossible," said James, holding out his hands. Snowflakes landed on his palms but quickly evaporated. "They aren't real. They aren't wet but I can still feel them."

Penny spun around with her arms spread wide. "I haven't been in the snow since I was little and we went to the mountains," she said when she stopped. "Remember Dad? Mama was still with us then." She stared down at me. "How are you doing this? Is this the same magic you used when you pretended you were my mom?"

"Yes." I willed the illusion to fade. The snow instantly vanished. "I told you this isn't a special effects trick. Well, it is, but not in the way that Realearth movie people do them."

James sank down onto Penny's bed. He took off his glasses and rubbed his eyes. "There has to be a rational explanation based in reality. I'd always thought magic wasn't real, that things that seem magical are merely tricks of the mind."

"That may be true in your world. But in mine it's possible. People can fly and form illusions. Not everyone, mind you, but some."

"Remmi, you're bleeding," Penny gasped. "Did that trick hurt you?"

I looked down. The cut on my finger had reopened and my blood dripped onto the carpet. I pressed the edge of Penny's shirt against it, staining it instantly. "Sorry."

"I'll get you a bandage." James dashed from the room.

Penny continued to stare at me, as if wavering between helping yet afraid to approach. "It's really true? You're from a different world? Is that how you also appeared in my dreams?" I nodded. "But I haven't seen you in my dreams. Not since you were here the last time, when I told you not to." A flush crept over her dusky cheeks. "Is Njim also from your world? Are you . . . are you a god too?"

I had to laugh at that last remark. "No. And neither is Njim." I stepped closer to Penny. She backed up, as if still afraid

I might cast some kind of spell on her, and bumped against her dresser. "But you must believe me."

"I believe you, Remmi." Penny's face had once again become impassive.

I gulped. Would she retain that attitude if I continued? "Njim manipulated your father in his dreams, where he inspired him to create the Dream Catchers. They're gradually mind-draining—"

James burst back into the room, breaking Penny's trance. He held a bandage and a narrow glass tube. "There is a way I can run a test and see if you're telling the truth, Remmi. Hold still." He pressed my finger against the vial. My cut stung as several drops of blood dribbled into it. Once he was satisfied with the amount, he wrapped the sticky bandage around my finger, "I'm going to test this immediately. The DNA from your blood will tell me once and for all if you are really an alien, as you claim. Oh. And you might want to change that shirt. Penny, give it a good enzyme soak." He hurried from the room with the blood-filled vial in his hand.

An uneasy sensation filled me. Is that how they discovered I was a Halfling before, by taking my blood?

"You took my clothes before, didn't you?" Penny said, handing me another shirt. I quickly replaced it with the bloody one. "I could have sworn you were in my room one night. You were naked, like how you materialized this time," my cheeks burned, "but then you turned into Mama." She didn't seem angry this time, merely puzzled. "That part of the dream wasn't recorded." She pointed to the Dream Catcher. I had an urge to hurl it to the floor. But breaking just one wouldn't help.

"Penny, we must stop people from using the Dream Catchers." Her face took on that look again. It didn't bother me this time. Hayden had said that partially mind-drained Realearthlings still retained their mental faculties. They just lost their free will, but it wasn't permanent. "Is there a way to do this?"

She nodded. "Dad gave me the security code that connects us to all Dream Catchers he's sold. I was the only one he really trusted." She puffed out her chest with pride.

"So you can shut them down?" Relief passed through me.

"It's a bit complicated but yeah. You realize Dad will kill me?"

"Countless people in Dreamearth will eventually die if you don't, Penny," I said. "Do it now."

She sat at her desk and began rapidly typing on the laptop. I stood beside her as several images flashed across the screen.

Something shone at the edge of my vision.

It was a ghostsilk. I thought I'd taken mine down. I slid my hand into the pocket of those borrowed jeans and felt the familiar wispy hairs.

A glowing, muscular man with long silver hair stepped through.

Hayden, hidden behind Njim's illusion.

Chapter 44

He was not building-high this time but tall enough for the top of his head to brush the ceiling. Penny stopped her work to gape up at him.

"Keep searching, Penny," I commanded. I hated ordering her like that but I was desperate. "Don't let him distract you."

"I see you've found your Realearth family," he said, crossing his arms and staring down at me.

"Go away, Hayden," I snapped. I had to remind myself that his great size was merely an illusion. "This doesn't concern you."

"Oh, but I think it does," he said. I pushed against him as he peered over my head to look at Penny's laptop screen. "Tell me what you are doing, Penny."

"No. Don't tell him."

Penny gazed at us, confused, not sure who she should obey.

I mentally slammed the laptop closed.

Hayden laughed, a sound that seemed to shake the entire house like an earthquake. "Too late, Remmi dear. She's trying to deactivate the Dream Catchers. We can't have that."

He clapped his hands. They made a noise like thunder. The laptop exploded, sending smoke and pieces flying everywhere. Penny flung her arms over her head and ducked under her desk.

A mixture of rage and despair filled me.

Rapid footsteps pounded the stairs just outside Penny's room. Seconds later, James slammed the door open. He glanced at me with a strange expression, which quickly turned to shock when he saw Njim. "What in all hell is going on here?" His face burned a deep red as he glanced at Penny and her shattered laptop.

Hayden ignored him. "Remmi, my dear, you've become quite cocky. We both are Halflings, true, but I've had years more practice and experience. You're merely a baby next to me."

Before I could react, he pointed upward. The ceiling disappeared in a shattering blast. James grabbed Penny and, to my shock, me, and pulled us to him as debris rained down. Acrid dust stung my eyes and clotted my throat.

Penny coughed. I felt her shaking beside me. James's strong arm was firm on my shoulders.

"This is merely a warning," Hayden thundered. "Thanks to your Dream Catchers, thousands of people throughout your country believe I am a real god. It's all over the news and Internet if you don't believe me."

"What do my Dream Catchers have to do with it?" he rasped.

I struggled to speak but my throat was so aggravated by the dust that all I could do was cough.

"That's what Remmi was trying to tell you, Dad," said Penny, pulling back. "Why I have to do whatever people tell me." She glanced up at Hayden. "This isn't permanent, is it?" Her voice was edged in panic.

"I'm destroying that blasted thing, Penny," said James, stepping over wood and cement fragments where the Catcher still lay on her nightstand. He picked it up, tore off the electrodes, and hurled it against a wall. It shattered, just like the laptop had.

"You got rid of just one, James," said Hayden in a mocking tone. "But there's still thousands out there, with more being produced every day. And you just gave your company approval to start selling them overseas. Imagine what will happen once millions, even billions, of people are using these Catchers every night, recording their dreams."

"There will be no more Dreamearth left," I finally managed to croak.

"I thought I told you, Remmi, there will still be a Dreamearth. Just not the one we knew."

I glared up at him. Njim's glowing eyes were ominous. "I won't let you do this."

"Ah, but you won't stop me. Especially when your father and little sister are the only ones that know how to disable the Catchers."

"Father . . . sister?" Penny looked from Hayden to me. "What's he talking about?"

"I think I know," said James, looking down at me with a strange expression.

"But they aren't going to be around to do so." Hayden pointed at us.

An invisible force pushed us apart. I was flung over Penny's bed and slammed against the wall. I crumpled to the floor, winded. It hurt to breathe, to move. One of her posters fell on top of me.

Penny's cry ripped through my ears. She and James shot upwards, through the enormous gap in the ceiling, past the trees, at a rapid pace.

"You know, when Visitors fall in Dreamearth, they merely awaken," Hayden said, his Njim image stretching even taller. The voice streaming from the glowing, godlike man was Hayden's, reminding me that this was just an illusion. I staggered to my feet. "But we aren't in Dreamearth, are we?"

He flicked his hand. Penny and James, now tiny dark dots against the distant clouds, stopped and hovered. They were several feet apart. I heard the sounds of traffic screeching to a stop, sirens, and shocked murmurs of a crowd gathering in the street below.

I focused on James and Penny, imagined them floating safely to the ground as if they were made of feathers. Nothing happened. They continued to hang in the air. I could hear Penny's screams.

Hayden laughed. "I told you, Remmi, you are much too young and inexperienced. You are no match for me."

The clouds. I knew that clouds in Realearth were merely banks of mist, not living creatures, but I still had to try.

"Please . . . if you can hear me, carry these two Realearthlings to safety." My mind burned with desperation. The clouds drifted lazily across the sky, giving no indication of having heard me. I didn't realize I had spoken aloud.

Hayden reached down and ruffled my hair. "Remmi, Remmi, Remmi, so simple. So naïve. You know Realearth clouds can't hear you. I've had enough of this. It's time to let the fun begin."

He clapped his hands. James and Penny plummeted, their distant screams ripping through me. I had to save them. But how? Even if I flew after one, the other would fall.

I pulled the ghostsilk from my pocket and tied its corner to Hayden's. Ghostsilk couldn't be *perceived* by Realearthlings, but that didn't mean it was nonexistent in their world. Like Halflings, it was the one substance that could cross worlds.

I leaped into the air and released the entwined ghostsilk portals. They floated horizontally in the air. I mentally pushed them beneath James as I sped toward Penny. She was a blur of motion, her limbs flailing.

Slow down, I thought, focusing on her as I strained to remain airborne. Her speed lessoned.

I pushed closer, ignoring my hair that whipped across my face. "Penny, stop kicking," I commanded and was relieved when she did. I grabbed her.

"Y-y-you can fly too?" She stared at me with wild, unfocused eyes. Her face was ashen pale.

"Yes," I gasped, struggling not to drop her. Despite her slender build, she was heavy. "Just hold on."

Penny clung to me with a painful grasp as I kicked toward James. Just as I'd hoped, the ghostsilk portals had caught him around the shoulders, forming a pair of makeshift parachutes that billowed over his head. He drifted now instead of falling, but was still going much too fast.

The crowd and houses below were getting larger by the second. Hayden as Njim towered above them. I ignored James's confused and panicked expression as I grabbed his arm and slowed him to a gentle glide.

Stunned people, including some in police uniforms, surrounded us as we tumbled onto the front lawn of James's damaged house. I let go of them. The ghostsilk tangled around James as he pulled Penny into his arms. They remained huddled on the grass, sobbing and shaking. He stroked her tousled hair, which had come free from its ponytail.

I barely caught my breath when I was instantly surrounded. "Is this some sort of stunt?" "I don't see any wires." "Are you an angel?" "Weren't you the same kid who flew on TV? You were with Njim then too."

"Yes, I was." It was an effort to stand. My legs wobbled, threatening to give way beneath me. "Hay—Njim and I are part of an act—"

"The child lies," he thundered. His massive illusion now blocked a part of the sky. "She's just a simple, weak mortal and I'm a god. A true god, appearing before you in the flesh. Who are you going to believe?"

"Didn't I tell you before? I can be a god too." I ignored the ache that filled my entire body and concentrated on taking on that beautiful goddess image I had formed once before.

The sensation of sharp, sticky needles stabbed my skin.

Before I had a chance to see if my illusion was successful, a chain of volcanoes formed around me. They spewed massive flames into the air. The heat seared my face, the acrid stench burned my nose.

It's just an illusion, I reminded myself. Through the smoke, I saw James pull Penny onto their porch. The ghostsilk was still tangled around his shoulders. I rose into the air to avoid being trampled by the panicked, screaming crowds.

"I originally planned to form a God Squad," Hayden said as I flew toward him.

"A God Squad?" I dodged the blast of a volcano as I fought to cancel out his illusions. Best to keep him talking. If he became distracted enough . . .

"A modern day pantheon, made up of Halflings. You weren't the only one I saved, just the only one I was able to find again. The others likely were killed off. Only the strongest of us survive in the current Dreamearth. But now I found I prefer to work alone."

I ignored the pain and exhaustion that seeped through me. Lengthy platinum hair and draping butterfly-wing sleeves danced at the edge of my vision. My illusion had been successful. Could I hold it and project another? Erasing Hayden's illusions proved impossible.

Sweat tickled my skin as I closed my eyes and thought of the Forest, my original home.

The bitter stench instantly vanished, replaced by the fragrances of pine and flowers. I opened my eyes.

We were surrounded by monstrous trees that reached upward for miles, dwarfing even Hayden's giant illusion. The leaf-heavy branches tangled far above our heads, forming a sky of their own. This was an image I remembered from my earliest childhood. Stunned gasps rose from the crowd below.

My limbs burned with the effort to remain airborne and maintain two illusions, but, I feared if I landed, I'd be mobbed.

I looked at Hayden. His Njim image had shrunk to nearly his regular size. He breathed heavily and his movements were jerky.

He waved one arm and grimaced, as if doing so was painful. The surroundings shook with a thundering noise. A great tidal wave, flashing against the sunlight, crashed over the tree illusions, washing them away as if they were simply water color paintings. The crowds below shrieked and ran for cover.

"It's only an illusion," I yelled down at them as I formed a new one. The water splintered into thousands of feathers that floated everywhere.

I drifted back toward James and Penny and allowed my goddess image to fade. Hayden was tiring. I could use that to my advantage.

They were huddled on the porch and gaped up at me with shocked expressions. "I'll explain everything later," I said, tugging at the ghostsilk that still wrapped James. "I just need something from you."

"What . . . ? I feel something tickling me but I can't see it," he said. He still had his arms around Penny.

"It's a portal into my world and was what stopped your fall," I said as I pulled the silk free. Both portals, Hayden's and mine, were still tangled together but they'd have to do.

Hayden had landed on the lawn, his Njim image flickering. He was naked beneath that illusion. I held the ghostsilk behind my back.

"Stay away from my family," I called to him. My voice rasped. "Go—"

The words died in my throat. He stretched back into the towering image of Njim. A fierce wind swirled around me. Debris from James's shattered roof battered me from all sides.

Chapter 45

I planted my feet firmly on the ground and, to avoid getting dust in my eyes, squinted as I concentrated on Hayden. No counter illusion this time. Just force.

I took a deep breath and gathered that tornado into me. I felt every inch of me swelling as the wind instantly calmed.

Focus, focus . . . I lunged toward Hayden and, using the force of his wind illusion, pushed.

He flew back at a blurring speed and slammed into a tree on the other side of the street. His Njim illusion faded completely, leaving only Hayden, lying naked, face down in the street.

Had I killed him? I felt a mixture of horror and relief.

"Get back!" I shouted, pushing my way through the gathering crowd. As I suspected, several people instantly obeyed.

I looked down at Hayden. Blood dripped from a gash on his forehead but his sides slightly moved with gentle breaths. He wasn't dead but, in moments, he'd wish he was.

I envisioned Penumbra's endless badlands and flung the entwined portals over him. He vanished. He would probably find a way out—I certainly had—but at least that should delay him for a while.

The people who remained gaped at me. "Where did he go?" "Was he just a hallucination, like those other things?"

I grabbed the portals, crumpling them into a single ball that I thrust in my pocket. Aside from lingering people wandering around in a daze, the neighborhood was back to normal. James and Penny's house was the only damaged one. There was no sign that Hayden and I had participated in a battle of illusions moments before.

"You didn't see anything," I said to everyone I could. "If you took pictures or videos, erase them instantly."

Those who most likely owned Dream Catchers did as I asked without hesitation. Others looked at me as if I were crazy.

I couldn't overthink this. I had one more task to complete.

I raced toward James and Penny, who were still holding one another and staring up at their damaged roof. Their hair was tousled, their clothes rumpled, and their faces, coated with dust, were ghastly pale. I was sure I didn't look any better.

"Y . . . you saved us, Remmi." Penny pulled me into a firm hug. "I'd never been so scared in my entire life. It was worse than a nightmare. I don't understand how you did it. This has to be a dream but it feels so real."

"It is real," I said. "But that's not saying much since, where I'm from, dreams are real too." I laughed weakly. It was only then that I realized how exhausted to the bone I was. "Which is why we must disable the Catchers. But I don't see how. Njim destroyed your laptop."

"That's not the only place I back up all my information on them," James said, herding us into the foyer, then his office. I shivered suddenly. This was where I'd first met him, where I'd angered him with Bianca's illusion.

"Will my mind get back to normal?" Penny asked as James sat down at his computer and began typing. "Or am I stuck obeying orders for the rest of my life?"

"Hayden—or Njim, as you knew him—said that the users' minds would return to normal in a few days, after they stop using the Catchers." *If only that worked on the mind-drained in Dreamearth,* I thought bitterly.

"But why should we trust him?" James stopped typing and looked up at me.

"He was the one who inspired you to invent the Catchers, along with the glitch that made all users lose their free wills," I said.

He stared at me for several moments. His stoic face melted into a smile. "I'll send out a mass email to every person who purchased a Catcher, recalling each one for a defect. Anyone who's used it will have to obey, right?"

I nodded.

He resumed typing. "And, in the meantime, I'll disable all the Catchers so they can't be used." He typed rapidly for several moments before leaning back, removing his glasses, and rubbing his eyes. Now all the excitement was over, I could sense his disappointment. "There. It's done."

"I'm so sorry, sir." I sank into a chair. My body felt as if it was made from the transparent gooey substance of fresh Thought Artifacts, before they harden. "I'm sorry you had to do that but you just saved our world."

"Don't call me sir." I stiffened. Was he angry with me again?

"Sorry?"

"Remember how I took your blood to see if it differed from ours?"

"Yes." I glanced down at my bandaged finger.

"Penny, you'll want to sit down for this too," he said, nodding to the chair beside mine.

"What is it, Dad? Haven't we all been through enough today? I just want to go to my room and collapse . . . On second thought I'll take the guest room. I don't have a ceiling anymore."

"I'll get that fixed as soon as I can, Pumpkin. I promise. But there's . . . Well, this is impossible to explain, even after all that's happened." His gaze settled on me. He cleared his throat and swallowed. "Of course, I suppose nothing is impossible if you really are from a parallel world, Remmi. And, after today, I believe it. I ran a DNA test on the blood sample I took from you and, well, it . . . it . . ." He shook his head. "I figured, if there is anything abnormal about your blood, it would prove you were telling the truth about your origins. I even compared it to a drop of mine.

"Your blood is perfectly normal, Remmi. It's human blood but that's not the strange part. It, well, it matched mine. There's no other way to explain it, except, just going by the blood sample itself, you're . . . well, you're my daughter. But that's absolutely impossible. Is one of your powers the ability to duplicate other peoples' DNA?"

"No." I was shaking so much with excitement I could barely speak. "You really are my father. That's why I tried to meet you."

"That doesn't make sense," said Penny. "Yeah, I believe you've appeared in my dreams, and even pretended to be Mama." I stiffened. "But how on earth can we be *sisters*?"

I focused on James . . . or Dad. "Several years ago, you had been my mother's client." He looked puzzled. "My mother lived in Dreamearth and she'd taken on your wife's likeness in your dreams. In those, you must have . . . you know." My face burned. I looked down and tugged at my fingers. "Well, that's how I was born and why I can travel between worlds. A part of me is from your world, the other half the dream world."

"How old are you, Remmi?" James asked, his gaze boring into me. "You had mentioned you were in high school."

"Fourteen."

He took a deep breath. "Bianca and I were engaged over fourteen years ago." He placed a hand over his face and shook his head.

"Dad, are you all right?" asked Penny, touching his shoulder.

"Then this must mean," he mumbled without uncovering his eyes, "that I was unfaithful to Bianca?"

"Not really. My mother *was* Bianca in your dreams. She'd taken on her likeness, just as I . . . I'd done to demonstrate . . ." My voice shook on that last part. "How could you have known otherwise? You can't overthink this. It's illegal in my world for Dreamearthlings to . . . to have relations with Realearth Visitors but it happens quite often." I thought of Periwinkle. "But that was Mother's fault, not yours."

James lowered his hand and stared at me. "This is too incredible to believe." He smiled. "I'm a scientist so I've always had to rely on evidence. But the evidence is here. We just have to figure out where to go from here. This isn't a situation one comes across every day."

I placed my hand in my pocket and pulled out the dual ghostsilks. "I have to return to Dreamearth for now," I said as I hung them in the air.

"How?" said Penny.

"I have an invisible portal." I stared at the twin ghostsilks, hanging side by side, their edges tangled together.

"Well, invisible to full-blooded Realearthlings. They are what saved you, Dr. Brooks."

"Call me Dad." He winked. Warmth filled me. "You're always welcome here, Remmi," he said, kissing my forehead.

"I hope you'll start appearing in my dreams again," said Penny, giving me a firm hug. "They won't be recorded this time. At least for a while, until Dad fixes that dumb glitch."

"I'll do my best." I turned to face the portals. "You'll get your clothes back when I step through, since nothing from your world can pass into mine."

"So you're going to step into a dream, right now, while we're awake?" asked Penny.

"Yes. But you won't be able to see anything once I'm through."

I stared into the portals as I formed an image of Periwinkle. They reflected James and Penny, staring at me with awed expressions.

My borrowed clothes fell away as I plunged through.

Chapter 46

A dim light shone overhead and the floor beneath my bare feet was cold. I was in a small alcove. Someone gasped.

"Remmi! My goodness, you startled me. And where are your clothes?" Periwinkle peered out from a barred window in the wall. I hurried toward her.

"I lost them when I returned to Realearth." She passed me a thin blanket through the bars. "Thank you." I wrapped it around myself just as Jenna and Peter burst into the alcove, flanked by a uniformed guard.

"You're back!" Peter picked me up and spun me around until he noticed I was only wearing a blanket. He set me down. His face burned a deep red.

"What happened?" Jenna gasped. "Were you . . . the Dream Catchers . . . ?"

"They've all been recalled. Visitor Thought Artifacts should start returning to normal. And Hayden," I had to catch my breath, "I defeated him. I sent him to the outskirts of Penumbra."

Jenna, Peter, and Periwinkle cheered.

"Get someone to bring Remmi some clothes," Jenna said to the guard.

"But first release Periwinkle," I said.

He gave me a brief nod and unlocked the door, before scurrying off.

"Remmi, dear one," said Periwinkle, folding me into her arms. I sunk into her warm, soft embrace. She still smelled of the sea. "I was so worried about you."

"Worried about me?" I forced a laugh and pulled back to look up at her. "I was so scared you'd be mind-drained."

"It looks like the only one who's going to be mind-drained is Father," said Jenna. "And that's only after he gets a fair trial."

"Malcent?" A plummeting sensation filled my chest as I said his name. "But isn't he Emperor?"

"Not anymore," said Peter. "There's been an uprising throughout Dreamearth while you've been away."

"Because of Hayden? What has this to do with Malcent?"

"People all over Dreamearth are furious at Father for what he did to you, Halfling or not," said Jenna. "Or almost did." I looked down at my scabbed finger. The bandage had disappeared when I returned to Dreamearth. "They don't want an Emperor who would do such things. They all fear they could be next."

A woman I assumed was a palace servant, but thankfully didn't seem to be a drone, entered with a pile of clothes. I shifted through it as everyone left to give me some privacy. Almost everything was too big, except for a dark green gown embroidered with colorful flower patterns. It looked as if it had been made for a child. It fit decently and came down to my ankles. None of the shoes fit so I remained barefoot. I slipped the portals into the dress's pocket.

I entered the meeting room with Periwinkle, Jenna, and Peter. The damaged section had been boarded up. "Where's Windstreaker?"

"I sent her home," Jenna said. "She was no longer needed after Father was arrested and taken to Nod's main prison. The leaders still didn't want to release Periwinkle until you returned but they assured us she wouldn't be mind-drained."

The men I recognized as Malcent's advisors sat at the table, joined by several well-dressed men and women. They were Dreamearth's province leaders. Malcent, I noticed, had been replaced by his eldest son Randal, but his purple cape was draped over a chair. The gurney he had tortured me on had been removed. A cameraman stood in the corner, filming everything. Police lined the walls.

I ran my fingers through my hopelessly tousled hair. Despite the pretty dress, I figured I looked terrible.

"Honored leaders," Jenna said, stepping forward with the regal grace of a Penumbran lady and dipping into an elegant bow. "Remmi Clearwater has succeeded in her task. She has stopped the Dream Catchers that have been destroying our world, and defeated the Halfling Hayden."

"And where is Hayden, if you caught him, as Lady Graystone has claimed?" asked Queen Lavonda.

Lady? I glanced at Jenna, who merely shrugged.

"Esteemed leaders," I said, following Jenna's example and lowering my head in respect. "I can lead you straight to Hayden." I pulled out of one the ghostsilks and hung it in the air.

"Go ahead, Miss Clearwater," said a pretty, dark-skinned woman I recognized as Queen Selene of Sandman Island. "The police will follow."

Before I stepped through, I grabbed Malcent's cape off the chair.

Hayden huddled at the base of a jagged hill. He moaned softly, with his hand pressed against the bloody gash on his forehead.

I hurried over to him, the rocks sharp beneath my feet, and flung the cape over his shoulders. I'd overpowered him but at least I could give him his dignity.

"So this is it, Remmi," he said as the police dragged him to his feet and cuffed his hands behind his back. He was still too weakened to fight back. "You've betrayed me and other Halflings and joined our oppressors."

"*I* wasn't the one who tweaked the minds of Realearthlings so they'd think me a god," I said. "Such actions were what inspired the mind-drains in the first place." The police pulled him into the portal. I stopped one of the police. "Is he to be mind-drained?" The thought, even if it was Hayden, filled me with dread.

"Most likely, miss," he said. "But it will be up to the judge to decide." He disappeared into the ghostsilk with the others.

*

Periwinkle and I stayed at the palace with Jenna for several days as we waited to see if shutting down the Catchers had worked. Peter came by each day after his collecting to inform us that, little by little, Visitor thoughts were returning back to normal. But it wasn't until over a week later that Dreamearth's leaders and their advisors met once again in the conference room to hear the outcome from Mr. Sparks. All cameras were aimed at him.

I held my breath as he stepped forward and bowed. "Honored leaders," he said, grinning. "I'm happy to report that all the Visitors who had previously shed blank thoughts are now producing again. Many of our Collectors are adding their essences to the River as I speak."

The room exploded in cheers.

"And don't forget, you have Remmi to thank," Peter said, grabbing my hand. My face grew hot.

"He's right," said Jenna. "I know my father is no longer Emperor, but I recommend that you grant Remmi full Dreamearth citizenship. Our world would still be in danger if she hadn't crossed over."

"Not just me, but citizenship should be granted to every other Halfling out there," I said, "provided they don't abuse their magic. And drones should be given full rights and privileges, as well as payment for their work."

Murmurs filled the room as the leaders and advisors drew close together to discuss our proposals. I shifted from foot to foot and tried not to fidget. At least I now had a potential home in Realearth, but what about Mother? And Dreamearth *was* my first home.

After what seemed an eternity, Lord Randel rose to his feet.

"We've all agreed to grant you amnesty and citizenship, Remmi Clearwater," he said in a firm voice. My companions cheered and hugged me. "As for the drones, well, that will take more deliberation. Many Dreamearth companies rely on the free labor drones provide, so there is liable to be unrest if we move too hastily with this."

"In the meantime," said Queen Selene, "we will pass laws that all drones are to be well treated and not overworked. That is the best we can do at this point, at least until a new Dreamearth emperor is selected."

"I understand," I said, pushing the words out. It wasn't a complete victory but it was a step in the right direction. "There's one other—"

Another ghostsilk suddenly appeared. Morphia stepped through it. She was clad in a sparkling gold gown and her streaked hair had been sculpted into an elaborate, upswept style.

"Remmi, love," she cooed, holding out her arms to me. Her draping sleeves brushed against the tiled floor. "You've been through so much. I've been following you over the Viewing Crystal news. It made me realize how much I missed you. Come back and train with me again. You had been doing so well."

I laughed. I couldn't help it. "You're joking, right? Why do you think I'd go back with you after what you've done? You're lucky I don't turn you over to the authorities." I brushed past her. "Oh, I see you purchased a new ghostsilk."

She grabbed my arm. "Remmi, love. Please." Her voice squeaked. "I caved in a moment of weakness. You can't . . ." She choked on a sob. "You can't hold this against me. My dear husband is in prison. He'll probably be mind-drained. I have nothing—"

"I thought you two weren't that close. You'd better take good care of Fiona and Mia. I'm sure you heard over your enormous Viewing Crystal that laws regarding treatment of drones have been passed."

I approached the province leaders and bowed. "I have one last request."

Chapter 47

I entered my portal with Peter, Jenna, and Periwinkle at my side. Seconds later, we stood in the Thought Dump, surrounded by those never ending, surreal hills.

The glowing, rainbow Life River, which snaked around them at a distance, already appeared fuller, more vibrant. In days, it should be back to normal.

My heart pounded as we moved closer to the drones. None of them, not even Mother, her face hidden behind a curtain of matted hair, noticed us. They continued to sweep up loose Artifacts and slowly piled them into a new hill. I felt both Peter and Jenna squeeze my shoulders.

"Mother," I whispered as we drew closer. The unwashed stench that emanated from her and the others was overwhelming but I forced myself to ignore it. Hopefully with the new rules, bathing facilities and other amenities would soon be built here. "Mother," I said again, touching her thin, scabbed arm.

She ignored me and continued sweeping. Of course she would. I hadn't given her a direct order. Although I knew it would do no good, I took a deep breath and pushed back her curtain of filthy hair. Mother's enormous eyes, watery and vacuous, gaped at me without recognition. Tears touched my eyes but I blinked them back. I had to be strong.

"Mother, it's me, Remmi." It almost hurt to pry those words from my tight throat. A hopeful part of my brain urged me to continue, giving me hope that my words could get through to her. "Your daughter." A stray tear tickled my cheek. I quickly brushed it away. "I came back for you, just as I said I would. You must come back with us."

Mother dropped her broom and straightened her shoulders, ready to obey. I took her hand.

"You've been freed from that, honey," Periwinkle said gently, taking her other hand. "You'll be given a new job, along with plenty of food and a comfortable place to sleep."

I wasn't sure if it was my imagination but I thought I saw a Mother's lips curve into a slight smile.

Before we entered the ghostsilk portal, I turned toward Peter and Jenna.

"You know where to find me." Jenna hugged me. "I can't wait to tell Mother all that's happened, although I'm sure she watched all of it on our Viewing Crystal."

She turned and disappeared into the ghostsilk.

"Dad and I will be all over Dreamearth, collecting thoughts," said Peter. I looked up at his brilliant eyes, which seemed even more intense against the drab surroundings. "Thanks to you, the Artifacts from now on will once again enhance our world." He pulled me close and pressed his lips against mine. Fleeting euphoria stirred through me. I longed to linger in his arms but I forced myself to pull back. My chest ached as I watched him disappear into the ghostsilk. I missed him already but couldn't focus on that. I would see him again.

*

Periwinkle and I clung to Mother as we stepped through the portal. I blinked at the sudden late afternoon sun that struck my eyes. Even though it was mid-autumn, Sandman Island's sea-scented air was balmy. The vivid colors, after the drab monotonous shades of the Thought Dump, were almost painful to look at. The iridescent ocean beyond glittered with countless sun-sparks that coated it like a layer of shimmering glass shards. I pulled down the ghostsilk and tucked it into my pocket.

Mother felt heavy despite her frail appearance, and my arms ached from struggling to support her. I was grateful to Periwinkle for helping.

"Let's take her to your cottage," Periwinkle suggested. "It's still empty."

A few resort guests, lounging in the sun, gazed at us with stark curiosity as we moved slowly down the sand-packed path, practically dragging a starved, bedraggled woman.

I drew in a deep breath of relief as we entered my familiar cottage. It looked exactly the same as I'd left it.

"I saved this place just for you, in case you ever wanted to return," said Periwinkle as we maneuvered Mother into the bathroom.

Warmth flooded me as I filled the seashell tub.

"Stand still, Mother," I said, removing her hopeless tunic. "We need to get you cleaned up."

"Yes, miss," she said softly, her eyes lowered in obedience.

Periwinkle helped me lower her into the tub. I winced as my eyes grazed Mother's bony body. Her translucent skin was mottled with bruises, welts, and oozing sores. She gasped in pain as the warm water brushed against them and dug her fingers into my arm. Her jagged, filth-clotted nails hurt but I forced a smile.

"I'm sorry, Mother," I whispered. "It stings at first but that will fade once your body adjusts to the temperature." Mother gazed at me through blank, dark eyes that looked too big in her pinched face. Did she understand anything that wasn't a command?

"You'll be all right, honey," Periwinkle said in a gentle tone as she ran her hands over Mother's greasy snarls. "Your daughter Remmi will clean you up." She looked at me. "I'll get her some fresh clothes and something to eat. Can you handle her alone for a while?"

I nodded. "Thank you."

I bathed Mother, careful to clean her sores with the least amount of pain. Our roles had been permanently reversed: I was now the mother while she was the small child.

At least I'd had practice with Penny. I wiped beads of moisture from my face. I wasn't sure if that was from the bath's steam or tears.

I spoke to Mother, my voice intermingling with the splashing of the water, telling her about James and Penny and how we were all a strange sort of family split between two different worlds. A twisting sensation filled my chest. I hoped she at least understood part of it.

"I will stay here for now, return to school, and help you and Periwinkle. I'm not sure I want to continue to be a Substitute. Maybe I'll become a Cloud Wrangler instead. Or maybe I'll decide to live mostly in Realearth. At least I have options." I smiled.

I stared down at the water that was now nearly black from the layers of dirt and sweat I had washed off Mother. I pulled the plug and helped her stand. I gently patted her dry and wrapped her in the soft towel.

The sinking sun painted the room a rich reddish-gold as I guided Mother to the edge of the bed. I noticed Periwinkle had replaced the brush and comb I had taken when I'd left to become Morphia's apprentice. I grabbed those and started to work on Mother's wet, knotted hair. I hummed tunelessly as I did so, separating the hair into narrow locks and slowly smoothing each snarl.

Mother gasped in pain a few times when I tugged too hard. I was tempted to grab the scissors and cut off her stubborn locks, just as I had done with my own. I forced myself to remain patient.

The room was nearly dark by the time I had finished and I turned on a light. Now that it was autumn, the day was shorter than I remembered and a slight chill tinged the air.

Mother's thick chestnut hair, now dry and wild with static, flowed tangle-free. It clung to my sleeves and hands as I gingerly stroked it. We have the same hair. A twinge of pride filled me.

I looked up as I heard footsteps approaching the cottage. Periwinkle entered with an armful of clothes, followed by a serving girl carrying a steaming bowl.

"We brought you some broth," Periwinkle said to Mother as I helped her into a soft nightdress. Periwinkle took the bowl from the girl and held it to Mother's lips. "Drink it slowly," she cautioned. "You may feel an urge to drink it down in one big gulp but that would be bad. You'd get sick since you haven't eaten for a while."

I watched as Periwinkle fed Mother, allowing her just a few sips at a time. "I'll gradually increase your food intake every day. You should have your strength back in no time."

Once Periwinkle and the serving girl had left, I snuggled next to Mother in the small bed, something I hadn't done since I was little. I pressed my head against her frail chest, listening to her heartbeat and the steady sound of her breathing. At least I had her back, in body if not mind.

Chapter 48

I stayed on Sandman Island, where I shared my cottage with Mother. We obtained a second bed, although I continued to snuggle against her when we slept. She grew stronger each day but her mind remained fogged. I clung to the hope that Dad would come up with a way to reverse the mind-drains. He had invented the Dream Catchers, after all, and recalled them just as easily. Anything was possible.

Periwinkle hired Mother on as a permanent staff member. She proved to be a dutiful worker and the staff applauded each simple task she completed. This filled me with both pride and sadness.

I continued to follow the Viewing Crystal news. Every Visitor was now shedding abundant thoughts and the River was restored. Cloud beasts grew plentiful again and the section of the Forest that had disappeared had returned.

Despite the fact I no longer worked as a Substitute, I managed to get the scripts of many of Dad and Penny's dreams tweaked so they could sometimes visit me. Dad had repaired the roof and continued working on fixing the Dream Catchers.

During one of Penny's dreams, she asked me to return to Realearth over her winter holiday and stay at her house as a guest for a whole week.

"It's okay with Dad," she had said. "In fact, he suggested it. We'll take you to the mall, movies, and amusement parks. We'll be like sisters are meant to be. In the same world. I'll lay out some clothes for you."

I approached Mother, as I did every day when I left for school, or to visit Peter and Jenna. She was clad in a bright sundress and her long hair, shining with reddish-gold highlights, was neatly tied back with a flower behind one ear. Her body was now more slender than frail and her lovely face held the hint of a healthy glow. She smelled faintly of lilacs.

"I'll be back soon, Mother," I said, kissing her cheek. "I want you to continue helping Periwinkle and Andrew while I'm gone." I had repeated this message countless times but my throat still ached whenever I said those words.

"Yes, Miss Remmi," she said. I thought I saw a flicker of a smile, a slight sparkle in her otherwise blank eyes, but it could have been my wishful imagination.

I turned, pulled out the ghostsilk, and hung it in the air. Without looking back, I formed an image of Penny's bedroom in my mind and stepped through.

Acknowledgements

Many thanks to my first readers Cacy Duncan, Maddie Rue, Sharon Bailey, and Glenn Jason Hanna for your detailed critiques.

I would also like to thank Lynne, Catherine, Monika, Robin, Cleo, Elaine, Paige, and Claire, and the CBW-LA (Children's Book Writers of Los Angeles) writers' critique group led by Nutschell Anne Windsor and Cassie Gustafson for all your helpful comments. You have all vastly improved *Halfling.*

And, of course, my husband Ron Atmur who read several drafts as well as my parents John and Rosalie Robb for having encouraged my dream to be a writer.

Donna Marie Robb works as a children's librarian and enjoys traveling around the world with her husband Ron Atmur. Several of her short stories have been published in literary magazines such as *Wild Violet, Skyline, Femspec, Tales of the Talisman,* and the anthology *Story Sprouts.* She has also reviewed children's books for *School Library Journal.*

Made in the USA
San Bernardino, CA
07 February 2017